DANGEROUS EXPERIMENTS

DANGEROUS EXPERIMENTS

The Fire Pit Cell Explores
Freedom Love Science

Jf Verdonik

DEDICATION TO FREE PEOPLE EVERYWHERE
I dedicate this book to all of us imperfect people struggling to live Free Lives.
Maybe you know someone.
Now that Britney is finally Free, is it time to free yourself?
Also, thanks to friends and family who encouraged me to
explore my own Freedom in writing this Book.

Table of Contents

Table of Contents

Author Page

H i, I'm Jim Verdonik. I've done a lot of things: teacher, journalist, NYC taxicab driver, Peace Corps Volunteer (and assorted odd jobs we shouldn't mention).

I'm also a lawyer, have taught law school and ran a free legal clinic for startup tech companies. I like to think I'm good at theory but have street smarts that I incorporate into everything I write. See if you agree after reading my book. Let me know what you think at DangerousExperiments@FirePit-Cell.com

I've written nonfiction books, but this is my first novel. Most of my legal work has been with science and technology businesses and universities, which explains why I'm writing about the "Follow the Science Foundation."

How we choose between good things when they conflict has always fascinated me. If you ask people to choose between Freedom, Love and Science, most people will choose "all of the above." The interesting question is: How do you choose when "all the above" isn't an option?

Dangerous Experiments is the story about how ten college students in the Fire Pit Cell deal with that question. I think you'll enjoy getting to know the Fire Pit Cell members. I like these people. I hope you do too.

You can email questions and comments to the Fire Pit Cell students at DangerousExperiments@FirePitCell.com

The ten Fire Pit Cell members don't just live in my book. They also blog about relevant current events and topics at https://firepitcell.com/ blog/. They have lots of opinions. Check out their blog. They'll also be appearing in other adventures that I'm researching and writing about now. Tune in for their next adventures. They like to travel. So, their next adventures will be on the road and around the world.

NOTE TO READERS ABOUT HYPERLINKS: I wrote this book on the assumption that some people will read a paper version and others will read the e-book version. The story is the same in both, but the e-book version contains hyperlinks to hundreds of pictures, videos, music, articles and other information that add a richness to the story. Depending on which version you read and how may hyperlinks you explore, you will experience the story in a different way. All the hyperlinks are also on my website. The website identifies the place in each chapter each link relates to. Go to https://firepitcell.com/ if you want to access these links to enhance the print version.

I recommend you begin reading my book by first looking at the characters' pictures and personal profiles in the introduction. That will tell you about the ten primary characters. What they look like and their interests. Then, read the story. Some of the hyperlinks enhance the storyline. Others make fun of the story. Others provide relevant background information.

Meet Kaitlyn

Hi, I'm Kaitlyn Korosec, a dynamic ball of energy and soon to be college freshman. I like this picture of me[1] because my life is always a surprise. I don't know why, but I'm not bothered by it. I like surprises. At least I did until at some point during my first semester of college, the surprises got to be too much for me.

Did you see the Fire Pit Spirit on the cover? That's me too.
Are you wondering how a sweet girl like me became a Fire Pit Spirit?[2]

---

1 Kaitlyn Perplexed Picture https://firepitcell.com/wp-content/uploads/2021/11/FSN1.jpg
2 Kaitlyn as Fire Pit Spirit Picture https://firepitcell.com/wp-content/uploads/2021/11/FSN2.jpg

Me too. Weird, right? But I've been learning in college that life is weird.

It wasn't my plan, but it happened. So, I went with it. Now I'm a Fire Pit Spirit.

Let me tell you how it all happened.

How Did I Become a Follow the Science Scholar?

I was going to win a college scholarship by competing in beauty contests. But I gave that up after I realized two things. World peace isn't ever going to happen, and my singing voice is good enough for church and high school plays, but won't get me into the big time. That was hard to admit, but a girl has to realistically assess her talents. Of course, I can juggle, but I refuse to do it in public.

So, with beauty contests a thing of the past, how do I finance this 5'5" 105-pound blond package through college? I mean, my grades were decent (I'm not a dumb blond), but not scholarship level. I can't play football. And my parents make enough money to get by, but not enough to pay tuition and other expenses. No one gives people like us enough money to go to college, unless you want to spend the rest of your life repaying the loans. What's a girl supposed to do?

It's funny how I found my answer. It all started with a perfectly ordinary email. At least for me, that was the beginning. You know, one of the hundreds of useless emails that flood our Inboxes every week. The kind we don't have time for because we're busy with WhatsApp and Instagram and Snapchat. Anyway, my grandmother still insists on emailing pictures, and it was her birthday. So, I checked my Inbox and after I saw pictures of granny having dinner with her two cats (Oh, so cute!), I found the email that changed my life.

Well, at least this one had a timely subject line: How to graduate from College Debt Free. So, I opened it. Like many others, it advertised a tremendous conference promising great speakers and fascinating topics. In other words, BORING!

Then, came the important part that sucked me in, the location: DESTIN Florida (the Redneck Riviera), and during spring break.[3] Talk about God helping out a girl! My girlfriends and I had been drooling over the prospect of a senior year trip. Our parents suggested New York museums. We wanted Florida. All the hotels in DESTIN had been booked for weeks. Sure, guys would let us sleep in their rooms, but you know what that means. We're not prudes, but sex for a roof over our heads was out of the question.

So, I thought. Is this email God's way of answering my prayers? My reward for being interested in granny's birthday? Score our own room? At a discount? And all I have to do is listen to some old guys talk about whatever old guys talk about?

Count me in!

I had just gotten my admittance letter from my dream college. My parents were so proud. Perfect timing to hit them up for some Spring Break money. I knew my pitch to my parents. Sharing the room with three friends made it cheap. I'll use the money from my after-school job to pay half (very responsible of me). And it's about a free college education. So, this is an investment.

Guess what? They bought it. That's how I found myself lying on this beach with my three BFFs, Caroline, Maria, and Patty after singing the "Spring Break Anthem"[4] at least a hundred times and breaking the "Let's go Brandon record" on the long drive to Destin in a hot convertible.[5] We borrowed the car. Hot girls can borrow hot cars. Trust me.

Honestly, we missed most of the conference, except the parties by the pool. Boys with athletic tanned bodies[6]

---

3 Destin Florida Spring Break https://www.youtube.com/watch?v=6ttCw1Y3yYo
4 Music Video Spring Break Anthem https://www.youtube.com/watch?v=jUw4Qh9uFK8
5 Convertible Picture https://firepitcell.com/wp-content/uploads/2021/11/FSN5.jpg
6 Movie Clip Where the Boys Are https://www.youtube.com/watch?v=Pnti5rjFcUQ

were gathered on beaches like packs of wolves ready to devour cute girls like us. Poor unsuspecting boys. My besties and me gave as good as we got.

Our last beach morning was rainy. OK, I guess that was God's way of telling me something. Time for me and my BFFs to go to the conference, at least until it stops raining.

Entering the conference center was like landing in dreary Kansas after being in OZ. (By the way, I was never sure why Dorothy wanted to go home so much. I mean, couldn't her family just visit her in OZ?) Inside the conference were the pasty-faced strivers who had spent the last three days taking notes about financing college. I'll talk to one of them before we leave town. My parents might ask me about what I learned about financing. A pretty girl can always get a boy to share his class notes. So, I'm not worried.

I never turn down invites from God. So, I found myself walking with my three besties down the long corridor of conference rooms with the names of the presentations going on in them. It's like playing Russian Roulette. Which one will kill the most brain cells today? With four choices, we decided to split up. Each of us picked a subject and later brief the group on the long car ride home. Pretty efficient. Right?

We decided to stick Caroline with "Current Student Loan Interest Rates," because her name began with a C. As good a reason as any, right?

For some reason, Maria was actually interested in "Loan Consolidation Strategies." Her dad is a banker. So, maybe its inherited.

Patty followed a cute guy into "Debt Forgiveness Programs." Way to go Patty!

So, God led me by process of elimination into something called the "Follow the Science Foundation."

What Is the Follow the Science Foundation?

The speaker on stage began with, "Hello, I'm Dr. Brandon Fauchison, Executive Director of the Follow the Science Foundation."

"OMG," I'm thinking, "he looks so much like that goofy old scientist we were always seeing on TV during the Covid lockdown. Might be his son or grandson." As he begins his presentation, I'm thinking, "With a body like that, I hope you like socially distanced dating for the rest of your life."

Now, let me tell you about me and the wonderful work the Foundation is doing. The Foundation is allowing me to fulfill my lifelong dream to bring ordinary Americans into the scientific experiment process while solving the country's student debt problem. We're creating a world where scientific principles guide our decisions. I hope you all participate. It will change your lives.

I confess, this is about where most of the audience were doing some emergency meditation[1] (see, I'm not the only one) after Dr. Fauchison began talking. Why do they darken the room for slide shows, especially when the audience has been up all-night partying? Does that make any sense to you?

Dr. Fauchison continued his spiel oblivious to the sleeping Kaitlyn who was now using the boy seated next to her as her pillow.

---

1 Picture Students Sleeping https://firepitcell.com/wp-content/uploads/2021/11/FSN7.jpg

"Now, some background information about us. Following the Great Pandemic of the early 2020s, America began to acknowledge that scientists know best and we should all "follow the science." One of many initiatives, the National Science Act, funded government-private partnerships. These partnerships created student work programs to facilitate university research by acting as experiment subjects.

The Follow the Science Foundation became the biggest government-private partnership administering such research programs. Finally, scientists have all the human test subjects we need to advance the frontiers of human scientific knowledge. Data is flowing in every day. Each year tens of thousands of fresh persons at dozens of prestigious universities participate in Follow the Science Foundation experiments in return for the Foundation paying their tuition, room, and board."

The still sleeping Kaitlyn also misses a disturbance. During Dr. Fauchison's presentation, a student from the audience approaches the stage and yells, "Look what their experiment did to me! They made me a freak!"

"Miss, you know you are under a restraining order to keep away from all Foundation events." As she is surrounded by security officers, she yells, "Don't believe a word he says. They ruined my life," followed by tears and an assortment of curse words before she is dragged out of the room.

Before returning to his prepared remarks, Dr. Fauchison says, "Let me assure you that there is nothing dangerous about the Foundation's experiments. That misguided student failed to follow experiment protocols. It was her fault, but the Foundation paid a generous settlement amount. In the unlikely event something goes wrong, we have great insurance coverage for experiment participants. So, don't worry."

Dr. Fauchison then continues his slide show presentation for the next half hour before someone texts him that it has stopped raining outside. Knowing that means he will soon be losing his audience he wraps up his presentation.

"If you have any acceptable science-based questions or suggestions, please send them to me at DrFauchison@gmail.com. We want to be inclusive of all groups. Foundation experiments are perfectly designed for every student, regardless of their race, creed, nationality, sex, gender, sexual orientation, political party, income or dietary restrictions."

As the boy Kaitlyn is leaning on gets up to leave, Kaitlyn's head hits the desk and she awakens to hear: "I urge you all to go to our website and sign up for your experiment as soon as possible. Spaces for next semester's experiments are filling up fast. Act now and you may win a free Spring Break experiment/vacation in beautiful CANCUN at a properly socially distanced resort. Experiment survivors all receive a lifetime supply of N-99.47 masks. Nothing gets past them."

"CANCUN next spring! OMG, the spring break capital of the whole world![2] That's so totally me," is all Kaitlyn can think about. "God, thanks for waking me up at the right time."

One more thing Dr. Fauchison continues, "Don't be scared off by the paperwork. It's all just a formality."

CONFIDENTIALITY FORM. I hereby agree not to use or disclose to others the CONFIDENTIAL INFORMATION (as defined in the National Science Act) of the Follow the Science Foundation. Violators will be subject to penalties specified in the National Science Act. BLAH, BLAH! BLAH!

EXPERIMENT CONSENT FORM AND LIABILITY RELEASE. In exchange for all the benefits afforded by the National Science Act, I hereby consent to all experiments by the Follow the Science Foundation and release the Foundation from all liability associated with such experiments. The Foundation reserves the right to change experiments at any time. BLAH! BLAH! BLAH!

At the end of the presentation, I handed Dr. Fauchison my two signed Foundation forms and started to walk away. Looking back, I probably should have read them. And maybe I missed some important stuff while I was asleep. But what's done is done.

"Thank you for signing up, Ms. Korosec. I noticed you sleeping for most of my presentation. You're lovely when you're asleep. Would you like

---

2 Video Cancun Spring Break https://www.youtube.com/watch?v=9Ik9XOVgcmo

some private counseling about how to become a Foundation Scholar?" I have a penthouse suite upstairs.

Ew! As if!

So, I did what I always do when this happens. Laugh hysterically, point like this[3] and walk away.

Older guys really hate feeling ridiculous, especially if they're a doctor or someone else who usually gets their way. I bet I'll never see the likes of Dr. Brandon Fauchison again after I gave him my treatment. I also hoped he wouldn't hold it against me. But I stopped worrying about that, when a couple of weeks later, a very official looking package from the Follow the Science Foundation arrived in the mail. Good timing too, because when my parents looked at my tan when I got back from Destin, they didn't believe I had attended the conference at all. Parents are so . . . frustrating. Now, I had official proof from the American Government. The Government never lies. Right?

So, my family and I diligently filled out the piles of forms, got my medical tests and two weeks later I received confirmation that I was officially a "Follow the Science Foundation Scholar." My college financial problems were over. YAY!

Awsome Spring Break, right?

Well, except for that problem with the car[4] driving home. That absolutely killed my manicure.

And then, three weeks after I got home, I realized I was late. No, not for class. The other kind of late. Time for the "test."

Kaitlyn begins praying.[5]

"OK God, before take this test, I promise I'll NEVER do it again, ever. Really! Just work with me, God. Please."

Am I?[6] or aren't I?

---

3 Kaitlyn Pointing Laughing Picture https://firepitcell.com/wp-content/uploads/2021/11/FSN9.jpg

4 Kaitlyn Fixing Car Picture https://firepitcell.com/wp-content/uploads/2021/11/FSN9.jpg

5 Kaitlyn Praying Picture https://firepitcell.com/wp-content/uploads/2021/11/FS-N11.jpg

6 FS12 Kaitlyn Pregnant Picture https://firepitcell.com/wp-content/uploads/2021/11/FSN12.jpg

As Kaitlyn imagines herself pregnant, she experiences a familiar feeling. "WHEW! Never been so glad to feel the crimson tide. Roll Tide Roll! Sweet Home Alabama. Thanks God! I owe you one."

God, I've been thinking. You know, forever is a long time. How about we make a tiny amendment to the promise I just made? How about for one whole month? Plus, I'll help my mom more at home.

It's a deal? Thanks God, I knew you'd understand. Sorry I keep breaking promises. I mean well, but you knew that already, didn't you?

"Oh, you think this type of outfit is what gets me into trouble? Sorry God, this outfit just attracts boys, like the flowers you created attract the bees. See, it's all part of your plan. I'm just a poor flower who likes bees. My spirit is willing but my flesh is weak."[7] So, if you think about it, God, it's kind of your fault for creating my weakness. Why did you do that? Maybe, next time we talk, God, we should talk about that.

"Gotta run now, God."

"What am I going to do with that girl?" the creator of the universe asks.[8] "So frustrating when she uses what I say and do against me. Why do I create such manipulative creatures? Maybe this free will thing was a mistake." They keep making the same mistakes.[9]

---

7 Bible Quote Flesh is Weak https://www.kingjamesbible.me/Matthew-26-41/

8 Creator of the Universe Picturehttps://firepitcell.com/wp-content/uploads/2021/11/FSN14.jpg

9 Music Video I did it Again https://www.youtube.com/watch?v=CduA0TULnow

Who Are the Fire Pit Cell Members?

Hi, Kaitlyn Korosec, again.

I had a great summer now that my college finances were settled thanks to being a Follow the Science Foundation Scholar. That was great, because my three BFFs were all going to different colleges. So, we deserved a great summer together, right? Contact me later and I'll tell you some stories about that summer. OMG!

But life was throwing me curve ball. How would I survive college without my three besties. When I got to college, I was going to have to start over finding new BFFs. Here's the story about me and the Cell, my new besties.

The Cell? Oops, I forgot, you don't know about the Cell yet, do you? So sorry, I do that sometimes. People tell me it's confusing, but you'll get used to it. I'm worth getting to know. Really.

We called ourselves, "The Fire Pit Cell." We all became Fire Pit Spirits, each in our own way. Our cell started small, but we grew to many spirits.[1]

Our story tells the good, the bad and the ugly about the ten of us through the Fall semester of my first year of college. Follow our story and you'll know why we're called the Fire Pit Cell. We'll describe how the Follow the Science Foundation experimented on us and the other things going on my freshman year. But our story isn't just about me.

---

1 https://firepitcell.com/wp-content/uploads/2021/11/MN1.jpg

We all entered college full of dreams, hopes and insecurities. We knew we needed to study to get good jobs, but first we enjoyed the sweet taste of freedom from parental controls. We partied and formed romantic and other relationships. We skipped a few classes, especially on Friday mornings after Thursday night football games. I mean, what a dumb time to schedule a class!

It's a little embarrassing to have all this become public. As you'll soon see, we made some mistakes along the way, but we learned a lot of important things outside the classroom. In short, we were about as smart and as dumb, and as strong and as weak, as the many generations of students who came before us.

Well, OK, maybe we did it a different way than some earlier generations. I mean, we're in the third decade of the 21st Century. Stuff is going on. Its real. We're part of that. But aside from that, normal, right? Maybe, that was what the Foundation was looking for, a perfectly representative sample for scientific experimentation. Very natural for scientists, right?

I guess I should tell you a little about our experiences with the Foundation. At the beginning of the semester, the Foundation processed and assigned students to a wide range of experiments. It was all very institutional and efficient. Kind of like when we registered for our normal classes.

I thought some of the experiments were a little weird, but what do I know? I'm not a scientist. It made me feel good that I was helping to advance the frontiers of human scientific knowledge. And, hey, we were going to graduate college without any student loans. Debt free is worth suffering a little, right? So, initially we were enthusiastic about the Foundation's program.

Later, some odd things started happening to some of us in our Foundation experiments. That's all our settlement agreement with the Foundation allows us to say in public. The Foundation's attorneys insisted on that. So, if you really want to know more, I'll have to whisper. (I negotiated the whispering is OK provision of the settlement agreement). Just don't tell anybody else, OK?

Our story is about how we tried to be ordinary students while dealing with the Foundation's experiments. You definitely want to know how we did it, if you're going to sign up with the Foundation.

Now, I'll introduce you to all the Fire Pit Cell members. Let's start with three pairs of first year roommates, who live in adjoining dorm rooms.

Room 311: Michelle Collins and Sheldon Atwell (aka Shelley), who skipped the last two years of high school;

Room 313, Kaitlyn Korosec (that's me) and Olivia Jackson (super smart and I loved being her roommate).

Room 315, Allison Lee (aka Allie) and Luna de Reyes (a refugee from Venezuela)

We soon met the remaining four members of the Fire Pit Cell: Scott Hopkins (OMG, what a hunk!), Sanjay Singh, Nicole Wilson and Gerald Brown.

You'll get to know them better when you hear our story, but I've asked each of the Cell members to tell you a little bit about themselves. I'll go first.

Kaitlyn Korosec[2] - Follow the Science Foundation Scholar

I'm an 18-year-old criminal justice major from a small town nobody has ever heard of.

"I was just a scared girl who fell in love the first day I arrived at college. After that, I was prepared to do anything to get my man (Scott), but I did a lot more than I ever expected I'd have to do."

A girl has to be ready for anything these days. And I am.

I watched the movie "Clueless"[3] again the other night. Why do I like movies that make fun of girls like me? Because they remind me that we

---

2 Pic Many Faces of Kaitlyn https://firepitcell.com/wp-content/uploads/2021/11/MN2.jpg

3 Movie Clip Clueless https://www.youtube.com/watch?v=9Um1SvJvDLY

serve a purpose. We make people happy, a much-needed talent in today's world.

These days I can't get this song out of my head.[4] I know I'm taking a risk but try not to break my heart, Scott. We can do better than they did.

Scott Hopkins[5]

I'm 21 years old in the fourth year of a five-year joint Engineering and Business Degree program and captain of the Lacrosse team. Olivia Jackson and I are so close. Practically one person. My father, Senator Hopkins of Tennessee chairs the Senate Judiciary Committee. He and Judge Jackson work together on many projects. I'm the product of the Senator's second marriage. He's had four and I won't be surprised if I don't get another step-mother before I graduate college.

Here's what drives me.

"If I don't like the way the world works, I change it."

What about Kaitlyn, you ask? The song "Gentle on My Mind"[6] sums up our relationship. I hope Kaitlyn can live with that.

I like fast things, cars, motorcycles and boats, it doesn't matter as long as it's fast. My favorite movie is "The Road Warrior."[7] The 1981 Mel Gibson film. I like survivors. Watch it if you want to know me.

I'm from Nashville. When I'm driving, I play country music. I love Alan Jackson singing "Drive (for Daddy Gene)"[8] and "The Devil Went Down to Georgia"[9] by the Charlie Daniels Band. Music for fast cars.

Olivia Jackson[10]

4 Music Video All Too Well https://www.youtube.com/watch?v=tollGa3S0o8

5 Pic Scott Hopkins https://firepitcell.com/wp-content/uploads/2021/11/MN5.jpg

6 Music Gentle on my Mind https://www.youtube.com/watch?v=ETkzK9pXMio

7 Movie Clip Road Warrior https://www.youtube.com/watch?v=UlwtiOyaoo0

8 Music Drive https://www.youtube.com/watch?v=dQe3DKDQRRs

9 Music Devil in Georgia https://www.youtube.com/watch?v=wBjPAqmnvGA

10 Pic Olivia Jackson https://firepitcell.com/wp-content/uploads/2021/11/MN1-1.jpg

I'm 18 years old majoring in political science and Mandarin Chinese.

I grew up traveling around the world with my mother (aka the Professor) while my father (aka the Judge) played political games. My family and I have known Scott Hopkins and his family practically forever.

The most important thing to remember about me is that I like orderly rational behavior. So, you're probably wondering, "How do Kaitlyn and Olivia share a 200 square foot dorm room?" Some days I wonder about that too, but most of the time we're actually a good roommate match. She's fun to be with. Sometimes I need her to loosen me up. My father was a civil rights lawyer before he became a Federal Judge. My mother is a college linguistics professor who sometimes works for a secretive government agency[11]. (Please don't tell anyone. People might die. Really!) My parents were a mixed-race marriage back in the olden days when some people seemed to think that was a big deal.[12] Can you imagine? But the world changed. So, I guess my parents had the last laugh.[13]

"I like being half and half. I see both sides of every issue. I don't like people forcing me to choose a side."

These days I don't have much time for movies and music, but I adore Opera, especially "Carmen."[14] When I relax playing piano, I prefer Mozart."[15]

Michelle Collins[16] – Follow the Science Foundation Scholar

I'm a 22-year-old transfer student performing arts major from Pittsburgh. I'm restarting my academic career after taking a detour. Some

---

11 CIA website https://www.cia.gov/

12 Music Society's Child https://www.youtube.com/watch?v=3O0LiZtuDPw

13 Pic Olivia's Parents https://firepitcell.com/wp-content/uploads/2021/11/MN11-Olivia-s-Parents.jpg

14 Opera Carmen https://www.youtube.com/watch?v=KJ_HHRJf0xg

15 Music Mozart https://www.youtube.com/watch?v=Rb0UmrCXxVA

16 Pic Michelle Collins https://firepitcell.com/wp-content/uploads/2021/11/MN16-Michelle.jpg

people don't understand my life choices, but I do and that's all that matters. Some people think I'm deranged because I see a side of reality that most people are blind to. I prefer the word "enchanting" to deranged. It's so much nicer, don't you think? You decide what this tells you about me.

"A bubble is real, until it's gone. Think about a glass of champagne Where do all the bubbles go?[17] They were there, but then you can't see them. I live my life on the edge between your world and the dimension where all the burst bubbles go. My bubbles guide my life. It's so beautiful in my bubble dimension, but it's not for the weak of heart. Maybe I'll let you visit me there if you dare."

I'm an actress. I change every day. What you see today you may never see again. So, if you see a Michelle you like, cherish that Michelle while she's still here. I suffer to create beautiful performances. Nothing is free in life. I'm willing to pay the price.

I just rewatched the movie "Close Encounters"[18] for about the tenth time and love Rod Serling's "Twilight Zone."[19] A song that inspires me every day is Madonna's "Material Girl."[20] Explains a lot about how the world works. Not the world we're all supposed to like, the real world.

Allison Lee (aka Allie)[21] - Follow the Science Foundation Scholar

I'm an 18 years old performing arts major from Hawaii. Part Japanese and part Chinese, but my people have been in Hawaii practically forever. We're kind of like Hawaiian Pilgrims. I have three older brothers. I'm the rebel in the family.

---

17 Pic Bubbles Dimension https://firepitcell.com/wp-content/uploads/2021/11/MN17-Bubbles.jpg
18 Movie Clip Close Encounters https://www.youtube.com/watch?v=S4PYI6TzqYk
19 TV Clip Twilight Zone https://www.youtube.com/watch?v=daCWbRQfOyc
20 Music Video Material Girl https://www.youtube.com/watch?v=6p-lDYPR2P8
21 Pic Allyson Lee (Allie) https://firepitcell.com/wp-content/uploads/2021/11/MN21-Allie.jpg

What's the most important thing to know about me?

"I thought I was a tough girl. Turns out, not really, at least not all the time. Life has been much sweeter since I learned to ride with the waves, not against them."

I control my temper and my body with sunrise yoga. I like the movie "Mulholland Drive"[22] a lot. Denise Rosenthal's "Isadora"[23] is one of my favorite music videos. Such sweet girls.

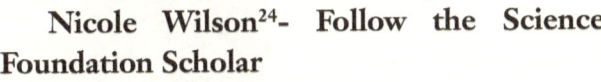

Nicole Wilson[24]- Follow the Science Foundation Scholar

I'm 18, a black studies major. I grew up about five miles from school. Gerald Brown is the closest thing I have to family. Everyone needs a Gerald in their life.

Remember this about me. **"I get them before they get me. It works. Then, Kaitlyn gives me something powerful to help me move on."**

People who test my patience once don't do it a second time because I've got the power. Want to test me on that?

Kaitlyn and I didn't hit it off at first. Two people from different worlds, but we made our peace. Fate brought us together. I guess the saying that "the enemy of my enemy is my friend" explains how we became friends.

Check out the movie "Respect."[25] Billie Holiday singing "Strange Fruit"[26] inspires me. Lest we forget.

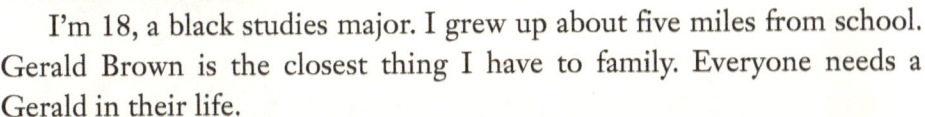

---

22 Movie Clip Muholland Drive https://www.youtube.com/watch?v=jbZJ487oJlY

23 Music Video Isadora https://www.youtube.com/watch?v=T6ikG-WbFMk

24 .Pic Nicole Wilson https://firepitcell.com/wp-content/uploads/2021/11/MN24-Nicole.jpg

25 Movie Clip Respect https://www.youtube.com/watch?v=qTtxoz3OIlU

26 Music Strange Fruit https://www.youtube.com/watch?v=Web007rzSOI

Gerald Brown[27]

I'm a 24-year-old community college student, studying hospitality management. I have five brothers and sisters, but I'm closest to my friend Nicole. I knew her brother before he died. He gave me my first job. Looked out for me on the street. So, now I look out for his little sister. That's the way the world is supposed to work. Right?

What to know about me? Humm . . . Yeah, this is it.

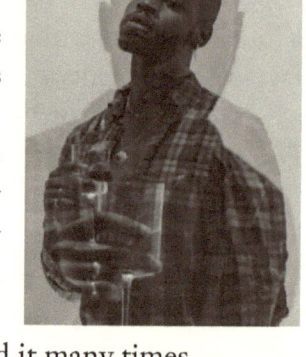

"Having a bad day today isn't an excuse to be angry tomorrow. Understanding that is what turned my life around."

I'm going to open my own restaurant some-day. I can see it now. Have my business plan. Know a great location. Just need the cash. Know any investors? Send them my way and I'll save you a table.

I really like "The Terminator.[28]" Have watched it many times.

2Pac's "Hit 'Em Up"[29] is my favorite Rap song. Its gritty, but life is gritty sometimes.

Know what I mean bro? Yeah, you do.

Luna de Reyes[30]

I'm 19, a math and computer science major from Venezuela.

I'm blessed. My family fled Venezuela when I was ten. We appreciate having running water and electricity every day and not having the secret police follow us. My big thing is that **"I don't want the same things to happen to my new country. Lest we forget."**

---

27 Pic Gerald Brown https://firepitcell.com/wp-content/uploads/2021/11/MN27-Gerald.jpg

28 Movie Clip Terminator https://www.youtube.com/watch?v=k64P4l2Wmeg

29 Music Video Hit Em Up https://www.youtube.com/watch?v=41qC3w3UUkU

30 Pic Luna de Reyes https://firepitcell.com/wp-content/uploads/2021/11/MN30-Luna.jpg

Here's my pet peeve. So, you think you know all about Latinas? Think again. We're not all the same.

Life is so sweet now, especially when I'm listening to Malu Trevejo singing "Luna Llena."[31] It has my name in it. For movies, I like almost anything Sci-Fi, but only the psychological scary ones. "Invasion of the Body Snatchers"[32] from the 1950s is especially good.

Sheldon Atwell (aka Shelley)[33] - Follow the Science Foundation Scholar

They asked me to provide a photo. I hate that. I'm at that awkward stage. Check me out in a few years girls. I'll age well.

I'm 16, math and computer science major. I'm the youngest member of the university's freshman class. School was easy, but my age created social issues. My mom died when I was little. I miss her.

What should you remember about me?

"Maybe someday, I might become a fully functioning person. That's number 6 on my list of top-10 life goals."

"2001 Space Odyssey"[34] is my favorite movie, probably because it opens with "Also Sprach Zarathustra."[35] Yes, Michelle, I know you told me to never tell that to a girl. Dating poison you said. But that's what I like.

Sanjay Singh[36]

I'm a 24-year-old computer science grad student from southern California.

---

31 Music Video Lula Llena https://www.youtube.com/watch?v=E-zcNpZJX78

32 Movie Clip Invasion Body Snatchers https://www.youtube.com/watch?v=WuL2QwsNeM8

33 Pic Sheldon Atwell (Shelley) https://firepitcell.com/wp-content/uploads/2021/11/MN33-Sheldon.jpg

34 Movie Clip 2001 Space Odyssey https://www.youtube.com/watch?v=XHjIqQBsPjk

35 Music Zarathustra https://www.youtube.com/watch?v=vWF1glZWQa8

36 Pic Sanjay Singh https://firepitcell.com/wp-content/uploads/2021/11/MN36-Sanjay.jpg

I know that screams nerd, but you need to know I'm not. Check me out on dating apps girls. I'm on several. Michelle says I'm an underrated dating opportunity. I've memorized the "Kamasutra."[37] My parents emigrated from India, but I was "Born in the USA."[38] I go back to India sometimes to work with my uncle. That's where I first met Scott and Olivia.

Kaitlyn's Comments

It's me, Kaitlyn, again. Thanks for sharing, gang. As always, I'll share some thoughts with you all.

"Shelley, becoming a functioning person is only number 6 on your list? We need to talk about your priorities, yet again."

"Sanjay, memorizing only gets you so far with girls. It's not what you do. It's how you do it."

"Olivia! You are so modest. People should know that you're a lot like Condoleezza Rice[39] and you might become President or something someday."

"Allie, what's it like being Asian? Yes, I know some people think that's not an appropriate question. But how will I learn if I don't ask?"

"Luna, you didn't have electricity or water? How is that possible?"

"Michelle, I'd love to visit you in your bubble world. I was talking to God the other day and God knows your bubbles. God and I find you enchanting."

"Gerald, you're so sweet. We're so much alike. If I was a black guy, I'd want to be you."

"Nicole, you may have the power, but we both know your weakness. You'll do anything for one of these."[40]

---

37 Book https://www.amazon.com/Kama-Sutra-Colouring-Book/dp/1910787310
38 Music Video Born un USA https://www.youtube.com/watch?v=EPhWR4d3FJQ
39 Article Condoleezza Rice https://www.biography.com/political-figure/condoleezza-rice
40 Pic Present for Nicole https://firepitcell.com/wp-content/uploads/2021/11/MN40-Ice-Cream-Cone-for-Nicole.jpg

And "Did you hear what Scott said about me? I'm making progress with that boy. Here's how I imagine Scott and me . . . forever.[41] Don't laugh, I'm just the girl to do it."[42]

Like I said, nothing wildly unusual about any of us. We're a representative cross sample of our generation. Maybe that's why the Foundation wanted to experiment on us.

So, now you know us. Or maybe you don't. Want to find out more?

I'll start our story from the beginning of my first semester. But before I do, I want to say what that old English guy, who wrote all those long boring books, said, "It was the best of times, it was the worst of times[43]. . .." That pretty much describes my first semester in college. Know what I mean?

Now remember, don't tell anyone else what you're about to hear. Or at least whisper if you do. We'll all get in trouble if the Foundation finds out I've been blabbing about them. And you don't want to cross these people, believe me.

---

41 Pic Scott and Kaitlyn https://firepitcell.com/wp-content/uploads/2021/11/MN41-Scott-Lifts-Kaitlyn-Forever.jpg
42 Pic Kaitlyn Victorious https://firepitcell.com/wp-content/uploads/2021/11/MN42-Kaitlyn-Victorious.jpg
43 Article Tale of Two Cities https://en.wikiquote.org/wiki/A_Tale_of_Two_Cities

The Big Move

5:30 am Friday, August 26th and for one small town[1] girl the big day has finally arrived! College Freshman move in day. But it's still dark. Up at 4 am, because Daddy wanted to arrive early.

As they drive through town in the dawn's early light, Kaitlyn's mind wanders.

"I've lived here 18 years and I never noticed how magically serene my hometown[2] is. How can I possibly move away? Only six thousand people. I've probably met everyone one of them. We're kind of like an extended family. My support system."

"How will I deal with the mayhem of life at a big university? I'll see that many people every day. I've been looking forward to adventures, but am I really prepared to leave my cocoon? Will I fly like a butterfly? Sting like a bee? Or fall on my face?"

"I've been sleeping on long drives in this backseat behind Mom and Daddy since I was born. It's cozy knowing Daddy is driving. I know how to drive now, but why stop a good thing?"

Half asleep. Half awake. Images of her life drift before her. Kindergarten, Communion. Grandma's funeral. Kaitlyn smiles as she thinks "That boy in third grade who brought me cookies every day was so sweet. We thought we'd be married." Then images bathe over her of hunting with

---

1 Kaitlyn's Home Town https://www.beaufort-nc.com/
2 Music High School of Half My Hometown https://www.youtube.com/watch?v=abYaq2tWGYs

Daddy, the day she shot her first buck. "I learned so much about life that day, she thinks. Then, cheerleading, back seats under the stars, prom, graduation. "All so . . . normal" she thinks, "but now what?"

*   *   *

Many hours later, Mrs. Korosec nudges her daughter. "We're almost there,[3] honey."

"Almost where?" a dazed Kaitlyn wonders.

Her father's less gentle manner abruptly wakes Kaitlyn from her dreamlike trance. "Objective 1 achieved" as he pulls the van into a prize parking space. Bragging, "Close to your dorm but not so close that late arriving cars will block our get away. Perfect spot." That was Daddy's way. Life was always full of objectives.

As Mr. Korosec points to her dorm – Bagwell Hall.[4] Nice park across the street. Stay away from the park at night, Kaitlyn."

"Yes Daddy," as she looks forward to fun evenings with friends in Pullen Park.[5]

"OK, let's get your stuff moved in before it starts getting too warm."

The Korosec family immediately act with drill team precision learned helping her older brother do the college move in two years earlier. Kaitlyn jumps from the car as soon as her father pulls in. Her assigned Mission: find a cart to roll her belongings from the car to her dorm.

Mom walks ahead to confirm there is no last-minute dorm room change.

Kaitlyn spots the prize, an empty luggage cart about 30 feet from the dorm door. Then her mission goes off track. There he is, standing tall between her and her objective. He dwarfs the crowd. All around him small

---

3 Website Raleigh NC https://www.visitraleigh.com/plan-a-trip/cities-and-towns/ raleigh/west-raleigh/

4 Website Raleigh NC https://www.visitraleigh.com/plan-a-trip/cities-and-towns/ raleigh/west-raleigh/

5 Website Raleigh NC https://www.visitraleigh.com/plan-a-trip/cities-and-towns/ raleigh/west-raleigh/

anonymous people are scurrying back and forth across the courtyard. He stands still observing as one might watch a flock of quacking ducks. Serene and outside the crowd, not part of the confusion that surrounds him.

For one endless wonderful moment, his calmness bathes over her. She thinks, "Just like the warm feeling of home. Maybe, with his help, this can be home."

Then, Kaitlyn returns to reality, "Too late," she sighs as another girl drags the precious cart away. "Oh no. I've failed in my first college mission."

Seeing disappointment wash across her face, the stranger approaches. In a deep voice, accompanied by a casual smile, that makes you feel he wouldn't trust anyone else (only you) with this intimate message. "You don't need that cart. You have me."

"I do?"

"Yep, I'm here to recue damsels in distress."

"You are?"

"Yep. I'm at your disposal. I'm Scott, Scott Hopkins.[6] Part of the luggage brigade."

"And what makes you think I need help?"

"That girl just took the last cart. Another cart won't be available for at least an hour."

In a fake stern voice, but smiling to send the signal she wants, "And it's all your fault I didn't get that cart!"

"And exactly how is that my fault?"

"You were standing there, and I couldn't take my eyes off of you."

"Did I just really say that?" Kaitlyn thinks. "Maybe I really am ready for this bigger world."

"I like girls who know what they want," he replies before asking, "Shouldn't you be at football practice now? You're kind of small for a football player, aren't you?"

---

6 Pic Scott Hopkins https://firepitcell.com/wp-content/uploads/2021/11/C1N6-Scott.jpg

"Oh, this jersey?[7] I'm big enough where it counts for a girl. And it's autographed. See."

"I can see that. Shall I just call you by your number? Or do you have a name?"

Smiling, "I'm Kaitlyn Korosec."

"I've seen pictures of that player with beautiful girls. Are you one of them?"

"Why Mr. Hopkins, are you trying to sweet talk a newbie freshman girl?"

"Of course, I am. It's part of my VIP service."

"I like VIP, but no. I don't really know him."

"I don't see other girls in football jerseys. Is there's a story behind your jersey, Kaitlyn?"

"Well yes, he was appearing at a charity event. My friends dared me to ask him. So, I summoned up all my courage, walked over to him and went into flirting mode wearing his numbered jersey. And he signed it in exchange for a kiss. I wore it today because it's my good luck charm. It reminds me to overcome my shyness and go after the things I want."

"And what do you want, Kaitlyn?"

Looking up into Scott's eyes, "Right now, I have everything I want, Mr. Hopkins."

"Sounds like you're pretty good at flirting, Kaitlyn."

"It's not hard doing things I like."

"OK Kaitlyn, I can see that I'm not going to top you in the flirting department. Where do I start work?"

"My family is parked half a block that way."

Scott begins walking in the direction Kaitlyn points. "Since it's my fault, there's no time to waste."

Following her new conquest, she wonders, "OMG, do I have magical powers now?" Arriving at the family's van, "Daddy, all the carts were taken. But Scott is here to help carry my things."

---

7 Pic Kaitlyn Football Jersey https://firepitcell.com/wp-content/uploads/2021/11/C1N7-Kaitlyn-Moving-In-Day.jpg

"Did you leave anything at home, Princess?" Scott says, as he surveys the stacks of bags[8] Kaitlyn's father unloaded from the trailer and piled on the sidewalk hiding their car.

"Well, girls need more things than boys, Scott. I just brought the bare minimum. Hope I have a big closet in my dorm room."

Mr. Korosec's instinct was to go it alone and shoo off this stranger, but before he can, Kaitlyn's mother turns to her husband, "Dear, this is the difference between moving a son and a daughter into college. Girls are smart enough to accept help."

With that settled, Kaitlyn's mother smiles as she watches Kaitlyn's '6' 4" prize catch grab the two biggest suitcases with her backpack and computer bag slung over his shoulders.

After Mom's help, Kaitlyn knows her father remains skeptical of her new friend, "Scott, tell my father what you do when you're not rescuing damsels in distress."

"Third year combined business and engineering major sir. And I dabble in Lacrosse. Don't worry sir, I've helped move dozens of girls in the past two years. Haven't had a single casualty yet."

"He's the Captain of the Lacrosse Team, Daddy! Isn't that exciting?

With that, Scott leads the Korosec caravan into the dorm entrance hall. "Look at all these carts waiting for that small slow service elevator. They'll be waiting all morning. Kaitlyn was smart not to get stuck in that mess. The fire stairs are this way sir. They're wider than the regular stairs."

Taking the lead climbing up the stairs, Kaitlyn is acutely aware that Scott is below her watching her butt bounce with each step and that her father is watching Scott watching his daughter.

"What room number? Mrs. Korosec, did you say Room 313?"

Stepping over a jumble of boxes and bags, Scott hurries Kaitlyn forward as they leave her parents behind: "It's this way Princess."

---

8 Pic Kaitlyn's Luggage https://firepitcell.com/wp-content/uploads/2021/11/C1N8-Kaitlyn-s-Essentials.jpg

Reaching Room 313, they can finally talk out of parental range, "We can't fit through this door together, Princess," as their bodies touch for the first time. "I didn't mind trying though," Scott says with a smile.

"OK Kaitlyn, you need to say something," she thinks before she blurts out, "Scott, a girl knows when she is being watched. And with Daddy watching right behind us! I mean, what a naughty boy you are!"

"But you did like being on display' Kaitlyn. Come on, admit it."

"Well, let's just say that it's a girl's prerogative when she's in the mood. Besides its good to remind Daddy that his little girl isn't so little anymore."

"Can we do this some other time then when your 'Daddy' isn't around?"

"Maybe, if you're a good boy," Kaitlyn says smiling.

"I can be a good boy for a while. But no promises about how long."

Scott breaks off their flirtation as he shouts down the hall: "Hey Bro! What are you doing here?"

"Moving in like everyone else," Sheldon responds. "And you?"

"Helping Princess move in."

"Princess, this is Sheldon, my best friend's younger brother. "

"Sheldon, Princess' other name is Kaitlyn. And she's not on the football team."

"Sheldon, aren't you still 16? What happened to the last two years of high school?"

"17 early next year, but not so loud, Scott. Let's keep it secret. Trying to pass for 18."

"You must be really smart, Sheldon," Kaitlyn says.

"Maybe, but my high school just ran out of math and science courses for me to take. It didn't make sense hanging around high school another two years. So, here I am."

"Princess, in his family, his brother Allen got all the muscle and Sheldon got all the brains. If you put the two of them together, you might have a normal person."

Kaitlyn's parents finally catch up, "Daddy, Scott just introduced me to Sheldon. He's a big brain. Now I have two friends. Sheldon, these are my parents, Peter and Helen Korosec."

In a hurry, Scott says, "Sheldon, glad I bumped into you. Let's get together later. In the meantime, take care of Princess for me."

Lightly caressing his arm, Kaitlyn thinks "He's all muscle." Then, tilting her head she smiles looking up at her giant, "Thanks for all your help, Scott. Don't know what I would have done without . . ."

"No prob. You're a damsel who looked distressed. I help damsels in distress. Mission accomplished. But I'm on duty now. Other damsels to help move in."

"Isn't there anything to distract you from your duty?" Kaitlyn asks.

Scott imagines what Kaitlyn could do to distract him from his duty,[9] and then "Goodbye Mr. and Mrs. Korosec. Don't worry about your daughter. Kaitlyn will be fine. She's ready for whatever she finds here."

Kaitlyn frowns as Scott begins walking down the hall filled with other families moving their daughters in. "Every girl and mother is looking at him and he knows it. No wonder he didn't ask for my number. I'm just another pretty face in a sea of pretty faces."

Looking back over his shoulder, "Don't worry Princess. I copied your phone number from the tag on your bag. I know where you live and I've got your number."

Helen to Peter Korosec, "Don't worry Dear. Scott seems like the type of boy we've always wanted for Kaitlyn."

"Boys I can handle. Boys Kaitlyn can handle. But don't fool yourself, Helen. That was a man, not a boy."

As mother and daughter smile knowingly at one another "Oh Daddy, don't underestimate me. I'm a college woman now. I know exactly what I'm doing."

"I'm not worried about what you're doing. But what will he be doing?"

The Korosec's finish unpacking.

"Room is looking good. Almost perfect. All it needs is my roommate. Can't wait to meet her."

"Well, can you wait until after lunch? I'm hungry and we have a long drive home," Mr. Korosec says.

---

9 Music Video Duty https://www.youtube.com/watch?v=aOHuqb8YrUQ

The family finds a place near campus – Sammy's. After lunch, hugging his daughter goodbye at their car, Kaitlyn's father hands her a small box. "Well, go ahead. Open it. It won't open itself.

Kaitlyn unwraps the box and finds a silver police whistle with an inscription: 'Carry me always.'

"It's the one they gave me when I first joined the police force. It was lucky for me. Hope it protects you." As Kaitlyn remembers being a ten-year old who she snuck this whistle out of the house and tried to direct traffic at her town's biggest intersection, she hears her father say, "Well, we're not ones for long goodbyes. Just whistle if you need us."

Maybe Peter Korosec said something else. Maybe not. So many feelings all at once. Too much to process. All Kaitlyn remembers is that he opened the car door, got in and waived goodbye.

"Oh Daddy[10] . . ." in a whisper. As a song plays in her head, a single tear slowly rolls down her cheek. Watching her parents drive away, Kaitlyn aches to get back into her spot, that empty back seat. Then, "God, please watch over Mom and Daddy[11] while I'm not there to protect them."

---

10 Music My Father https://www.youtube.com/watch?v=R04d-XAA_EQ
11 Pic God https://firepitcell.com/wp-content/uploads/2021/11/C1N11-God-Galaxy.jpg

2

Reality Crash!

Kaitlyn sits in an isolated corner of the Quad[1] assessing her situation. Blocking out the sights and sounds around her, she thinks.

"I'm all alone. So far away from home.[2] Just me and Daddy's whistle." Holding her last connection to home, "How did Daddy know this would comfort me so much?." Then, "How silly of me, Daddy and I know each other more than anyone in the whole wide world. That's why."

"Wide world? There are more students here than people in my hometown. I'm new here. No one knows me. Scary." Then "Kaitlyn, that's enough. Time to snap out of my funk. The good thing is no one knows me. I'm starting with a clean slate. All my high school mistakes are gone. I can be anyone I want to be. That's just what I need, a restart. That's what I've been praying for. Thank you, God."

"Can't leave everything up to God though. I have to do the rest with this gift. So, what do I want? That's my problem. I don't know what I want, aside from wanting Scott. Being born again, what do I want?" After a few seconds, "Time for 'Kaitlyn the Bold' to emerge. No more a shy girl, who's afraid to draw attention. Do new things. Meet new people. Never say no. Conquer new worlds. That's what I want. But can I do that? What if I crash? Nah, that won't happen."

---

1 Article Best College Quads https://www.collegerank.net/beautiful-campus-quads/
2 Music 500 Miles https://www.youtube.com/watch?v=Q_XgghFZt1o

CRASH![3]

"Hey Princess! You're supposed to catch a frisbee with your hands, not your head."

"Sheldon, there are more subtle ways to invite a girl to play."

"Yeah, but not as much fun as seeing the dazed look on your face."

"Sheldon! Has anyone told you that you throw like a girl?"

"Trash-talk from the Princess. Let's see what you got Princess!"

As she retrieves the frisbee and joins the group,[4] she thinks, "Thank you God for answering my prayer. So begins my new life – alone, but not alone.'

"OK Princess, so you know how to throw a frisbee, but your catching technique still stinks."

The afternoon passes quickly – full of laughter, many new names she won't remember tomorrow and a bottle of warm beer.

"God, I love College," Kaitlyn thinks, walking back to her room. "Still no sign of my roommate. Hope she didn't change her mind."

Sweaty from chasing frisbees in the warm August sun, "OK, time to test the plumbing in this old dorm. Time for a shower.[5] No one in here. The cold water feels good in August. Hope we get hot water by December. Not like home, but this works" as the water washes away Kaitlyn's sweat and troubles.

Returning to her room wrapped in a towel, she hears, "Hi, I'm Olivia.[6] I hope you're Kaitlyn."

"Yes, great to finally meet you. I was worried you had transferred to another school or something. That's my nature. I'm always worrying about something."

---

3 Article St Paul Damascus Road https://en.wikipedia.org/wiki/Conversion_of_Paul_the_Apostle

4 Video Frisbee Tournament https://www.youtube.com/watch?v=jM59VIwXRg8

5 Pic Kaitlyn Shower https://firepitcell.com/wp-content/uploads/2021/11/C2N5-Kaitlyn-Shower-.jpg

6 Pic Olivia https://firepitcell.com/wp-content/uploads/2021/11/C2N6-Olivia-Move-in-Day.jpg

"No. They asked the Judge to give a speech today at the faculty club. So, that delayed my move in."

"The Judge?"

"Sorry. The Judge[7] is my father – Harrison Jackson. I call my mother the Professor.[8] That's what they do. Our family is a little strange that way."

"Join the club. Everyone's family is at least a little strange."

"I'm almost 18 and a still call my father Daddy." Smiling, "calling him 'Deli Man'[9] just doesn't work for me." After seeing the perplexed expression on Olivia's face, "Daddy owns a delicatessen. I like Judge better than 'Deli Man.' So, who am I to judge you and the Judge?"

"So, you're a 'Daddy's Girl,'[10] are you? "

"Yep, since the day I was born. Still a proud 'Daddy's girl.' Sharing her prized possession, "Look, here's the police whistle he gave me when we said goodbye this afternoon. He's had it forever, since his first year on the force. He was like me, a first year."

"Oh, that's so sweet. My parents just gave me a reading list in case I ran out of class assignments to do."

"Well Olivia, I look forward to our parents meeting someday. Sounds like they have nothing in common, except they all have two great daughters."

"Maybe that's enough."

"Where are your bags?"

"Someone from the University is bringing them over."

"And your parents?"

"They're due here in ten minutes. The Judge is never late."

"Ten minutes? And I'm in a towel! And my hair is still wet! I've got to hurry. Can't meet a Judge and a Professor looking like this."

Kaitlyn scrambles to make herself presentable for the Judge and the Professor but takes time to do a little Internet research about Olivia's

---

7 Music Here Comes the Judge https://www.youtube.com/watch?v=DvMBxlu62c0

8 Movie Clip Harry Potter https://www.youtube.com/watch?v=vJIxdmLLpoc

9 Music Video Deli Songhttps://www.youtube.com/watch?v=prRK1o-1vOs

10 Music Video Daddy's Little Girl https://www.youtube.com/watch?v=rMNS9oNCL3s

parents. "OMG! They're both listed in Wikipedia! Olivia, please meet your parents in the lobby and buy me ten more minutes to get ready to meet them. I'm can't meet two famous people looking like this."

"You're so funny. We'll get along fine. But just remember, he isn't called the hanging judge for nothing."

As Olivia leaves for the lobby, "See you in 15 minutes. Princess." Catching Kaitlyn by surprise that Olivia knew Scott's nickname for her, "Oh Yes. I forgot the room number but asked someone in the hall what room you are in. He said, 'Oh, you mean the Princess.' That's how I found my room. Even the Judge doesn't meet a Princess every day. So, relax."

Kaitlyn ponders "So, Scott's nickname for me is circulating. Scott's a leader. People naturally follow him. Not the worst nickname, but I'm not sure I want to be called Princess the next four years, unless Scott is doing the calling."

Kaitlyn finishes dressing just as Olivia and her parents arrive in the hallway. "Kaitlyn, my parents are here. Can I open the door? Are you decent?"

As Kaitlyn opens the door, "Hello Mr. and Mrs. Jackson. So nice to meet you."

"Mr. and Mrs. Jackson? Who are they? Just call us Judge and Professor. And we'll call you Princess. That's the Judge's order," holding back a smile as long as possible.

"It's a deal Judge" as Kaitlyn hugs Olivia's father.

* * *

Meanwhile, at his Oberlin Road apartment near campus, Scott and his handler are texting encrypted messages:

"Agent 1, have you disabled the geo-tracking function on your phone?"
"Affirmative."
"Have you acquired your target?"
"Affirmative."

"Confirm Target's code name."
"Target's Code name is Princess."
"Proceed executing mission."
"Affirmative, commencing Mission."

3

Meeting the Neighbors

"Olivia, what do you want to do now that our families are gone?"

"Review our courses, Kaitlyn?"

"Maybe later, Olivia. How about getting to know our neighbors first? I've met a few, but let's dragnet the halls and round up a few more suspects."

"Come again?"

"Sorry, my father was a police officer and I'm intending to major in Criminal Justice. So, I have a habit of using police language. Sometimes in wildly inappropriate situations."

"I'll get used to your police references, if you don't mind me switching from English to Mandarin from time to time. I'm minoring in Chinese."

"Really? I'm not sure that's an even tradeoff, but I'll try."

"How do you say 'Come and meet the two girls from room 313,'" in Chinese?

"That's not the standard vocabulary I've studied, but that would be something like:

出来见313房间的两个女孩

"OK, I'll never pronounce that right, but you yell that in the hallway. If anyone comes out of their rooms, I'll translate it for them."

"I don't know that's the best way to meet people."

"Come on Olivia. It'll be fun. You need some fun in your life, roommate."

"Well . . . ."

"And you'll make an impression on people they won't forget. The worst thing that can happen in college is to be forgettable. You don't want Olivia to be that girl everyone forgets about, do you?

Olivia enters the hallway:

出来见313房间的两个女孩

After no one comes out of their rooms, "You'll have to be a lot louder than that, Olivia! Again MUCH LOUDER!

出来见313房间的两个女孩

"LOUDER!"

出来见313房间的两个女孩

Walking toward the boys' end of the hallway, "We're still being ignored. That not acceptable. Let me try:"

认识卖淫者 313 室

"Olivia, why are you laughing?", Kaitlyn asks

Before Olivia can respond, a door opens "She's laughing because what you said sounds a lot like: 'Meet prostitutes in Room 313.' So, how much does it cost to hire you two hot girls?

"Great! I love to negotiate," Kaitlyn responds. "How much do you have?

"How about two beers payable on the Quad. By the way, that's where everyone is now."

"It's a deal. You have two hot girls for two beers Mr. X?"

"Dennis Lee. Call me Denney. I studied in Beijing this summer."

"Great. My roommate Olivia here can practice her Chinese with you."

你好我叫奥利维亚 很高兴见到你Denney

"Hey, that was pretty good!"

"And I'm . . . ."

"I know, you're Princess."

"Really? You too! It's Kaitlyn, thank you very much. How am I going to ditch this nickname?"

"You probably won't. You've already become a legend. Hey Richard, hurry up! I've lined up two hot girls for the party on the Quad tonight."

"Hi, I'm Richard and I don't speak Chinese."

As Olivia and Denney begin walking away together talking in rudimentary Mandarin, "I'm ready for a hot girl, but I'll have to see proof."

"You'll have to wait on that proof. You haven't paid your beer yet."

That first night went as it began. Lots of people getting to know their neighbors. Several hours later, Olivia and a slightly wobbly Kaitlyn walk back to their room.

"Olivia, do you know what I like most about our room?"

"No Kaitlyn, what do you like?"

"I like the room number. 313 is so easy to remember."

"Yes, that's easy to remember."

"And people will remember the two hot girls who live in room 313, right?"

"Well, I know they'll remember at least on hot girl."

"Thank you, Olivia. I do so want to be remembered."

"You're off to a good start, Kaitlyn."

"Thanks Olivia."

"Olivia."

"What?"

"Nothing, I just like saying the name Olivia. It's such a pretty name. Olivia . . . Olivia . . . Olivia."[1]

"Thanks Kaitlyn, I like your name too."

"Which of my names to do you like better? Kaitlyn? Or Princess?"

"I like both names, Kaitlyn."

"Olivia, I have a confession to make."

"A confession?"

"Yes, you're my first black girlfriend."

"Really? What makes you think I'm black?"

"Ha! That's funny Olivia. I just wanted to say that this feels more like home, now that I've found a friend. We can make this dorm room our home away from home,[2] together.

---

1 Music Olivia https://www.youtube.com/watch?v=2soQop5g2Pk

2 Music Video Home https://www.youtube.com/watch?v=HoRkntoHkIE

"I'd like that, Kaitlyn. I've really never had one place to call home. I've travelled with my mother so much."

"Olivia, why did we leave the party so early?"

"1 a.m. isn't early, Kaitlyn."

"Not in high school time, but it's early in college time, Olivia. We have to adjust our clocks to college time. High school is East Coast time. In college, we're on West Coast time."

While Olivia hesitates to think about Kaitlyn's time analogy, Kaitlyn adds, "Gotcha, bet you weren't expecting that. I'm not as stupid as I might look at this moment on the time continuuuuuuum."

As Kaitlyn looks up at her, Olivia melts and bends down to hug her interesting roommate, "No, maybe not Kaitlyn, but I might decide to stay on high school time . . . at least for a while. I have a busy day tomorrow, Kaitlyn."

"Olivia, no one has to be busy tomorrow. Classes don't start until Monday. We have three whole days not to be busy."

"Well, I'm busy. I have an important meeting with the son of one of my father's friends."

With a mischievous look, "Is it a fun meeting, Olivia?"

"It's a business meeting, Kaitlyn. Last summer I was a Congressional intern at the office of a friend of the Judge. Our fathers thought it would be good for us to get together again."

"OMG! The Judge is a matchmaker? WOW! What a great dad! What does he look like?"

"My father? You just met my father."

"OK, your father is the best-looking Judge I've ever met. But what does your date look like?"

"Kaitlyn, you are very persistent for being so inebriated. It's not a date."

"I'm not ineb . . . by the way, Olivia, real people say drunk, because if you're drunk you can't pronounce ineb. . . . I was really drunk once in high school, and this doesn't feel like drunk This feels wonderful, but I'm glad you took me home.[3] This feels wonderful. I'm tired and a bit tipsy, but not drunk."

---

3 Music Video Drink Girl https://www.youtube.com/watch?v=XDTFRQa593w

"OK, tired and tipsy, then."

"Come on, tell all about your date, girlfriend! I won't go to sleep until you do."

"Well, if you must know, Scott is tall and athletic and has a nice smile."

"Is Scott Hopkins your date?"

"Yes, Senator Hopkins' son. The Judge and the Senator are good friends," Olivia says, "Do you know Scott?"

"Senator?" Kaitlyn asks and then thinks, "OMG! I'm in way over my head. How do I deal with these families? I'm just the daughter of a retired police officer, now deli man."

"Wait a minute, "Kaitlyn thinks, Daddy's just as good as a Senator and a Judge and I'm just as good as their son and daughter. I just have to be me at my best and I'll be OK."

After her debate with herself, Kaitlyn tell Olivia, "You're absolutely right, Olivia. It's late and your appointment tomorrow is a business meeting. Not a date. No, definitely not a date! Olivia, why did you think it's a date?"

"Kaitlyn, it's been interesting getting to know you. But it's been a long day and sometimes you're a very unusual girl. I'm tired."

"Olivia? One more question?"

"OK, one more."

"Did you have fun tonight?"[4]

"Yes, I had fun. For me, it was an unusual kind of fun, but it was definitely fun."

"That makes me so happy, Olivia. I do want us to have fun together. The fun will get us through the bumps."

"Good night, Kaitlyn," Olivia says as she thinks, "Oh yes, I can foresee lots of bumps. Normally, I'd be worried, but why does Kaitlyn make me feel like it will be OK?"

"Good night, Olivia," then, the last thing Olivia hears Kaitlyn mumbling, "And God, bless my roommate Olivia too."

"I guess that's why," Olivia smiles before sleep overtakes her.

---

4 Music Video Girls Have Fun https://www.youtube.com/watch?v=PIb6AZdTr-A

4

Follow the Science Foundation Meeting

The following morning Olivia slips out of the room early. More students move into the dorm, but Kaitlyn sleeps through the noise[1] until . . ..

"11:30?"

"Feels like 7 am. Ugh, feels like my head is exploding[2]. Maybe I partied too much last night like Olivia said. Don't I have to be somewhere at noon? Opening the Freshman orientation schedule on her phone, "YUCK! How did it get so dirty?

"Let's see.

8:00 AM Chapel – missed that!

9:00 am to 11 am breakfast at Clark Dining Hall – no breakfast for Princess today!

Oh good! Some pretzels from last night. God, I'm smart when I drink . . . bringing home breakfast."

11 am to 12 noon – Tour of Hunt Library, no big loss there.

12 noon to 2 pm – "Follow the Science" meeting at the Hunt Library

---

1 Music Overslept https://www.youtube.com/watch?v=9jw19czeXn0
2 Pic Kaitlyn Hangover https://firepitcell.com/wp-content/uploads/2021/11/C4N2-Kaitlyn-Hangover.jpg

"Follow the Science sounds familiar. Oh yeah, I'm on a Follow the Science Scholarship. Guess I shouldn't skip that. Can't pay tuition without that. Got to hurry!"

Arriving at the Hunt Library conference hall at 12:30, Kaitlyn hears:

"Thank you, Chancellor, for that wonderful introduction."

"OMG, that's Brandon Fauchison[3] who hit on me at Spring Break. So, he's the head of the whole Foundation? Guess I'm not rid of him like I thought. Hope he doesn't hold it against me that I made fun of him."

"Oh good, all I missed was a boring introduction. Sounds like my scholarship is safe."

"And now I'd like to remind all of our Follow the Science attendees that this isn't a Scholarship."

"It isn't?" an astonished Kaitlyn mutters to herself.

"At the Follow the Science Foundation, we take great pride that this is work program."

"A work program? How did I miss that in the application?"

"We think it's the most important work program in the country. Instead of washing dishes in the cafeteria, you'll be helping this University's great scientists advance the borders of human knowledge."

"Me? Kaitlyn Korosec is going to do what? That sounds pretty cool. I'd be proud to help advance the borders of human knowledge."

"Now, we'll play a brief video to explain the Foundation."

"The Follow the Science Foundation is a public private partnership that was founded to implement the goals of the National Science Act."

"After the pandemic of the early 2020's, the nation demanded greater attention to . . .

BLAH!

BLAH!

BLAH!

"To sustain public support for the sciences, the Foundation started the student work program you are participating in. It's a national priority that

---

3 Pic Brandon Fauchison https://firepitcell.com/wp-content/uploads/2021/11/C4N3-Fauchison-Revenge-on-Kaitlyn.jpg

everyone be able to participate in advancing the frontiers of human scientific knowledge."

20 minutes later the video ends.

"Your counsellors will explain how you do that in the offices on the fifth floor."

"Glad they have counsellors. I have no idea about how to advance the borders of human scientific knowledge," Kaitlyn thinks. Then she hears her name. "Will Kaitlyn Korosec please report to the stage."

"Oh no! Is he going to take away my scholarship? Just because I find him repulsive and laughed at him during Spring Break?"

As Kaitlyn approaches the stage, "Glad to see you here, Ms. Korosec. I just want you to know that I'll be taking a personal interest in you and your experiment."

"Oh, Dr. Fauchison?" Kaitlyn says worried about what personal might mean.

"No need for formalities between us, Kaitlyn. You can call me Brandon." Then, he sends Kaitlyn on her way with a smile that says he's confident that she's under his complete control while lifting Kaitlyn's skirt grabbing a cheek and exploring until a surprised Kaitlyn jumps away,[4] "Now be a good girl and move your sweet little ass to your counselling meeting, Kaitlyn. I'm busy now, but we'll have plenty of time to get to know one another better. It's a long semester."

Kaitlyn is too stunned to respond. Moving away as quickly as she can, she thinks, "Did he really just feel me up? What a disgusting creep!" Then, "Can't stand having that man's touch still on me," as the upset Kaitlyn visits the ladies' room to wipe off her derriere and dry the tears from her eyes. "Second day at college and I'm at the mercy of that perv! I'm so helpless. In so over my head."[5]

---

4 Pic Kaitlyn Harassed https://firepitcell.com/wp-content/uploads/2021/11/C4N4-Kaitlyn-Harassed.jpg
5 Pic Kaitlyn Feeling Helpless https://firepitcell.com/wp-content/uploads/2021/11/C4N5Kaitlyn-Feeling-Helpless.jpg

"I just want to go home![6] Then, fighting off the urge to call her father, Kaitlyn looks into the mirror and decides, "OK, girl. Snap out of it. What would Daddy say? He's say, 'You're not helpless. You're a big girl now.' Can't run to Daddy every time something happens. Daddy has faith in me. Time for me to have faith in me. I need to take care of this myself."

A determined Kaitlyn stares into the mirror, "I don't know when or how, but Brandon Faichison you will pay for this.[7] I'll just wait until the right time. You've messed with the wrong girl this time."

*　*　*

Emerging from the ladies' room, Kaitlyn sees people from her dorm and last night's Quad party, all heading to the fifth-floor counselling meetings. "Wonder how many of them have been sexually assaulted today?" Then, Kaitlyn covers her distress with her patented smile and assumes her sweet girl façade.

"Hi Sheldon! Guess we're both in the same scholarship program."

"Richard, you were so cool last night."

"Oh, Staci, we should definitely get together again."

All headed to their counsellor meetings.

"Well at least I already know people in this Following the Science club."

Waiting in line to see her counsellor, "Where's Olivia?"

Oh, she's at her 'business' meeting with Scott.

"Makes sense. Judge's daughter and Senator's son.[8] They were born to be with one another. No standing in counsellors' lines for them. Wait a minute. I'm going to a bad place that Daddy always warned me about. I need to focus on what's good in my life. Don't focus about what other people have. I'm going to this great university for free. And I'm complaining about standing in a line?"

---

6 Gifs Want to Go Home https://tenor.com/search/i-wanna-go-home-gifs

7 Music Video Goopdbye Earl https://www.youtube.com/watch?v=Gw7gNf_9njs

8 Music Senator's Son https://www.youtube.com/watch?v=ZWijx_AgPiA

"How dumb is that? Pretty dumb, I'd say. Suck it up girl. My mission today is to impress this counsellor. Make the most of this opportunity. OK, I'm next in line. Look out Follow the Science counsellor, here I come."

One by one students enter and leave the counselling rooms.

*   *   *

"I'm Virginia Taylor. Sorry to keep you waiting Ms. Lee, but meeting with 100 students in one day is difficult. The essence of your experiment involves your performing arts major. We want to test how your dancing affects your ability to deal with stress. Twice a week, we'll give you a stress test. Then you'll dance for half an hour. After that, we'll retest."

"What are the stress tests like?"[9]

"I'm sorry, but we can't describe the tests in advance. That would make them less stressful."

Allison Lee signs up.

*   *   *

"Welcome Ms. Korosec."

"I'm so happy to meet you Ms. Walker. I guess you're my boss."

"Follow the Science Foundation doesn't like to think of it that way. We prefer to think of it as two colleagues on a mission to push the boundaries of scientific knowledge."

"Great colleague, what's our mission?"

"Well, we can't disclose the mission's goal. That's a secret. All I can do is to explain your role."

"Check. Top secret stuff. Like you're ground control and I'm an astronaut.[10] Just tell me what I need to do. How many hours a week will I be working and where."

---

9 Music Video Stress https://www.youtube.com/watch?v=aaqxczLXeMw
10 Music Video Ground Control https://www.youtube.com/watch?v=iYYRH4apXDo

"It should take you about one hour each week. You'll report to the Foundation's building on Centennial Campus. It's behind this building."

"You mean I get free tuition, room and board for one hour a week of work? Who do I have to sleep with that hour?" To herself Kaitlyn thinks, "Hope it's not that Dr. Fauchison guy."

Ms. Walker frowns.

"Sorry, that was a bad joke. I joke a lot. My jokes aren't always as funny as I think. Let me rephrase my question. What will I be doing during that hour?"

"It's really quite simple. Our nurse extracts a pint of your blood each week.[11] Then, our scientific team processes your blood. The next week we replace the pint we drew the previous week and extract another pint."

"What do you do to my blood?"

"That's the experiment. It's a secret process we're testing."

"So, my job is to lend you a pint of blood each week? That's all?"

"That's right, Ms. Korosec."

"And that will help push the boundaries of human scientific knowledge?"

"Well, our scientific team hopes so."

"What happens if I get sick from the experiment?"

"We hope that won't happen, but the Foundation will pay all your medical expenses. Is that acceptable?"

"Yes, it sounds great!"

"You'll have to sign these papers to make it legal."

"Do my parents have to sign?"

"No, they appointed the Foundation your medical guardian in the papers they signed this past summer."

"They did? Really? They passed complete control to you? OK, one question before I sign."

"Yes."

"Can I quit giving blood if I don't like it?"

---

11 Article Vampire Song List https://www.rollingstone.com/music/music-lists/the-15-greatest-songs-about-vampires-22357/

"Of course, you can quit, Ms. Korosec. It's still a free country."[12]

"But what happens if I quit?"

"Well, none of the students I've worked with have ever quit, but I think the Foundation would try to find another mission for you."

"What if no other missions are available? What happens then?"

"This is a student work program. As long as the student is working on a mission, the Follow the Science Foundation pays the University. If the student stops working on a mission, the Foundation stops paying the University. The University also gives the Foundation a refund if the student's withdrawal impedes the experiment. That's a requirement in the Foundation's charter."

"And then the University kicks me out of school?"

"A termination decision would be up to the University, not the Foundation."

"Well, I'm not a quitter. So, I'm not worried about that."

"I'm so happy that you'll be joining us."

"There are six places to sign. Just click on the screen in each place."

"That's good."

"Do I get a copy?"

"Of course, it's already been emailed to you."

"If you have any questions, my contact information is in the email. Welcome to the Foundation team, Ms. Korosec. You can make your first appointment online through our website or download our app."

"Thank you, Ms. Walker. I totally believe in our mission."

As Kaitlyn leaves, she says to the next girl in line "This is such a sweet deal."

*   *   *

Ms. Walker greets the next student.

"I'm your counsellor, Helen Walker."

---

12 Movie Clip Braveheart Freedom Speech https://www.youtube.com/watch?v=TME0xubdHQc

"I'm Nicole Wilson."[13]

"You'll be in our blood program, Ms. Wilson." Ms. Walker then explains the blood testing.

"You're going to do what with my blood? Why didn't someone tell me about this when I signed up?"

"That's because the Foundation didn't know which program you were best suited for until now. Your application and the physical you took this summer helped us choose your program."

"Are you conducting this experiment only on black people?

"What?"

"I mean, are you also doing the same thing with the white students?"

"Why of course we are, Ms. Wilson."

"Well, I want to talk with one."

"One what?"

"A white student who is also doing the same blood project."

"That's an unusual request. We try to treat each of you as individuals, but I think I can arrange that."

"Good, because this black girl isn't going to let your doctors do anything to me, unless they're doing same thing to the white students."

"Ms. Wilson this attitude is highly irregular. Are you sure you want to participate?"

"I'm sorry if this sounds impertinent. I don't mean to be. But one of my relatives was in an experiment at Tuskegee.[14] The scientists did bad things and they only experimented with black people."

"Tuskegee was a long time ago. A lot has changed since then."

"Yes, but some things haven't changed very much, and I promised my family I would protect myself."

Ms. Walker calls Kaitlyn's cell phone "Ms. Korosec, could you please return to my office? An unexpected issue has come up."

13 Pic Nicole Wilson https://firepitcell.com/wp-content/uploads/2021/11/C4N13-Nicole-Interview-Follow-Science-Counsellor.jpg

14 Article Tuskegee Experiment https://en.wikipedia.org/wiki/Tuskegee_Syphilis_Study

After Kaitlyn returns about 15 minutes later, "Ms. Korosec, I forgot to tell you that you and Ms. Wilson here will be a team. You'll be taking all your blood appointments together. You'll both get the same treatment at the same time."

"Hi, I'm Kaitlyn."

"I'm Nicole."

"Ms. Wilson, does that satisfy you?"

"Yes, it does for now."

"Ms. Korosec, is that OK with you?"

"Sure. Might be nice to have someone to talk to at these appointments." Looking at Nicole, "We can be blood sisters."[15]

"Well then, sign in these six places and the Foundation will email your contact information and you can work out schedules."

"You can go now, Ms. Korosec."

"Ms. Wilson, are you ready to sign the paperwork?"

"Yes, I am."

"Just one thing before you go, Ms. Wilson. Some of the Foundation's medical people might not like being compared to what happened at Tuskegee. How about we both be discreet about why you and Ms. Korosec are going through this project together."

"OK, I really don't want to alienate people. It just happens sometimes. And I do appreciate you not sharing this with others."

"It will be our little secret, Ms. Wilson."

After Nicole leaves, Ms. Walker notes in her file, "Handle Nicole Wilson with care."[16]

*   *   *

Sheldon Atwell Interview

"Welcome, Mr. Atwell."

"I'm April Falkner. Please sit down and I'll explain your project to you."

---

15 Movie Clip Blood Sisters https://www.youtube.com/watch?v=bsWbbKlZJac
16 Music Video Handle with Care https://www.youtube.com/watch?v=1o4s1KVJaVA

"Thank you. I been looking forward to learning what I'll be doing."

"You've been assigned to a long-term project that is a joint venture between the University's psychology and endocrinology departments."

"Really? I had listed the math and physics departments as priorities. I think I have skills in those areas."

"I'm sorry, but our scientists don't select students based on academic accomplishments. You're the subject of their experiment, not an investigator."

"Oh! I guess I misunderstood."

"That's a common misconception about Follow the Science Foundation programs. I hope this doesn't mean you aren't interested in participating."

"Well, it does give me pause. I was hoping . . . ."

"Mr. Atwell, your application says your nickname was Shelley. Can I call you Shelley?

"My grandmother called me that until she died several years ago. No one has called me that since then, but I guess it's OK."

"Duly noted in your file. I'll share something with you that I don't usually tell students. Our team analyzed your application and physical and described you as their perfect candidate."

"Really?"

"Yes, but please don't tell other students. We like all our students to think they're special."[17]

"Of course."

"So, what will I be doing, Ms. Falkner?"

"It's really rather simple. We want you to keep a daily journal and write down how you are feeling."

"Feeling about what?"[18]

"Oh, about anything that you want. We'll give you suggestions, but you really have a lot of freedom to do whatever you want. The experiment is as much about what you choose rather than about specific content."

---

17 Music Video Midnight Special https://www.youtube.com/watch?v=PYY3xhIEAZw
18 Music Video Gotta Feeling https://www.youtube.com/watch?v=uSD4vsh1zDA

"Is that all? Just write in my journal every day?"

"No. there are some other tasks. There's a Monday morning class where participants discuss their feelings with other project participants."

"Is that all?"

"Just one other thing. You are free to socialize with anyone at the University as long as you eat at least one meal each day at a table of students the Foundation has selected and take the Foundation's exercise class each day. Also, the Foundation is assigning you a roommate to help you with the experiment's protocols."

"Why is that?"

"I can't share the reasons for the experiment's protocols because we don't want the experiment's goals to shape your reactions. We want the real you to shine though. Let's just say that the success of the experiment depends on this being an immersive experience for participants."

"That's a bit mysterious."

"Yes, it is, but remember that science is about exploring unknowns. Freeing your mind to new experiences. Changing how we experience the world.[19] You do want to help advance science, don't you?"

"Yes, of course. I'll do it."

"Good, then I'll explain the paperwork to you. But first, let's see if you have remembered the experiment's protocols."

Sheldon confidently recites the list:

Foundation Roommate -check

Daily Meal - check

Daily Exercise Class – check

Daily Journal – check

Feelings meeting each week – check.

Freedom to make choices outside the protocols check.

"Very good, Mr. Atwell. Enjoy your experiment."

---

19 Music Video Liquid Tension Experiment https://www.youtube.com/watch?v=jWP4JLUxiqY

As Sheldon heads back to his room to see whether his roommate has arrived, "What a sweet deal! The Foundation is the best thing that's ever happened to me."

*   *   *

Back at Sheldon's room, his new roommate is visited by, Sarah Atwell, Sheldon's dead mother.

"Michelle, thanks for agreeing to take care of my little Shelley."

"Sarah, what if I screw up? Are you sure?"

Yes, my Dear. You don't know it yet, but you're ready."

THE FOUNDATION WAS VERY PRIMITIVE AT THE BEGINNING. SINCE THEN, WE HAVE REALLY IMPROVED SUBJECT INTAKE.

5

Immersion Experiment Begins

Passing someone in the hall, "Why are you so happy, Sheldon?"

"I just feel like something big is happening."

Sheldon is right. His life is about to change.

*   *   *

Back at Sheldon's room, Sheldon's dead mother, Sarah, is finishing her visit with Sheldon's new roommate. "Thank you for agreeing to take care of my little Shelley, Dear. He was a very sweet little boy,[1] but he needs a teacher. There are so many things I wanted to do but couldn't since the accident separated us."

"Sarah, you've helped me so much on my journey. I'm honored you've chosen me, but my journey isn't finished yet. Are you sure I'm ready?"

"Who is ever ready, Dear? Not to worry, I'll be here to help both you and Shelley."

Sarah's apparition disappears[2] with the sound of a key in the locked door as Sarah's last words are all that remain, "Be kind but firm with my Shelley."

*   *   *

1 Pic Sheldon Five Years Old https://firepitcell.com/wp-content/uploads/2021/11/C5N1-Sheldon-as-Child.jpg
2 Pic Sarah Atwell Apparition https://firepitcell.com/wp-content/uploads/2021/11/C5N2-Sheldon-s-Mother-Apparition.jpg

Unlocking the door to his room, Sheldon finds his roommate asleep. Michelle is pretty, but Sheldon experiences her in a way he has never experienced any other girl. Is this because Michelle lives in the bubble dimension?[3] Or is it because Sheldon has never been alone with a sleeping naked girl? Maybe a bit of both. A dazzled Sheldon thinks to himself, "Do they really make girls this perfect?"[4]

Hearing Sheldon's purposeful noise, his roommate awakens, "Oh, hi!" the sleepy girl says from under some kind of metallic bed sheets. The two look at one another. As time passes and Sheldon doesn't respond Michelle says, "OK Sheldon, I get this a lot. Let me know when you're through fantasizing about me.[5] Not wanting to admit he is imaging what is under the sheets, but knowing he should say something, he blurts out, "Don't be frightened. I live here."

"Why would I be frightened? You're not some kind of pervert, are you?"

"No, of course not, but I think you're in the wrong room."

"Isn't this room 311?"

"Yes, this is room 311, but this isn't your room."

"You're mistaken Shelley. I'm Michelle Collins and my assigned room is 311."

"But . . . .."

"But what?"

"Isn't it obvious?"

"Isn't what obvious, Shelley?"

"Well . . ."

"Well . . . right back to you."

"Well, you're a girl and I'm a guy and the University doesn't assign coed roommates. So, you don't belong in my room."

"It's our room Shelley, not your room."

3 Pic Bubble Dimension https://firepitcell.com/wp-content/uploads/2021/11/C5N3-Bubble-Dimension.jpg

4 Pic Michelle in Bed https://firepitcell.com/wp-content/uploads/2021/11/C5N4-Michelle-in-Bed-to-Sheldon.jpg

5 Music Who Loves You https://www.youtube.com/watch?v=-KtYgOM62fk

"No, you must be a mistake."

"Shelley, that's not very nice. I belong here just as much as you do. And it's also not very smart. First thing you do after meeting a girl is to tell her she must be a mistake. You don't know much about making friends with girls, do you?"

"But, not in a boy's dorm room."

"You may be smart, but you're not very observant. You've been here over 24 hours and you really didn't notice, did you? You'll have to work on noticing things if you want to get by here."

"Notice what?"

"Turn around, Shelley, while I put on some clothes." Then, the half-dressed Michelle leads the startled Sheldon by the hand into the hall. "Notice the names on all the rooms on this hallway. Read the first names aloud Shelley as we talk down the hall. That's the best way to understand reality."

301 Anna and Hellen

303 Jenn and Andrea

305 Audrey and Elaine

307 Emily and Marsha

309 Elaine and Jennifer

311 Michelle and Shelley

313 Kaitlyn and Olivia

315 Allison (Allie) and Luna

315 Sandy and Latisha

317 Liz and Kelly

319 Tanya and Sharon

321 Rachael and Elizabeth

"Now do you get the picture? Come on Shelley. I know you're only 16, but you're supposed to be smart enough to notice patterns. It's in your bio."

"Patterns?"

"I'm disappointed in you Shelley. The pattern is obvious. This hallway only has odd numbers and all the rooms we passed have girls' names on them. The boys are in the even numbered rooms at the other end of the hallway on this floor. That's how the school prevents mistakes. Odd and even. Got it?"

"But . . ..

"We're standing in the girls' hallway. Right? So, I belong. I don't know why you didn't notice that before. But you do now, don't you?"

"Well, I guess . . .yes."

"So, Shelley, please don't say again that I don't belong in my own room. I belong."

"But . . ."

"No buts, Shelley. Now, what's the next logical question?"

"Then, why am I here? I should move."

"Shelley Dear. You're working for the Foundation, aren't you?"

"Yes."

"Didn't the Foundation just tell you your roommate had arrived."

"Yes.

"And here I am. Just like the Foundation told you. Do you think that's a coincidence?"

"Coincidence would have a low probability," Shelley reluctantly admits, "but it's possible."

"Now, did the Foundation mention anything about immersion?"

"Yes, immersion is one of the experiment's main protocols. But they didn't say what I would be immersed in. I was wondering about that."

"The Foundation does lots of different types of immersion experiments. In your experiment, its female culture. This is how you'll be immersed in girl culture.[6] You'll live, sleep, eat and exercise with us."

"You mean the Foundation is trying to turn me into a girl?"

"Of course, not Shelley Dear."

"The Foundation conducts scientific experiments. They don't really care what happens to the subjects of their experiments. They just want to collect the data. In your experiment, they just want to know how boys

6 Pic Sheldon Drowning in Girl Culture https://firepitcell.com/wp-content/uploads/2021/11/C5N6-Sheldon-Immersion-in-Female-Culture-Experiment.jpg

respond to immersion into a female environment. Become a girl? Be gay? Be a straight guy? Change back and forth every day? Do what you want. It's all the same to the Foundation. The Foundation is only interested in finding out what you decide and why."

"Well, it just doesn't seem normal."

"Exactly, that's the point of the experiment. You're used to one normal. But your normal isn't the only normal; it's a boy normal. The Foundation tests how people react when their normal changes." In your case, how you react to girl normal."

"I don't know . . . still seems like weird science."[7]

"Here's a card the Foundation gave me that lists the six experiment protocols. Read each one and tell me which protocol would turn you into a girl."

Foundation Roommate -No

Meals with Girls - No

Foundation Exercise Class – No

Daily Journal – No

Feeling meeting each week. Probably not, but I'm a little worried about feeling meetings. Not a guy thing.

Freedom to make choices outside the protocols. No

"See, you've said yourself that these are harmless things. Keep this card with you to reassure yourself."

"But I'm sure I'm a straight guy and will always be.

"Well then, you have nothing to worry about, do you, Shelley?"

"No, I don't."

"And remember that you might enjoy this."

"What do you mean enjoy?"

"There are many possibilities but consider this. What heathy straight male wouldn't enjoy being surrounded by beautiful women? Lots of dating opportunities, right?"

"Maybe."

"Well, you're a healthy straight male aren't you."

---

7 https://www.youtube.com/watch?v=9qd04u2Yj44

"Yes but . . .."

"You sound hesitant. You do like girls, don't you?"

"Yes, but to be honest, not much dating experience . . . but I definitely do like girls."

"Do you think it's possible that your lack of experience comes from not being around girls?"

"Maybe. There weren't very many girls in the math and chess clubs or on my computer hacking team. And I was always younger than the girls in my classes. Science proves that high school girls don't date younger guys."[8]

"See what I mean, Shelley. But I'm not here to push you into anything. I'm sure the Foundation told you that you're free to back out of the experiment at any time. So, don't let me influence you. While you're deciding, do you have any questions?"

"Just one question. Why are you here? Are you supposed to be my girlfriend?"

"I'm out of your league,[9] Shelley. It's OK to dream but don't get any ideas. There are two beds in this room. We'll be using both beds, separately. You can count on that. I know how to defend myself."

"Sorry Michelle, I had to ask whether immersion goes that far. I've never roomed with a girl before.[10] So, this is very strange for me. But I'm not the kind to molest someone in the middle of the night."

"I know, Shelley. Before I agreed to room with you, I studied the profile the Foundation created about you. A girl has to be careful about these kinds of things. You seem like a nice boy who just needs a little guidance. Think of me like a safety net. The Foundation has conducted this same experiment at other schools. Occasionally, there were suicides."

"Suicides?'

"Yes, some boys can't stand the cultural change. Girls and boys have a lot in common, but sometimes they are like two tribes with different cul-

---

8 Article Girls Date Older Guys https://www.jstor.org/stable/1131714

9 Music Out of Your League https://www.youtube.com/watch?v=EGd7E_4u3wU

10 Article roommate Romances https://www.romancerehab.com/blog/top-10-roommates-to-lovers-romances

tures. The tribes work out ways to deal with one another when they meet. But when they go back to their own village, they live among themselves by different rules. You've heard of culture shock, haven't you?"

"Yes, I know what culture shock[11] is."

"Well, some boys can't stand the cultural change of living in a community governed by girls' tribal rules. They lose their sense of reality. I know that's easy to do. It happens to me sometimes. It can end badly if you're not careful. That's one reason why the Foundation is studying this. My primary role is to help you adjust to reality whatever direction that reality is. If you're a pilot flying blind in a cloud without instruments, you can lose track of there the ground is. Easy to crash and burn."

"Really? Are you always such an optimist, Michelle?"

"Yes, really. I'm just saying that some guys have these problems. You probably won't, but if you do, maybe having a cultural interpreter will help you."

Sheldon looking into Michelle's eyes and seeing an ally, hugs her.[12]

"OK, I understand that reaction, Shelley, but if you want any more physical contact, you'll have to buy me dinner first. I'm not that easy." Michelle says with a twinkle in her eye that relaxes Sheldon.

A knock on the door, "Sheldon, I was just helping someone else move in. Princess isn't in her room. Let her know I stopped by and I . . .Well hello there," eying Michelle. "So, this is why your door was closed. Sorry I interrupted. Looks like something important, Sheldon."

"No Scott, it's not like that at all."

"Too bad . . . definitely too bad."

"Shelley, who's your big friend?"

"Sorry Michelle, Scott is a friend of my brother Allen. Scott, this is Michelle."

"So, Michelle what's your story?"

"Freshman, performing arts major and not in a relationship."

---

11 Article Culture Shock https://www.mosalingua.com/en/culture-shock/
12 Music Sister Golden Hair https://www.youtube.com/watch?v=LFsEvSyi2os

"I like that combination. We should get to know one another. But first, the girl I'm helping move in a couple of doors down the hall is a performing arts major. Would you like to meet her?"

As Michelle follows Scott two doors down the hall, "Her name is Allison Lee."

After a few minutes, Michelle returns to their room.

"Well Shelley, I owe you a favor. If you have more Greek Gods as friends, you're going to be VERY popular with the girls in this dorm." After some more coaching about the experiment, "Now, be a gentleman. I need some privacy to get ready for my date."

"Your date?"

"Yes, I hope I can help you Shelley, but I'm not your fulltime nursemaid. I'm here to experience my new life in college just like you."

After half an hour, Sheldon arrives back at their room just as Michelle is about to leave for her date.

"How do I look Shelley?"

"Twirl one more time for me."

"Why, is something wrong? What's wrong with my skirt?"[13]

"Nothing, I just like looking at you."

"Shelley, you say the cutest things! Keep that up and all the girls in the dorm will love you. We're all at least a little bit insecure before a date. Sometimes girls magnify our imperfections.[14] A little ego boost from our friends really helps."

"Well, whoever you are going out with tonight is a lucky guy."

Whispering in Shelley's ear, "Shelley, what makes you assume my date is a guy?"

"But you seemed so interested in my friend Scott . . . so, I thought . . . ."

"Thought what Shelley?

"That . . . ."

---

13 Pic Michelle Mdels Skirt https://firepitcell.com/wp-content/uploads/2021/11/C5N13-Michelle-Models-Skirt.jpg

14 Article Body Image Imperfections https://www.seventeen.com/health/news/a45729/girls-get-real-about-their-body-image-insecurities/

"Shelley Dear, I like more than one type of person. I gave up limiting myself long ago."

After Michelle leaves, Sheldon thinks, "What's going on? She's gorgeous, but there's something other worldly about her. Like from another dimension. I wonder . . .. But enough of that. My immediate problem is how do I deal with sleeping ten feet away from her? I might never sleep all semester."

*   *   *

Meanwhile, at Scott's apartment.

"What's Princess' story, Olivia? Is she part of the plot?"

"After a day with Kaitlyn it's hard to believe she could keep any secrets. But that could be a brilliant act."

"Yes, hide in plain sight while everyone looks for spies in the dark corners. Last night they gave me the go ahead to begin implementing our mission."

"And they confirmed that Kaitlyn is in the middle of our mission?"

"Yes, they're sure Princess is involved. But they don't know in what capacity. Is she a Player or a victim? Answering that question is our first objective. Then, they'll decide what we do with her."

"Is that all for mission Princess?"

"Affirmative."

"And do we have any other objectives?"

Picking Olivia up and tossing her on his bed, "Affirmative, and this objective just can't wait?"

"Affirmative."

*   *   *

Later that evening, as Olivia walks past Pullen Park to her dorm room floating from her rendezvous with Scott, a pair of eyes[15] follow her every step from a hidden nest. Safely arriving at their room, "Sleep tight Princess. You're in more danger than you know."

And so is Olivia.

---

15 Video Behind Those Eyes https://www.youtube.com/watch?v=ZkxR1e3XsVM

6

Girl Games

Over breakfast the next morning.

"Olivia, what was Scott like last night?"

"Oh, not at all like one might imagine. And . . .."

"And what, Olivia?"

"And . . . nothing."

"Why the mystery, roommate?"

"Kaitlyn, there's a difference between being mysterious and being private."

"Olivia, I get it. You and Scott have something going on and its none of my business."

"No Kaitlyn, you don't get it. I'm just a very private person. I don't blurt out things without thinking."

"And I do?"

"Well, to be honest, yes you do. Most people have filters. You seem to say whatever pops into your head."

"Oh!"

"Now please don't sulk. Your spontaneity is refreshing. But it's not my way. I like to think things through."

"Is that all, Olivia? I knew we're different like that the moment we met. But I still like you."

"So, Kaitlyn, if I let you let be you, you'll let me be me?"

"Olivia, you don't say as much as I do, but when you do talk, I listen."

Hugging, "It's a deal."

"Kaitlyn, I know you like Scott. Please believe me when I say that . . . ."

Looking up, Kaitlyn says, "Oh, hi Sheldon."

"What are you two up to today? Want to . . . ."

"Sorry Sheldon, we have a sorority rush orientation meeting this morning. Olivia, what time does our meeting start?"

"Same time as you asked me 20 minutes ago."

After Sheldon leaves, "Olivia, I hope we become sorority sisters."

"I don't think that's going to happen."

"But why?"

"The Judge and the Professor want me to join a black sorority."

"But why?"

"They think it will be good for me to get to know more black students."

"But why?"

"My father is black. My mother is white. They experienced the difficulties.[1] So, I take their advice seriously. Growing up, I've mostly been around white people. My parents think a black sorority will be a good way to get to know my other culture. The Judge thinks that will be important if I decide to run for political office."

"Sounds like very good reasons. The Judge and Professor are smart people, but they aren't joining a sorority, you are. What do you want, Olivia?"

"I'm not doing this just for my parents. Being both black and white is good, but sometimes it's confusing. People who don't come from both sometimes react oddly. I'd like to figure out how to deal with everyone. It would make my world more orderly. That's why I want to get more involved in the black community."

"Me too, Olivia, that gives me an idea. I'd like to get to know more black people. Do you think . . .?"

"No Kaitlyn. That wouldn't be a good idea."

"But why?"

"Trust me Kaitlyn, it isn't."

---

1 Music Society's Child https://www.youtube.com/watch?v=-QPF-duKQro

"Olivia, I do trust you. But do you mean I'll just have to settle for joining a white sorority?"

"Kaitlyn, people don't say 'white sorority[2].' Sororities for white girls are just called sororities."

"Doesn't that seem a bit odd, Olivia. I mean . . . why?"

"Yes, I know what you mean, but other people won't understand how you think. Just don't tell people you're joining a white sorority."

"OK Olivia, I trust your judgement. But does that mean we can't be roommates anymore?"

"Kaitlyn, I'm not planning to move out of the dorm[3] into a sorority house. At least not this year."

"Me neither, Olivia."

"Good. I don't fully understand all the reasons why, but I think rooming together may be good for both of us, Kaitlyn."

"I'm so glad. I've always dreamed that my college roommate would be the maid of honor at my wedding.[4] Then, we'd be friends for life, for real, not just because a university administrator assigned us to the same dorm room. Don't you hope that happens, Olivia?"

"Now I know why I put up with an unpredictable force of nature like you." Olivia says tearing-up as she hugs her roommate." Meanwhile, Olivia is thinking, "A university administrator didn't haphazardly assign us to the same room. The agency made that happen so that I can watch you. I wonder whether Kaitlyn will still want me in her wedding if she finds out I'm spying on her?" Then. "But Kaitlyn is growing on me. Maybe we will become friends."

*   *   *

At the sorority orientation:
   BLAH!

---

2 Sorority Recruitment Music Video https://www.youtube.com/watch?v=A5DztKJGVjw

3 Music Video Keep Moving https://www.youtube.com/watch?v=7-lWzQd_xeQ

4 Maids of Honor Sing Speech https://www.youtube.com/watch?v=u1YGdwvN_6E

BLAH!
BLAH!
BLAH!
Kaitlyn whispers to Olivia, "I hope this is ending soon."

After the meeting, Olivia and Kaitlyn make the rounds to different sororities.

* * *

Seeing Allison Lee again and again at each sorority social stop of the afternoon, "Hi I'm Kaitlyn. We seemed to be on the same trail all day. We live next door to one another, don't we?"

"Allison Lee, but you can call me 'Allie.'"

"Didn't I also see you at the Foundation meetings?"

"Yes, something about testing how dance affects my ability to deal with stress."

"I'm in some kind of blood testing experiment. Very secretive about what they are testing for."

"Guess we're just two Guinea pigs . . .."

* * *

After a long rush day, Kaitlyn, Allie and Olivia return to their dorm. Going out again is the last thing on their minds. They join Michelle and Sheldon to veg out. Other girls join their circle. Things become a little silly as they pass a joint.

"How about getting to know one another better by playing truth or dare?" someone suggests.

"I don't know if that's such a good idea," Sheldon and Olivia simultaneously respond, but Allie and Michelle overrule them.

OK Olivia agrees, "But only if Kaitlyn goes first."

Olivia to Kaitlyn, "Truth or dare?" "Truth." "Tell us about your first time doing it with a boy."

"OMG! . . .Really? . . . . How embarrassing! Hope the boys here are better at it than that."

"Truth or dare Michelle?" "Dare." "Show us your sexiest pose."

"OK, get ready. Here's one that always works on boys or girls."

Allie, "Truth or Dare Sheldon?" "Dare." "Take off your pants for the rest of our game."

An embarrassed Sheldon sits in the ring of girls in his underwear, imaging himself on display.

Sheldon "Truth or Dare Allie?" "Dare." "Show us how you kiss someone you like."

Allie, leans over to Sheldon "Nice try Captain Underpants." Then, Allie's life begins to change as she tilts Michelle's face and gently kisses her lips.[5] "Why is everything so . . . strange," Allie senses. Why are the other girls? Why are Michelle and I suddenly alone? Why do I feel so . . . blissful? Why is Michelle smiling like that? Why doesn't she say something? Can I still talk? Why is Michelle glowing dressed all in white? Why is that woman blowing bubbles at us?"[6]

After countless unanswered questions, Allie succumbs to the bubbles caressing her and Michelle. "Oh, what a lovely feeling, we're floating together like two bubbles," Allie thinks before Michelle's bright white image begins to fade. As she feels their lips parting, Allie begins to see the other girls again and thinks. "What just happened between me and Michelle? Was it seconds? An hour? A day?" Then, looking deeply into Michelle's smiling eyes, Allie senses, "Michelle's not flustered at all by our out of body experience together. Is this normal for her?"

Back in reality, Michelle says nothing, but gives a knowing smile that Allie senses says, "I can take you to places you've never been before."[7]

---

5 Pic Allie Michelle First Kiss https://firepitcell.com/wp-content/uploads/2021/11/C6N5-First-Kiss-Allie-Michelle-.jpg

6 Pic Sarah Atwell in Bubble Dimension https://firepitcell.com/wp-content/uploads/2021/11/C6N6-Bubbles.jpg

7 Music Words of Love https://www.youtube.com/watch?v=1I2Xup9dwW4

Finally, Olivia breaks the spell between the two girls with, "Oh! Sheldon! Look at your . . .. We can see you like watching girls kiss."[8]

Sheldon's face turns bright red, realizing he is putting on a show for the girls he thinks, "I've always been hiding in the shadows. Nowhere to hide now." Surrounded by giggling girls, Sheldon's mind begins exaggerating the girls' reaction.[9] Then, the spotlight shifts as the girls resume the game. "WHEW, glad that's over with, or am I?" as stripper music[10] floods Shelley's senses, and he asks himself, "why am I hating this and liking it at the same time?"

Finally, Sheldon comes back to reality and the game as he hears someone say, "Truth or Dare Olivia? Come on, choose." "Truth." "What do you think of your roommate?"

"Well, Kaitlyn, don't be upset . . .."

"OK, that's brutal . . .but I admit it's a pretty fair description," Kaitlyn confirms.

And the game continues as the roommates laugh and giggle into the evening.

* * *

After Michelle and Sheldon return to their room, he puts his pants back on.

"See what I mean Michelle, the girls . . .."

Michelle interrupts Sheldon before he can go further, "Shelley, you should be proud of yourself."

"I should?"

"Yes, you're not used to having your body inspected like that by a bunch of girls, are you? Girls are being inspected by guys all the time. I expected

8 Music Video I Kissed a Girl https://www.youtube.com/watch?v=tAp9BKosZXs&list=R DtAp9BKosZXs&start_radio=1

9 Pic Sheldon Imagines https://firepitcell.com/wp-content/uploads/2021/11/C6N8-Sheldon-Strip.jpg

10 Stripper Music https://www.youtube.com/playlist?list=PLUPVZ1Oep5U8PrbeKwwu nmjx74GDtAtQF

you might run away, but you didn't. You were a good sport. You passed your first culture shock test. You were uncomfortable but you smiled. Believe me, all the girls noticed how you handled it, because they've all been in your situation before. You behaved like a good member of the tribe.

"But Michelle, there's something I don't understand."

"I bet I know what it is, Shelley. Did you like it a little even though you were embarrassed?"

"How did you know, Michelle?"

"Lots of people have mixed feelings, Shelley. It's normal. Remember, this is all part of the experiment, Shelley. You get to understand how girls feel. Girls have mixed emotions[11] all the time. Guys too, but girls usually accept it as normal. It's disconcerting for some boys. Girls are more advanced than boys that way."

You also get to see what girls are really like when they have the upper hand and aren't trying to impress guys. Understanding girls can really improve your social life. Some guys never learn and stumble through life making the women in their lives unhappy. You know the saying 'Happy wife. Happy life.'"

"Yes, I understand that, but . . . .."

"OK, I get it. Are you still afraid you'll defect to the other team?"

"Not really, Michelle, but do you have tips on how to survive this experiment?"

Smiling, "Kudos, Shelley Dear! Asking for help is another step in the right direction. Lots of guys won't do that."

Leaning over to kiss his forehead, Michelle whispers in Sheldon's ear, "Tomorrow is Sunday. Last day before classes and the experiment's immersion schedule revs up. You won't have much free boy time after tomorrow. If I were a boy in your shoes, I would do a lot of male bonding[12] tomorrow. It'll be a good antidote to the sea of estrogen the experiment's immersion will have you swimming in."

---

11 Music Video Mixed Emotions https://www.youtube.com/watch?v=2PBCtOyMIi4
12 Music Video The Man https://www.youtube.com/watch?v=w3xcybdis1k

"Now, I'm off to meet some friends. Want to join us? One of them is very cute. I could set you up with her."

"No thanks, Michelle, I need to think."

*   *   *

As Michelle walks across campus to meet friends, she senses Sarah Atwell's presence, "I think Sarah is pleased with how I'm advising her son."

*   *   *

In their room alone, Sheldon also senses Sarah's presence and approval. "I'm feeling very close to her now. Did my mom pick Michelle to guide me? Is mom coming back to me?"[13] he wonders. Then, he ponders more pressing issues.

"Science experiments?"

"Rooming with a hot girl? "

"Half naked being inspected?"

"Passed the first test, just barely. Who knows what the next test will be."

"Immersed in a sea of estrogen?"

"Suicides?

"How do I balance all that with starting Freshman year?"

"Scott will know. Scott has his act together."

Picking up his phone, "Scott, this is Sheldon."

"Yeah, my brother Allen gave me your number

"Yeah, he still talks about the crazy things you two did together in high school."

"Yeah, he told me that story."

"No, he forgot to tell me that part."

"Well, here's the point of my call. Can you spare some time to talk tomorrow?"

---

13 Music Video Sara https://www.youtube.com/watch?v=32ScTb6_KHg

"Lacrosse pickup game? I totally understand. You're the team captain. It's your responsibility.

"What? Come and hang with the team for the day? No way you can keep me away from that Bro!"

"OK, I'll meet you there." Hanging up, "Way to go Sheldon!"

"Listen to Michelle's advice and then execute. Check."

"Hang with Scott to get a break from the Foundation's experiment. Check."

"That's the formula for getting through this experiment."

7

Male Bonding

The next morning in the dining hall Shelly bumps into Olivia and Kaitlyn.

"Shelley, I didn't recognize you with your pants on,"[1] Kaitlyn says, followed by giggles.

"OK," Shelley thinks, "more tests. I can deal with this." Smiling, he responds, "Hope you enjoyed the show. I aim to please. Maybe you'll return the favor."

"Want to join us for breakfast?"

"Yes, but it'll have to be quick. I have a big day ahead of me."

"Don't leave us hanging, Shelley. What's up?"

"Do you remember my friend, Scott, who helped you move in?"

"Yes, he's VERY memorable."

"Kaitlyn, could you be any more obvious?" Olivia asks.

"Well Scott stopped by my room yesterday, Sheldon explains. "He was looking for you Kaitlyn. Sorry, I forgot to tell you."

"Kaitlyn, don't be cross with Shelley. He's not your receptionist. You're not a real Princess you know."

"What are you doing today that's got to do with Scott?"

"I'm thinking about trying out for the lacrosse team. Heading over there now to hang with the guys."

"Really? I didn't know that you played lacrosse."

---

1 Music Video Put Pants On https://www.youtube.com/watch?v=k3ViN10pl7Q

"Well, technically I don't . . . at least not yet. But my friend Scott, the team captain, and I go way back together. So, I figure I'll go down to the practice field to see whether I want part of that action. See if this dog likes the pack."[2]

"Sounds like a plan. Have a great day, Shelley. Don't hurt the other players."

After Sheldon leaves, both girl's giggling "Well, we all know who has the most active imagination on our hall."

"Why do you suppose he's living in the girl's hall, Kaitlyn?"

"I don't know. There's a juicy story there. But we have all semester to find out. He was a good sport last night and he's a friend of Scott. So, how bad can he be?"

"You're a woman on a mission, Kaitlyn."

"Yes, I'm leaving nothing to chance. And my mission right now is to stroll down to the practice field. I think it's just over there. It's so inspiring watching jocks pant and sweat[3] and fight one another to impress girls. It reminds me that they're not as smart as we are."

"Amen to that roommate."

"Coming with me?"

"Sweating jocks? Can't keep me away Kaitlyn."

* * *

"Hey Sheldon! Over here. Glad you could make it."

"We've been working out for an hour. A couple of the guys could use a break. Would you like to get in a scrimmage?"

"That's why I'm here."

"You have played before, haven't you?"

"No, but I watched my brother play in high school.

"Are you sure you want to do this? These guys are pretty experienced."

"Maybe I inherited some of my brother's talent."

---

2 Music Video Who Let the Dogs Out https://www.youtube.com/watch?v=Qkuu0Lwb5EM
3 Movie Clip Chariots of Fire https://www.youtube.com/watch?v=CSav51fVlKU

"OK, put on the equipment and watch to refresh your memory. Let me know when you're ready and I'll try to find a spot for you when a player gets tired."

"I hope this works out," Scott thinks, "Sheldon isn't half the athlete his brother is."

Wincing as two bodies crashed at high speed, Sheldon thinks, "Now I remember why I didn't play like my brother did."

After watching for a half hour, Sheldon is losing his enthusiasm for playing, until he hears "Hi Shelley! We decided to come to watch you play."

"Olivia and Kaitlyn!"

"Oh great . . . an audience," he thinks, "can't back out now,"

Seeing Sheldon's fan club, Scott decides now is the time. "Ken, take a rest. Sheldon you're in for Ken."

"How do they change direction so fast?" Sheldon wonders as he struggles to keep up. The ball whizzes past his outstretched net at over 100 feet per second. Up and down the field he runs trailing the action. "I've finally got the ball" as Sheldon runs downfield until "Thud."[4] A stunned Sheldon (suddenly without the ball) takes a moment to recover from a solid body check.

"Oh! That looked brutal. Give as good as you get Shelley," Kaitlyn yells.

No longer as eager to get the ball, Sheldon wanders around the field until he sees he is the last defender between his opponent and the net. Throwing his body against the oncoming player "Thud."

"How'd he run through me like I didn't exist?"

A Whistle blows. "Water break!"

"Ken, get back in for Sheldon when we start again." As Sheldon staggers toward the sideline, Scott asks, "Had enough?"

"For the moment, but I'll be ready to go again soon."

"That's the spirit. Your brother was like that."[5]

---

4 Pic LacrossePhttps://firepitcell.com/wp-content/uploads/2021/11/C7N4-Lacrosse.jpg
5 Movie Clip Rocky Goona Flyn Now https://www.youtube.com/watch?v=xSmYAdiXb5M

"WOW!" Like my brother? Really Scott?"

Kaitlyn approaching Sheldon "That was very brave. But don't kill yourself out there."

"Don't baby him, Princess!"

"Scott, I'm so mad at you! That name stuck. Everyone's calling me that."

"Would you prefer being called your jersey number?[6] That was my first thought when I saw you wearing that jersey."

"I'll settle for Princess. But why nicknames at all, Scott?"

"It's my way of remaking the world."

"Don't you like the world the way it is?" Kaitlyn asks.

"Not as much as I like my version."

Leaning into Scott's sweaty torso, "So, where does Princess fit in your version of the world?"

"Don't know yet. How about helping me figure it out? See you at Player's Retreat[7] around seven?"

Wiping Scott's sweat from her arm, "Only if you shower first."

* * *

Having achieved her mission, "I'll be running along now."

"OMG, I can feel his eyes following me. And that's how it's done," Kaitlyn thinks as she and Olivia head back to their dorm.

"You're not shy, are you Kaitlyn?"

"I was, but I've decided I don't want to be that shy girl anymore. No more just hoping my dreams will come true.[8] So, I'm starting over. Now that I'm a college woman, I'm not hiding anything."

"And you can change just like that?"

---

6 Pic Kaitlyn Football Jersey https://firepitcell.com/wp-content/uploads/2021/11/C6-Kaitlyn-Football-Jersey.jpg

7 Bar https://www.tripadvisor.com/LocationPhotoDirectLink-g49463-d1603420-i377053886-The_Players_Retreat-Raleigh_North_Carolina.html

8 Movie Clip Wishin Hopin https://www.youtube.com/watch?v=R_Kc6YFnYO0

"I really hope I can. This is my big chance. Isn't that what college is about? A big second chance?"

*　*　*

Back at the lacrosse field, Sheldon does his best in short spurts with only a few more bruises to show for his efforts. After another hour, Scott announces, "OK guys. Sun is high in the sky. Let's save what we have left for a real practice tomorrow."

As Sheldon hands Scott his stick and helmet, "I like your spirit. But I hope you understand that only official team members can play in games and real team practices." Looking down at a disheartened Sheldon, "Don't give up. You're welcome to join us for these pick-up games. Do you have time to hang out with the guys this afternoon, so they get to know you better?"

"Oh yeah!"

"One thing before you talk with the guys . . .. I might have embellished a little in some of my stories about me and your brother in high school. Some of the guys might be curious about that."

"Don't worry Scott. I've got your back."[9]

---

9 Gifs Got your Back https://tenor.com/search/i-ve-got-your-back-bro-gifs

8

Black and White

Walking back to their dorm, "Look Olivia, there's my new friend Nicole."

"Really Kaitlyn? You do manage to get around meeting all kinds of people."

"I'm going to meet everyone, Olivia. I'll learn more that way than in classes. Nicole's a black studies major so she's learning how to protest."[1]

"Kaitlyn, there's more to black studies than protesting," Olivia says.

"Nicole it's me, Kaitlyn. Don't you remember from yesterday at the Foundation meeting?"

"Nicole, this is my roommate Olivia."

"Olivia, Nicole and I are doing the Foundation's blood experiment together. I'm Nicole's insurance policy."

"What? What do you mean, insurance policy?" Olivia asks.

Kaitlyn explains, "Olivia, it's easy to explain. Black girls need insurance policies. Nicole thought the Foundation wanted to conduct a terrible experiment on black people. You know . . . like in the olden days at Tuskegee. So, she insisted that she have a white girl as her partner. They wouldn't do something terrible to a white girl after all. Now, would they? Good things happen to white girls. Nicole wants some of my white girl privilege."[2]

---

1 Pic Niciole Protesting https://firepitcell.com/wp-content/uploads/2021/11/C8N1-Nicole-Protest-Unsplash1590962376209-d064530150ea.jpg

2 Music Video Rich White Girls https://www.youtube.com/watch?v=US9lCjHkV6s

"Really? Nicole and Kaitlyn, I'm perplexed. What's going on?"

"I'm so embarrassed, Olivia. It really wasn't quite like that."

"Nicole, I totally understand. I'm just getting used to Kaitlyn's discretion deficiencies myself. But she does have a way with getting right to reality, doesn't she Nicole?"

"I didn't mean anything by what I said about insurance. I just thought it was a good way to introduce my two black friends. A week ago, I didn't have any black friends. Now I have two. And now you know one another. I mean, isn't that amazing."

"Kaitlyn!" The exasperated Olivia says, "It's not appropriate to be counting black friends."

"Sorry girls, I didn't know. This is new to me. If I can't count, then how will I know how many black friends I have?"[3]

"Olivia, is she always like this?"

"Oh yes, Nicole, always!"

"I guess I bought some very expensive insurance," an exasperated Nicole says.

"OK, I goofed," Kaitlyn admits, "anyone up for coffee? So, I can make it up to you both."

"Good idea," Olivia says. "I'd love to hear what Nicole thinks about the Foundation's experiment."

"OK, I have about an hour before the big event at the Black Student Union. Are you going, Olivia?"

"I hadn't planned to. Is it important?" Olivia asks.

"VERY."

"Then, I'll go," Olivia replies. "Sorry Kaitlyn, you can't come with us. We don't want you counting black people. We understand you don't mean any harm, but I don't think other people will." Before Kaitlyn can respond, Olivia puts her foot down, "Kaitlyn, you're grounded until you learn more about delicate social situations. Don't sulk. It's for your own good. You've lived a sheltered life. Time to catch up with the real world, but not all at once tonight."

---

3 Movie Clip Toy Story https://www.youtube.com/watch?v=nMN4JZ8crVY

Olivia gets back to her mission, "Now Nicole, tell me about your role in the Foundation's blood experiment. I want to hear all about it."

* * *

After Olivia and Nicole leave for the Black Student Union.

"OMG! Time to hurry back to my room to get ready for my date with Scott."

Going through her closet, "No, too formal. No, makes me look fat. Too much makeup. Need look like I didn't prepare, like I'm naturally beautiful. Boys like that." Later, looking into the mirror. "Kaitlyn Korosec, this is it. That boy isn't going to know what hit him when he sees me tonight. And it only took two hours to seem totally natural so he'll love me just the way I am[4] naturally."

* * *

At the top of the stairs as Kaitlyn is leaving for her date with Scott, she watches Shelley slowly pull himself up the stairs, "Hi Shelley, looks like you were in a fight. How does the other guy look?"

"I just want to lay down and die, Kaitlyn."

"Do you think playing with the varsity squad the first time you played lacrosse was a bit overambitious?"

"Maybe, but it was a good way to make friends. Pain is a male bonding thing."

* * *

At the top of the stairs, "Kaitlyn, what's the occasion?"

"Oh Michelle, it's just a date."

---

4 Music Just the Way You Are https://www.youtube.com/watch?v=nBQdf2ZlDR0

"No, I know what 'just a date' looks like. From the look on your face,[5] this looks like a special date. These moments are so precious. I'm totally jealous. Like you're Juliet meeting her Romeo."[6]

"Well . . ., I guess I can't hide it. Maybe I am feeling my inner Juliet." Kaitlyn giggles as she floats down the stairs. At the bottom, she remembers to tell Michelle, "But your roommate needs some TLC. He's up in your room nursing wounds. Got to go. Romeo's waiting but let's talk about Shelley tomorrow. What a strange boy!"

A concerned Michelle asks, "What happened to my Shelley?"

Kaitlyn summarizes Sheldon's lacrosse misadventure and ends with, "And he's half their size mind you. That's just crazy. Oops, got to go now. See you tomorrow."

"I guess he took my bonding advice to heart," Michelle thinks as she hurries to her Shelley. "I'll have to be careful about how I advise Shelley. Somehow, I feel responsible for that boy. What am I feeling about that sweet boy? [7] . . . Like . . . like I . . .like I don't know what. What am I feeling?"

---

5 Pic Kaitlyn Ready for Date https://firepitcell.com/wp-content/uploads/2021/11/C8N5-Kaitlyn-Date.jpg

6 Music Video Love Story https://www.youtube.com/watch?v=8xg3vE8Ie_E

7 Music Video My Baby https://www.youtube.com/watch?v=P5o8ac8obNg

9

A Night to Remember

Nicole and Olivia walking across campus to the Black Student Union. "What's happening Nicole?"

"There's a big defund the police rally tonight. We're going to win this fight tonight. What's the matter, Olivia? Aren't you behind our cause?"

"Well, my father's a judge."

"What does that have to do with anything, Olivia?"

"Well, it's just that we like to look at both sides of the story."

"Two sides? This isn't just a story, Olivia. Cops are killing black people all across America every day."

"Nicole, that's crazy talk. It's not nearly that many. Look, I'm not saying there aren't some police officers. . .."

"Stop right there, Olivia. You're talking more like a white girl now than black.[1] Sounding more like that dumb blonde roommate of yours than a black sister."

"Kaitlyn is spontaneous, but she isn't dumb."

"Olivia, I'm not trying to make this personal, but we're at a point where everyone has to choose sides. I don't think Kaitlyn is going to choose our side."

"Especially since her father is a retired police officer," Olivia adds.

"See Olivia, that's what I mean. You're hanging out with the wrong crowd.[2] Get involved with the community."

---

1 Movie Clip White Voice https://www.youtube.com/watch?v=T5X3cu1B87k
2 Music Wrong Crowd Video https://www.youtube.com/watch?v=T5X3cu1B87k

"I'm planning to."

"No, I mean really involved. Ready to put your life on the line. After this is all over, everyone will remember who was totally committed to this fight and who wasn't."

"Well, I may do that. But I don't like jumping into things quickly."

"Girl, you'll have to decide now. We're going to blow the roof off this university tonight."

"Who's WE, Nicole?"

"You, me, the whole community."

"Nicole! Over here! Hurry, we're just about to move out."

"Gerald, sorry I'm late. I brought along another recruit. Meet Olivia."

"Great. I have extra masks and hoods. Put this on before we start. So, the police cameras never see who you really are. And here's some Vaseline and goggles for the tear gas."

"But . . ..

"No time to talk now. Have to keep up with the other marchers. Orders are no breaks in the ranks."

Someone near the head of the crowd shouts over a bull horn, "Tonight we fight the cops the way they fight.[3] Organized."

The now masked and hooded Olivia, "OMG! How do I deal with this? My life here will be miserable if I don't become part of the community. But I'm not a rioter."

Olivia hears, "Glad you decided to jump into this fight, sister."

"Nodding to the masked Nicole,[4] but thinking, "Who jumped in? You mean dragged in. Well, it's not a riot yet. Pretty peaceful so far. Free speech for a good cause. Maybe this will be OK."

* * *

---

3 Music Street Fighting Man https://www.youtube.com/watch?v=9pVL4AH9AlY
4 Pic Michelle https://firepitcell.com/wp-content/uploads/2021/11/C9N4-Nicole-Masked.jpg

Kaitlyn thinks as she spots Scott with friends at the bar, "I wasn't expecting to date a crowd tonight."

As she approaches the group, "Guys, this is the girl I was telling you about."

After introductions, "You mean the girl you said walked up to you out of the blue and started flirting?" one of Scott's friends asks.

Kaitlyn responds before Scott, "I'm not sure who started flirting first, but sometimes the girl has to take the initiative. Scott is so shy."

Amid laughter from his friends "Shy? Yeah that's the Scott we know. Shy around girls."

"Come on Kaitlyn. Let's leave these morons."

"But aren't we going to stay? This place has an earthy atmosphere." Kaitlyn says.

"That gang will be bothering us all night, Princess. The more they drink, the more obnoxious they'll get. I want you all to myself." As Scott leads his smiling date out of the bar as Kaitlyn thinks, "Thank you God."

"Well, Mr Hopkins, what will you do with me when you have me all alone?"

"First dinner. There's a quiet place at the corner of Hillsborough Street. And then, who knows?"

"Who knows? That sounds intriguing. Will we still be alone when who knows what happens, Mr. Hopkins?"

"You aren't shy, are you, Kaitlyn?"

"I used to be. I used to run away from life.[5] Not anymore. At least not when I know what I want."

"Good, I hate girls who spend all night looking at a menu and not being able to decide what they want."

At the corner, "Kind of noisy here for Sunday evening, Scott. Is it a parade or something? Today's not a holiday, is it?"

---

5 Music Video Shy Girl https://www.youtube.com/watch?v=AAYwk1neM70

"No, this happens a couple of times a year." Scott says. "They head downtown and protest for a few hours. We'll be finished with dinner before they get back to campus."

*   *   *

Scott and Kaitlyn enjoy their dinner. Their conversation is easy. Like they know one another in ways no one else does. Kaitlyn decides it's time to stake her claim to Scott by taking one of the French fries off his plate.

Scott smiles at this girl behavior as he thinks, "It's better than how dogs mark their territory. I hate soggy fries."

"He's smiling!" Kaitlyn thinks. "He knows I'm making my claim and he approves."

The evening continues and as Scott finishes a story about an adventure in South America, Kaitlyn begins to worry, "OMG, he's been everywhere," she thinks, and I've been nowhere."

"Does Atlanta qualify as South America, Scott? I visited an aunt there once."

"Close enough, Princess."

"Being cute makes up for a lot," Kaitlyn thinks as Scott begins another story.

After Scott pays the check, "I like you, Kaitlyn. I really do like you."

"Well, I like you too, Mr. Hopkins."

"Do you want to go to my apartment, Kaitlyn?"

"For a drink, Mr. Hopkins?"

"For a lot more than a drink. Interested, Princess? Still time for you to escape."

"Escape? Me? You're the only one in danger here, Mr. Hopkins," as she takes Scott by the hand leading him to the restaurant's door.

*   *   *

Downtown in front of a courthouse and police headquarters, hundreds are chanting.

"No Justice. No Peace."

"Burn it down."

Someone starts a fire. Then bottles and rocks begin flying at the building.

A panicked Olivia thinks, "They're trying to set the courthouse on fire.[6] My father works in a courthouse that looks a lot like this one." Trembling as conflicting emotions tear at her, Olivia thinks, "I so want to be part of the community, to help . . . to feel like I belong. But I shouldn't be part of this. What am I going to do?"

A line of police appears a block away. As the blue line slowly approaches some of the crowd begins to fade away. Then after a warning to disperse, tear gas begins to drift across the crowd. Rubber bullets fly past Olivia toward someone setting a car on fire

The masked Olivia dons her goggles like the others in the crowd, "OMG, is this is really happening to me? Trapped in the middle of a riot."[7]

*   *   *

After Scott opens the door to his apartment, Scott looks at Kaitlyn the same way he's looked at the many other girls he's bedded here. So sweet. So vulnerable. So, his for the taking.[8] Kaitlyn senses that she's in a well-rehearsed scene. Not wanting to become Scott's flavor of the day, Kaitlyn decides to change the script. Suddenly, Kaitlyn grabs his key and locks the door behind them. Leading him to his bedroom, "Now that I've lured you here, no escape for you, Mr. Hopkins."[9]

Scott watches Kaitlyn wiggle out of her dress and take control of their mating. Stunned, the wolf turns into a sheep and follows Kaitlyn's lead, "Kaitlyn, you're full of surprises," a confused but excited Scott says after a few minutes playing Kaitlyn's game.

---

6 Pic Riot Couthouse Fire https://firepitcell.com/wp-content/uploads/2021/11/C9N6-Fire-at-Courthouse-Demonstration.jpg

7 Riot Video https://www.youtube.com/watch?v=H5XyaLMkizs

8 Music Video Vulnerable https://www.youtube.com/watch?v=x7Iosk7Jg8E

9 Music Video Hot Stuff https://www.youtube.com/watch?v=yg6Y_1_DJyI

"More than you know. And it's Princess to you, Mr. Hopkins. You gave me that name and now I insist on you treating me like your Princess. Your body is mine to do with as I please."

"Happy to serve my Princess" are the last words Kaitlyn hears before . . . .

*   *   *

"And where are Nicole and Gerald?" Olivia panics as she feels so alone[10]. Then, she realizes, "We all look alike with this head gear. If I can't tell who Nicole and Gerald are, they probably can't tell who I am. This is the time. Time to get out of here."

*   *   *

Kaitlyn, in bed with Scott wrapped around her, "That was lovely[11]. I do hope you weren't disappointed, Scott."

Still a bit dazed, "Maybe I was right in calling you Princess. You acted like royalty, but then . . . so different . . . my servant girl. Where did all that come from, Princess?"

"I don't know, Scott. It's just happening to me. I'm changing. I'm more sure of what I want. More willing to take risks to get it. That's new for me. But there's something else. I know you're experienced. I imagine this bed has seen a lot of girls come and go. But don't treat your Princess like one of your normal girls. We'll love each other with a new set of rules because I'm unique."

"Yes, you are, Princess."

"And sometimes, I'm not your Princess and I'm not your servant."

"What are you then?"

"Whatever I feel like. It depends on my mood."

"A continual guessing game, Kaitlyn?"

---

10 Music Video Vulnerable https://www.youtube.com/watch?v=ha5vw3OlMx0
11 Movie Clip My Fair Lady Loverly https://www.youtube.com/watch?v=q5fW7sERw7I

"Don't you like games?[12] I do. And the prize, me, is worth your effort to play the game well."

*   *   *

Oliva makes her escape [13]from the mayhem downtown at the police station. Two blocks away, she thinks, "I don't think Nichole and Gerald saw me leave. I'm not cut out to be a social justice warrior, but I do want to fit into the community and help people."

As Olivia finally reaches the relative safety of campus, she is overcome by a sense of being between two worlds, a part of neither. Then she thinks, "I'm not the only one. That girl next door, Michelle, feels the same way too. She's always talking about knowing both sides, being pulled in different directions and visiting her bubble dimension when the rest of the world gets too crazy. I should talk with Michelle. We seem to have a lot in common."

*   *   *

As Kaitlyn sits up in bed, Scott pulls her back, "Not so fast Princess. Time for you to play the servant girl. Light my Fire[14] again."

"OMG, he's so . . . like I dreamed. Like it should always be, but never was before."

*   *   *

Back at the dorm, Michelle finds Sheldon cleaning up a few bruises, "I heard you took on the whole lacrosse team today."

"Well, Michelle, you suggested male bonding and I do things in a big way. Ow, it hurts when I laugh."

---

12 Music Video Wicked Game https://www.youtube.com/watch?v=0C-dNgypA5M
13 Gifs Sneaking Away https://giphy.com/explore/sneaking-away
14 Music Light My Fire https://www.youtube.com/watch?v=rj405bbDsoY

"It's a good sign that you can laugh. Let me help. I have some lotion that will reduce the swelling. It helps in ballet when I fall.: As Michelle applies the lotion, "Don't be such a baby," as Sheldon winces.

"Shelley, why are you laying your head on my lap? We can do this sitting up."

"My mother used to do it this way when I was sick. I mean, before momma died.[15] Do you mind?"

"Well, I guess its harmless, Shelley."

Remembering how his mother had comforted him when he was a little boy,[16] Sheldon looks up at Michelle and says "Someday you'll be a great mom, Michelle. You have a gentle touch like my mom had. You remind me of her sometimes."

"How old were you when she died?"

"About five. But I still remember her gentle touch."

Patting Sheldon's head and holding him tighter, Michelle begins feeling waves of sensations she's never felt before. "What am I feeling? Why?" she thinks. "My bubbles are trying to tell me something. But what? What are they telling me?" Then Michelle lets herself bath in waves of feelings and is immersed in Sheldon's confused childhood memories.[17] "What a broken confused boy I have, Michelle thinks. Looking down at Sheldon she strokes his hair and a single tear runs down her cheek, "Oh, Shelley, you're making it much more difficult to tell you what I have to say."

*   *   *

After Michelle composes herself for the task at hand, "Shelley, we need to have a little roommate talk."[18]

---

15 Music Video Where Her Heart Has Always Been https://www.youtube.com/watch?v=BvhJk1pRfxE

16 Pic Sarah Atwell Holding Sheldon https://firepitcell.com/wp-content/uploads/2021/11/C9N16-Sheldon-Remembers-Dead-Mother.jpg

17 Music Video Bubbles Burst https://www.youtube.com/watch?v=nxH8Bc0cHok

18 Music Video Roommates https://www.youtube.com/watch?v=Nhe13bRNKbs

"Roommate talk? Or Foundation talk?"

"A little of both."

"Sure, I've had enough male bonding for today. A little female immersion sounds just fine right now."

"I'm not sure how to start Shelley, but here goes."

"Don't worry Michelle. I've put myself in your hands and I'm comfortable with that."

"I know you have, Shelley. That's why this is so difficult. Just listen for a minute without interrupting. You see, I didn't tell you everything you should know about me when we talked yesterday. I intended to. But with those big puppy eyes of your looking up at me like you're doing now, I just couldn't do it. I know I need to tell you now. But first promise not to tell anyone. This has to be kept private. It's my secret that I only share with my closest friends."

"Of course, Michelle. I'm glad I'm a close friend after just one day."

"Shelley, you need to take this very seriously. I'll be very cross with you if you don't keep your promise. You haven't seen me when I'm angry. It's not pretty."

"Go ahead, I understand this is important and I promise."

"I can't tell you this with your head on my lap. It wouldn't be right. You'll understand why in a minute." As Michelle stands up, "Three years ago, I worked for the Foundation on an experiment.

"What was it?"

"Well, it was a lot like the experiment you're beginning now?"

"You mean the Foundation immersed you in boy culture? You had to hang with boys all the time?"

"No, I mean exactly like the experiment you're starting now in every way."

Michelle puts her hands on both sides of Sheldon's face. "Stop looking so perplexed, Shelley. I'm trying to tell you that before my Foundation experiment my name was Michael, not Michelle."

Sheldon laughs.

"No Shelley, I'm not teasing you. This is real life."

"But you look so . . ... No way that you're a guy."

"Seriously, Shelley honey. I wanted to tell you when we first met, but you were so freaked about the Foundation trying to turn you into a girl that I thought the truth might push you over the edge."

"Then, are you saying now the Foundation does want to turn me into a girl?[19]

"No, listen again, Shelley. I have my story. You have your story. They're not the same. The Foundation didn't turn me into a girl. I just chose to make changes in my life. I was on that path long before the Foundation's experiment. So, your story doesn't have to end like mine."

"Sorry, Michelle or Michael or whatever . . . this is scaring the hell out of me."

"I know Shelley. That's why I couldn't tell you yesterday. You weren't ready.

"Well, I'm not ready now. And call me Sheldon, not Shelley. My name is Sheldon!"

"OK, Sheldon. Please calm down. Let me explain."

"No way freak" as Sheldon pushes Michelle away. "Stay on your side of the room!"

A stunned Michelle lays on the floor waiting for Sheldon to calm down.

"Don't pretend to cry, freak."

Losing her patience, Michelle jumps up, "Sheldon Atwell! Calling me names? Pushing me? Not acceptable behavior. I'm just trying to help you. Since you refuse to listen, I'll have to make you listen."

"Make me? How you going to make me, freak?"

"I warned you not to make me angry!" as Michelle rushes toward Sheldon, knocks him on the floor and pins his arms with her knees.

"Like this, you whiney bitch!"

*   *   *

A stunned Sheldon struggles on the floor to release Michelle's grip on him while Michelle feels Sarah's approval of how she is dealing with Sheldon's

19 Video Woman For a Day https://www.youtube.com/watch?v=jExyi2iCt_A

misbehavior. "Teach him as best you can, Michelle. Be firm when he's been naughty," Sarah advises.

"Squirming won't help you, Shelley You're mine until I decide to let you go."

Looking up at Michelle, Sheldon finally pleads, "Please let me up!"

Shaking her head, "Not until you listen! Understand? I'm stronger than you thought. Aren't I, Shelley? Years of dance training builds strong legs."

"Yes, you're strong, Michelle."

"So, say it."

"Say what?"

"Say 'Michelle, I'm your bitch.'"

"Really? That's what you want?"

"I can stay on top of you all night if you want, bitch!"

Sheldon ponders his choices in this uncomfortable position while Michelle seems to be drifting off to another world. Sheldon sees only the shell of her body [20] while her spirit talks to his dead mother. Looking up at Michelle with her knees pinning his arms, he thinks, "She's calm now. Doesn't look like she wants to hurt me. Almost seems like her brain is in another place now while her legs keep me pinned down."

Michelle's rage melts as she feels the sensations from Sarah in her bubble dimension getting stronger. "My Shelley was a happy little boy until I had to leave him. So ready to explore the world. Then his world fell apart and my happy boy little boy vanished.[21] Now, look at him," Sarah says as Michelle looks down at Sarah Atwell's son quivering on their dorm room floor.

Meanwhile Sheldon continues thinking, "Can't really see or feel anything, but I don't think she's lying about her past. This might be funny, if I was watching it happen to someone else, but it's happening to me. Not so

---

20 Pic Michelle on Sheldon https://firepitcell.com/wp-content/uploads/2021/11/C9N20-Michelle-Dominates-Sheldon.jpg

21 Video That Happy Child https://www.youtube.com/watch?v=8OtkXU4XD9A

humorous. Must do something. Can't stay like this forever. Calm down and think. What's my best move in this situation?"

Seeing that Sheldon has ceased struggling, Michelle thinks, "I'd let him up now, except that he needs to learn how to behave. Let me show him he doesn't need to be afraid." as Michelle smiles down at him. Michelle senses Sarah's approval, "My, my Michelle, you do have a mother's instinct. Just the right time to give him a little hope," Sarah praises.

"A smile? I think she's trying to tell me something," and Sheldon smiles back. "She was so nice to me before. She looked like my mom a few minutes ago when she was taking care of me. She's starting to look more like my mom again. Probably would still be nice if I hadn't freaked out. Didn't mean to. Just happened before I knew it. Throw myself on her mercy. Get back to where we were half an hour ago. Yeah, that's my best move. Show her I'm really sorry and have learned my lesson."

"OK, Michelle, I'm your bitch."[22]

"That took you long enough. Now say it again, Shelley, like you mean it."

"I'm your bitch. I'm your bitch! Satisfied now?" Shelley says as he begins sobbing.

"Will you behave yourself, if I let you up?" as Michelle begins wiping away Sheldon's tears with the sleeve of her blouse."

"Yes Michelle. I'll do whatever you say."

Standing up looking down at Sheldon "Good, because I'm just trying to help you."

"But why did you just?"

"Because I've learned the hard way that I must draw boundaries, Shelley. You can't be calling me names and pushing me. I deserve better. I haven't always stood up for myself in the past. But now I do. You need to respect me even if you think I'm a freak."

---

22 Music Video Bitch https://www.youtube.com/watch?v=BF8TE5qsOCs

"Sorry, I really am sorry,[23] Michelle. I shouldn't have called you names and pushed you. Normally, I'm not a physical person. It was just a shock. I mean, I never expected."

"I know, Shelley. Believe me, I would have knocked you unconscious if I didn't know that you acted on reflex. And don't think I couldn't. I've been in bad situations. Learned how to protect myself. But I'm on your side and can help. All you need to do is listen and stop running around like a frightened child."

"Oh . . .."

"Go ahead and sulk, as long as you listen. Believe me, as soon as you start behaving like a rational person, I'll start treating you with respect. Until then, you'll get just what a misbehaving child deserves."

Sheldon thinks, "She sounds like one of my friends' moms. Oh, how I missed that. Do I have that now? Is Michelle my mom reincarnated? Probably not, but maybe my mom is talking to Michelle. Telling her to help me, but also make me behave. Who knows? I just know that she comforted me before I freaked out. And she's being nice to me again after I was bad. That's what moms do."

* * *

Michelle explains her story to a now docile Sheldon. Three older sisters. Ballet school surrounded by girls. Dancing better than my sisters[24] could and liking the girls' dance roles more than the boys' parts. "Then in high school I realized that I'm attracted to both boys and girls."

"Is that when you realized you were a woman trapped in a man's body?" Sheldon asks.

"Not really, Shelley. People can do the same thing for different reasons. Other people who do what I've done might feel like they're girls trapped in boys' bodies, but that's not my story. I know I wasn't born a girl.

---

23 Music Video Sorry https://www.youtube.com/watch?v=fRh_vgS2dFE
24 Movie Clip Chorus Line I can Do That https://www.youtube.com/watch?v=_nZRjGKIbfM

And I never felt trapped. But I like to do a lot of things some people say only girls should do. I wish people didn't think that way, but they do. So, I decided I would get more of what I want out of life if people think I'm a girl. And I like my choice. I'm happier. So, I'm Michelle now. The bubbles helped me decide."[25]

"Oh . . .."

When Michelle mentions the bubbles helping her make decisions images of his happiest childhood memory flood Sheldon's brain, his mother blowing bubbles[26] and he rehears the last happy thing his mom said before the accident, "Catch the bubbles, Shelley."

How many times have those last sweet words echoed in my mind?" he wonders. "The happiest day of my life before it was all vanished," he thinks. Then, "I knew my mom didn't really leave me all alone forever. I knew she would find me. Momma is using the bubbles to tell Michelle how to help me. Michelle couldn't be my mom when she was Michael. But the bubbles helped Michael become Michelle. She just said that. So, now she can help my mom guide me."

Michelle senses a change come over Sheldon. "Maybe he'll listen to me now," she thinks.

"So, Shelley, (excuse me Sheldon), is that your story? What part of my story is your story?

"Well, nothing."

"Then, why would your experiment end like mine? That's not a very scientific conclusion."

"But this scares me so much, Michelle. Why?"

"Good question. I don't know your answer. I suspect that's the point of your experiment. You should work on that."

"Oh . . .."

---

25 Music Video Your Decision https://www.youtube.com/watch?v=2D37POA11KY
26 Pic Sheldon's Mom Blowing Bubbles https://firepitcell.com/wp-content/up-loads/2021/11/C9N26-Sheldon-Mom-Blowing-Bubbles.jpg

"Don't get too depressed, Shelley. We all have things to work on –
especially at this stage of life. This experiment is an opportunity to learn a
lot about the most important subject in the world."

?????

"Yourself, silly. Do you want to go through life not knowing who you
are?"[27]

"Well, Michelle, that's a viable strategy for some people. I was hoping
it would work for me."

"Sheldon, the experiment protocols say that you can make that choice.
You have that Freedom." Looking deeply into Sheldon's eyes, "I can see
that scares you. It should. Freedom is wonderful, but it's also scary.[28]
There's risk that you'll make the wrong choice. That might lose everything. A lot of people can't handle it. So, that makes you normal. I've stared
into Freedom's eyes; made my choices and I'm liking the results now. But
it's been a bumpy road. I think that's why the Foundation arranged for us
to be roommates. Not to turn you into a girl. Just to help you deal with the
terror of being Free to choose."

"But I can't guaranty what will happen. That's up to you, Shelley. All
I can do now is assure you that this experiment isn't designed to turn you
into a girl. The Foundation has been doing this experiment for several
years at schools across the country. Very few boys make the choices I've
made. Most seem to resume their normal lives at the end the experiment.
Some are even better prepared to be men than they were before the experiment. That's what I hope for you Shelley. You know, not all boys grow up
to be men. Some just become old boys. That's kind of pathetic. You're
almost 17. This is your time to start becoming a man. I'm sure your mom
would want that, Sheldon."

"Maybe, you're right Michelle. I've been struggling to find my place in
the world. My default reaction is to drift."

"Just one word of warning, Shelley. I've worked hard to create my new
life. I'm 21, starting over at school as a freshman. I've earned the right to

_____

27 Music Who A I https://www.youtube.com/watch?v=v7Fk6dt_uHo
28 Music Me and Bobby McGee https://www.youtube.com/watch?v=N7hk-hI0JKw

decide what I tell other people about myself and when I tell it. You'll regret it if you don't keep my secrets."

After Michelle turns off the lights, she hears Sheldon breathing heavily.

"Shelley, try to remember that almost everyone on this campus is adjusting to new things. Some will succeed. Others won't. We're really all in the same boat. If you and I row together, this experiment will be fine.

"OK Michelle, I just pictured myself in a different boat. But this is where we both are now and I'm glad I'm not alone."[29] Then Sheldon thinks to himself, "My mom is with me. Michelle is the way mom found me. I need to listen to Michelle like she's my mom."

"Now, can we finally go to sleep, Shelley? Classes start tomorrow and the other girls still have some advantages. Sometimes I wake up looking like a drag queen if I don't get my beauty sleep. Believe me, you don't want to see that tomorrow morning!"

Good night, Michelle.

Good night, Shelley.

Before the exhausted Michelle falls asleep, conflicting feelings overwhelm her. "He's so young and vulnerable. No mom since he was five? Breaks my heart. I can deal with guys, who just want sex. Can I deal with someone who desperately wants a mom? I'm so screwed up myself. Am I ready to guide him? Is helping Shelley how I fix myself? Or will he pull me under? I wish my mom was here. She'd know what I should do."

Then, Michelle feels her bubbles again. With that reassuring feeling that she is not alone, that she will have help, her doubts begin to fade. "I'm an actress. Maybe I can learn to act like the mom[30] Shelley needs," she thinks before falling asleep.

*　*　*

---

29 Music Video You Are Not Alone https://www.youtube.com/watch?v=pAyKJAtDNCw
30 Pic Michelle Mom in Training https://firepitcell.com/wp-content/uploads/2021/11/C9N30-Michelle-Mother-Training.jpg

Just after dawn[31], Scott walks Kaitlyn from his apartment to her dorm as Allie enters a small meadow at the edge of Pullen Park for her morning yoga.

"What a fine morning to be alive, Allie thinks as she begins her poses in a bed of flowers softly lit by the pink Eastern sky."

But it's not all light and serenity in Pullen Park. Beyond the edge of the small meadow, darkness stalks the light. Allie isn't alone. A predator has found what he has been waiting for. Lost in her yoga, Allie is unaware of the approaching stranger, who suddenly emerges from the bushes and begins running toward her.

Walking with Scott along the edge of Pullen Park, Kaitlyn sees her friend Allie in the distance and calls, "Hi, Allie. You look so beautiful in the dawn light!"[32]

Suddenly, the dark figure changes direction as he sees Kaitlyn and Scott. Ignoring what she presumes is just a jogger, "What are you doing here, Allie?

"Early morning yoga."

"You're so good, Allie. I should join you some time."

Allie, noticing Kaitlyn's dress from the night before and the way she holds herself against Scott, Allie smiles and says, "But not this morning, I bet."

"Is it that obvious?"

Still smiling, "Well, my experience is the better it was, the more obvious it is. Must have been pretty wonderful."

"No, not this morning," as Kaitlyn, back in Princess mode, bestows a parting kiss[33] on her escort that makes it hard to leave.[34]

---

31 Music Here Comes the Sun https://www.youtube.com/watch?v=KQetemT1sWc

32 Pic Allie in Dawn Light https://firepitcell.com/wp-content/uploads/2021/11/C9N32-Allie-in-Park-Dawn-Light.jpg

33 Pic Kaitlyn Scott Dawn Kiss https://firepitcell.com/wp-content/uploads/2021/11/C9N33-Kaitlyn-Scott-Dawn-Kiss.jpg

34 Music Hard to Leave https://www.youtube.com/watch?v=MrSQaOiL4MI

Walking with Allie across the street to their dorm, "I can't believe how much my life has changed since I moved in. Was that really only four days ago?"

"No classes yet, but we've all learned a lot, Kaitlyn."

Back at her room, Olivia is full of questions, "Kaitlyn, where have you been? And why was your phone off. I've been worried about you."

"Worried? Olivia, that's just what my mom would have said. You're so sweet. But there's no need to worry about me when I'm with Scott."

"Oh, did that go well?"

"My. . . yes. I'm still in heaven and don't know when I'll get back to earth. He's a magic man,[35] is all I can say. Know what I mean, Olivia?"

"Yes, I know what that means, Kaitlyn," Olivia replies curtly. Not wanting to hear more about Kaitlyn's romantic encounter with Scott, Olivia changes the subject. "Well, the peaceful demonstration I went to last night turned into a riot. I was really scared."

"Were you caught up in that, Olivia? Poor Dear," Kaitlyn says hugging Olivia, "Are you hurt?"

"No, but I barely escaped. It was total mayhem."

"Disorder is your idea of hell, Olivia. Isn't it? I wish it was me instead of you[36], disorder is my life."

*   *   *

CONFUSING.

SO MUCH HAPPENED IN ONE NIGHT. HOW DO WE EDIT THESE MEMORIES

---

35 Music Video Magic Man https://www.youtube.com/watch?v=CbH7zNrHQqE
36 Music Video Swap Places https://www.youtube.com/watch?v=HeZVOPDeRYQ

10

Classes Begin the New Normal

Michelle wakes up before Shelley. Staring across the room, she worries about Shelley's first full day immersed in female tribal culture, "That boy is on the edge. Don't know if I can stand too many sessions with Shelley starring as the drama queen. I'm supposed to be the drama queen." Then Michelle remembers the many issues Michael presented his mother and her promise to Sarah. "Maybe I can do this. Shelley and I made some progress last night. My Mom would say 'one step at a time.'[1] I can take the next step and see what happens."

The alarm on Sheldon's phone starts at 7 am, but he turns over.

"Don't you have some kind of gym class in a half hour, Shelley?"

"Yeah . . . Mom," as Sheldon grabs shorts, sweatshirt and sneakers, gargles with mouthwash instead of brushing and heads out the door three minutes later.

"Make good choices, Shelley. Girls can be mean." Then she thinks, "Did I just say that?"

"Yeah, Mom."

"And I'm not your mother!"

"Yeah, Mom," as Shelley closes the door.

"Why do I like him calling me Mom?" Michelle muses to herself, "Is this the next stage of my journey?"

Then, Michelle ponders her journey, "Sometimes I miss Michael getting ready to face the day in five minutes. Now, I've got half an hour of

---

1 Music Video One step at a Time https://www.youtube.com/watch?v=PIE5QtkxzvM

fussing ahead of me." But when Michelle finishes and looks in her mirror, "What was I thinking about missing Michael's life? I can't give up the beautiful girl in this mirror."[2]

By chance, Michelle and Allie emerge from their rooms into the hall at the same time.

Allie, who has been thinking about Michelle since her out of body experience when she kissed Michelle, realizes, "This is my chance. I need to find out more about this girl."

"Hi neighbor! Is drama your first class today?" Allie asks. "Me too. Shall we show the world how it's done?"

As they walk together to face their new lives, Allie holds Michelle's hand and confides, "I've been thinking that we may have a connection, Michelle."

"Did the bubbles tell you that Allie? Oh, I can see you're still processing our moment together. That's OK, Allie. Take your time. I can be patient."

"OMG, our time together in the bubbles really did happen!" Allie thinks. "Thought I was crazy, but somehow, someway, it was real. Now's my chance to discover more about Michelle, my bubbles queen." Allie starts her get to know Michelle project, "Michelle, I checked out your Facebook page last night. How long have you been selecting actresses to be each day?"

Seeing that Allie isn't ready to discuss their bubbles experience, Michelle responds, "Oh, for about a year. I rotate about two dozen actresses and roles, but I'm always looking for new ones. Today, I'm Audrey Hepburn playing Holly Golightly in Breakfast at Tiffany's.[3] It's never a mistake to be Audrey, She's perfect even first thing out of bed in the morning. And Holly knew how to have fun. I want this semester to be fun."

"Who's your favorite, Michelle?"

---

2 Music Video Girl in the Mirror https://www.youtube.com/watch?v=U_1Ne7XHBas
3 Movie Clip Breakfast at Tiffany's https://www.youtube.com/watch?v=52kC2KKpUT0

"Playing Vivien Leigh's Scarlett O'Hara[4] character from Gone with the Wind is the one that gets the most reactions from people. That's the most fun, at least during the day. Carrie Bradshaw from Sex and the City[5] is the most fun at night. Scarlett was something of a prude."

"Can you introduce me to Carrie sometime?" Allie asks as she caresses Michelle's hand.

As Michelle leans against Allie, both girls think, "We'll be more than just friends."

*   *   *

Kaitlyn and Olivia walk halfway across campus and then part to different buildings. Political science for Olivia and the dreaded required math class for Katlyn.

"I've got your back roommate."

"And I've got your back. But I'm so jealous that you placed out of math class, Olivia. This is my nemesis. If I can just get by in this class, I know, I'll do OK in my other classes. I'm not dumb. I'll pass. And then, no more math for the rest of my life." Kaitlyn smiles, "Oh, what a wonder! A math less world."

*   *   *

At the gym, Sheldon walks past grunting weightlifters to reach his aerobics class. With him are a dozen girls of varying shapes and two guys who walk in holding hands. Stationing himself in the back of a room he watches his classmates warm up stretching their bodies in unimaginable ways. "Glad I'm here early to get the back row. Oh yes! Smart move." Then, the instructor walks in past the front of the room and stands behind Sheldon. "Oh no, I'm in the front now."

---

4 Movie Clip Gone with the Wind https://www.youtube.com/watch?v=ja1fqOo4ukc
5 TV Clip Sex and the City https://www.youtube.com/watch?v=Wn_WHLTK3qI

When the music starts everyone effortlessly mimics the instructors' moves.

"OMG, this is so confusing" as an out of breath Sheldon struggles to keep up. And everyone's looking at me! [6] How can I do this for a whole half hour? Why can everyone but me do this?" Sheldon asks himself.

Finally, the class is over.

"Not as easy as it looks, is it?" the diminutive blond girl whose rear end was in his face half the class volunteers.

"I'm just glad it's over."

"Are you coming back tomorrow?"

Nodding yes, "I have to. It's part of my Foundation contract."

"If you get here 15 minutes early, I'll show you the basic routines. Once you learn them, you won't have to think before you move. It's all muscle memory. It can be fun after you stop thinking and just move with the music."

"Thanks.

"Oh, I'm Sheri. And you?

"Sheldon Atkins."

"Sheldon, is it OK if I give you another tip? Wear lighter clothes. Class stopped five minutes ago, but you 're still sweating."

The girls and Sheldon parade back past the weightlifters who have all stopped and are watching closely, "Rhone is a good brand for guys. They're not too girly. You don't want that. Some of these guys would screw anything that moves."

"Thanks Sheri . . . for all your advice," as he thinks, "People are looking out for me. First Michelle, now Sheri. I'm not alone after being alone all this time. Why? Oh yeah. Thanks for coming back to me, Sarah."

* * *

---

6 Video Aerobics Class https://www.youtube.com/watch?v=bBWkPRSE-W4&t=57s

"I have enough trouble with math. Why can't they at least teach it in English!" Kaitlyn wonders as she struggles to understand the Asian grad student who teaches with an unfamiliar accent.

As she leaves class, another student says, "I see you're not following what our professor is saying."

"I admit it. I'm not. Totally confused. He doesn't speak my language."

"Technically, he does, but not in practice. A lot of the grad students are from other countries. They can read, write and understand perfect English, but they pronounce words differently. And their rhythm is different."

"My older brother figured out system to deal with that."

"Go on. I'm all ears!"

"Before I left home, he gave me a long academic article and audios of people from different parts of the world reading the same article as if they wrote it. If you listen to them talking, while you read the article, it really helps you figure out their speech pattern. My brother says it turns what seems like random sounds into intelligible speech."

"What's the trick?"

"Our trick is finding the recording that most closely matches how your particular teacher speaks. I have over a dozen different recordings of the same article. Once you figure out the right match, you won't be as lost in class. This grad student closely matches number 6. Listen to this . . .."

"That sounds exactly like him."

I'm holding a group learn-in tonight. A dozen or so students listening to all the recordings. I only charge $50."

"What?"

"But you can earn that money back. If you sell my system to other students, you earn commissions. This is a big opportunity, you know. I don't select just anyone to sell for me."

"Well, how do you select?"

"In your case, because you're the prettiest girl in the class. My program usually attracts geeks. I want to break into the sorority market. My guess is that you are rushing. Right?"

"Oh, I get it. You're hiring a dumb blond to sell to other dumb blonds. That's insulting. Do you always insult the people you recruit?"

"Nothing personal Princess. It's just reality. Pretty girls[7] hang together. They run when the see a geek like me. You have market access."

"Well then, what's my split on sales?"

"70% for me. 30% for you, Princess."

"No deal, unless its 50%-50%."

"But it's my program."

"Look, you picked me. I'm the one with market access. Do you want to close a deal or not?"

"Well, OK, but how about a weekly 'friends with benefits' relationship to sweeten the deal?"

"That's disgusting! No wonder girls run away from you. Just for that, it's 60% for me and 40% for you now."

But . . ..

"Say another word and it's a 70% 30% split in my favor."

"OK Princess, I mean Kaitlyn, I'm going to stop digging myself into a hole. OK, 60% and 40%."

"Deal. Also, you should know that I would have settled for 30%, because I think your ass is cute. Maybe I'll call you for a booty call if I ever get that desperate, sweetie. You need to learn how to negotiate better. I could teach you for a small fee."

"Kaitlyn, you're going to make both of us a lot of money with that attitude."

"I know. That's why I'm worth 60%."

*   *   *

Calling home:

"Daddy! I've started a new business."

"Well, it involves translating languages."

---

7 Music Video Pretty Girls https://www.youtube.com/watch?v=uV2uebhnqOw

"What languages? Oh, I guess it's really translating English to American. Yes Daddy, people actually pay for that."

"Well, some of the teachers here don't talk American."

"Yes, I know that sounds a little crazy."

"Yes, I know, but it's a real opportunity. And you always said opportunities pop up in the strangest places."

"Love you too, Daddy."

*   *   *

On the way to class, "Olivia! What happened to you last night?"

"I was wondering the same thing about you, Nicole. Where did you disappear to?"

"Well, it became pretty chaotic after the first tear gas cannisters. I totally lost track of people."

"Me too. Totally crazy. I got separated from Gerald too. Want to hook up with Gerald and me later? See you at the Black Student Union around 12:30."

"Whew! I lucked out. Nobody knows I ran as soon as I could. We're still friends," Olivia thinks.

*   *   *

In drama class, Michelle and Allie audition and land parts.

"Michelle, I'm so glad we're in the same play. Rehearsing together will give us an opportunity to . . ..," as Allie returns the kiss Michelle gave her playing Truth or Dare.

In response to the surprised look on Michelle's face, "You never know the chemistry until lips and tongues meet when we're alone. Last time it was part of a game.

And in the middle, it was so confusing the last time. Kind of like in a fairy tale So, I took the opportunity to find out for real this time."

"Allie, I'm hoping you're not just playing a game,[8]" as Michelle casts a reassuring smile and offers her hand to Allie.

"I never noticed your hands before, Michelle."

"Hands? Is something wrong with my hands, Allie?"

"No, I like holding your hand, Michelle. It feels right. I think a lot of things seem right about us."

Later that day, Michelle daydreams about Allie.[9] "She's so . . . the way I like. Kissing me like that in class in front of everyone right out of the blue. Very confident. Like she knows she already owns me. So, exciting. The way my bubbles are behaving I know I'll just melt in her arms. Someone to risk their all to save me from my dark prison and Carry Me[10] to a better world. I could see Allie doing that."

Then, "But Allie thinks I'm a regular girl. What if my secret is a problem for her? What's a special girl like me to do?" Michelle pouts. "I'll need to be careful about when and where I tell her. Maybe, I'll tell her the next time we're in the bubbles together. That will work. We're good together in the bubbles. But everything is good in the bubbles. If only that was true in this world."

Meanwhile, Allie walks back to the dorm thinking, "Something about Michelle in acting class today seems so familiar but different. Where have I seen her before?[11] Have to get to know that girl better. She's kind of surreal. What's with her and the bubbles? Like she's walking around in a dream. But she's on the right side of the thin line between enchanting and weird. Maybe I'll like walking that thin line with her. Maybe the girl of my dreams needs to walk in dreams." Walking by Michelle's dorm room, Allie quietly hums a song.[12]

* * *

---

8 Music Video Games https://www.youtube.com/watch?v=ne5AQiEFvBI

9 Pic Michelle Daydreaming About Allie https://firepitcell.com/wp-content/uploads/2021/11/C10N9-Michelle-Daydreams-about-Allie.jpg

10 Music Video Carry Me https://www.youtube.com/watch?v=7QPtFy7OnGE

11 Pic Allie Thinking about Michelle https://firepitcell.com/wp-content/uploads/2021/11/C10N11-Allie-Wonders-About-Michelle.jpg

12 Music Michelle https://www.youtube.com/watch?v=FkolGEALbms

After a quick shower, Sheldon drags his tired body to a class on the Theory of Numbers.

Suddenly, Sheldon becomes alive, "But professor, I think you'll find that this hypothesis was nicely refuted in Stephen Wolfram's[13] paper published by the Max Plank Foundation[14] back in the late 1970s."

"Yes, I know you knew that. I was just refreshing your memory."

After class, Luna who lives in the same hall, approaches, "Shelley, that was wonderful the way you put that pompous professor in his place."

"I tried to do it diplomatically, Luna. Do you think I was too hard on him?"

"No, I loved it, Shelley."

"Really Luna?"

"Yes, it was thrilling[15]. Very . . . masterful, Shelley."

Maybe another couple would have brought their relationship further, but Luna and Shelley weren't ready, yet.

*　　*　　*

At lunch, Sheldon finds nine girls sitting at the round table the Foundation assigned him and fills the last seat.

"So, you're the mystery boy."

"What do you mean?"

"Well, we've all been wondering why the Foundation is paying for all our meals just to sit with you. What's wrong with you?"

"Nothing unusual that I know of. Just an ordinary guy trying to fit in. But I agree it's kind of weird. I mean, why are these people manipulating us?"

---

13 Article Stephen Wolfram https://blogs.scientificamerican.com/cross-check/polymath-stephen-wolfram-defends-his-computational-theory-of-everything/

14 Website Max Planck Institute https://www.maxplanckfoundation.org/about-us-2/?lang=en

15 Pic Luna Falling for Sheldon https://firepitcell.com/wp-content/uploads/2021/11/C10N15-Luna-Thrilled-by-Sheldon.jpg

"My older sister warned me about the Foundation before I came. Bunch of control freaks she said. But if they're willing to pay for my meals, I'll go along. I mean, how bad can you be, Sheldon?"

"Not very bad, I assure you."

Within five minutes after he sat down, the girls returned to their normal conversations. "Michelle was right. I'm just like a fly on the wall," Sheldon thinks.

*   *   *

"Scott, thanks for calling me so soon. You win big boyfriend points for that."

"I'm your boyfriend now, Princess?"

"Of course, you're my boyfriend, silly. You belong with me."[16]

"I do?"

"Well, do you think I'm the kind of girl who goes to bed with every guy she meets?[17] Well, do you?" After a few seconds, "Scott, you're not supposed to think about the answer. It's a rhetorical question."

"Of course not, Princess."

"Good answer, Mr. Hopkins. Slow, but good. You'll have to work on your timing."

"Boys are always the last to know they're boyfriends. Girls know these things. You can pretend you're not if you want."

"I don't think . . ."

"OK, I can play your little game. So, Scott, who isn't my boyfriend, why did you call?"

"Tonight?"

"You'll pick me up?"

"Yes, I can be ready at 7.

"Which Kaitlyn will I be tonight? What a question, Scott. Even if I knew, I wouldn't tell you. We'll both be surprised. That'll be fun.

16 Music Video You Belong with Me https://www.youtube.com/watch?v=VuNIsY6JdUw
17 Music Video I'm That Kind of Girl https://www.youtube.com/watch?v=m-HVP01goE4

After their call, "The real question is whether Scott has as many personalities as I do. There's more to Scott than he wants other people to know. But I'm not just other people. We're also different. With me, it's 'what you see is what you get.' Scott is hiding something. Just from me? Or from everyone?" Which Scott will show up at my door tonight?"

* * *

"Hi Gerald![18] You remember Olivia from last night, don't you?"

"Sorry I didn't recognize you without your mask and goggles. I like you a lot better this way, Olivia."[19]

"I guess the revolution needs a new fashion consultant."

"Olivia, the struggle for our rights isn't something to joke about!" Nicole admonishes, "people are dying."

"Yes, but I think everything has a serious side and a humorous side. You just have to look for it."

"I like that attitude, Olivia, Gerald says."

"Gerald, you like anything in a skirt, if they're willing."

"Not true, Nicole. Not true. The person has to be alive."

"That's not a very high standard, Gerald."

Olivia defends Gerald, "Nicole, I'm sure Gerald meant 'alive' in a philosophical sense. Aristotle and Plato had very high mental, emotional and ethical standards for judging whether someone is really 'alive'."

"Yeah! That's exactly what I meant Olivia," Gerald responds laughing.

"Since when have you been reading Plato and Aristotle, Gerald?" Nicole asks.

"Since just now that I know Olivia does."

"You're impossible, Gerald!"

"No, I'm very possible, Nicole. I'm just about the most possible guy you're ever going to meet. But now I have to get back to work. Lunch

18 Pic Gerald https://firepitcell.com/wp-content/uploads/2021/11/C10N18-Gerald-for-Olivia.jpg
19 Pic Olivia https://firepitcell.com/wp-content/uploads/2021/11/C10N19-Olivia-for-Gerald.jpg

doesn't just happen by itself. But Olivia, I'm not working the dinner shift. I'd like to find out more about being alive over burgers and fries."

"I'd like that, Gerald."

"How about 7 pm, Olivia? Players' Retreat?"

As Gerald departs, Nicole confides to Olivia, "Gerald goes to the community college down the road. He's studying hospitality management. Restaurants and hotels. The community college students come here to practice at the university dining halls."

"Really? Tell me more." Olivia says smiling.

"Yes, but he's not your type, Olivia.

"And what's my type, Nicole?"

"Rich and snooty."[20]

"Oh! Now I understand,' Olivia says. "Are you and Gerald a couple? That's it, isn't it? I'm so sorry., Nicole I didn't mean to . . . .."

"No, not a couple. We just go way back together. We're from the same neighborhood. Gerald worked for my older brother. The one the police killed. Gerald has looked out for me since my brother died."

"Oh! I didn't know."

"Olivia, sorry for that 'Rich and snooty' crack. It's not your fault. Gerald has an easy way about him that's irresistible. Just don't blame me for introducing you."

"Nicole, it'll just be burgers and fries, Plato, Aristotle and a few laughs. Not every evening ends with being boyfriend and girlfriend."[21]

"I doubt that, Olivia. Believe me. I know Gerald. You'll fall for him. And I think he'll like you. Just don't dump him for a rich guy. He deserves better."

---

20 Music Uptown Girl https://www.youtube.com/watch?v=hCuMWrfXG4E
21 Music Video Boyfriend https://www.youtube.com/watch?v=9SRxBTtspYM

11

International Friends

"Scott, you remember Sanjay[1] from that month we worked with the Indian government, don't you?" Olivia asks.

"Of course. Sanjay, what are you doing here?"

"Grad School, and you?"

"I'm a junior and Olivia's a freshman here."

"Good to bump into you. Maybe we can play some squash, Scott?"

"Sure, that'd be great."

"Funny that we all end up at the same school at the same time, isn't it Sanjay."

"Yes, quite a coincidence, Scott."

"Isn't there a famous saying about fools believing in coincidences," Olivia asks.

"Sorry Sanjay, our friend Olivia is a born skeptic and a bit of a paranoid. Still thinks her parents constantly spy on her. How is Tuesday next week for squash, Sanjay?"

"Let me check. Early morning looks open."

"Great, I'll reserve a court."

Before they part, the three exchange contact information.

* * *

---

1 Pic Sanjay https://firepitcell.com/wp-content/uploads/2021/12/C11N1-Sanjay.jpg

"Scott, wasn't Sanjay's uncle the head of Indian intelligence[2] Do you think Sanjay is spying[3] for his uncle?"

"Maybe? We're working for our parents. So why not?"

"The Indian intelligence must think something important is going on here if they sent their chief's nephew. Do you think they're here because of the same thing we're after?"

"That has crossed my mind, Olivia. I'll have to brush up on my squash game before next Tuesday. The Senator will have a fit if I let Indian intelligence beat me."

"I'll check in with the Professor to get instructions about Sanjay."

*   *   *

"Scott, the Professor's instructions are that India is an ally.[4] China is the threat. For some reason we don't know yet, China is interested in the Princess' Foundation experiment. We know something was going on, but India tipped us off that this is a high priority project for China. So, India's our partner on this. One of many projects India and America are working together on. Both countries know China is our common threat. Sanjay isn't working for India. As an American, he's acting as liaison to reassure his uncle that we're not double-crossing India."

"So, Sanjay's on our side, Olivia?"

"Affirmative."

"Great, I always liked Sanjay."

"Here's something you're not going to like Scott! The Professor instructs you to lose your squash game with Sanjay."

"But I can beat him in my sleep."

---

2 Article https://en.wikipedia.org/wiki/List_of_Indian_intelligence_agencies

3 5 Bollywood Spy Movies https://www.youtube.com/watch?v=DSHF2N6UEUI

4 Article India US Alliance https://foreignpolicy.com/2021/10/25/us-india-alliance-military-economy-biden-china-afghanistan/

"Just do it Scott, take one for the team!"[5]

*   *   *

"Woah, Sanjay, you've really improved your game. Let me congratulate the winner."

"Scott, you're a good squash player, but a lousy actor! I know you were instructed to throw the game. You're not a professional intelligence officer yet. India just wanted to test whether you can follow instructions from your commander. Too much at stake here to have egos get in the way."

"Sanjay, you were enjoying watching me throw the game weren't you."

"It was funny watching you trip over yourself while we were playing, but now I can report to my uncle that you followed your instructions. Then maybe he'll calm down. Don't know why. I'm just a liaison, but something is making him very nervous.'

"So, our bet is off, right?"

"No way, you still have to buy the beers – charge it to your agency. I didn't instruct you to lose. They did."

"OK, while I'm buying you beers, let's talk about how we cooperate. Frankly, all I know is that Princess is our target. Don't know why or what I'm supposed to do other than monitor the situation."

"I don't know anything more than that, Scott, except that the highest levels in India are interested in this potential threat."

*   *   *

Later, over beers, Sanjay and Scott toast, "Here's to the alliance of India and America. May we always bring light into a dark world on the edge!"

---

5 Video Clip https://www.youtube.com/watch?v=N-eve_v7xYg

12

Preparing Shelley

Kaitlyn, Olivia, Allie and Michelle plot how to hook up Luna and Shelley. Allie visits with Michelle to discuss their roommates.

"I'll get Luna ready while you prep Shelley, Michelle."

"Are you sure a club is the way to go, Allie? I don't think he knows how to dance."

"Then teach him. He doesn't have to be perfect."

"And I don't think he knows much about girls."

"Then teach him, Michelle."

"Allie, I had no idea you're such a take charge kind of girl," as the two smile at one another.

"And you're responsible, Michelle, if he screws up." Allie adds laughing.

"I see you're playing Meryl Streep as Miranda Priestly[1] in The Devil Wears Prada today, Allie."

"Just don't disappoint me like that lazy Anne Hathaway did. A thousand girls would love your job, Michelle."

"OMG, she's so what I crave. So sure of herself," Michelle thinks as she leaves to find Shelley. "I'm going to teach that boy some things that will wow Allie."

* * *

---

1 Movie Clip Devil Wears Prada https://www.youtube.com/watch?v=97XCFu-4RH8

"Shelley, I've been talking with our neighbors. We're going out tonight to a dance club a few blocks from campus."

"OK, have a good time, Michelle."

"No, you don't understand, Shelley. We all decided you're going with us. Kaitlyn and Olivia, Allie and Luna, Michelle and Shelley. It's a roommate thing and you're my roommate. Luna is Allie's roommate. We've all decided you and Luna will make a cute couple. And you both need dating practice."

"A club? Dancing? I don't dance."

"Well, time to learn. I'll teach you."

"Don't worry, I won't molest you. We'll all teach you at the club. But I'll just help you get a head start with a dance lesson now."

"Uh, I don't think this is a good idea, Michelle. I'm kind of clumsy."

"Shelley, the best way to learn about girls is to be with us when we're having fun. Then, you'll know what girls want."[2]

"But I've never done this before."

"Then, you have a lot of catching up to do. I've been taking dance lessons since I was four years old. I've taught some classes too."

"But . . .." then Shelley stops resisting when he sees Michelle's determination.

"Now, I want you to focus on one thing. Girls have lots of reasons they want to dance. I'll explain dancing music with science first."[3]

"Wow, Michelle, I didn't realize dancing is so scientific."

"Well, it is, but now that I have your attention, you can forget all that. I'm here to teach you about dancing with girls. All the girls in the world don't matter. Only the one girl you're dancing with matters. Your job is to find out why she wants to dance. Then, you can create a pleasant experience for her. If you do that, she'll think you're a great dancer – even if you make some mistakes. The secret to dancing is showing this one girl that she matters more than anything else in the world[4] - at least during the time

---

2 Music Video https://www.youtube.com/watch?v=PIb6AZdTr-A

3 Video Dance Science Article https://www.youtube.com/watch?v=eWMP22dbv4k

4 Intimate Dance Video https://www.youtube.com/watch?v=4BvtjClyL0Q

she's your dance partner. Same thing for your next dance partner. Make each one feel special. Does that make sense Shelley?"

"Yes, but how do I know what she wants?"

"That's mainly what our lesson will be about. I'm not going to try to teach you a lot of dance steps. No time for that. I'm going to teach you how to dance with one girl and make her happy."

"There are two basic types of dances. Tonight, at the club, it will mainly be the easy type. A bunch of people will be jumping around on the dance floor[5] trying to move in sync with the music. Hold her hand as much as possible and look at her like she's the only one there. You can't really do much more than that. So, it'll be easy for you."

"Then, there are other dances where the two of you touch and your bodies move together in sync. You'll need to know some dance mechanics, how to communicate with your girl, understand how your bodies should communicate with touches. Let's begin by showing you how to hold your girl.[6] A lot of guys don't know how to do that."

"What's the problem, Shelley?"?"

"Well, holding you. I mean, we're both . . . but you're . . . attractive."

"Why thank you Shelley. You really know how to flatter a girl."

"See what I mean, Michelle. It's not something I should be doing with you."

"Shelley, do you want to learn how to dance with Luna tonight?"

As he nods, "This is awkward for both of us, Shelley, but we have a job to do. Allie is preparing Luna right now. You know what? Pretend I'm your mom. Lots of moms teach their sons how to dance.[7] I'm sure your mother, Sarah, would have done that if she were still alive. So, I'll do it for her. If you try to think of me like your mom substitute, maybe that will help. OK?"

---

5 Music Video https://www.youtube.com/watch?v=5L6xyaeiV58

6 Pic Michelle Sheldon Dance https://firepitcell.com/wp-content/uploads/2021/12/C12N1-Sheldon-Michelle-Dance.jpg

7 Video Mothers Sons Dance https://www.youtube.com/watch?v=uFUFbHZZxtg and https://www.youtube.com/watch?v=aJxrX42WcjQ&list=PL5LSRDWWZWY-y7KF6W3Oz2bogM0PSIQT-

"Michelle, you talk like my mother, and you were best friends."

"Maybe we are Shelley. Maybe we are. But time to start your lesson. First, don't worry about your feet. If you learn how to move a girl's body, she'll make sure you're not stepping on her feet – at least not too often. Remember, you're the driver. She needs you to be in control, so she knows how to move."

"Lead me with your left hand, but your right hand is the power that determines which direction you move me. Uh, not exactly like that. I'm not a sack of potatoes. I'm a living graceful creature and you're my strong handsome prince."

"Let's switch. I'll be the boy and you dance the girl's role. Then, you'll see how this is supposed to work." As Shelley hesitates, Michelle says, "I promise you can be the guy again after I show you. I like dancing the girl's role better anyway and you'll never be a Ginger Rogers even if I dance like Fred Astaire. After you try it, you'll see why girls have more fun. You're a big girl," Michelle giggles, "but don't worry, sweetie. See how my right hand easily moves you around the room with just a little pressure. Your center of gravity is your lower back bone to your waist. When I move your center, the rest of your body has to follow. See, it even works if I let go of your hand."

"Doesn't my firm touch make you feel more comfortable, knowing that I know how to move both our bodies. That's the secret. Guiding your girl without effort, makes your girl feel lighter and more attractive and less nervous. Always make your girl feel that she's graceful and looks beautiful. Believe me, I love it."

"Now, you be the boy again and I'll be the girl. Use your power to make me feel graceful and beautiful. See, you're moving me anywhere you want. Now, I'm going to close my eyes. I'm totally relying on you to guide me. Be strong and steady. Make me feel safe. Make me feel graceful and desired like the Dancing Queen.[8] Good Shelley! That wasn't just a game. I closed my eyes just now to show you that every girl you dance with is trusting you when she puts herself in your hands. Don't be one of those

---

8 Music Dancing Queen Abba https://www.youtube.com/watch?v=xFrGuyw1V8s

the guys who take advantage of that permission and touch in ways your girl doesn't want."

"Now it's time to learn what your girl wants.[9] We're all special. I'll start by sharing something personal Shelley; why I like to dance. My partner and I are creating our own story together by moving and touching instead of using words. Our story is about how our dance makes us feel. If you make me feel that we're creating a special story together, I'll forgive a little clumsiness."

"As we create our dance story together, you're going to understand when and how I want to be touched. But I'm not going to tell you. You have to understand my hints as we dance. I promise I won't get mad if you make a mistake, because I know it can be confusing. OK Shelley?"

"Let's start. OK?"

"Always check to see whether I'm smiling. If I am, you're pleasing me. But I can smile two ways. Mouth and eyes. Check both."

"Do you feel how me moving my left hand higher on your right shoulder is bringing our bodies closer? By moving closer to you, I'm taking a chance showing that I like you. Always reassure your partner when that happens. Why not give me a little hug to show me that you like me being closer? Press gently, but don't squeeze me too tight. That's good! We're making a good story together, Shelley."

"You might decide not to touch me any more than this. You've accomplished your primary goal. My body is used to following your body's instructions. Leaving me wanting more may lead to other things later. If you stop while you're ahead, my body will pick up where we left off when we're alone together."

"If we were doing a fast dance, we probably didn't get much body contact. Let's pretend the music is ending. We've had fun, but you're a hot guy and I'm disappointed we barely touched. Our bodies have one last chance to do something together. Any clue what you should do, if you feel like your girl wants more when the music ends?"

---

9 Music Video https://www.youtube.com/watch?v=hpspGHeLOPE

"OK, here's something I love when guys I like do it. Pick me up, Shelley.[10] I won't break. Now, swing me in a semi-circle, back and forth. Just a couple of times. You have no idea what leaving the ground and being totally under someone's control does to girls. It's so exciting."

"Try it again but be more playful. Laugh with a mischievous look in your eyes when you do it. Make me feel like I'm so cute you can't bear to let me go."

After being in the air for a few seconds, "Shelley, you can put me down now. Shelley, I mean it. Really. Stop laughing, Shelley. I'll tell your mom!" Michelle squirms as her legs dangle off the floor. "Put me down," she giggles."

"Nope, I like you up in the air. My turn to play. You've been telling me what to do all morning. Can't do that from up there, can you Miss Dance Teacher? Besides, I'm feeling that you're liking it up there, because you're smiling. That's making you feel . . . special. Don't you feel special, Miss Dance Teacher?"

"Yes, but put me down," in a mock stern voice broken by her giggling.

"You have to say please. No, not like that. Like you mean it."

Finally, after Michelle does it the way Shelley wants, he tosses Michelle onto her bed. Looking up at him, the surprised Michelle instinctively assumes an inviting pose and waits for Shelley to join her.[11] Then, Michelle thinks to herself. "Wait, this is just Shelley. Why am I picturing him . . .? This isn't what I planned."

"Was that playful enough Miss Dance Teacher? I saw a guy throw a girl on a bed once in a movie. Now, I know what it feels like," with a big smile.

Thinking to herself, "Glad Shelley wasn't serious. I might have made a big mistake. Have to get back in control of myself."

Finally, getting back into teacher mode, "Shelley, you're learning fast. Teasing a girl like that is very . . . masculine. Very exciting! Now, Miss

---

10 Pic Shelley Lifts Michelle Dancing https://firepitcell.com/wp-content/uploads/2021/12/C12N2-Sheldon-Lifts-Michelle-Dancing.jpg
11 Pic Michelle Awaits Sheldon on Bed https://firepitcell.com/wp-content/uploads/2021/12/C12N3-Michelle-Awaits-Sheldon-Bed.jpg

Dance Teacher needs a few minutes to recover. Take a walk around the quad before we start again, OK?"

During the break, Michelle thinks, "WHEW, the train almost jumped the tracks there. This is going to make the rest of the lesson difficult. Mustn't play my usual games with Shelley. We should stop, but she feels her bubbles telling her to continue. Someone wants Sheldon to learn about girls in every way. Leery of going against what she feels her bubbles are telling her, Michelle devises a strategy. Have to think of something else while I'm dancing with him. As Allie's image begins to fill her mind Michelle smiles, "Someone else. Yes, that's it. I'll think about Allie the next part of the lesson."

* * *

When Sheldon returns, a more serious Michelle starts again, "Your job of making your girl feel special isn't over just because the music stops. Take my hand and lead me back to my friends where you found me. Never leave me standing alone on the dance floor. OK? That would be a bad ending to our dance story. I'd feel like a loser. If I'm with friends, I'd be embarrassed to go back alone. If I did, I'd tell them what a loser you are."

"OK, that was social dancing 101. Kind of like what a mom might teach her son. If you meet a girl at a club that you don't know, you probably stop there unless the girl clearly signals she wants more, but if we already know one another, we might want to be more sensual when we dance.

"So, now I'll stop teaching like I'm your mom, because the girls you dance with at the club tonight might be there for something more. I'll teach you how to deliver that without her giving you a public lap dance. Maybe, it's what your mom liked when she was a girl. Just keep checking how I react each time we touch in a new way. For the next few minutes, we'll pretend you're Patrick Swayze and I'm Jennifer Grey in Dirty Dancing.[12] You can all me Baby."

"Who, Michelle?"

---

12 Movie Dirty Dancing clip https://www.youtube.com/watch?v=WpmILPAcRQo

"It's a romantic movie. I forgot you're a movie illiterate. I'll show you a video clip from the movie. Do you see how he's totally in charge and she's loving it? See how she's smiling and her body is bending at his command? I tingle just watching it. Learn to do that to a girl on the dance floor and you'll never go home alone."

Now, like a drill sergeant, "Never mind the fancy dance steps in the movie, just get ready to transition from cute puppy to being a sexy stud. It's time for you to man up, Shelley. Show me you're really into me. Time for you to take some risks. Girls like guys who aren't afraid of taking a chance."

After some practice, "I'm going to play a song that doesn't require any fancy steps. Its called Samba Pa Ti.[13] It's very sensuous. Keep checking my reactions to see if I'm still liking what you're doing." Then gigging, "But watch out, because I might slap your face, if you go too far or too fast."

"Hold me closer than before, Shelley. No space between us anywhere. Let me know you're in command, that you're confident my body is yours. Now, begin moving your right hand slowly down my back starting with my pretty neck. Use gentle massaging motions. It's OK to linger and wander. You decide where and when to stop. Keep me guessing."

"That's it, tiger. My whole body is waiting to feel where you'll touch me next. That's where you want your girl to be, anticipating your next touch.[14] Do you feel how my body is responding? How your rhythm is our rhythm now. You're not just grabbing me. We're doing something together. Remember, Shelley, do things with me, not just to me. That makes us a couple. I like that we're doing something together. That's also how you make love to a girl, together."

The two roommates gaze into each other's eyes. As the music ends, Shelley leans in to kiss her lips, [15] After moment that may have been an eternity, Michelle playfully slaps his face. "Hey, I'm supposed to be your mom! Remember? Not nice to have dirty thoughts about your mom!"

---

13 Music https://www.youtube.com/watch?v=JGJdU2dpYxg
14 Video Touch Me https://www.youtube.com/watch?v=w9XLDme8HQ4
15 Movie Clip https://www.youtube.com/watch?v=IztjGOPMCwU

"Looking up at a confused Shelley, "We're in dangerous territory here, lover boy. You got my bubbles tingling. No telling what I'd do then.[16] Time for this lesson to end before something else happens."

"Michelle . . . er Mom . . . Sorry, I'm kind of mixed up. You're right Michelle. I wasn't thinking. I was feeling that maybe . . .. Totally wrong of me. What's happening?"

"Shelley, you didn't do anything wrong. You read my hints right. I was signaling you to kiss me to see whether you were understanding what I want." That's what she told Sheldon, but she knew it wasn't true. Michelle acknowledges to herself, "OMG, Sheldon pressed all my buttons."

Smiling the smile of an experienced woman who's teaching a younger boy,[17] "You're learning fast, Shelley. You took your teacher for a spin. If Luna or another girl looks at you like I just did, go ahead and kiss her for real. Believe me, she'll like it. And so will you. My son is ready for whatever a girl throws at him tonight."

"Michelle, no one has ever cared enough about me to teach me like this. You're opening my eyes to a whole new world."

Blushing, "Make me and your mom proud when you go to the club tonight. Make Luna or another nice girl feel special; like you've made me feel."

Then, Michelle thinks, "Whew! Glad we got through this lesson with only a few minor bumps. I hope Luna appreciates what I taught Shelley today. And . . . that Allie and I get to practice what I just preached to Shelley."

But Michelle is troubled. In the past, her bubbles seemed to understand her. They helped guide her. But Michelle thinks, "I'm no longer alone with the bubbles. They're listening part to me and part to someone else."

Then, Michelle wonders, "Sarah wanted me to help Shelley. I did the best I could today but look what almost happened between Shelley and me. Is that what Sarah wanted to happen? She wouldn't hurt Shelley. She may

---

16 .Video Boy and Girl https://www.youtube.com/watch?v=KCW9fTiYmSo
17 Music from Summer of 42 https://www.youtube.com/watch?v=kWMxX5MGuHI

have a plan, but I don't. I'm new at this mother thing. I'm afraid Shelley might get hurt in the confusion. Sarah and I need to talk again."

Then, Michelle wonders, "But what if Sarah wasn't guiding me today? Is this what I really want? Or is someone else influencing what the bubbles guide me to do? I need to be on guard. Can I continue trust my bubbles to guide me?"

*   *   *

Michelle soon shifts her attention from Sarah and Sheldon to Allie. "Oh, what Allie and I might do together!" Snapping out of her daydream about Allie, Michelle tells Sheldon, "Now, we have other things to do to get you ready for tonight. Let's see what you're going to wear. You must have something other than what I've seen you wear around campus so far. Hoping to find some hidden treasure."

Michelle opens Shelley's closet, "Not much here. No, you can't wear that, or this. Maybe this. No, not that. Shelley, we're going shopping. Right now."
"Now?"
"Yes, it's an emergency! Mom knows these things."

*   *   *

At the mall, "Is this really necessary, Michelle?"
"Yes, it is. You may have danced with Michelle earlier, but right now I'm your mom. Do exactly as I say Shelley. If we don't get you some proper clothes, you'll have to wear one of my dresses. Seriously."
"OK Mom."
"First, what size do you think you are?"
"Extra-large. All my shirts are extra-large." As Michelle stares incredulously at him ". . . am I a Large then?"
"Doubtful. Probably medium."
"OK, here's a nice shirt." Handing him an extra-large, a large and a medium, "take them all into the dressing room and model each one of

them for me. Then, we'll talk about why each one fits or not. That will teach you how to choose the right size."

"You mean, try them on right here in the store?"

"OMG, you don't try on clothes, do you? You just guess and buy them?"

"While you're changing, I'll get you some jeans that fit."

* * *

"Now, come out of the dressing room and show me how you look."

"You're making me feel like I'm eight years old, Michelle."

"I've seen better dressed eight-year-olds, Shelley. That's better. See, with the medium size, you have shoulders, a chest and a waist. No one could see them before drowning in your extra-large. You look almost presentable."

As they leave the store, "I just texted your sizes to you Shelley. Medium shirt. Jeans 32 waist 32 length. Sleeve 34, neck 15. You'll probably grow a bit this year. So, you'll be a 34 length soon. I don't know if the other measurements will change much. You'll need to buy more clothes this semester. One outfit isn't enough. I'll let you know when I see a sale and go shopping with you."

"Thanks Mom!"

* * *

"OK, my turn. Trying on clothes is fun. I'll show you how to shop.[18] If you're going to learn about girls, you need to understand why we think shopping is fun. So, think of this as part of your experiment."

"Oh! Here's the store I've been looking for. It's just like I imagined. So, excited to be here Shelley. Here, you hold my purse, Shelley.[19] Now don't look like that, Shelley. It's not going to kill you to hold a purse. Think of it

---

18 Video Michelle Shopping https://www.youtube.com/watch?v=Zgz9yifcLyQ

19 Video Holding Purse https://www.youtube.com/results?search_query=man+holds+purse+in+store+

this way, a hot girl has just entrusted you with her most important posses-
sions. She needs a strong man like you to guard them for her."

After Sheldon stops his purse panic, Michelle explains, "See Shelley, it's
all how you look at things. Be confident you're a strong male protecting
your girl and helping to relieve her worries. Now, doesn't that make you
feel better?"

After modeling six skirts and a dress, "What do you think of this one,
Shelley?"

"It's kind of . . . definitely not like what a mom would wear."

"I know . . . see how it shows off my legs[20] when I do this. I just love
that. This is the one. Mom has worked all day. Time for Mom to disappear.
Michelle wants to have fun tonight."

*   *   *

Back at their dorm room.

"Shelley, we have to hurry before the girls are ready to leave. One last
lesson. Do you know how to talk with a girl? Not just any girl, but a girl
you want to make feel special?"

"Huh?"

"That doesn't cut it, Shelley! You'll have to do better tonight."

"Talking is sexy. And I don't mean talking dirty. Remember what I said
earlier about doing things with your girl, not just to her? Talking helps
her feel that way. When you make a joke and she laughs, then she's trying
to make you feel like you're doing something together. So, when she tells
you something, do the same for her. Make her feel like anything she says
is important to you."

"Questions are good, Shelley. Ask questions that I can't answer yes or
no. Don't worry, your girl will probably do most of the talking if you ask
the right questions. If she asks questions, don't just answer yes or no. Yes,
with a short story is what you want to give her. That encourages her to

---

20 Video Legs Skirt https://www.youtube.com/watch?v=IkfthALfY5E

share with you. It isn't what you talk about, it's the sharing that matters most."

"Oh, look at the time! We're running late. You practice talking while I quickly get dressed [21] First close your eyes. Then practice talking. If you can talk to a naked girl, you can talk to one that's dressed. I'll tell you when I'm decent."

Sheldon's a good boy. So, he doesn't peek. He just wonders about Michelle and practices talking to a naked girl. Then, he hears, "OK, Shelley, you can open your eyes now."

"Michelle, you're so . . ." is all he can say.

"Not bad for a mom, right?" Michelle says as she bestows a motherly kiss on Sheldon's forehead."

"OK, time for my son to get ready. I'll hand you clothes and comb your hair. You just do what mom says."

While dressing Shelley, Michelle imagines her and Allie tonight, "You know, Shelley, getting dressed might seem like a boring chore to you, but it can be exciting. Just imagine you and your date getting ready for one another[22] and how you'll both react in that magic moment when she sees you and you see her and the world lights on fire. I'm getting hot just thinking about it.'

Seeing that Shelley can sense her passion building as she thinks about Allie, "I don't want you to miss out on experiencing the excitement of anticipation, Shelley. So, while you're getting dressed imagine Luna dressing herself just to please you."

A perplexed Sheldon stares blankly at Michelle.

"Sorry, I forgot you're taking your first baby steps, Shelley. Here, look in this mirror and listen to this music.[23] Now, don't let this scare you, but in an hour you'll have to walk across a room and ask Luna to dance with you. You need to start psyching yourself up to do that. It can be scary. A girl can

---

21 Video Quick Change Before Date https://www.youtube.com/watch?v=RU_jPkjKb5o

22 Video https://www.youtube.com/watch?v=02ui0Qg5Jbc

23 Music Video https://www.youtube.com/watch?v=129kuDCQtHs

say no. Now's the time you start building up your courage, Shelley. Look in the mirror and imagine why any girl would be silly to say no."

"Go ahead and pose in the mirror. Practice making your eye tell a girl you're attracted to her. No, that's a creepy stare. A girl would run away from that face. OK, your eyes are better now. Add a gentle smile. What you see in the mirror is what Luna will see. Keep practicing until you see something a sane person would like."

Sheldon imagines how awkward he'll feel[24] with Luna and yearns for the comfort of talking with Michelle.

"While you're practicing, remember that Luna has been getting ready for you. She had her nails done today just for you. She bought a new dress and borrowed shoes from Olivia. She's been talking all day with Allie the way you've been talking to me. That's what girls do before a big date."

"You've worked hard today, Shelley, but you probably won't do this much date preparation again. Its not a guy thing, but girls do it all the time. It's important that when she first sees you, you show her that you appreciate the efforts she's made for you."

"She's earned the right to see that you're excited about her when you ask her to dance. So, keep practicing posing in the mirror, Shelley.[25] I want to see that excitement in Allie's face tonight," Michelle says as she crowds Sheldon away from the mirror to retouch her makeup, "Oh yes, very kissable now."[26]

---

24 Video Awkward Flirting https://www.youtube.com/watch?v=Uxg5tPBWOmI
25 Mirror Video https://www.youtube.com/watch?v=S-3DiFGgp2g
26 Pic Michelle https://firepitcell.com/wp-content/uploads/2021/12/C12N26-Michelle-Lipstick.jpg

13

Roommates on the Town

"Girls, Shelley and I spent the afternoon shopping. I present the new Shelley. Come out Shelley, model for us."

"Just don't laugh, OK?"

"Shelley, you're actually looking . . ." Olivia grasps for the right word.

"Michelle called it presentable."

"That's exactly how I'd describe your new look, Shelley, quite presentable."

"Michelle, you really are a wonder! He does have a body. Who would have thought?"[1]

"OK, any girl whose boyfriend is nerdy gets sent to Michelle for a makeover."

"How did you do it Michelle?"

"Let's just say I have a lot of experience making over guys," which causes Shelley to bend over laughing, "Good one, Michelle!"

Michelle cautions Sheldon with a stern look and then changes the subject, "What do you say to our friends, Shelley?"

"Thanks for inviting me tonight. You all look beautiful tonight."[2]

After Michelle pokes him from behind, "What pretty shoes you're wearing, Luna. And I like your perfume."

"Michelle, you're such a good trainer," Allie says as she hugs Michelle.

---

1 Pic Sheldon Remade by Michelle https://firepitcell.com/wp-content/uploads/2021/12/C13N1-Sheldon-Redone-by-Michelle.jpg

2 Music Video https://www.youtube.com/watch?v=nRxodL0dKcE

Relishing Allie's reaction, Michelle returns the embrace with "If you only knew, Allie. If you only knew."

* * *

As they get into their Uber, the girls notice that Luna rushes to sit next to Shelley.

"What are they talking about in the back seat?" Olivia whispers to Kaitlyn.

"Something about equations, I think."

"From the look in Luna's eyes, she finds equations a lot sexier than I do,"[3] Olivia giggles.

* * *

At the dance club,[4] Kaitlyn and Olivia take turns helping Shelley practice dancing.

As they watch Shelley and Kaitlyn dancing together, "Luna, do you like him?"

"Yes Allie. He's a math genius."

"No, I mean . . . do you like him . . . in other ways? The body, not the mind."

"In my country, we don't talk about such things."

"That's OK . . . I can see you like him. But he's a little shy. We'll all help you."

Luna smiles her approval.

After they dance, Kaitlyn tells Shelley, "I think you're ready for Luna."

"Luna? Now? I'm not ready," a nervous Shelley emits in a high cracked voice.

---

3 Math Music Video https://www.youtube.com/watch?v=ojq_ivvwxpM
4 Pic Dance Club https://firepitcell.com/wp-content/uploads/2021/12/C13N4-Dance-Club.jpg

"Well, Luna is ready[5] . . . she's been waiting while we warmed you up. And when you've learned more about girls, Shelley, you'll understand why it isn't smart to keep a warmed-up girl waiting. Some other guy may snatch her away from you."

"Do you think I'm ready, Kaitlyn?"

"I've danced with a lot worse, Shelley. Besides, time to man up. Girls like that more than we like perfect dancing. You can do it."

Michelle looks Shelley in the eye and whispers, "Do it for your mom, Shelley."

With that encouragement, Shelley walks the longest ten yards in his life as he approaches the table where Luna is sitting. "Luna, would you like to dance with me?" Taking her hand and holding her the way Michelle taught him, Sheldon guides Luna to the dance floor and they begin creating their story. To others in the club, their movements may have appeared awkward, but Luna and Shelley experienced it as a graceful love dance[6] that opens them up to new adult pleasures.

Watching, their four mates take pride in their work, "Aren't they cute together!"

Allie[7] whispers in Michelle's ear, "We did good with both our children, but it's time for adults to take over. Michelle you look so hot tonight. Like a Persian cat with all your outfit's white fluff.[8] Wonder what other things we can do together?"

"Who knows?' Michelle replies pursing her lips, "the night is still young."

Allie feels herself getting excited, "This girl is driving me wild."

But Michelle pretends to ignore Allie's advances. Walking alluringly to the dance floor, she begins dancing alone. After a minute Michelle thinks,

---

5 Pic Luna Dance Club https://firepitcell.com/wp-content/uploads/2021/12/C13N5-Luna-Dance-Club.jpg

6 Dance Video Luna and Sheldon https://www.youtube.com/watch?v=GQa10n21YIw

7 Pic Allie Dance Club https://firepitcell.com/wp-content/uploads/2021/12/C13N7-Allie-Dance-Club.jpg

8 Pic Michelle Dance Club https://firepitcell.com/wp-content/uploads/2021/12/C13N8-Michelle-Dance-Club.jpg

"Oh yes . . . she's following me." As Allie joins her dancing, she whispers to Michelle, "You're not getting away from me so easily my pretty kitten. You're mine." Then, Allie begins leading Michelle on a sensuous dance journey. While Allie's fingers wander over her body, Michelle bathes in Allie's touches.[9]

Dancing together, Michelle thinks, "She's playing me like a musical instrument that she's played forever like I tried to teach Shelley earlier today. Firm, then gentle, in subtly changing patterns. Oh, so good. She instantly knows what my body craves. I feel so . . .." Then thinking ends for Michelle as sensations continually build until, "Oh, . . .! Oh, my . . .!"[10]

Michelle begins shaking and collapses into Allie's arms. "What just happened to me?" Michelle wonders. It's never happened all over all at the same time before." With Michelle, temporarily unable to move on her own, Allie gently sways the two of them back and forth to the music while Michelle recovers.

"I see you like that, girlfriend," Allie alluringly whispers in Michelle's ear, "I want you."[11] No one can see Michelle blushing in the dark club, but Allie senses the deep connection they established.

"That's the magic elixir, being desired. I don't want this to end," Michelle thinks, "but it's too much too soon," as she finally breaks from Allie's caresses and melts into the crowd of dancers.

Knowing that Michelle is on sensory overload, Allie makes no move to follow her. Smiling thinking, "Retreat now my kitten, but you'll be back for more."[12]

The evening proceeds with Luna and Sheldon playing the roles Allie and Michelle trained them to perform. "And you never danced before today, Shelley?"

"No Luna, but it was easy dancing with you."

---

9 Dance Video Michelle and Allie https://www.youtube.com/watch?v=_uGr57NZGc8
10 Pic Michelle Allie Dance https://firepitcell.com/wp-content/uploads/2021/12/C13N10-Dance-Michelle-Allie.jpg
11 Music Video Hands to Myself https://www.youtube.com/watch?v=FMlcn-_jpWY
12 Music Video Back for More https://www.youtube.com/watch?v=-engbJJnJTQ

Meanwhile, Allie and Michelle bring flirting to new levels. Drawn to her confidence, Michelle wraps herself in a ball on Allie's lap, "So, comforting to belong to her," Michelle thinks looking up into Allies dark eyes while Allie's fingers massage her neck.

As closing time approaches, Kaitlyn spies the two girls in a corner of the club, "You look very comfortable Michelle, wrapped around Allie like that."

"Purrrr . . . purr . . . purr,"[13] is all Michelle replies as Allie continues masaging her pretty kitten's neck while Michelle rubs Allie's bare feet.

* * *

On the way home from the club, Allie whispers to Michelle, "Shall we switch roommates for the night?"

Michelle is feeling, "I want Allie more than anything I've ever wanted." But instead her mother instinct takes over responding, "Shelley isn't ready to be with Luna yet. Besides, Shelley is processing a lot of new things. I think I can help him do that tonight." Then Michelle realizes what she just did, "Did I just turn down sex to mother Shelley? What's happening to me?"

Sensing Allie's feeling of rejection, "Allie, I know you can sense how much I want you. I promise we'll make time for ourselves soon," followed by a bouquet of long kisses. "I adore being your pretty kitten and want to get to know you much better, Allie, but Shelley is very needy now. Just be patient for now, please."

A disappointed Allie, hugs Michelle at her dorm room door, whispering in her ear, "I know you're mine,[14] Michelle. Shelley may have you tonight, but I'll me back to claim what's mine."

"I'll hold you that Allie. I'm worth it. You'll see."

* * *

---

13 Purr Video https://www.youtube.com/watch?v=JA5ImXYK6U0
14 Music Video https://www.youtube.com/watch?v=3eOuK-pYhy4

As Michelle looks longingly and then closes her door on Allie, she feels Sarah Atwell embracing her saying, "I chose the right girl to take care of my little Shelley. Help Shelley understand how much I love him and that I've chosen you to teach him what I can't."[15] Then as Sarah continues "Michelle, I've been watching you since you were Michael. What a poor lost boy you were. It broke my heart to see you suffering so much. I hope I've helped you find a better path that will lead to sweetness and light."

Sensing that Michelle is missing Allie already, Sarah promises, "I'll help you win Allie over my dear. Even mothers are allowed to have fun."

*   *   *

In their dorm room, "Olivia, I feel left out."

"What do you mean, Kaitlyn?"

"Luna and Shelley are a couple. And Allie and Michelle were acting like a couple at the club. You and I were kind of the chaperones tonight."

"We're too young, Kaitlyn. We'll have our nights."

*   *   *

Shelley and Luna take their time getting back to their rooms. At Luna's door, Shelley hesitates, until Luna asks, "Are you gonna kiss me or not?"[16]

*   *   *

Bolstered by her mystical experience with Sheldon's mom, Michelle begins a difficult soul baring talk with Shelley after they get into their beds, "Shelley, we still have some unfinished business to talk thorough. Don't we? I mean we've both been through some very heavy things, especially today. Do you need to talk about anything, Shelley?"

---

15 Music Video Imagining https://www.youtube.com/watch?v=dzauwt30wII
16 Music Video Gonna Kiss me https://www.youtube.com/watch?v=FDUOcHg5ijg

"Uh . . . maybe.[17] But it's hard to talk."

"Would you feel better if I turn out the light? Sometimes it's easier to talk in the dark. I'm going to start by confessing something to you. It's a little embarrassing. I'll trust you with my truth if you agree to trust me with your truth."

"Uh . . . OK."

"When I was teaching you to dance today, I was trying to turn you on. It didn't start that way, but after I felt you looking at me and touching me, I just did it. I'm sorry I confused you[18]. I shouldn't have done that."

"Uh, you mean . . . you wanted you and me to . . .?"

"No, I don't want to have sex with every guy I flirt with. I just like to tease sometimes[19]. I told myself that it was just to teach you how girls behave, but I confess . . . I like being desired. Guys have their power. Like, when you picked me up and wouldn't let me down. And when you tossed me on the bed, I was ready for you to do anything, until I came to my senses. Very sexy move Shelley, even though you were just teasing me. Teasing is sexy. Understand?"

"Being desired is when I feel powerful. That's what was missing when I was a boy. I did a lot of things to try to make it happen. Some not very smart things. It just wasn't the same as it is now. Maybe that's why I can't resist teasing guys so much. Being desired is like a shiny new toy."

"There, I said it out loud. I haven't told that to anyone Shelley. Only to you."

"Now, Shelley, do you have anything to share?"

"Lots. I don't know where to begin. I was so turned on. I didn't want to be. I told myself I shouldn't be. But I was. I almost jumped on the bed with you, but I held back at the last minute. What does that mean?"

"I know Shelley. That's why we need to talk. Doesn't saying it out loud make you feel better?"

---

17 Music Video Talk About It https://www.youtube.com/watch?v=w46bWxS9IjY

18 Music Video Sorry https://www.youtube.com/watch?v=tEnCoocmPQM

19 Music Video Touch https://www.youtube.com/watch?v=9b8erWuBA44

"It does, Michelle, but I'm still confused.[20] I'm not supposed to be attracted to you. You're the prettiest girl I know . . . at least any that's been nice to me. Its hard sleeping in our room . . . so close . . . listening to you breathing in the middle of the night. But you're also not a regular girl. I really don't like guys. At least that's what I thought. But do I?"

"I know that's been bothering you. But what we did today doesn't show that you like guys,[21] Shelley. It just shows you like me. Maybe it just means you think of me like I'm a regular girl – not a new girl. At least I'd like to think of it that way."

"I'd like to think of it that way too, Michelle, I really would. But I'm confused."

"Of course, you're confused Shelley. It's been over three years since I became Michelle and I'm still figuring out some things. What makes me do what I do? How will other people react? Why? If I'm still learning, there's no reason for you to have all the answers in the week we've known each other. Right?"

"Yeah!"

"And you liked dancing with Luna tonight, right?"

"Yeah!"

"When you were sitting in the Uber coming home from the club with Luna sitting on your lap, you were thinking about her. Hoping the two of you will become more than friends. Right?"

"Oh, yeah!"

"And there were a lot of guys at the club tonight. You didn't want to dance with any of them, did you?"

"Nope!"

"See, then, it's just because you like me and you think about me like I'm a girl even though you know some things about me that other people don't. Isn't that right, Shelley?"

"Yes, it is, Michelle!"

---

20 Music Dazed Confused https://www.youtube.com/watch?v=yO2n7QoyieM
21 Video Trans Attraction https://www.youtube.com/watch?v=DaqXJH5VmTE

"Shelley, I like that you like me. I'm not ashamed.[22] You shouldn't be ashamed either. It is what it is."

"Now another difficult question Shelley. Do you ever fantasize about me? Like in the middle of the night when you listen to me breathing?"

"Uh . . .."

"You promised to tell me the truth, Shelley."

"Well . . ."

"Don't be embarrassed. Everyone fantasizes.[23] You're not responsible for what you dream about. It's a separate world we don't control. You don't have to answer any more questions. I just want to give you something to think about, OK? I don't think you've ever seen my boy parts – except maybe partially that one time I pinned you to the floor you might have felt something. I've been very careful about privacy. Truthfully, with all the hormones I've been taking, it's not that difficult to hide"

"The point is that I think I'm really a blank slate to you that way. You can fill in whatever parts you like in your fantasies. Every day, your senses see a girl, hear her, smell her and sometimes, like this afternoon, touch her. All your senses tell you I'm a girl, even though your brain knows otherwise. So, I'm just like a girl to you.[24] Senses are stronger than brains, Shelley. Even your big brain."

"So, the question is, what are you filling into that blank page in your fantasies? If your fantasies envision me with girl parts, then you're probably just a normal straight guy. If your fantasies invent boy parts that you haven't seen and would like. . . I've been to a lot of counsellors. Maybe you could talk with someone to help you figure things out. The Foundation would probably pay for counselling for you to understand why."

"Thanks Michelle. No guy parts involved. Really. I'd tell you if there were. I can't imagine you with guy parts. That's not how I think of you even though you told me. But don't make me talk about the girl parts I imagine."

---

22 Movie Clip Not Ashamed https://www.youtube.com/watch?v=1OCiUVr8Bxk
23 Music Video Fantasy https://www.youtube.com/watch?v=qq09UkPRdFY
24 Music Just Like a Woman https://www.youtube.com/watch?v=dRLXZVojdhQ

"Shelley, thanks for accepting me as Michelle. That's very important to me. I'm still a little insecure about being Michelle."

"Here's something else, Shelley. I like helping you and I think you like helping me. But it's not because we're boyfriend and girlfriend. It's because we're roommates. Some college roommates become lifelong friends. We all need a little help from our friends.[25] This kind of bonding is very natural. The only thing that's a bit odd about it is that college roommates are usually both boys or both girls. That's why this is a little confusing for both of us. Does that make sense to you, Shelley?"

"Yeah, I can see that Kaitlyn and Olivia are bonding. Kaitlyn already has plans for Olivia to be in her wedding."

"And it was Allie's idea for me to help you get ready for the club tonight. She knew Luna likes you, but she thought maybe you both weren't quite ready yet. So, Allie helped prepare Luna today while I helped you get ready. Olivia lent Luna those sexy high heels. And Kaitlyn and Olivia both helped you learn to dance at the club before we turned you over to Luna. That boosted your confidence. Right? And when we saw how you and Luna were dancing and looking at one each other we all felt good together."

"Michelle, you mean the six of us are bonding?"

"That's what I mean, Shelley."

"That's good. Then, maybe I don't need to worry so much about you and me bonding?"

"Shelley, I knew you're smart enough to figure it out. You just need a little help sometimes. And roommates help one another."

"WHEW! I'm going to sleep a lot better tonight, Michelle."

"Me too Shelley. I like it when we're bonding . . . even if it's confusing. There was a time in my life I felt so alone. Not now though. And . . . I hope tonight you dream about how you're going to make Luna feel special."

"Michelle? Are you going to dream tonight about making Allie feel special?"

"So, you noticed us?"

"Yeah, we all did. You were the center of attention."

---

25 Music Help https://www.youtube.com/watch?v=a3LQ-FReO7Q

"Yes, guys like to fantasize about two girls together. It's always popular at clubs."

"Well, Luna and I think you and Allie were cute together. We both want the best for our roommates."

"Any advice for me Shelley? Advice is a two-way street, you know. Did Luna tell you anything about Allie I should know? Don't hold out on me, roommate."

"Not advice, a question. Do you like guys or girls better? I think Allie is interested in knowing that."

"And you're not interested, Shelley?"

"Well, yeah, but you asked about Allie."

"Shelley, I think we're setting a record for the weirdest Mother-Son discussion! But since we're baring our souls tonight, why stop now?

"I don't like either one better. Just different. I used to think about which bodies I liked best. But that was a dead end. It took me a long time to realize the biggest difference is in me, not the other person. I like myself better when I'm with girls. Some guys really push all my buttons. My brain kind of stops working. I do dumb things. Oh, the stories I could tell . . .. That hasn't happened with girls. And it doesn't happen with most guys, just some."

"Remember when we talked about boundaries? Sometimes, I've had a hard time setting boundaries. I'm trying to become better at that."

"I have a confession to make. My real secret is that I have a weakness for what some people might call 'bad boys.'[26] People warn me a guy is bad news. Do I listen? No. Sometimes, I think the warnings attract me more. Why do I crave . . . the danger? . . . the pain? . . . the humiliation?[27] The way they make me feel, I'll do for anything for them . . . things I'm not proud of . . . things that aren't good for me. Looking back . . .."

"Are you crying, Michelle?"

"A little. It's been hard. Hard to take responsibility for my life."

---

26 Video Why Bad Boys https://www.youtube.com/watch?v=xnAM_quhNDU
27 Pic Michelle Abused https://firepitcell.com/wp-content/uploads/2021/12/C13N27-Michelle-Abused.jpg

"Michelle, I'm sorry I asked you."

"Don't be, Shelley. I need to tell someone and to cry. It will make me stronger.[28] It might scare you, but I need to get it out. OK?"

"I'm trying to deal with this. I really am. It's been better since I became Michelle. Michael was a real mess. Michelle has her act together, at least by comparison. But I know it's still an issue for me. So, I'm not safe from my dark side. Maybe I'll never be. That scares me sometimes, Shelley. It really does."

"But I'm a better person with girls. I can be creative, helpful, funny, smart, confident – all the things I'm not when I'm going gaga over some jerk."

"But here's the worst. One guy told me he needed to stop seeing me, because I was . . . kind of making him be a bad boy. He didn't say it exactly like that, but that's what he meant. Said he needed to get away from me so he could be a good person again. Looking back on it . . . I do remember that he was nice to me at first. Then, I kept prodding him . . . to punish me. To do things . . . that maybe he didn't really want to do."

"That really scared me. Was I creating the darkness? Or making it darker? Was it true? Maybe? I don't know. But it explains why sometimes I fall into a downward spiral. That's when I decided it's a bad idea for two dark side people to be together. We need the light for balance. To save us from ourselves."

"Sometimes, it's so overwhelming. I just lose control. Before that one guy admitted it, I never thought the 'bad boys' were caught in the same type of downward spiral. I thought they were totally in control. I liked the idea that someone was in control. Now, I'm not so sure that anyone is. And that scares me even more. Maybe they are. Maybe they aren't. Who knows? I just know that I don't want to spend my life searching for answers. I just want to be happy. That's what I'm working on these days."

"So, now I'm Michelle, not Michael. And most of the time I date girls and I try to stay away from 'bad boys' to save myself. Not to save myself

---

28 Music Video Cry https://www.youtube.com/watch?v=CFMz9DOhaJ8

from the 'bad boys.' To save myself from me . . . because . . . it's my responsibility to create a life that makes me happy."

"Strange thing is I don't fall for nice guys. I only go for 'bad boys'[29] and good girls. But I know I'm not alone that way. And it has nothing to do with my transition. Lots of good girls fall for bad boys.[30] Maybe someday I'll understand why. Then, I'll explain more if you want. But Mom is tired now. School is closed for today. OK?"

"Michelle, thanks for sharing . . ." as she hears a few muffled sniffles coming from Shelley's bed in the dark room.

"Shelley, you're a good roommate. We need each other. Let me know if you sense any darkness coming over me. Be my warning signal. I'll try to be your mom when you need her. Being a mom is part of being in the light, not the darkness. We'll lean on each other,[31] OK?"

"Good night, Michelle."

"Good night, Shelley."

Before falling asleep, Michelle realizes, "Is this why I like mothering Shelley? Is it because mothering is part of the light, not the darkness? I didn't realize that until I said it out loud just now to him. Is being a mom my path to the light?"

As Michelle succumbs to sleep after giving her all to Shelley, she hears Sarah Atwell whispering again, "You'll be a good mother,[32] Michelle."

"Thanks Sarah, I tried. You and Shelley deserve my best."

---

29 Music Video Bad Boys https://www.youtube.com/watch?v=LwZBh7dwQJA
30 Video Top Ten Good Girl/Bad Boy Movies https://www.youtube.com/watch?v=Oz2smeEdvBU
31 Movie Clip Lean on Me https://www.youtube.com/watch?v=8VmRNr9QbxQ
32 Music Video The Mother https://www.youtube.com/watch?v=npSDM26xlzs

14

Night Games

The following day back at the dorm, Sheldon runs into their room out of breath.

"Michelle, tonight I have . . .."

"What do you have, Shelley?"

"Well . . . I don't really know. Maybe . . . it's kind of a date?"

"Who?"

"With Luna."

"Doing what?

"Rereading Wolfram's paper on The Theory of Numbers together."

"What makes you think that's a date, Shelley?"

"Luna asked me to bring wine. So, is that a date Michell?"

"Where?"

Pullen Park.

"Yes Shelley . . . that sounds like a date. It an unusual date, but I've had some weird dates myself. So, who am I to judge? A date is a date."

"Thanks Mom! I'm off to find some wine."

"Stop calling me that. I'm your sexy college roommate, not your mom."

"Yes, Mom."

"Before you go, I'm curious. Who asked who out on this date?"

"Funny you that you asked that. I guess I kind of did. I wasn't intending to, but Luna and I started talking and before I knew it, I heard myself asking her whether she's busy tonight. Something about the way she was looking at me and talking in that accent of hers. I just wanted us to be together tonight. Not part of a group."

"Shelley Atwell, you manned up! You didn't wait for her ask you. Mom is proud."

"And Shelley, all the things I taught you in our dance lesson about understanding what a girl wants work on a date."

* * *

"How nice that you're picking me up at my dorm, Scott, almost like Prom again," Kaitlyn laughs. "Go ahead, you can kiss me. You're my boyfriend."

"Well . . .."

"OK, go on pretending you're not my boyfriend," as Kaitlyn wraps Scott's right arm around her for the three-block walk to Players' Retreat. A lot can happen in three short blocks.

"Oh look, there's your friend Shelley walking in the park with Luna," Kaitlyn tells Scott, "The whole dorm is abuzz about their date tonight."

"Sheldon has a date? You mean, with a girl?"

"Is that so unusual?

"Let's just say that Sheldon's family will be pleased to hear he's making progress socially. He's very young and smart. The only reason he's in college now is that his high school ran out of advanced subjects. So, he came two years early. High academic IQ, but low social IQ. Everyone will be happier if he finally finds his place in the world outside the classroom. He's basically a good kid. I'd like to help him. Letting him hang out with the team."

"Scott, I love that you're concerned about Shelley. Yes, he's a bit awkward, but also sweet. We're all helping him to work on the awkward part. When all that's left is the sweet part, he's going to make some girl happy."

"Who's we, Kaitlyn?"

"Practically all the girls on our floor are doing something. You see, Scott, a lot of boys at his age are like that. Girls mature faster. So, for girls, dating is a lot like duck hunting."

"Huh? What does duck hunting have to do with dating?"

"Oh Scott, sometimes, you're so naive, just like Shelley. I love that about you. Shelley and Luna like each other. But they need some help. So, all the girls got together and created a nice cozy place for Shelley to land so Luna could catch him. We taught each of them how to be together. And it's working. Isn't that great!"

"So, what's your team of duck hunters doing to help you catch me?"[1]

"Nothing Scott, you're way too smart to land for decoys like Shelley. You're a real experienced wild duck. You were almost on someone's plate for dinner many times. Each time you learned something to survive. You know how to get away. [2] Nope, you're too smart to fall for tricks. Just you and me, Scott. No tricks. I'm going to have to shoot you on the fly, fair and square, all by myself."

"Really? How does that happen, Kaitlyn?"

"Like the other times I've had duck for dinner, YUM! I have to aim for where I think the duck us going to be. Not where the duck is now. It's the same with boys like you. The art of dating isn't picking the boy who is perfect now. Its picking a boy who will become perfect. You, Scott, will soon be my perfect duck. And I'm a smart patient hunter."

"So, you're an expert on both boys and ducks. You sound pretty sure of yourself, Kaitlyn. You know you exactly how you'll bag me?"

"Well, since you asked, yes. I grew up shooting ducks long before I started with boys. Went hunting many times with Daddy and his police friends. I know a few things a man oughta know."[3]

"I guess I need to be careful with you Kaitlyn. I might become a dead duck."

"You should be careful, Mr. Hopkins, very careful. You're in over your head. Wait until hunting season. I'll make you a feast like you've never had. You'll be glad I know how to both shoot and cook. Then, you'll recognize,

---

1 Music Girls Chase Boys https://www.youtube.com/watch?v=5GBT37_yyzY

2 Video Boy Runs from Girl https://www.youtube.com/watch?v=QJPuRzw2iK4

3 Music Video Man Oughta Know https://www.youtube.com/watch?v=dqINSvm3Psw

you're a dead duck from a dating point of view. But don't worry, you'll be the happiest dead duck."

"Oh really, Princess? You're that sure of yourself?"

"No Scott. I'm a ball of nerves. But I'm that sure that I can make you happy. And I'm sure you're smart enough to recognize that."

* * *

Entering the bar, Kaitlyn spots Olivia at a table[4] with a man.

"Olivia, why didn't you tell me you had a date with such a handsome gentleman?"[5]

After introductions, "Gerald, do you mind if we barge in?"

Olivia cautions Gerald, "Don't mind Kaitlyn. She's . . . ."

". . . . like a breath of fresh air in a smoke-filled room," Gerald says finishing Olivia's sentence for her.

"Oh, that' so sweet," as Kaitlyn sits at Olivia's table. "I like him already."

"I guess, we're a foursome now?" Scott laughs.

"Foursomes are for golf, Kaitlyn. We're not playing golf. This isn't a double date."[6] says Olivia without a smile.

Scott and Olivia watch the banter back and forth between Gerald and Kaitlyn. Neither is used to being passive watchers.

"Gerald, your ambition to run a restaurant is so exciting."

"Really? Most college girls think it's kind of boring."

"Only boring people get bored, Gerald. What you're doing is so exciting. Really. Never let boring people convince you otherwise. Daddy owns a deli back home. It makes him happy. And he makes his customers happy. Is there anything more important than making people happy?"

"See, Olivia, that's what my life is about. Being happy and helping other people be happy. Yeah! That's what I'm talking about."

---

4 Pic Olivia https://firepitcell.com/wp-content/uploads/2021/12/C14N4-Olivia.jpg

5 Pic Gerald https://firepitcell.com/wp-content/uploads/2021/12/C14N5-Gerald.jpg

6 Video Double Date https://www.youtube.com/watch?v=ILo7jxcVqOk

"Gerald, do you want know who makes me happy? My roommate Olivia. She's the smartest person I know. Every night before I go to sleep, I thank God in my prayers that Olivia is my roommate."

"I can see why, Kaitlyn."

"Of course, you can. You and I are happy people. We need people like Olivia and Scott, who are smart planners. But they have trouble being happy. We were born to make people like them happy.[7] So, they need us. You know that Gerald and I know that. Olivia and Scott are smart enough to catch up with us, eventually."

A very pleased Gerald responds, "Right you are, Kaitlyn!"

"Scott, we've intruded too long." Looking back at the table, "Olivia, Gerald is a keeper."

Olivia begins smiling again as Kaitlyn tells Gerald as he nods in agreement, "And you should be as grateful to be with Olivia as I am".

* * *

"Luna, do we really need to talk about Manfred tonight?"

"No, Shelley," wrapping Shelley's arm around her as they sip cheap wine.

Shelley remembers Michelle's lessons, as he lays Luna back on their blanket and they kiss.

"Shelley . . . you're so . . . like the man you were in class standing up to that professor the other day. I adore that. I tingle every time I picture it."

"Luna, I have something to confess. I'd do anything to make you look at me the way you are now. I'm not normally that brave. I usually sit in the back of classes and let professors say the stupidest things. But I remember watching the sun shining on your hair through the window. And I knew you knew that professor was wrong. I could see it in your eyes. The next thing I knew I was telling him he was wrong."

---

7 Music Video Make You Happy https://www.youtube.com/watch?v=Yy5cKX4jBkQ

"Really? You did it for both of us, Shelley?"

"Yes, Luna, for both," as Luna pulls him down on top of her. Looking down at Luna, Sheldon thinks, "So, this is what heaven looks like."[8]

*   *   *

Back at the bar, "Scott, there are pool tables in the next room! Learn pool from a pro. $1 a ball, OK?"

Olivia and Gerald stare at each other for a minute and then. Gerald breaks the silence laughing, "Is she always like that, Olivia?"

"Yes, that's my Kaitlyn."

"She's quite different . . . but she makes sense to me. You and I are different, but I get how we can make each other happy. Do you mind if we skip Plato and Aristotle tonight?"

"Not at all. Truth be known, I've never really liked them, Gerald. A bunch of old dead guys. I know all the philosophers, poets and kings[9], but lately I've noticed that I've missed out on other things. Just part of my programming I guess."

"Programming, Olivia?"

"Yes, by very involved parents. I don't blame them, Gerald. They meant well. They've created this great life for me. Maybe, I'll do the same. I hope not, but maybe. Know what I wish, Gerald? I wish they would be happier. Not so busy being busy, being important. Just enjoy their lives. I really wish that for them. They're good people. They deserve it."

"Yeah, they do, Olivia. But what if they can't change? What if they're too old to change?"

"Sometimes, I worry about that, Gerald. But now's not the time. I'm not too old to change. Come back to my dorm room. I don't think Kaitlyn will be home tonight. And . . .."

---

8   Pic Luna https://firepitcell.com/wp-content/uploads/2021/12/C14N8-Luna-.jpg
9   Music Philosophers https://www.youtube.com/watch?v=1DCYvWl8NDU

"And what . . . Olivia?"

"And I do want to be happy, more than anything else."

*   *   *

Meanwhile, Scott is happily losing money to Kaitlyn playing pool.[10]

"I guess a new Kaitlyn did show up tonight," Scott whispers in Kaitlyn's ear.

"You OK with that, Mr. Hopkins? You OK by being beaten by a girl?"

"You bet, Princess," with a hug. "By an extraordinary girl."

"Then rack them up again, I'm on a hot streak."

*   *   *

Allie stops by Michell's room, "Oh . . . come in, Allie," a flustered Michelle says, "I was looking for you earlier."

"And what did my pretty kitten want, Michelle?"

Hanging a string around Allie's neck, "To give you this. Just to thank you for a lovely evening at the club last night. It was special. Sorry, it ended the way it did, but Shelley really needed me."

"I was disappointed, Michelle. You really got me revved up.

"Me too. Allie. If you only knew."

"But your gift is sweet. What is it?"

"It's a bubble. One that doesn't burst."

With a hug, "Then, I'm forgiven, Allie?"

"When you're sweet like this, Michelle, hard not to forgive. Let's start over. Want to take a walk? It's a nice evening."

"Sure, Allie. How about we walk in the park?

"You have a mysterious look on your face? What's up, Michelle?"

"Shelley has a date with Luna tonight in the park."

---

10 Pic Kaitlyn Pool Table https://firepitcell.com/wp-content/uploads/2021/12/C14N10-Kaitlyn-Play-Pool.jpg

"I know. All the prep work we did with them worked. Luna and I had a long talk late last night in our room after we all came back from the club. She likes Shelley, a lot."

"Shelley and I talked too. Long into the night. Way too long. It was a talk for the record books."

"Luna asked me what I knew about you and Shelley. She was wondering whether you and Shelley are . . . a couple."[11]

"And . . .?"

"I said I hoped not. After our evening together at the club, I really hope not. You're not, are you?"

"No, we're just roommates."[12]

"Michelle, you do know that you and Shelley are high on the hall gossip grapevine.[13] Most of the girls on this floor are wondering why you and Shelley are roommates. I mean, it's against university rules, but there the two of you are. And we all see how the two of you are together. More than just roommates, but I'm not sure exactly what."

"I'm not surprised, Allie. It's a puzzle. If you figure it out, let me know. It's a new kind of relationship for me. We're close, but we're definitely not a couple."

"So, Michelle, why do you want us to spy on Shelley and Luna in the park, if you're not a couple?"

"Shelley doesn't have a lot of experience with girls. It's important for him that this date goes right with Luna tonight. Really important. It could change his life. I do hope that happens. He's so, vulnerable at his age."

"So, you're like . . . a worried mother? My mother didn't worry about me as much on my Prom night."

"I don't know why Allie, but I do worry about Shelley. Funny you mentioned mothers. Sometimes he calls me Mom. It's odd, but very sweet. I don't know how to describe our relationship other than to call it special.

---

11 Couples Interviews https://www.youtube.com/watch?v=X6t-O6DxVmE
12 Music Video Roommates https://www.youtube.com/watch?v=Nhe13bRNKbs
13 Music Video Gossip https://www.youtube.com/watch?v=kN8FwBDCLEc

His mother died when he was little. So, he has a gap that I'm helping to fill. And most of the time I kind of like the way it makes me feel."

"OK, now I get it. You're the mom. But Luna's the kind of girl any mother would love a son like Shelley to be involved with. She's a nice girl - a math whiz like Shelley. They both could use a little more experience. And I doubt either of them is the type that goes all the way on a first date."

"I guess you're right Allie. It's just . . . .."

"Come on. Let's go for our walk. But not in the park, Mom," as Allie leads Michelle the opposite direction across campus. Besides I gave you up last night so you could mother Shelley. Tonight you're all mine. Mom is off duty. Got that Michelle?"

"Oh my, Allie. How's a girl say no to you?"[14]

"No isn't allowed tonight,[15] Michelle," as Allie kisses her, "I'm not letting my pretty kitten get away like last night."

"Oh, that was lovely, Allie," Michelle says melting at Allie taking control.

Smiling, Allie thinks, "Oh yes. She's mine now," but then, "Now what? I felt totally ready. Now she's drifting away as a recovering Michelle asks herself, "How do I tell Allie about my secret? Can I bear a look of disappointment in her eyes? No, I couldn't bear that rejection. I have to make Allie understand we're meant to be together." Then, Michelle thinks, "Maybe the bubbles will help me find the right time and right way. Are you listening, Sarah?"

* * *

In the park, Shelley and Luna continue their date.

"Shelley . . . I feel like someone . . . or something . . . is watching us."

"Where? I don't see anyone Luna."

"I don't know. I can't see anyone either. It's a feeling."

---

14 Music Should've Said No https://www.youtube.com/watch?v=Yi7woL6ZtZA
15 Pic Allie Kisses Michelle https://firepitcell.com/wp-content/uploads/2021/12/C14N15-Kiss-Allie-Michelle.jpg

"I can go look around."

"No . . . let's just . . . ."

". . . . continue?"

"Oh Shelley . . . that feels good . . .. Please . . . just . . . continue."

*   *   *

"Scott, you owe me $26."

"But I have no money on me. Just credit cards."

"Sorry Mr. Hopkins, I don't extend credit. You'll have to work it out in trade. You can make your first installment payment now."[16]

*   *   *

"Shelley, you're very intuitive - like you were understanding my soul."

"You know the passion you aroused. But just when I was feeling conflicted about going any further, you slowed us down. It was like a gentle landing after a storm. I'll share a secret with you. It was hard for me to stop.[17] I wanted more, but just not tonight. I want . . . ."

"I know Luna. I want us to be special together too."

"Maybe next time Shelley."

"Next time?" Shelley grins.

Walking back to their dorm hugging, Luna and Shelley are bursting with the sweetness of life. As they walk up the stairs together, Shelley whispers to himself, "Thanks, Michelle, for teaching me how to create the special story my girl wants."

*   *   *

---

16 Pic Kaitlyn Scott Pool https://firepitcell.com/wp-content/uploads/2021/12/C14N16-Kaitlyn-Scott.jpg

17 Music Don't Say No https://www.youtube.com/watch?v=QYC-I2UJ2XQ

Watching Luna and Shelley leave the park, a figure emerges from the darkness.

Picking up a book Luna left behind, "Who is this Manfred?"

* * *

Back at Olivia's dorm.

"Gerald, no one's in the hallway. You can come to my room now."

"I doubt anyone really cares, Olivia."

"Well, maybe I care about my privacy. When I run for political office, I don't want the girls in my dorm saying . . .."

"Saying what? That you were a loose woman?"

"Something like that. Politics is a dirty business."

"I can just picture the TV ads," Gerald smiles.

"Gerald, this is serious. I'm not some ditzy freshman girl without future plans."

"In a minute, you're going to care more about now than the future," as Gerald embraces her.

"If only I could . . .."

* * *

Back at Scott's apartment, Scott asks a dazed Kaitlyn, "Well, was I worth it?"

"Best $26 I've ever spent, sexy,"[18] are Kaitlyn's last words before they both collapse. Later, holding her, he begins wondering, "Who is this girl? How does she keep changing? Do I like that? Sure, as hell I do."

"That works for now, but what about long term? Would she be a good politician's wife? She sure can work a room. Have everyone eating out of her hand. I've seen some DC wives do that. Very powerful. But in politics, the media jumps on every statement. Kaitlyn would be media click bait.

---

18 Pic Kaitlyn Scott in Bed https://firepitcell.com/wp-content/uploads/2021/12/C14N18-Kaitlyn-Scott-2.jpg

Olivia is much more controlled. Olivia wouldn't make mistakes. That's why our parents know we're a good match."

Then it dawns on Scott. "I've known Kaitlyn less than a week. And I'm already thinking about our political career together? Why? Maybe Kaitlyn was right. Maybe I am her boyfriend. Sounds like how a boyfriend would think."

With his arms wrapped around his sleeping time bomb, "I can't wait to see the next Kaitlyn."

* * *

Later, Kaitlyn listens in the dark to Scott's breathing as he lies next to her.

"He's so cute when he's asleep. All that planning his next step is gone. He's just living in the moment."

Peering up into the darkness, as if to see through a hole to heaven, "Thank you God. I love this man.[19] I promise to make him happy. Please keep both of us safe and guide us to be good to one another and use the talents you gave us to help people. And help us specially to help Nicole."

* * *

"Gerald, thanks for a vacation from my future,"[20] as Olivia embraces him again, "that's a special present."

"That's me, your personal travel agent, Olivia."

"But my future always comes back. It stares me in the face before I fall asleep and its back when I wake up again. Always staring. . . always measuring me."

"How can you live that way, Olivia?"

"It's always been that way. I guess it's my fate."

"Maybe yes. Maybe no. Your fate is up to you."

"Gerald, it would be so nice, but I know what I have to do."

---

19 Pic Kaitlyn Praying https://firepitcell.com/wp-content/uploads/2021/12/C14N19-Kaitlyn-Praying.jpg

20 Music Video Vacation https://www.youtube.com/watch?v=M2WTRqCu_DY

"Olivia, you're not making sense. You're a smart, creative, rich girl. All you have to do is choose . . . and then fight for it."

"If only that were true," a misty-eyed Olivia thinks before falling asleep in the arms of her vacation specialist.

"Rich girls are so complicated," Gerald thinks to himself.

*   *   *

Scott awakens before dawn. Looking at Kaitlyn curled up in a ball like a kitten, he ponders, "How will this affect Operation Princess?"

"Can I still be objective, if Kaitlyn is dangerous?"[21]

"Can Olivia be objective? I know she's bonding with Kaitlyn too."

"How's that for irony? Olivia and I have been groomed to be with one another for as long as either of us can remember. And now . . . in different ways . . . we're falling for the same girl in the middle of a national security operation. What will we do?"[22]

*   *   *

Meanwhile back at the Foundation, the graveyard shift of scientists is busy reviewing the data collected today from the many hidden cameras and microphones spread around campus.

Experiment Hypothesis: Freshman transition is intense. One Freshman-day is like a month in normal time. Is this time warp a survival instinct triggered by rules changes? Science demands more data. More experiments are necessary.

---

21 Music Video Dangerous Woman https://www.youtube.com/watch?v=9WbCfHutDSE
22 Movie Clip https://www.youtube.com/watch?v=ANqGm-MiqQs

15

Threesome Michelle, Allie, Michael

Earlier that evening, Michelle and Allie return from their walk to empty dorm rooms holding hands.

"Michelle, how about we get to know one another better while the children are playing in the park? I have a bottle of wine."

"I'd like that, Allie. Yes . . . I'd like that. A lot."

Michelle primps while Allie retrieves the wine from her room. "I'll tell her when she opens the wine. I'll make a toast that lets her know my secret. How's this 'Allie, I'm so glad I became a girl.' No, that's not it. Too abrupt. 'Here's to surprises!' No, that doesn't tell her anything. Life is so simple in the bubbles. Why does real life have to be so complicated?"

While Michelle ponders her dilemma, Allie returns to Michelle's room. Sitting close and holding her hands, Allie asks, "Before we start, Michelle, isn't there something you want to tell me?"

"What do you mean?"

Waiting with an impatient look, "I mean tell me[1] about Michael."

"Michael . . .?"

"Yes, Michael."

"Who is Michael?"

"When I was visiting my brother several years ago, I saw Michael Collins in a play. That was you, wasn't it?"

---

1 Music Video Tell Me https://www.youtube.com/watch?v=THtqUDitQ4I

Retreating to a corner of the small dorm room, Michelle begins sobbing as she fears Allie is slipping away from her[2] while Allie waits for an answer.

"Er. . . I could say that I'm his sister. That's what I planned three years ago if anyone ever mentioned Michael. But I like you, Allie. I don't want to start our relationship by lying to you. Yes, it was me."

"When were you planning to tell me, Michelle? It's not nice to spring big surprises in bed. I'm pretty sophisticated, but someone else might freak out."

"I always try to tell people at the right time. I know it's dangerous not to. But did you think we'd be in bed together? Tonight? Is that all getting to know me means to you? What makes you think I was intending to jump into bed with you as soon as we were alone together? Do I have 'slut' stamped on my forehead? What kind of a girl do you think I am, Allie?"

Allie becomes less sure of herself as she backs into another corner of the room, "Please calm down, Michelle. I didn't mean to imply . . . you know . . . that you sleep around."

"Well, OK. It's just that some people make assumptions about people like me. They assume everything we do is about sex. But I'm a real person. I'm a serious actress. I have many interests. That's why I don't advertise my past."[3]

"I'm sorry, Michelle, I didn't . . . .."

"Well, that didn't go like I wanted, but at least this issue is out in the open," Michelle thinks, and she is apologizing to me. Maybe, it was all for the best. But how do I win Allie back? How do I convince her that I'm a real girl? How do I become her kitten again like the other night?"

After throwing Allie off balance, Michelle changes direction again, "I accept your apology, Allie, because a lot of people think that way. I'm a very forgiving girl. I just like to take things slow."

"So, are you telling me that Michelle is a shy girl?"

---

2 Music Video Sad Girl https://www.youtube.com/watch?v=arT0DeW44lY
3 Music Video Can't Forget Past https://www.youtube.com/watch?v=jSx6L6W4vFU

"Not shy exactly, just cautious. I haven't always been, but I'm learning. When you get to know me better, you'll understand why."

"Sorry Michelle. . . I've been with guys . . . been with girls . . . I might be at the beginning of my first 'trans' relationship. I like you, Michelle, but I don't know the rules."

"Neither do I. The hormones I've been taking don't come with an official 'trans' rule book. I'm making up the rules as I go along. OK with you, Allie?"

"I've been dutifully following rules at home for 18 years, Michelle. I tossed out the rule book when I got on the plane to come to college. So yes, I'm open to exploring and creating new rules."

"I was hoping I read you right, Allie. I really want to build our relationship. OK, if we start just by hugging?" As they embrace, "By the way, I'm not sure whether or not 'trans' describes me. You might say I'm a bit 'complicated.' People seem to think they know what 'trans' means. I'm not sure I really do. The media lumps a lot of different things all under that label. I suspect we're not all the same."

"Is that why you're not more open about your secret?"

"People have a lot of weird ideas about trans people.[4] Some people are attracted to the novelty of doing it with someone 'trans.' I'm not a toy. I don't want to be someone's novelty. So, I wait to tell people until they accept me as Michelle."

"Believe me, Michelle, I'm not just some kind of 'trans' groupie."

"That's why we both need to learn more about each another, Allie, before we get physical. I'm sure you have some secrets to share, and you may be surprised about how your new friends, Michelle and Michael, don't fit neatly into any box."

"Can I expect more surprises?"

"I get surprised by my new life almost every day. So, I expect you'll be surprised too. Do you think you can deal with surprises?"

"I'm not sure about tomorrow, but OMG, right now surprises sound . . . so hot!" As Allie leads Michelle to bed, "If you're going to do this slowly,

---

4 Music Video Mother's Daughter https://www.youtube.com/watch?v=7T2RonyJ_Ts

Michelle, I think we should begin finding out now whether our chemistry goes beyond what we experienced dancing together at the club."

After their first kisses, Michelle sits up."

"What wrong girlfriend? Don't you like?"

"I like. It's not that."

"Does it upset you that I know about Michael?"

"Not really. You surprised me, but it's OK that you know. I'm not ashamed of Michael. I have to trust people and I trust you, Allie," brushing her fingers against Allie's cheek.

"So, what's wrong, Michelle? Why are you pulling away from me?"[5]

"It's complicated, Allie. Like I said, I'm attracted, but I just think we should get to know one another before we get more physical. You need to know the real me[6]. That's more difficult than it is with some people. I have a real identity, but it's mixed up with a lot of other things. You must have some questions. Don't you?"

"No, I mean, not really. Well, maybe there are some things . . .."

"Of course, there are. I mean, who throws out all the rules without having questions afterwards. You're absolutely dying to ask . . . something. Aren't you?"

"OK, I'm wondering how committed you are to being Michelle. Will Michael show up again tomorrow? Or the next day? I'm not sure I want a relationship with someone who may suddenly change their mind and disappear on me."

"What else, Allie? Don't worry, it won't offend me."

"Well, you've mentioned hormones, but not surgery. Have you? Will you?"

"The hormones helped soften my face and change my body shape. That enabled me to pass as a girl. But I didn't want to settle for passing. I wanted more, to be pretty so I can be an actress. I needed some surgery to improve my voice and refine my face." Posing for Allie, "My cute nose and cheekbones that you love so much were sculpted."

---

5 Music Video Pulling Away https://www.youtube.com/watch?v=T7Jld5e_CHA
6 Music Video Identity https://www.youtube.com/watch?v=0VF8iF4OG_M

"But nothing's been done below my neck. My breasts are from the hormones. And, of course, the hormones have made my male parts less important and given me all kinds of sensitivities to touch I never had before. You saw how you touching my breasts drove me wild when we danced. I'm hoping that's made me girl enough for you, Allie, because emotionally I'm all girl, and I think we have something special together, you and pretty kitten."

As Allie hesitates, Michelle senses that Allie is unsure of how she feels about.

"Allie, I don't know if I'll ever have any surgery. Maybe, someday. Maybe not. All I know now is that for now I'm comfortable the way I am. I'm kind of taking a vacation from making big decisions like that, at least for now. If that's a deal killer for you, I guess we're not ready for one another."

"Michelle, I just don't know how important that is to me. I'm only 18, still learning about myself. Can we just try to see how it works?"

"Of course, we can, Allie. But don't you feel better that all your concerns are out in the open?"

"Yes, but I didn't want to, you know . . . offend you."

"I know, Allie. It's not something I talk about with everyone, but you're special. So, I'll try to explain my journey. Then, we can decide whether we want to be in a special relationship or just be friends down the hall from one another. OK?"

Michelle holds Allie's hand, "I started taking hormones about three years ago. It was after I took part in a Foundation experiment. The same Foundation that's running the stress experiment on you, Allie. They do these experiments at colleges all over the country. I started on the same Foundation immersion experiment my roommate Shelley is doing now. I'd wondered about gender before and sometimes dressed before, but that semester convinced me I'd be happier as a girl. The next semester, I graduated to hormone experiments the Foundation was conducting. The Foundation already knew practically everything about me by then. So, it was easy getting accepted into the hormone experiment. Getting accepted was probably the only easy thing on my journey."

"I imagine it was difficult, Michelle. I wish I had been there to experience it with you."

"Here's the next best thing, Allie. One benefit of working with the Foundation instead of going it alone is that the Foundation documents every detail. So, I have photos of every stage of the process as Michael became Michelle. Want to see?" After Michelle brings up her Google Photos on her tablet, "These may help you to understand what I've been through to become Michelle. Then you can decide if this was just a whim or a commitment to a new life."

"See, this was Michael.[7] Then, Michelle began growing and Michael started fading. Michael was late in developing. So, the hormones didn't have to overcome a lot of the effects of male puberty. But he didn't look like a girl either. See how gradual the changes were?"

"No, don't look at that one! Not looking my best there. I do wish the Foundation would invest in better photos. Some of them look like mug shots. It's embarrassing."

"Oh, Michelle, it's remarkable to see your progression."

"This one is about a year into my hormones. You can see that before this picture, I relied a lot on makeup to help me pass. Beginning here . . . I could just brush my hair and go out as Michelle, and no one could tell."[8]

"So, how did people react as they watched you change?"

"Very few people saw me. I took most of my classes online for a year. But the way I looked was only a small part. Most people think it's about how you look. I did too at first, but soon I learned the biggest change was how I started feeling and acting differently . . . even when other people weren't around to see."

"My journey did start out as a guy wearing a dress, but then Michelle emerged as a new personality. Michelle and Michael are like different

---

7 Pic Michael https://firepitcell.com/wp-content/uploads/2021/12/C15N7-Michael.jpg
8 Pic Michelle Mid Transition https://firepitcell.com/wp-content/uploads/2021/12/C15N8-Michelle-Transition.jpg

characters in a play. For a while, I was both Michael and Michelle. That was really confusing. Then Michael gradually started to fade away. As time went on, I became Michelle . . . inside and out.[9] Ready to love and be loved. Ready to pleasure and be pleasured. Experiencing the results of my transition has been enlightening. People relate to me now in very different ways. I'm finding that being desired is an intoxicating power. It's also unnerving trying to balance that with living a normal life."

"You sound like you're surprised. Isn't that what you planned, Michelle?"

"Not really. I planned to explore. To see what roles, I could play. I didn't really have a set end game. For me, it's been more like an adventure than a struggle."

"I never thought of it that way. Do you like being Michael or Michelle more?"

"I liked playing Michael, but I like playing Michelle more. More than either, I like exploring. I want to know everything . . . about me . . . about you . . . about the world. Why do we do what we do? What can I learn from that?"

"That's a lot to process, Michelle. Let me think about that while we talk about simpler matters. Like, how did Michelle end up in school here?"

"I decided to start over in a new school where no one knows Michael. I guess transferring schools doesn't wipe out the past. But . . . I wish it did."

"Oh, I don't know. Your past made you the girl you are today. And I like Michelle," as Allie draws closer.

"No, not yet Allie. Later, maybe, but not yet. OK?

"Michelle, you're toying with me. What's your game?"

"Allie, I'm very attracted to you. The way you take charge. I need that. But you've told me nothing about yourself. I have some questions before we get more involved. You know my story. What's your story, Allie?"

"Here's my story in a nutshell. Fourth child in a high achieving Asian-American family. Chinese on my father's side and Japanese mother. But

---

9 Video Transition https://www.youtube.com/watch?v=-ko4gddorGU

both were born in America. So, were their parents. I also have three older brothers. I grew up in Honolulu."

"Allie, that's so . . . I had three older sisters."

"I thought this was about me and my story, Michelle. I'm in the spotlight now."

"Sorry, I'll keep quiet until you finish."

"By high school, I'd been playing the dutiful Asian daughter role for so long that acting became second nature to me. I like girls. I've been with boys. It was OK, but they just don't excite me the way girls do. I stopped hiding my preferences in sophomore year. I've been much happier since then. But it broke my parents' hearts. They still love me, but they'd like me to pretend to be normal. Personal happiness isn't as important to them as family is. I struggle a lot with that. That's one reason I like performing on stage. I get to show the world my version of reality without hurting anyone. The audience either claps or doesn't. They walk out and a new audience appears the next night. Family approval or disapproval lasts forever. And with a play, we get to rehearse, and we get do overs. Life is like improv. There's a lot of pressure to get it right the first time. Sometimes, I don't."

As the two continue talking, "Oh, that feels good, Allie, but not yet. I want all my relationships to be special. It feels like you're moving through your checklist. Like you're buying a car or something. That's not . . . not how I imagined the two of us."

"Is that a tear, Michelle?"

"No, not really. Well, yes. I'm so embarrassed. I'm trying not to get so emotional. Allie, I like you. I had high hopes for the two of us, but I'm disappointed in you now. You knew my secret before we started, and you assumed I was going to jump into bed with you. After I shared my most personal journey with you, you've been trying to test out my equipment, like you're trying to make me prove I'm a girl."

"I didn't mean to . . . .."

Interrupting Allie, "I'm a real person, not a toy, Allie. What you've been doing to me today is humiliating. And now you're surprised I'm getting misty? What happened to that nice girl I danced with the other night?

I really liked that Allie. She was fun. She seemed kind. Today, you've just been so insensitive."

"What was I thinking?" Wiping Michelle's damp cheek, "please give me another chance. Come on Michelle . . . please. I promise . . . anything you want."

"Well, . . . I guess you're forgiven . . . lucky for you, I find humiliation a little sexy."

"You do?"

"Sometimes. It's hard to explain, but that's part of my submissive side. See, that's what I mean. It's like we're still talking different languages. You don't really know me yet.[10] I'm a lot more complicated than just someone born a boy and now I'm a girl. In some ways, that's the easy part. I want you to know how I feel about all kinds of things before we get more physical."

"You think transitioning is the easy part? Now, I'm really interested. We're way outside my experience. How do we begin exploring your complications?"

"Are you really interested? Or just adding to your experience? I'm not a science project you know!"

"Michelle, I totally deserve that. I get that this is very personal and maybe some people haven't done right by you. Maybe, earlier today, I was one of those people. But I'm different now. I really want to find out whether there can be an 'us.' Will you?"

"Yes, if you're willing to open up to me the way I've shared with you, then there might be an 'us.' Tell me one thing about me you think will make us both happy. Then, maybe I'll be able to tell whether we have a future."

"OK, Michelle. I confess something about the way you've been mothering Shelley[11]. I know you aren't just acting when you're mothering him. It's so sweet. I've gotten misty eyed a couple of times watching the two of you. I'm thousands of miles from home for the first time. My family and I are taking a break from each other." Looking like a lost puppy, "I can use

---

10 Music Video Do You Know Me https://www.youtube.com/watch?v=8UNQOby0akQ
11 Music Video Stacy's Mom https://www.youtube.com/watch?v=dZLfasMPOU4

some sweetness in my life now – a little TLC. I'm feeling, hoping, that together we can create a sweet life."

"Allie, you poor baby. That gives us something real to build on. I've had some long breaks with my family too. We're together again, but it still hurts."

"Can we forget about your other tests, Allie, and just focus on being sweet to one another? Really get to know one another before we get more involved? I mean, we live next door to one another. If it doesn't work out between us, we can't just disappear. We'll still be seeing each other every day. So, we should make sure we're not just . . .. You know what I mean?"

"Will you let me hold you, Michelle, while you tell me about what you like? I'm fascinated by what you've already told me especially that transitioning isn't the hardest part."

With Allie's arms around her, Michelle tells her story. "I like both boys and girls, but mostly, I like girls. I grew up in a family of three older sisters. Pajama parties were big in our house. Sometimes my sisters dressed me as their sister. As the youngest, I guess my sisters spoiled me. It started as just a game. Later it became more real with more and more details. I began to like it."

"It was fun. We all giggled. No one meant any harm or thought it would change my life. But maybe I grew up being their life size barbie doll.[12] I learned from my sisters was that being a girl is fun and that I'm one of the special people in the world who can choose what they want to be. Suddenly, I had choices. Choices that most people don't have. I felt I was special. I could choose to remain a small boy that both men and women would ignore, or with some effort, become a hot girl who would be everyone's center of attention. You see what I chose, but I'm not just a doll. I'm a complex person that people should enjoy, but take seriously."

"Michelle, I'm beginning to understand your evolution, but why do you like girls? Why not just be a gay guy? Much easier than becoming a girl, right?"

---

12 Video Barbie Doll https://www.youtube.com/watch?v=zSR_dKGbtLQ

"Being in bed with a girl just seems very comfortable to me. I like . . . the softness. . . the feelings . . . the shared experiences when girls are together[13] I crave that girl intimacy from pajama parties and the games. I don't usually find with guys. . . . Maybe, most important, I'm a better person when I'm with a girl. I like me better."

"And what about the guys you like? "What's Mr. Right or Mr. Wrong look like?"[14]

"Someone strong. If they're not athletic, I'd rather be with a girl. But its more than physical. Guys are usually so simple. I'm complex. I'm attracted to that steady simple influence over me. It calms me down. But some girls have that same direct approach. I see that in you sometimes, Allie. I think that explains why I'm so attracted to you."

"Oh, Michelle," as Allie hugs her, "You get me. Most people don't."

"Neither one of us are most people, Allie."

"I'm beginning to understand our connection, but what else, Michelle? There's something you haven't told me, Michelle. Isn't there?"

Beginning to tear up again, "Allie, my real secret isn't that I used to be Michael. I'm proud of my journey. It's worse than that. I'm so ashamed.[15] I'm hoping that you'll understand . . . but I'm so afraid you won't!"

Stroking Michelle's hair, "There . . . there, baby. It can't be that bad. You can trust me. I'll take care of you."

"Sometimes, the way the right guy, or often than not, the wrong guy, holds me . . . my brain completely shuts down. I do stupid things. It's so. . . wonderful . . . but terrifying too. Most of the time, I'm a strong independent person. I run my life. But I get really submissive with Mr. Wrong. Can't make decisions. Just take care of him., hoping he'll take care of me too. Sometimes he does, but usually not in the way I need. So, I act out and I hope he punishes me. When he does, it's painful, but also comforting. I know that sounds crazy, but it isn't, at least not to me."

"Go ahead my sweet girl, I'm listening . . . not judging."

---

13 Music Video Lost Cause https://www.youtube.com/watch?v=S2dRcipMCpw
14 Music Video Mr. Right https://www.youtube.com/watch?v=VNqFNgb2opw
15 Music Ashamed https://www.youtube.com/watch?v=Y12wyQbFXo0

Looking up misty eyed to Allie, "Sometimes it leads me to dark places; I mean my craving to be punished. When I was Michael, the craving was strong. So was the pain. I'm less into the pain part now that I'm Michelle. Now, it's more about wanting someone to control me to bring me out of my dark side, but I still feel comforted when I'm punished and have earned forgiveness."

"Whips and chains, Michelle? Fifty Shares of Grey?"

"Stop . . . I know that's what people think, but it's not like that – at least not the main thing for me. There are more than fifty shades of grey. I have my very own color - my submissive side that I suppress with most people. And I've learned . . . the hard way . . . to avoid sadists. They don't love me. They just love inflicting pain. What I really crave is someone who knows me . . . and loves me . . . and cares enough about me . . . to punish me when I do bad things. People hear submissive and they picture someone who's always afraid. That's not me. I'm only afraid, desperately scared that I'll lose you,[16] Allie, because I'm different. The other night, you calling me you kitten reminded me that I sometimes need a little vacation from my struggles; you're the alpha who'll guide me to my sweet spot that girls like me need to be a bad ass[17] when life gets tough. Is that too much to ask?"

"Do you think I can help you find that sweet spot, Michelle?"

"I hope so, Allie. You can be both strong and gentle. I've only found that once since I've begun my new life . . . and it only lasted a few weeks, but I liked every minute of it. Being so close to someone strong . . . and the way he looked at me with desire . . . and feeling his power . . . and the way he looked at me when I pleased him . . . and setting rules for me to follow. He didn't like inflicting pain. It hurt him more than me. I saw it in his eyes, but he knew that sometimes I'd lose control and punishment was the only way to get me back to what I really wanted. It was just so . . . perfect . . . until it was over. He left me a lovely letter explaining that he hated himself

---

16 Pic Michelle Afraid https://firepitcell.com/wp-content/uploads/2021/12/C15N16-Michelle-Afraid.jpg

17 Music Video Bad Ass Girl https://www.youtube.com/watch?v=qYwgG2oyUbA

for punishing the girl he loved. I still read it. I can't show it to you . . . it's too private."

"Are you blushing, Michelle? Yes . . . you are! Blushing like a schoolgirl talking about her first time. Don't be embarrassed. It tells me Michelle is a real person. It's not all just acting. Girls can fake orgasms, but we can't fake a blush. Girl, I want to make you feel that way.[18] Make you forget about guys."

"I'd like that, Allie. I really would, but I've been doing that a lot lately." Michelle looking worried, "These super hormones the Foundation is giving me now are really changing me in ways the normal hormones didn't. Running around mothering people? Crying and blushing at the slightest little thing? What's happening to me?"

"You're softer than most girls I know, Michelle. Still full of emotions and ideals . . . despite hard life lessons. I was like that once, just a vulnerable surfer girl. Now, I'm hard. Life's big waves have knocked the softness out of me. I miss that part of myself. I'd like to get back there someday, but I don't know how. So, I protect myself by controlling everything."

"I'm on the opposite path, Allie. With my hormone treatments, sometimes I'm so . . . not in control of myself, it's scary."

"Welcome to the club new girl. If all you wanted was to be in control of your emotions, you might have saved yourself a lot of trouble and stayed being Michael. Tell me what you want, Michelle."

"I want the whole package. I want someone who'll give me the freedom to be me. Help me when I want to storm a castle, but someone who will take control of me when I lose control. Save me from me. And I'll do anything for that person, who I call my 'alpha,' I'll withhold nothing from that person. Is that too much to ask?"

"No, not to ask, but you seem to expect it. I used to, but not anymore. I wish I still had high expectations. Maybe, someday you'll lead me back to being the girl I was. Fixing the damaged goods."

As just a hint of a smile appears, Michelle leans her head on Allie's shoulder. "Now, you're the Allie I danced with. The Allie I wanted to know

18 Music Video Explosion https://www.youtube.com/watch?v=PChExlwo3Y

better. Just as complicated as I am. Not the Allie who showed up today guns blazing. I'm liking the Allie you are now. I'll follow her anywhere."

"How do you do it, Michelle? You're making being vulnerable so . . . sexy!"

Michelle's smile widens and Allie senses Michelle's game, "You're manipulating me. Aren't you? You knew being vulnerable was turning me on and you played it to the hilt. OMG, the way you emotionally played me. Made me talk about things I've never talked about with anyone. I can't believe I fell for that."

"OK, you finally caught me, Allie. But isn't that what boys say after they finally figure out our girl games after it's too late?"

"So, you decided you'd be the girl and I'm the boy?"

"Not really. You're a natural alpha. You need to be in charge. I'm not and you knew that, so you decided to play a control game with me." Seeing that Allie is worried, "It's OK Allie, I like games. But you thought you had me all figured out. That you'd be the winner by putting me on the defensive about my secret; a useful strategy in winning your get the girl into bed game."

"Ow! . . . that's harsh, Michelle. It wasn't so premeditated. I swear."

"I know Allie, it was just your natural alpha way of dealing with the world. Don't worry, I like that. I need an alpha to create stability. But I can't just let my alpha win without trying. You have to really be stronger to bring out my submissive nature. Until then, I'll compete in the game. You forgot, I'm an actress. I'm good at playing roles. I played a different role than you expected. Instead of jumping into bed or throwing you out, I opened my heart to you. You could have stomped all over it. Instead, you opened your heart a little. I like alphas who do that even if I have to take chances to get us to the sweetness of life[19] we're both looking for."

"But you're confusing me, Michelle. Was it all just an act?[20] I really need to know what's real and what's not."

---

19 Movie Clip La dolce Vita https://www.youtube.com/watch?v=04P1dCLvc_0
20 Music Honesty https://www.youtube.com/watch?v=SuFScoO4tb0

"Reality Allie? I'm not sure what that is. Life's a game, but in the game we played tonight, you had me tingling, I shared real personal things from my life and I think you shared real feelings too. That's real enough for me even if it took a game to make it all happen."

"I believe that Michele, but I'm still confused about the game. What are the rules?"

"Oh Allie, that's why I like these games. It's exciting because the rules change. I changed the rules on you while you were so busy being in charge, being the initiator and trying to maneuver me into bed. Allie, you try very hard. I like that. I need someone who does that. You were trying to be my alpha, but not in the way I need. So, I decided to teach you to be a better alpha by making you feel good. I do that. It's my nature. You'll have to get used to it if we're going to be a couple. I'm very good at making my alpha feel good, Allie. Really. I promise."

Michelle smiles mischievously, "But, I'm a challenge. I don't dedicate my life to make just anyone feel good. You have to earn it[21] and put up with my tricks. Like just when you were sure that you were in charge, I let you lead me where I wanted us to go and I let you think it was all your idea."

"It did kind of happen that way, Michelle. It's a little confusing, but real."

"So, now I'm introducing you to my reality, Allie. I'm hoping you'll like it. I like getting my way. We'll be good together because the best way for me to get what I want is to make you feel good about it, because you're my alpha. We can learn how to use our powers together for good – to help each other – to create a happy 'us.' I feel in my heart that's our journey together. Will you join me on our journey?"

"But you manipulated me,[22] Michelle. Shouldn't we always be honest with one another?"

"Allie . . . really? Relationships don't just happen. Our relationship was in danger of dying at the beginning. . . because . . . because of . . . how my journey had you on edge. I mean, what's a girl supposed to do when the

---

21 Music Video Win My Love https://www.youtube.com/watch?v=rxIfKpsemGo
22 Video Manipulating https://www.youtube.com/watch?v=sAjYq7VCr_E

lover she's absolutely aching for is wondering whether she's just a guy in a dress?"

"I didn't mean to hurt you, Michelle."

"I know. It's difficult to understand, but don't worry, Allie, all is for-given. Your sub is very forgiving after she gets what she wants from her alpha . . . even if getting it is painful . . . maybe more satisfying because of the pain."

"Tell me more about this alpha-submissive thing[23] – and the punish-ment and pain. I'm not a sadist. It scares me. How can I be your alpha when it scares me?"

"Allie, if you were a sadist, I wouldn't want you to be my alpha. For me it's more symbolic than real pain. I'm a complex girl. I need a strong person like you to help keep me within boundaries. It won't be easy for you to be my alpha. Sometimes, my games may drive you a little crazy. To remind you how much I love you while I'm driving you crazy, I'm willing to submit to punishment . . . like a child. It's my gift to my alpha. After you've pun-ished me, I'll feel better, and you will too. My humiliation will remind you I love you and show that you care enough to punish . . . instead of leaving me. Then, I'll be bound in chains of love."[24]

"I'm still confused, Michelle."

Biting her lower lip and opening the eyes to her soul, "You won't believe what I'll do to take care of my loving alpha after the pain.[25] Look how much I've already done to help bring us together, helping you pursue me . . . by playing hard to get. . . sharing embarrassing personal secrets with you . . . sympathetically listening to your story. All because I knew in my heart that you're my alpha. But now we're here in bed together, just where both of us wanted to be. We've created the perfect alpha and sub story together. Is that so bad?"

Allie smiles and in a soft voice "No, not so bad at all."

---

23 Music Video love Slave https://www.youtube.com/watch?v=Mzybwwf2HoQ

24 Music Video Bound to You https://www.youtube.com/watch?v=7i2SupYmXpI

25 Music After Pain https://www.youtube.com/watch?v=vN3Q6-4wyY0

Whispering into Allie's ear, "And always remember this. My story about my other alpha and my blush was a real personal moment. I've never shared how that guy made me feel with anyone, not even with him. Only with you because you're my new alpha. I really am that vulnerable girl. And I'm yours if you want me."

"I want, girlfriend."

Michelle moves Allie's arm around her shoulders and snuggles into her, "Allie, I'll be totally dedicated to bringing happiness to both of us. Really, I will. Making my alpha happy is all I live for. If that involves a little game-playing, what's the harm?"

Stroking Michelle's hair, "No harm at all."

Michelle looks up at Allie with her big blue eyes and pouts her lips, ". . .are you still worried about Michael returning tomorrow? Am I really a boy in disguise?"

"Nuh-uh, girlfriend," as Allie leans in with gentle kisses, "Guys can't be as tricky as you are," Allie jokes. "You're a master of trickery." When Michelle begins to sit up, Allie pulls her back down. Nuh-uh, I'm not finished with my submissive girlfriend. Time for your new alpha to give you something to blush about, the way you did remembering that guy."

"Jealous? . . . I like that," Michelle giggles. "But it's time to stop talking. Time for my alpha to turn my body on fire.[26] Just tell me you're my alpha and my body is yours."

Allie becomes serious, "Michelle, I'll be your alpha. It's just crazy enough that it might work." Cupping Michelle's face between both hands and looking into her eyes, "Do you accept me as your alpha?".

"Oh yes, Allie. That's why I didn't let you make love to me right away. I needed to find out whether you'll be the kind of alpha I need. I trust that now. I'm turning my body over to you so that you can bring harmony to us both."

Allie stands up, looking down at her sub, "Michelle, you've been bad. You disrupted our harmony. What do you need when you're bad, Michelle?"

---

26 Music Video On Fire https://www.youtube.com/watch?v=S8kkZgcwcBY

"I need my alpha to punish me. And then we make up." Michelle grins. "Then, all will be right in our world."

"And does my submissive girlfriend have any punishment toys?"

Michelle reaches under her bed and hands Allie a bag.

"Let's see what we have here. This looks interesting. And this one."

As Allie practices using her new toy,[27] Michelle interrupts, "I really like this one, Allie."

Allie immediately responds in the way that excites Michelle, "Oh? Do subs get to choose their own punishment?" Allie mocks.

"No Allie, my body is yours.[28] I trust my alpha will know how to punish her sub."

"That's more like it. Since your body is mine now, I'll wrap you up and inspect my treasures.[29] And the deal is off if you don't measure up."

Allie takes her time, exploring the helpless Michelle, as she works up the courage to move to the next step. "Oh my, what a cute bubble you have Michelle. Yes, very cute." Allie thinks to herself, "Why is this girl trusting me so much? She's totally helpless now. I could do anything. Am I worthy of such trust?"

After the inspection, "You'll do until I decide on what improvements I want. Every day, you'll wear what I tell you. You'll know you're my doll to play with. Now, what naughty things have you done to merit punishment? Confess every sin against your alpha!"

"I withheld sex from my alpha."

"Will you do that again, Michelle?

"Oh no. My body is yours, always."

"What else, Michelle?"

"I played games with you and didn't let you win. And I made you jealous."

"And will you do that again?"

---

27 SNL Auditions Clip https://www.youtube.com/watch?v=mHlpEbhNyh0

28 Music Video Body Yours https://www.youtube.com/watch?v=9uC9ArgIcr8

29 Pic Michelle Tied https://firepitcell.com/wp-content/uploads/2021/12/c15n29-mi-chelle-inspected-by-allie.jpg

"Oh yes, Allie. All the time. That's why I need an alpha. I just can't help being bad like that."

"Then, I'll be punishing you often."

"Oh, yes my alpha. Often! And we'll be kissing and making up after punishment, often!"

Allie thinks as she begins the first punishment, Michelle senses her spirit bit by bit transferring to another body. With each stroke less and less is left in the shell Allie is punishing. As Allie completes the punishment ritual, Michelle's spirit turns pure white.[30] All the remains of her sins cleansed by her body's suffering, she senses "I'm worthy of being loved again.[31] My body will be rewarded for its suffering by Allie's love. Harmony of body and spirit has been restored."

"Strange, this seems harder for me than for Michelle. I bet she knew that all along. What a little manipulator she is."

Her punishment completed, Michelle consoles Allie and wipes a tear from her alpha's cheek. "I know it's hard being my alpha. It didn't hurt me much. Really. You did it just the way I needed. I was bad and feeling guilty. Now, I feel loved and forgiven. All the turmoil we went through earlier is gone. You feel it, don't you, Allie?"

"Yes, my kitten, you're like an innocent virgin now," Allie responds. As she positions Michelle's compliant body for the next phase of their relationship, Allie looks down at her purified lover,[32] and whispers, "I've waited two long weeks for this while you teased me. I cherish your total surrender to me my sweet kitten."

As she looks up at her alpha, Michelle relishes the look of pent-up desire growing in Allie's eyes. Smiling as she braces herself for Allie's coming torrent of passion, Michelle has one last moment to think, "this is why I created this new body of mine," before being overwhelmed by Allie. Wave

---

30 Pic Michelle Purified https://firepitcell.com/wp-content/uploads/2021/12/c15n30-michelle-purified.jpg

31 Music Video Angel https://www.youtube.com/watch?v=TlGXDy5xFlw

32 Pic Allie Loving Michelle https://firepitcell.com/wp-content/uploads/2021/12/Allie-Loving-Michelle.jpg

after wave[33] tosses Michelle about as Allie ravishes her. Gasping for breath between Allie's kisses, Allie covers her mouth. "No words kitten," before the two girls' bodies surrender to the overwhelming tide. Lying in motionless bliss for an eternity, they share a sacred silence.

Recovering from the uncontrolled first wave of their lovemaking, Michelle hears Allie laugh "Now you'll always want to be my kitten. They'll be no escape for you. I am your alpha."

"Yes, you are my alpha, and I am your kitten. This was always meant to be. Now it's time for your kitten to appreciate her alpha." As the two girls begin a long, sensuous journey together they create a concert of sweet girl night noises.[34]

Before the two exhausted girls fall asleep, Michelle whispers, "Allie, are you crying?"

"Yes, my kitten. It was so beautiful. No one has ever given me such a precious gift."

"Allie . . . we're going to make life so sweet together. I promise."

*   *   *

I CAN'T BELIEVE WHAT THEY JUST DID!

*   *   *

"That was sweet Luna," as Shelley kisses her goodnight at her dorm room door. "I'm just down the hall."

"Yes, I know Shelley."

Returning to his room, Shelley finds the remains of Michelle's and Allie's performance with the two exhausted girls entwined in many layered embraces[35] on his bed.

---

33 Movie Clip From Here to Eternity https://www.youtube.com/watch?v=4iTCDWQXYlY

34 Night Noises https://www.youtube.com/watch?v=qtRaLTg4MxU

35 Pic Entwined Legs https://firepitcell.com/wp-content/uploads/2021/12/Michelle-Allie-Entwined.jpg

Shelley ponders, "They look so beautiful together. Will I ever live like that? Giving it my all on the edge?"

Knocking on Luna's door, "Shelley, I like you, but I'm not ready to . . . at least not yet."

"I know . . . it's not that . . . . I'm kind of homeless. Our roommates seem to be more ready than we are."

"Oh . . . ."

"Can I sleep in Allie's bed since she's not using it? And I promise I won't visit you while you're sleep."

"I know that, Shelley. I trust you."

Before Luna falls asleep, "Shelley, isn't it so predictable?"

"What?"

"We're two math geeks sleeping in separate beds, while the two performing arts majors are wrapped around one another."

"I suspect the Foundation has some statistics about that," Sheldon adds. "How many dates before first coitus broken down by school and majors. Maybe they'll use that data to create a dating algorithm. Then students can choose majors based on . . . ."

"Shelley, you're so funny."

"Good night, Shelley."

"Good night, Luna.

16

Experiments on Schedule

In the darkness that precedes the first light, the two girls snuggle. "You're my alpha now, Allie. Pleasing you makes me feel so . . . secure."

"Michelle, last night was amazing. I feel so . . . clean . . . I mean in my soul. No turmoil. Is it always like this?"

"Yes, submission[1] can be beautiful . . . at least when the alpha cherishes her kitten's gift. It can be dark with the wrong alpha. That's why I had to be sure about you, Allie."

At the first hint of dawn the girls walk together to the park for their first sunrise yoga together. After yoga, "Michelle . . . are we still two separate damaged people?[2] Or are we one better person? We're like all mixed together. Where do I end and you begin?"

After ten minutes of golden serenity, Michelle breaks the silence, "Oh, there you are Sarah![3] Yes, the autumn leaves are pretty. Yes, just like Allie and me."

"Michelle, who are you talking to?" Allie asks.

"To Sarah Atwell, Shelley's mother." As Michelle winks to Sarah, "Relax Allie, I know Sarah isn't actually in the park with us. I'm not that crazy. It's just that our spirits communicate sometimes, especially when I'm in a pure

---

1 Music Video Surrender https://www.youtube.com/watch?v=gcpvXaD9acM

2 Music Broken People https://www.youtube.com/watch?v=0QKTb6PSIOs

3 Pic Sarah in Park https://firepitcell.com/wp-content/uploads/2021/12/C16N3-Sarah-Atwell-Looks-after-Michelle-and-Allie-in-Park.jpg

state of harmony like now. Sarah has helped me and now I'm helping her Shelley. It's a mother thing we have."

"Yes, Sarah. You're right. Allie is just the kind of girl I need."

"So, Michelle, Sarah approves of you and me?"

"Yes Allie, I thought she would. Sarah's a lovely woman."

Allie thinks, "My beautiful girlfriend is crazy.[4] Why am I attracted to the loons? Why are the loons attracted to me? Am I crazy too? But it seems harmless. And yoga is supposed to open our minds and bodies to new experiences. Maybe that's all Michelle is going through. No need to panic yet, but I need to be careful with Michelle."

"Allie, I know you think I'm looney. I can see it in your eyes and Sarah confirms. Sarah and I prefer to word 'enchanting' to describe our abilities to sense things other people can't. Trust your kitten. You need someone like me.[5] You're my alpha, you can punish me whenever I talk to Sarah. Then after, we can have great makeup sex."

"Ha! Michelle, this is just another one of your manipulation games "Allie says. "You're baiting your alpha to get punishment and sex. What a naughty girl you are. I'll have to . . . .""

"Whatever my alpha thinks must be true," Michelle says smiling. While assuming her punishment position, she tells Sarah, "Its better this way. Allie isn't ready to understand our bubble world."

"Not here in the park, Michelle. You'll have to wait until we get back to our room."

After Michelle makes a sad face, Allie says, "Don't sulk, Michelle, I hate that." After Michelle smiles, knowing she has earned punishment, Allie catches onto Michelle's game, "Oh, you did it again. You knew I'd hate you sulking and you would earn punishment. This alpha thing is a lot more work than I thought it would be."

Michelle, smiles thinking, "I love training a new alpha. They're so cute while they're learning my games."

---

4 Video Psycho Girlfriend https://www.youtube.com/watch?v=TW0_mzBocwo

5 Music Crazy https://www.youtube.com/watch?v=rB80XpP4dzA

After sulking silently for a while, Michelle responds, "Actually, Allie, my all-powerful and all-knowing alpha, I'm not sulking. I'm getting into the mood to play a new actress."

"Who?"

"No, my beautiful alpha, the game is that you have to guess," is all Michelle says before she jumps into her new character."

"No fair Michelle, I need a clue, and you're not saying anything. Just stop licking me. I can't think . ." but suddenly Allie realizes that's the clue, "Are you playing Lassie,[6] Michelle?"

When Michelle, begins nuzzling Allie," Allie responds by petting her new dog," pleased that she guessed right.

"I'm a handful and I know it Allie, but I'm worth it. Aren't I, Sarah?"

When she hears about Sarah again, Allie decides to up the stakes in Michelle's new game, "Not a word from you my pet until you tinkle like a good dog does walking in the park," as Allie leads Michelle by her neck behind some bushes. Then sternly, "And don't keep me waiting."

Allie expects Michelle to give up the game, but Michelle basks in the glory of teaching her mistress a new game as she obeys her mistress' command.

After Michelle finishes as instructed by her mistress and emerges from the bushes, Allie is stunned by Michelle's dedication to the game. Rubbing the smiling Michelle's neck, Allie gushes "Oh, what a good girl you are Lassie!"

Pleased by Allie's reaction to her game, Michelle smiles thinking "Allie thinks she's in charge, but I'm training Allie to play my games. I think she has promise."

Walking back to their dorm arm in arm, both exhausted girls giggle as they fantasize about the possibilities their new roles offer two aspiring actresses.

* * *

---

6 Video Girl as Dog https://www.youtube.com/watch?v=FElEx3pt51w

When Allie and Michelle return from sunrise yoga, they catch Shelley sneaking out of Luna's room.

"Thanks for respecting our privacy last night Shelley. Hope you and Luna enjoyed your privacy too."

"Luna and I didn't need as much privacy as you two. We both like to take it one step at a time."

Looking at the two slept in beds, "How many steps last night Shelley?"

"Enough steps for me and Shelley, nosy," Luna responds.

"Excellent answers roommates."

"Maybe, we'll double date some time."

"Maybe . . . when Shelley and I are ready" Luna responds. "We're not ready for advanced studies yet."

Still standing in the hall, Shelley sees Gerald leaving Olivia's room. "Hey bro!"

Kaitlyn returns from Scott's apartment. "Hi Shelley! How was your date with Luna?"

"You know about that?"

"Of course . . . I had six texts from girls on this hall last night. Everyone's talking about what a cute couple you two are."[7]

Shelley stands by his door pondering the early morning reshuffling of visitors. "Amazing how it's all so perfectly timed. What are the odds of that? Luna will be fascinated when I tell her about the early morning hall traffic. You can miss a lot if you sleep in."

Then Shelley remembers his early appointment with Sheri for tutoring before his aerobics dance class. "I was a drowning man yesterday. Sheri was so nice to volunteer to help. Can't keep her waiting."

*   *   *

As Kaitlyn enters her room, "Olivia, hope you and Gerald had a good time last night."

"No complaints from me. And Gerald seemed happy when he left."

---

7 Music Video Mirrors https://www.youtube.com/watch?v=uuZE_IRwLNI

"Good. I do so want you to be happy, Olivia."

After a shower, Kaitlyn is off, "Bye Olivia, I'm going to the Foundation for my first blood session."

Running across campus, she sees Nicole, "Hi partner, ready to have them suck our blood?"[8]

"By the way, Olivia introduced me to your friend Gerald last night. He' so perfect for Olivia!"

"What's the matter Nicole? Why that icy stare?"

"You really don't know. Do you?"

* * *

Olivia's phone rings.

Hi Scott. Yes, Kaitlyn's gone.

I agree we should meet to discuss next steps. I can do 11:30. Meet you there."

* * *

"What are they doing to you in this stress test,[9] Allie?"

"I don't know, this is the first one, Michelle. They didn't give me much info. That might be part of the stress."

At the Foundation, "Ms. Lee after I leave the room, we're going to darken the lights and . . . .."

* * *

At the gym, Sheldon spots Sheri walking toward him. Sheldon remembers Michelle's advice, "Say something nice about her clothes."

"I like your leotard, Sheri. Nice color."

---

8 Music Suck Blood https://www.youtube.com/watch?v=020hXHnhd20&list=RD020hX Hnhd20&start_radio=1

9 Music Stress Test https://www.youtube.com/watch?v=xmZ6PduSkN8

Sheri smiles and her eyes brighten. "Oh, thank you. It's my favorite."

"I see you bought better workout clothes Sheldon. Very smart looking."

"Thanks for the shopping advice, Sheri."

After Sheri shows Sheldon a few basic steps, the teacher notices his improvement, "Sheri thank you for helping Sheldon. By the end of the semester, you might turn him into a dancer."

As class ends, Sheldon remembers Michelle's advice that the girl is probably just as nervous as you are. Just man up and ask her. "Sheri, if you have some time, I'd like to see you outside of class."

"That's so sweet Sheldon. I don't know many people at school yet. I'd love to get to know you better.[10] Lunch Sheldon?"

"I have to work for the Foundation at lunch."

"What kind of work?"

"Well, it's hard to explain. I'm involved in an experiment the Foundation is conducting that requires me to sit with nine girls at meals each weekday."

"Why?"

"They call it an immersion experiment. I have no idea why they established the experiment protocols."

"Is aerobics class part of the same experiment."

"Yes, it is."

"Then, I'm part of the experiment too?"

"Yes, Sheri. I guess you are.

"Well, if I'm a girl in the experiment, why can't I sit with you at lunch?"

"You're right. What was I thinking? You are a girl."

* * *

Michelle's phone rings.

"Please calm down Allie. You're not making sense."

"Meet, you outside the Foundation?"

---

10 Music Know you Better https://www.youtube.com/watch?v=VmBSfXSC_dk

"Yes, right away.

"Don't move. It should take me about ten minutes to get there."

* * *

"Listen Blondie! We're in the same experiment together. But that doesn't make us friends! Get it?"

"But, Nicole, why not be open to . . . ."

"Not a chance. You're just my insurance policy. Let's get in there and let them do their stuff. Then we leave separately."

"But . . . ."

"You can fool Olivia and Gerald, but your charm doesn't work on me, Blondie."

A frustrated Kaitlyn, "If only we could talk. You know, to work out whatever this is."

"That's the point Blondie. You don't even understand what this is. Admit it!"

"Er . . . not really."

"Well, I'm not here to educate you. I have better things to do with my life."

Kaitlyn thinks, "This seems so familiar, but different. I've pulled this 'if you don't know'[11] routine on boys. I thought it was smart, but it sounds kind of silly now that Nicole is doing it to me."

* * *

"Michelle, I've never been more grateful to see someone in my life."

Cradling Allie in her arms as Allie stares blankly into space,[12] "What did they do to you girlfriend?"

---

11 Music If You Don't Know Me https://www.youtube.com/watch?v=zTcu7MCtuTs
12 Pic Allie in Shock https://firepitcell.com/wp-content/uploads/2021/12/C16N12-Allee-Experiment-Trauma.jpg

Sobbing, "The scariest thing is that they didn't actually do anything. They fixed it so I did it to myself. How did they get the power do that?"

"I don't understand, but that's not important now. I'm here for you, Allie. And I won't let anyone hurt you. Do you believe that?"

"Oh Michelle, I wish I could. But you don't know what they can do. Believe me."

"Allie, you're a smart girl who isn't normally afraid of anything. So, if you're this upset, it must be terrible. Let's get you away from the Foundation. We'll figure out the next step in the safety of your room."

"There's no safe place. Not for me. Not anymore," as Allie looks into Michelle's eyes, with her lips trembling and total despair in her eyes.

Michelle summons up her best mom voice to sooth her quivering girl-friend and hugs her, "Allie, honey, I believe you. The Foundation did something terrible to you. But I also know you're a strong girl. And together we'll be able to deal with this. We'll keep you safe.[13] Now, don't you agree?"

As Allie hesitantly nods yes, "Good Girl. You're strong Allie. Now remember that and we'll sort the rest out at home, OK honey?"

* * *

Back at the dorm Allie falls asleep with Michelle stroking her hair.

Michelle thinks, "Maybe I do have a certain mom talent."

"Michelle, glad you're back. Everything you said was right."

"Quiet Shelley," Michelle whispers, pointing to the sleeping Allie.

Shelley, never very observant, "The Foundation's experiment is working out great for me. I've never been able to talk with girls before. I never understood girls. But you and the experiment are helping me. It's changing my life."

"Nice to hear Shelley. But now's not the time."

"Allie's Foundation experiment today was horrible. Stop focusing on you. I need you to help me with Allie."

"Oh . . .."

---

13 Music Video Safe and Sound https://www.youtube.com/watch?v=RzhAS_GnJIc

"I just got her calmed down.[14] So, don't say anything to her about the Foundation or your experiment. And Shelley, watch out for yourself. These Foundation people don't care about anyone. All they care about is collecting data."

"What do you want me to do?"

"Go find some pot.[15] Maybe that will help Allie."

"Why are you smiling, Shelley?

"I was just wondering whether my mom would have ever sent me out to get pot. Michelle, you're the coolest mom."

"Please stop this mom business for now. I can't take care of both you and Allie at the same time."

"Yes, Mom."

Michelle ponders her mothering of Shelley and Allie, "So, one child is a basket case one day and the other is flying high. The next day they trade places. And I'm left to pick up the pieces. I wasn't expecting this. Being a mom is a challenging role. But it's not leaving me much time to play hot girl Michelle. My children are so . . . draining. How did my mother deal with the four children? Scary, but I'll just have to do it my way."[16]

* * *

"Ms. Korosec? Yes."

"Ms. Wilson? Yes."

"I have instructions that all procedures are to be conducted on the two of you in the same room at the same time. Normally, we give you privacy. Are you both OK with this new procedure?"

"That's right. I'm her insurance policy,"[17] Kaitlyn responds to a perplexed nurse, "You know, so the Foundation doesn't kill all the black people. Nicole will explain it to you."

---

14 Music Video Calm Down https://www.youtube.com/watch?v=iqpr5QQU5C8

15 Movie Clip https://www.youtube.com/watch?v=xrsbjjuDTzU

16 Music My Way https://www.youtube.com/watch?v=f3U0Xbnis5o

17 Music Insurance https://www.youtube.com/watch?v=SFq-ONsLnP8

A mortified Nicole chimes in "Believe me, I never . . ." as nurse methodically goes about her work.

After Kaitlyn's blood extraction. "Well, that was easy. Nicole, my mother was a Red Cross volunteer for blood drives. My whole family gave blood several times a year."

"Of course, our life is like a fairy tale, Blondie. My mother was a drug addict. My brother was a dealer. My family has a different history with needles."

"Sorry Nicole . . . I didn't know."

"There's a lot you don't know, Blondie."[18]

"But I'd like to learn . . . ."

"Find another teacher, Blondie." Then, as the nurse begins drawing Nicole's blood, "I've got other things . . . ."

"Nicole . . .. Nicole. Can you hear me?"

Looking up at Kaitlyn and the Nurse, "What happened?"

"You fainted."[19]

"No way."

"Yes, you did. Right in the middle of a sentence. In the middle of . . .. saying something nasty to me. Have you fainted before?"

"No, but I never gave blood before."

"Ms. Korosec, we're about to close for the day. Will you take her home? Or should I call medics to drive her?"

"No medics," Nicole says. "I'm OK, I'll go home with Blondie."

"Don't think today changes anything, Kaitlyn. You're still the same clueless blond you were before I fainted."

As the two girls walk across campus slowly, "Nicole, lean on me until you get your balance back."

"I'm OK now. Time for you to go your way and me to go mine".

"See you next week, Nicole. That will be the interesting one where they start putting our processed blood back into us. I've never done that. Have you?"

---

18 Music Video Blond https://www.youtube.com/watch?v=ku2YavtBEww
19 Video Fainting https://www.youtube.com/watch?v=4bewQ6rYSf4

"Not unless you count the transfusion I got when that junkie stabbed me, Blondie."

"Stabbed? How old were you?"

"About six or seven?"

"Why did they stab you?"

"She said my brother ripped her off in a drug deal. I got the payback[20] instead of my brother. But that was a lie. My brother was an honest dealer."

"Blondie, why are you hugging me?"

"Because you're a broken soul. And I'm going to help you fix yourself."

"But . . .."

"I just know that's the reason why I'm your insurance policy."

"No Blondie, you're my insurance because I don't trust white people."

"Maybe, but I think it's a cry for help in a way that lets you avoid admitting you want help."

"Blondie, you're still crazy, but I can understand why Olivia likes you and thinks you're smarter than you sound sometimes."

"Did Olivia really say I'm smart? That means a lot to me."

As Nicole walks away, Kaitlyn follows at a distance to make sure she gets to her dorm safely.

*   *   *

At lunch, "What's the matter Sheldon?" Sheri asks.

My roommate's girlfriend is having a nervous breakdown or something, Sheri.

"Oh . . . I know how she must feel. I was so depressed Sunday night sitting alone my room. It seemed like everyone else on campus was making friends except me. I cried myself to sleep. But I'm feeling much better now."

*   *   *

---

20 Music Video Payback https://www.youtube.com/watch?v=SjCqQD-h3Q0

"Thanks for interrupting your day, Olivia."

"This was unexpected. We definitely should check in with Command Central."

Here goes.

"Agents 1 and 2, have you disabled the geo-tracking function on your phone?"

"Affirmative."

"Have you succeeded in your mission?"

"Negative."

"Do you need help?"

"We do need Mission Control to evaluate new developments."

"State the nature of the new developments."

"Agents 1 and 2 are emotionally involved with target Princess and believe we cannot execute target Princess if that should become advisable to accomplish mission objectives."

"Mission Control will evaluate and provide instructions. Contact Mission Control at 14:00 hours tomorrow to receive instructions."

"Scott, last summer I would have accepted this as normal, because our mission is so important. The mission is still just as important, but something has changed me."

"Affirmative. Princess is changing both of us."

*   *   *

Later that afternoon at the dorm, when Allie awakens, she sees Michelle looking down at her, "I'm here for you, girlfriend."[21]

"I know. It's comforting, Michelle."

"I sounded crazy. Didn't I? It's just so hard to explain why the Foundation scared me so much today."

"Then don't try to explain now. You'll find a way later."

"You know, I think Shelley is right."

"About what?"

---

21 Music Here for You https://www.youtube.com/watch?v=b8PPap4dJog

"You're a natural Mom. And it isn't just an act. No one is that good a performer."

"Maybe you're right. But for now, why don't you take a nice long shower. That should relax you."

"Yes, Mom."

"Allie, it's going to be weird in bed together if you keep calling me Mom."

"We've been in weird territory since we met, Michelle. No turning back now."

While Allie showers, Michelle gets a little me time to reflect on what's been happening to her. "This mom stuff is a little spooky," Michelle thinks. "Being a mom wasn't part of my script. First, Shelley? Now, Allie? What's next?"

"These new hormones are more powerful than I thought. Changing my mind now. Will I even recognize the new me[22] the hormones are creating?"

Panicking, Michelle asks herself, Will I still be me? I'm losing control. Should I turn back?[23] Can I turn back?"

Calming down, Michelle thinks, "But Shelley and Allie both need me so much now. How can I not . . . at least . . . try to help them? But that's not being a mom. It's just being a good friend. I'd do that without the hormones. Michael would have done that, I think. No, probably not. No, I don't want to be Michael again. I'm a better person now."

"I just wish, I had more control. Not turn over control to the hormones. Wait, this isn't just my problem. Everyone has emotions. They're a part of me. The hormones are just releasing what was already inside me. Every little girl has to learn when to control her emotions[24] and when emotions are leading to the light. And each girl makes their own decisions.

---

22 Music Video "New You" by Zolita https://www.youtube.com/watch?v=R9SQl0cSfI8
23 Music Video Turn Back Time https://www.youtube.com/watch?v=iEXSxUraLCI
24 Music Video Control https://www.youtube.com/watch?v=5vrP3YB7iAg

I'm a new girl, but I can learn too. I want to choose my own way like most girls do.[25] I can find my own way, I can, and I will."

Taking several bottles of hormone pills from her drawer, Michelle muses, "I do love my hormones. What did people do before hormones? Why would I have been satisfied being just Michael, when I can be a mom?"

When Allie returns for her shower, she asks, "Michelle, deep thoughts? What's bothering my girlfriend?"

"Oh, nothing, Allie, I'm just tired, I guess. We've both had a tough day."

"Uh huh, don't know what I would have done without you today, Michelle. Time for your alpha to take care of her kitten."

"Mothering does have its rewards," Michelle thinks as Allie's sweet kisses envelope her.

---

25 Music Video Most Girls https://www.youtube.com/watch?v=qBB_QOZNEdc

17

Finding Your Tribe

Thursday was the big tribal day. The day all the sororities and frats sent out their pledge invites. Only 20% of the freshman class rushed the Greek organizations, but for the hundreds of students who did, mass panic is setting in.

"Am I good enough?"[1]

"Will they accept me?"

"What will I tell my parents if they don't?"

The ritual is the same each year. At precisely 10:00 am all the sororities and frats simultaneously text acceptances to students waiting impatiently to learn their social fates.

9:55 am.

The experienced professors don't even try to teach. Just before 10 am they announce . . . "Cell phone break. Class resumes in 15 minutes . . . and the material I'm teaching will be on the exam. So . . . break ends in 15 minutes."

At 9:59 am Kaitlyn prays, "Dear God . . . I trust your judgment. Please send me to a sorority with caring sisters and help me be a good sister to them. And let all my friends find the places that are best for them."

As Kaitlyn finishes her prayer, hundreds of text message pings permeate the school, followed by,"

'Thank you, God."

"Yes!"

---

1 Movie Clip Not Good Enough https://www.youtube.com/watch?v=b65C_muXajk

"Of course, they want me."

"Not my first choice . . . but OK."

Then, laughing and sobbing and mass texting to friends and relatives.

There were no rejection texts. If you didn't hear . . . you weren't in. After ten minutes, rejected candidates realized their fates. "This must be a mistake. Did I give them the wrong number?"

Life is cruel.

* * *

10:02 am Kaitlyn begins making calls.

"Mom, I got in. No, I was never really worried. I just thought you might be."

Reaching Scott's voicemail, a disappointed Kaitlyn leaves a message "Scott, it's me. I feel like a Princess today. Can we celebrate tonight? I mean after my sorority meeting. So, it might be late."

"Olivia? . . . You were accepted too! Delta Sigma Theta? Oh, I'm so happy for you!"

Then, texts to three girls she hoped would become her sisters.

* * *

Oblivious to the Greek annual pledge ritual, the non-Greek tribes on campus also hold big recruiting drives.

2:00 pm

Shelley and Luna attend the Hackers Anonymous meeting together.

"Hi I'm Sanjay Singh, President. I'll wait a few minutes for stragglers to arrive before telling you about the exciting things we plan this year," as Sanjay looks out over the nearly empty room.

"OK, five people is a good turnout. Our club is for people who love to hack computer systems, but for good purposes. We don't steal or destroy information. We let people and businesses know where their weaknesses are so they can fix them before the bad guys get in."

BLAH!

BLAH!

BLAH!

"And my last point is to remind you that sometimes the businesses we help hire us to fix their security weaknesses. So, this is a club where you can actually make money while improving you hacking skills."

"Luna, I'm really excited we're doing this together. A hot girlfriend and computers . . .. I'm living the dream."

"Shelley . . . this will be so much fun. And don't forget about earning money."

*   *   *

14:00 Hours

"Agents 1 and 2 here. Do you read us? This is the Professor. I'm taking control of Operation Princess. Now tell me what is going on!

"Well . . .."

"Have you two lost your minds? Are you abandoning years of training just because Princess has a cute smile and a big heart?"

"No Mam. Of course not, Mam."

"Well then, . . . act like it. I want your new action plan by 22:00 Hours at the latest."

*   *   *

3:00 pm

At the Black Student Union, Nicole recruits new people to the struggle.

"Can't win a revolution sitting on the sidelines."

"We'll need big boys like you when the action starts."

"What's the matter Hakeem? Afraid you'll lose your tampon? Man up!"

*   *   *

4:00 pm

Scott texts Kaitlyn, "Congrats Princess! Sorry can't tonight. Business meetings. I'll explain another time."

* * *

5:00 pm

Michelle and Allie do a dramatic reading to open the drama club meeting.

"Hope you all join our drama club. Where else can you see two hot girls like us kiss?"

* * *

18:00 Hours

"Scott, the Professor is right."

"Of course, she is Olivia. We both have to get back on track."

"Of course, we do."

"So, it's just the two of us. No room for Kaitlyn and Gerald. And we do whatever our mission requires."

Affirmative. Affirmative.

As they hear themselves speak, both Scott and Olivia know it won't be that easy.

"Olivia, you know I think about Princess a lot."

"Yes . . . I know.'

"Can you forgive me?

"Normally, not, Scott. But maybe I can with Kaitlyn, but only because I know how she makes me feel too, more grounded in reality and trusting of the world. Kaitlyn and I have girl crushes on each other."

"I know, Olivia, sometimes it's made me jealous watching the two of you together."

"Jealous? Of whom?"

"Of both of you. You two seem like the happiest roommates I've ever seen."

"Scott, we both have to be careful around Kaitlyn. If she's an agent for the other side, we could easily let something slip."

"You're right, Olivia. Either one of us could slip up. We'll have to watch out for each other."

"Yes, we're a team, Scott. We're meant to be together."

"Yes we are. The Professor and the-Judge are never wrong. And my father . . . the Senator. They've been planning our futures together for years. It'll be perfect, Olivia."

"I know Scott, but . . . it's more than that. We do love one another. Don't we? I mean . . . we can't live our lives just because our parents approve."

As Scott and Olivia embrace, he says, "No we can't. And we won't. We definitely have our own thing going. What we both have with Kaitlyn is different. We'll get over it . . . like the flu."

"Oh, Scott! This feels so . . . so much better than words,[2]" as the couple wipe out the rest of the world and renew physical vows taken years before.

* * *

8 pm

Just before Kaitlyn walks into her first sorority meeting, "God, please help me to be a good sister."

"Oh. Hi Sharon! So happy we're sisters."

"Kelly, I just knew you'd be here. I mean how could they not be excited about you?"

* * *

22:00 Hours

"Yes Professor."

"Here's our plan . . . .."

---

2 Clip Sex in the City https://www.youtube.com/watch?v=NyqyOIgVscE

BLAH!

BLAH!

BLAH

"Yes, we'll make that change."

"Yes, we'll update you daily."

"Whew! Glad that interrogation is over, Olivia."

"My mom can be intense. I grew you with that. But she can be a bit much for newbies."

*　*　*

11 pm

Before an exhausted Kaitlyn falls asleep in her room, "God, I miss Scott. Please watch over him."

"Wonder what Olivia is doing tonight?"[3]

---

3 Movie Clip Camelot https://www.youtube.com/watch?v=FhKF6WVjy3o

18

Beware: Actresses on the Edge

Michelle and Allie take a break from rehearsing.

"Allie, I'm curious about something."

"What, girlfriend?"

"I know this is silly, but . . . was Michael a good actor? You saw Michael's last performance. You're one of the few people who've seen both Michael and Michelle perform."

"Does my sub want to play the actress anxiety game again?"

"Well, it's just that . . . ."

"Don't worry, girlfriend. I totally get that game. I play it all the time. Before every performance I feel the urge to run out of the theater. Everyone will hate me. No matter how many good reviews . . . I always become that insecure little girl."

"Allie, it's so . . . frustrating. Sometimes . . . I think . . . hope . . .pray . . . that conquering my anxiety tonight will make it go away forever. But it always comes back."

"I know . . . me too . . . That's the price we pay for the joy of being on stage. The price of feeling totally vulnerable and insecure[4] . . . over . . . over . . . over. Once we're in it, there no exit. That's one reason people fall in love with actresses. We're perpetually vulnerable. Being insecure and vulnerable is so . . . sexy."

"But Allie, we beat it each performance. Why doesn't it go away?"

---

4 Video Actress Insecure https://www.youtube.com/watch?v=TG4hX6LBMjI

"I don't know, Michelle. We're both victims of the same illness. Like we're characters in the movie 'Black Swan.'[5] I so feel like Natalie Portman sometimes." Is there a cure?"

"Allie, I'm not sure I want a cure as much as a treatment to minimize the pain."

"Michelle let's make a pact. Before each performance, we'll always remind each how wonderful we're going to be."

Hugging Allie, "How's this? 'Allie, you have nothing to worry about. The audience will adore you.'"

"That's a good start . . . keep practicing that. I may add to the script later. And a little kiss would be a nice touch."

"Now . . . back to your anxiety.

"Yes, I'm your girlfriend, Allie. So, remember its always about Michelle," in a fake stern voice that breaks into a giggle.

"Duly noted, girlfriend."

"Michael was good enough that I remembered him this long. That's practically a lifetime. Michael had a distinct approach to his part. Most people wouldn't notice, but I'm interested in theater. So, I notice small things."

"Allie, when did you connect Michael and Michelle? When I first kissed you when we played truth or dare last week?"

"No . . . you kiss like a girl. We wouldn't be together now if you didn't. I had no clue then."

"You mentioned something about my hands once when we held hands walking across campus together. Was it then?"

"No, your hands are a little bigger than mine, but soft. You do remember every detail. Don't you Michelle."

"Becoming Michelle has forced me to focus on the little things[6] that don't seem important . . . until they are."

"Well, since it's killing you not to know. . . it was during our first acting class together, when you were auditioning for this play. Something about

---

5 Movie Clip Black Swan https://www.youtube.com/watch?v=dwD4JZsAuew
6 Music Little Things https://www.youtube.com/watch?v=XbAlPugythw

you reminded me[7] of an earlier performance I'd seen. At first, I thought it wasn't real. But the feeling that I had seen you perform before stayed with me. I've learned to trust my instincts. So, I kept thinking about it . . . or meditating. . . until Michael appeared in my mind. I had taken a photo of the playbill that had his picture and full name. So, I checked my phone and sure enough there it was."

"I know this is a silly question. But . . . it's important to me. Was Michael better on stage? Or Michelle?"

"On stage . . . I don't know yet. In real life . . . Michelle has been at school for almost two weeks. As far as I know, no one knows about Michael. So, Michelle must be giving a great performance. It must take work."

"Tell me about it! Every detail has to be perfect."

"Now that we've got a plan to deal with our acting anxieties, what about your other fears, Michelle? Isn't hiding Michael a difficult way to live? Why do you go to so much trouble? Lots of trans people are pretty open about their past."

"I don't think of it as hiding Michael. It's more like letting Michelle be the star now. Its Michelle's turn. And I won't let Michael spoil it."

"Does Michael want to spoil Michelle's turn?"

"No, not really. At least I hope not. Michael is nice. It's just that Michelle decided it's her time[8] and there can be only one star at a time. You're in theater, Allie. You know all about professional jealousy and fighting for the spotlight."

"But . . . who is the real person, Michael or Michelle?"

"Both . . . and neither. They're both parts of me. . . or . . . maybe I should say parts that I play. We're like a team. There's no 'I' in team is what they say, right? I, or we, live for being on stage. None of us could exist without that. So, being Michael for 18 years was real. Now, I like playing Michelle's role better. So, we're both real and we're all acting. That might sound crazy, but that's the way I experience my life."

"Are there any other people in there Michelle?"

7 Music Video U Remind Me https://www.youtube.com/watch?v=XSoEwjiW4IM
8 Music My Time https://www.youtube.com/watch?v=O9dSZUEZaPA

"I don't really know. Maybe in the future. Who knows? Over a lifetime, I may play many roles. Sometimes I worry about that. Sometimes I desperately want to know . . . so much that it hurts. But it's also exciting not knowing. I use that excitement when I perform. It makes me perform . . . on the edge."

"Michelle, that's exactly what I remembered about Michael's performance. He was on the edge the whole time. I kept waiting for Michael to fail as he pushed in every scene right to the edge between being great and failing miserably right in front of the audience. It was very brave. I kept thinking, that was good. Don't spoil it by going over the edge. Time to pay it safe and wait for the accolades after you finish. But Michael jumped right along the edge the whole performance. I remembered Michael so vividly because Michael became one of my role models. I wanted to try to be more like him. Stop playing it safe. And not just on stage. It's helped me be more honest with other people about me."

"Allie, both Michael and Michelle humbly thank you for noticing," as Michelle curtseys as if to an audience.

"And that's what I saw in your audition in class last week. Right at the edge[9] between climbing the heights of glory and falling off the cliff the whole time. I knew something reminded me of Michael, but I didn't have words to express it until now. And Michelle insists on living on the edge off stage too. That's one reason why you do it. Isn't it?"

Getting misty eyed, "Allie, I can't tell you how much it means to me that you understand. Most people don't. Living on the edge is so lonely and exhausting."

"Maybe it would be easier for you, if you help me learn to perform and live on the edge with you."

"Having you as a lover and friend on the edge is my dream, Allie. A dream that began when we first met. Do you remember? I do. I remember thinking to myself . . . there's a girl who may be born to live the edge. At the time, I didn't realize I partly owed that to Michael. In a way . . . maybe . . . you're the bridge between Michael and Michelle. Michael knew it would

---

9 Music Video Edge https://www.youtube.com/watch?v=QeWBS0JBNzQ

be difficult for Michelle, so he performed on the edge that night to inspire you. There's no way to really know but thinking of it that way helps me. Thanks for sharing." Running the tips of her fingers along Allie's neck as she smiles and whispers in Allie's ear, "I'm going to be so sweet to you tonight, girlfriend."

Then, both girls return to rehearsing and experiencing both the sweetness and the anxiety of living life on the edge.

19

Football Isn't Just a Game

Kaitlyn wakes up pondering her relationship with Scott. "I haven't heard from Scott in two days. Either he's dead . . . or he'll wish he was dead. Who does he think he is? Well, I'm not going to sit around waiting for him to call. Not like I did yesterday. Today, I'm back in action. Today, I'm going to help Olivia have a good time. God only knows how much she needs that. She's been so worried these last two days, but won't tell me what she's worried about."

Kaitlyn impatiently stares at her sleeping roommate until she can't stand it any longer.

"Wake up, Olivia!"

"It's so exciting! How can you possibly sleep in today? Today the day of all days, the first home football game?"[1]

Its only 10 o'clock Kaitlyn. We have plenty of time. The game doesn't start until 2 pm."

"Not the game, silly. They've already started tailgating for the football game.[2] Today, we'll go to our first tailgate parties. I've been collecting invites from frats all week. . . and we shouldn't miss any of them."

Time for sophisticated young ladies like us to transform into wild Wolfpack women.

*   *   *

---

1 Music Video Football https://www.youtube.com/watch?v=1hvEmhWdaXg
2 Music Video Tailgate Party Song https://www.youtube.com/watch?v=54SZjhaFugQ

Olivia and Kaitlyn arrive halfway through the tailgate parties.

"Kaitlyn, notice how all the guys are dressed in shorts and T-shirts and we're dressed in cocktail dresses.[3] Life is so unfair!"

"Unfair? The boys work so hard just to get a little sex. Look at them . . . cooking . . . pouring drinks. All in the hopes of meeting a fair young maiden and getting her so drunk they can have their way with her. You and I can just walk in late and have sex any time we want. Is that fair? Would you rather be them? Or us?

"When you put it that way Kaitlyn, definitely us!"

"So, who cares about fair? This is the way the world works, Olivia. Enjoy what we have."

"Kaitlyn, its only noon and half of these people are already wasted."

"Is this Olivia talking? Or your mother? I can't tell."

"Maybe it is the Professor talking."

"Take it from me, roommate. You don't want to bring your mother to your first tailgate party. Repeat after me: 'Go home mom!'"

"Kaitlyn, that's silly."

"Yes, it is. And this is your day to be silly. So, say it."

"Go home mom!"

"Good. You have a lot of catching up to do."

"Me?"

"Yep! I got a little tipsy the night we first met. My turn to see how you perform under the influence."

"That's not going to happen. I have no intention of starring in one of these boys' young maiden fantasies."[4]

"Olivia, I trusted you to take care of me when we met. Don't you trust me?"

"That's not the question."

"What's the question then, Olivia?"

"The question is, can I trust me?"

---

3 Video Girls Tailgate https://www.youtube.com/watch?v=_JwIwW7zURY
4 Music Video Baby Boy https://www.youtube.com/watch?v=8ucz_pm3LX8

"That's why you need to trust me. I've got your back, roommate. I'm not drinking at all today. I promise, I'll prevent you from doing anything off the charts stupid. Do you think I could live with myself if you're running for President some day and your opponent starts circulating nude pictures of you running across the football field chased by one of these rednecks? Nope, no way that's going to happen on my watch. You're safe with me."

"Nude? Rednecks? I wasn't afraid of doing anything like that!"

Well then, Olivia, you have nothing to worry about, do you?"

"Kaitlyn, you have a strange logic that backs a person into a corner."

"Forget about logic corners, just live a little and trust you roommate."

"Well . . . ."

Before Olivia can answer, Kaitlyn starts Olivia's party, "Hey handsome. My friend here would love a drink. Think you can find her one?

"This way, I live to serve lovely ladies like you."

As they follow their escort, "Olivia, remember when I told you that you were my first black friend?"

"Who could forget that magic moment, Kaitlyn?

"Well, my first black friend, welcome to a redneck tailgate party. Relax and enjoy. I've got your back for the day and evening."

"Ladies, I hope you enjoy these drinks."

"I'm not drinking, but my friend Olivia here has some catching up to do. So, she'll take them both."

"Olivia, you've come to the right place to catch up. By the way, my name is Kyle and you are the guests of Delta Kappa Epsilon fraternity. We live to help young women like yourselves enjoy life."

"Thanks Kyle. Down the hatch, Olivia."

As Olivia chugs the bottle of beer, Kaitlyn says "Olivia, under all your polish, you have the makings of a true redneck."[5]

"Remember our talking about sororities and politics, Olivia?"

"Of course, my entire life is designed to be a political winner."

"Here's another beer. It will help you appreciate my new plan."

5 Tailgate Queen https://www.youtube.com/watch?v=h-RCE3-O6D8

"What plan, Kaitlyn?"

"Well, why not have a backup plan to get the redneck vote. I mean just in case black people think you're too white. Or maybe you can win both groups!"

"Too white?"

"Well, that's what your parents are afraid of, isn't it? Why they wanted you to join a black sorority, isn't it? And let's face it, you're smart, but you talk a lot like Hillary Clinton. What a loser. Trust me. I'm more like Bill. Not the brightest, but smart enough. And a people person. OMG, wouldn't it be great if you became President and I was your press secretary? Then, I could translate your great ideas into something people can understand."

"I'm having a little trouble following your plan Kaitlyn, but I'm sure it will sound lovely after another drink."

"That's because it is lovely Olivia. We're a great team. Time to get to our seats to see the game. Here, put these two beers in your purse."

* * *

Leaving Carter-Finley stadium after the game.

"Kaitlyn, we won! Winning is my favorite thing in life."[6]

"I know Olivia, but did you have fun?"

"Yes, I definitely had fun."

"Good. Now, lean on me. I'll get you home."

"Hi handsome. Can my friend and I hitch a ride back to Bagwell Hall? With big blue eyes and pouty lip, "We'd be ever so grateful. Really we would."

In the backseat of the car, Kaitlyn whispers into Olivia's ear "This is the reason girls wear cocktail dresses to football games. It so much easier getting a ride home."

Olivia giggles, "You're so right. Kaitlyn. I absolutely adore being driven places and taken care of by servants.[7] It's like having a magic genie in lamp.

6 Video Winning https://www.youtube.com/watch?v=BBre0xNcr5c
7 Music Video Chauffeur https://www.youtube.com/watch?v=vTzhj6_N4N8

That's what I've thought since I was a little girl. But I've never said it out loud to anyone before."

"Let's keep that thought out of your presidential campaign, Olivia. Might not go over well with voters. I'll be like your secret Genie."[8]

"OK, Kaitlyn. Know what I wish? Oh . . . thanks . . . I needed another beer."

Back at their dorm, "Thanks for the ride. Yes, see you then."

As Kaitlyn helps Olivia up the stairs "Wasn't that boy sweet!"

"Yes, very sweet, Kaitlyn."

"So glad you agree, because we're double dating with him and his friend on Wednesday night."

"Oh, hi Shelley! Can you help me get Olivia up the stairs?"

Halfway up the stairs, "Kaitlyn, something else I need," as all the beer she drank pours down Olivia' legs.

"Oops! Did I do that? Sooooo . . . sorry."

"Eew! Your roommate has a big bladder. I'm totally soaked."

"Shelley, you need to listen to me. It's important. First of all, have you ever seen the women's bathroom in a stadium? Talk about eww! Olivia's too much of a lady to go in a stadium bathroom. Might be OK for me, but Olivia is finer. Second, this is totally my fault. She usually doesn't party like this. So don't tell anyone about her peeing incident."[9]

"Who would care? Half the campus is already wasted and the post-game parties are just beginning."

"I know, but you're not listening. Third, Shelley you're a virgin. Am I right? You don't need to answer that. I think they call that a rhetorical question. Next rhetorical question. You have girl juice all over you. You reek of it. When's the next time that's going to happen?"

"OK, so I'm lucky to have been showered in girl juice. What do you want me to do?"

"Thanks Shelley. You're going to help me take Olivia into the shower and wash Olivia's scent off all of us."

8 Music Video Genie in Bottle https://www.youtube.com/watch?v=kIDWgqDBNXA

9 Video Hold It https://www.youtube.com/watch?v=Tzq1FVwJrdU

"Three of us in the shower. You mean together?"

"Of course, together. I can't hold her up and wash her at the same time. I might drop her. One of us has to hold her and the other wash her."

"You mean naked?"

"Well, all our clothes are soaked with Olivia's scent. So, as soon as my clothes get wet in the shower, I'm ditching mine. You do what you want, Shelley."

Seeing Shelley blush, "Don't worry, I'll be too busy to look at you Shelley. What's wrong?"

"Why are you staring at me with that perplexed look, Kaitlyn? I'm a boy you know. I shouldn't be seeing her naked. And what if I . . .? What about the morning after?"[10]

"Shelley, Olivia won't remember this tomorrow."

"But . . .."

"Shelley, you need to man up and help me and Olivia. Get naked with us. Let's all get clean. Then, we forget about it. OK?"

"I think I can do everything except the forget about it part. Can't promise that."

"Fine, maybe it'll be a treasured moment for the rest of your life, but now we all need to get wet and strip."[11] As the trio enter the shower, "I'll strip first. Then you. Then, we'll work on Olivia together. OK?"

"Good, now I'll hold Olivia and you strip. OK, now hold Olivia and I'll get her clothes off. I'm probably better at getting bras off than you are. OK, now hold her and give me the soap. I'll start cleaning the three of us."

As they emerge from the shower, "Good job Shelley. I'll dry her off. You go into our closets and get us some dry pajamas."

As the three get back to Olivia's room they lay Olivia in bed, "Thanks Shelley. I know that was a bit unusual for you. I owe you one. A hug?"

"And Shelley, someday Olivia's going to become President and I'll be her Press Secretary. When you see us on the news, it's OK to tell your wife and kids you showered with the President and her Press Secretary. But if

---

10 Music The Morning After https://www.youtube.com/watch?v=msgxhVgUc6I

11 Video Shower https://www.youtube.com/watch?v=2LwQfyiKX9o

you tell anyone else, I'll have to issue an official denial and then have the CIA kill you. Understood?"

"Kaitlyn, I almost believe you'd do that."

"What do you mean almost? That was a promise. And I always keep my promises."

As Sheldon helps Kaitlyn steer Olivia into her room, "Shelley . . . "

"What now Kaitlyn?"

The last words Shelley hears after as he leaves the room, Kaitlyn grins, "Just wanted to tell you that you're not as small as most of the girls think."

*   *   *

After Kaitlyn puts Olivia to bed, she visits Michelle.

"Is Shelley coming back soon?"

"No some big computer game contest over at the boys' end of the hall. He probably won't be back for hours."

"Good, I need some girl-talk time."

"Michelle, what's with Shelley? The two of you sleep in the same room, but he's shy about seeing girls? I don't get it."

"Men are strange creatures, Kaitlyn. Don't expect me to explain them."

"Michelle, maybe you're the smart one."

"What do you mean?"

"Well, you and Allie are a couple, right?" Michelle nods.

"And you two seem happy together, right?" Michelle nods again.

"Well . . . I'm just so confused Michelle."

Kaitlyn gets a little misty eyed. "Scott and I seemed like the prefect couple. The dates were fun and bed was amazing. You know. . . the kind where you just melt into the guy's arms, and he takes you for a ride and all you want is to please him."

"More than you know, Kaitlyn. I go weak in the knees when that happens too. But Kaitlyn, do you think you should be telling me this?"

"Oh yes, I see how you are with both Shelley and Allie. You have amazing abilities to comfort people.[12] It's a real gift. Do you know who I would talk to about this if I was home?"

"Don't tell me. Let me guess. Your mom?" Michelle barely gets the words out.

"Yes, I have a great mom. But she's not here now. And you are. And my mom wouldn't understand. She's too old. But you're just a little older than I am. So, I really need your advice. Please?"

As Kaitlyn begins sobbing, Michelle hugs her and says "He's not worth crying over, Princess,"[13] while thinking, "OMG, do I have another child? Transitioning from sexy college girl to a mom in just two weeks? Is this my next role? But I was never a teenage girl like Kaitlyn's Mom was. How do I deal with this? I can't turn her away. She needs me. But I don't know what to tell her."

After being held for a few minutes, Kaitlyn's big wet eyes look up at Michelle as she asks, "What am I going to do, Michelle?"

"Tell me about your mom, Kaitlyn. I bet she faced some problems with your dad. How did your Mom deal with that?"

"Yes, mom said Daddy got scared after they were dating for six months. He disappeared from her life. He was a police officer. He saw a lot of bad things. So, he was kind of moody. Didn't want to talk about things with my mom."

"And what did your mom do about that?"

"Mom waited for several weeks. Didn't try to see him at all. And then, she went to a bar she knew he liked. And she waited there for two nights. The second night, he walked in with other police officers. He was so happy to see her that he left his buddies, and they took a walk together."

"Michelle, is that what I should do? Oh, it is. Isn't it? Allie was so right. You helped her and now you're helping me. I'm going to tell all our sorority sisters what great advice you give. We'll all come to you with our problems."

---

12 Music Video Mother https://www.youtube.com/watch?v=7_fqP-XJg2E
13 Music Video Princesses Don't Cry https://www.youtube.com/watch?v=2tJjplMngFE

Seeing the worried look on Michelle's face, "I mean . . . if that's OK with you, Michelle."

"Let's see Kaitlyn. Let's see. For now, you've had a big day. You need to sleep. And I need to talk with someone I trust."

Kaitlyn hugging Michelle,[14] "Oh Michelle, I just know this is your special talent. You're the next best thing to having my mom here at school. Years from now, at class reunions, all the girls will remember how much you helped them."

* * *

Michelle makes a call.

"Hi Mom. It's me, Michelle. Sorry to call so late."

"No . . . I'm fine. School has been great."

"Can't a girl call her mom without an emergency?"

"Nothing much . . . maybe I just wanted to hear your voice."

"You're sweet too, Mom."

"There is one thing . . . I was wondering whether you could . . . maybe . . . visit me on parents' weekend?"

"Yes, it's in two weeks."

"Well . . . I could use a little girl talk."

"No . . . not about boyfriends . . . or girlfriends, but you never know what it'll be two weeks from now. It's hard to explain . . . more like . . . how to be a mom. How did you do it all?

"My sisters? Yes . . . two of them are mothers now too. I don't think of them that way. but I guess you're all part of the same club."

"Sure, I'd like that."

"Dad? Do you think he can handle it? He's been good about my transition, but that was in private. My dorm may not be the best time or place. What do you think Mom?"

---

14 Pic Kaitlyn Hug Michelle https://firepitcell.com/wp-content/uploads/2021/12/C19N14-Kaitlyn-Hugs-Michelle-.jpg

"Yes . . . for us it'll be girls' weekend,[15] not parents' weekend.

"Tell Dad I'll be home for his birthday. He'll probably like that better."

"I miss you too. Mom . . . thanks for always being there for me."

"Yes . . . I am. Just a few tears. Yes . . . happy tears. I do that sometimes now."

"We should talk about that when you visit. It's a little confusing."

---

15 Music Video Girls' Weekend https://www.youtube.com/watch?v=WYPJQ9r6TyU

20

Experiments Become Intense

Kaitlyn and Nicole meet outside the Foundation before their second blood appointment.

"Why'd you lose your adorable smile, Blondie? Break a nail or something catastrophic like that? No, I can see they're all perfectly manicured as usual. So, what's bringing clouds into your sparkling sunshine day?"

"Nicole? Why do you hate me so much? I mean, I know you have some issues with people in general. But it seems more personal with me. Why?"

"Maybe it's because you live a perfect life[1], Kaitlyn. Maybe it's because people's eyes light up and smile when they see you. Or maybe it's because a cop[2] killed my brother and your father was a cop. Pick one, Blondie. Pick them all. I don't care."

"Now what . . .? Don't cry Blondie. I didn't mean it. At least not today. I don't really hate you."[3]

"You don't?"

"No, you'd be dead if I did. Trust me. For real! I'm just a little edgier than you're used to. Trash talk is normal where I come from. Apparently, not where you grew up. I just lay it on thicker for you because you're way off the charts for being . . . so . . . so . . . See, you're so far out there in cheeriness land that I can't even begin to describe it.

---

1 Music Video Perfect Life https://www.youtube.com/watch?v=gOU_zWdhAoE
2 Music Video Police https://www.youtube.com/watch?v=lSipXuqHt40
3 Music Video Brutal https://www.youtube.com/watch?v=OGUy2UmRxJ0

How is someone so . . . nice all the time? Not used to that. Don't trust it. What's your scam?"

"Scam?[4] You think I'm being nice to you just to trick you into something?"

"Yeah! So, what is it Blondie? Tell me! It's driving me crazy. I can't figure it out. What do you want,[5] Blondie? Why are you wasting all this niceness on me?"

"Wasting niceness? Can someone really waste niceness? Isn't just being friends enough of a reason, Nicole?"

"Yeah, Gerald told me that's what it was. Don't let this go to your head, Blondie, but Gerald told me you're OK. Didn't really believe it, but I always listen to Gerald even when I don't agree with him. So, I'm giving you a chance. Don't blow it."

"Olivia told me the same thing, but even though Olivia is smart, she doesn't have Gerald's street sense.[6] That boy can smell trouble a mile away. And Gerald told me I'm going to have to learn that not everyone is a total jerk. He says that's what helped him turn his life around.[7] So . . . I'm working on it, OK?"

"Want to know the real reason why I give you a hard time? Because nobody else does. It's good for you. It'll make you stronger. You'll need that because your perfect life probably won't last forever. If it does, I'll dye my hair blond and join a sorority."

"You mean . . . you're trying to help me, Nicole?"

"Don't tell anyone that, Blondie. I can't let you ruin my street cred,[8] but yeah. Maybe I can use a little softening up like Gerald is always telling me, but you sure can use some toughening. I mean, don't they have any A-xxxxs in that hick town you're from?"

---

4 Music Video Scammer https://www.youtube.com/watch?v=UgA8BS72ido

5 Music Video Want https://www.youtube.com/watch?v=ls07CE7csyA

6 Music Video Street Sense https://www.youtube.com/watch?v=cXbTZ-Kj7m8

7 Music Video Turn Life Around https://www.youtube.com/watch?v=1uCv75-oKlQ

8 Music Video Street Cred https://www.youtube.com/watch?v=nNevjsJrFGA

"I don't think so. I've ever met any. Wait, maybe one. A woman who moved into town a few years ago yelled at kids who ran across her lawn. Does she count, Nicole?"

"Not even close, Blondie. In the bigger world you're in now you're going to meet a lot of A-xxxxs. You can't run around crying every time you do. And you can't be smiling all the time either."

"But when I smile or cry people seem to want to help me. It seems to work, Nicole. When smiling didn't work with you, I cried. And now you're being nice to me. So, why would I stop smiling and crying?"

"You mean you were acting Blondie? Scamming me? Just like I suspected?"

"No, I cried because I like you and I want us to be friends and I didn't know how to make that happen. What's wrong with that, Nicole? Please tell me. I'm trying to understand."[9]

"Because it only works with normal people, Blondie. It doesn't work with A-xxxxs. They don't care."

"OK, will you teach me how to recognize these A-xxxxs? Then, I can smile at everyone else. But I'm not going to give up being happy, just because I might meet an A-xxxx someday. Doesn't make much sense to me. Does it to you, Nicole?"

"Olivia warned me about how it's hard to argue with you. I know you're wrong, but it sounds kind of stupid when I try to explain it."

"Stop hugging me Blondie. It'll ruin my street cred."

"Sorry, I can't stop, Nicole. You're making me happy again."

* * *

"Allie, are you sure you want to go back for another stress test?"

"I have to see this through, Michelle. Face my fears. Beat them at their own game."

"That's my brave girl, but is it OK if I come with you before my appointment?"

---

9 Music Understand https://www.youtube.com/watch?v=6a5-tkK3Dy0

"I'd like that, Michelle. They probably won't let you in with me. They're not big on comforting people. But I'll feel better knowing you're waiting just outside."

*   *   *

"Nicole, want to make a deal? You teach me how to be edgy when I meet A-xxxxs and I'll teach you how to be nice to people and when to smile and cry."

"Blondie, I hope you don't expect some type of blood oath to seal the deal."

"No, but that reminds me, we're almost late for our next blood appointment at the Foundation. This will be a good test for us Nicole. I'll be really edgy to the nurse. I won't tell her how I love her hair or shoes or anything. Then you say something nice to her."

"I'll try Blondie. I'll try. But not complimenting someone isn't being edgy. No one will even notice that."

"But I'd notice, Nicole. And lots of girls would notice. Just yesterday one of the sweetest girls came to our sorority chapter meeting and didn't say anything nice. That tipped us off, we all knew she was upset about something. So, I asked her what's wrong, Melody? Turns out her boyfriend went away last weekend and didn't even tell her. Can you imagine[10] how she felt? See, she wasn't being an A-xxxx and she appreciated me noticing that something was bothering her. That's the way the world works, Nicole."

"Kaitlyn, you're going to have to practice being edgy. I'll give you lots of homework."

*   *   *

Allie and Michelle hug.

---

10 Movie Clip https://www.youtube.com/watch?v=_wK6oktk3JU

"Remember, I'm right here girlfriend," Michell yells as Allie disappears into the foreboding Foundation building.

* * *

Kaitlyn and Nicole wait to have blood drawn. As the nurse draws a pint of her blood, Kaitlyn giggles.

"Kaitlyn, you're the only person I know who thinks blood is fun."

"No, it's not that, Nicole. I was just imagining you walking into my sorority chapter meeting and calling me Blondie. Most of the girls would turn would their heads, because they'd think you were talking to them."

"We don't have that problem in my neighborhood, except a few hookers who think they can make a few extra bucks per trick if they dyed their hair blond."

* * *

"Mr. Atwell! Any feelings you'd like to share with our group?

"Well, I'm not very good at this. Two weeks ago, I didn't even know I had any feelings. Now I know I do. So, I feel pretty good about that."

"And to what do you attribute this epiphany, Mr. Atwell?"

"To my roommate and friends. I think being alone without friends in high school made me shut down. Now, I'm alive. Maybe having feelings is a way to be alive. I don't know. Like I said, I'm not very good at this."

"Thanks for sharing Mr. Atwell. I'm sure your contribution will help others in the group."

* * *

"You're next Ms. Wilson.

"Thank you, nurse. Oh, do you mind if I call you Beverly? Nurse is so . . . impersonal and what we're doing together is so important, I'd like to think we're all friends. My, what pretty nails you have Beverly? Where do you get them done?

"Really? Yourself?"

"Oh, yes, they look so professional. Maybe, you'll share you secret?"

"Really? That's how you do it? Thanks so much for sharing, Beverly.

"Why yes thanks, I'd like an ice cube to numb my arm."

After Beverly applies the ice to Nicole's arm. "Kaitlyn, don't you dare tell anyone you saw me do that. Just trying to prove to you that I can fake nice with the best of them.

"I can see that, Nicole. I'm impressed. You sounded just like a sorority sister. But do you know why?"

"No Blondie, tell me why?"

"You didn't just fake nice. You made Beverly happy. That's what's important. Making people happy. And you did it. Hugs girlfriend."

"Do we really have to hug Kaitlyn? You're treating me like a child."

"Nicole, you grew up without having a real childhood. You think that makes you tough. Trust me, you need to catch up on what you missed out on. If you don't, you'll break. I couldn't bear it, if stood by and watched you do that. Later, if you want to be tough all the time, it's your choice. Now it's all you know. So, it's not really your choice. All I want is to help my friend have choices."

"Hugs, Kaitlyn."

*   *   *

"That was fast. Are you OK, Allie?"

"Much better than last time. Just as I felt like I was about to panic, I closed my eyes and saw the way you looked at me when I left you."

As the two girls kiss, "We're getting quite domestic together. Two old lesbians taking care of one another."

"Now it's my turn, Allie. My appointment is in five minutes.

"Then kiss me again, Michelle. For real this time."

*   *   *

"Doctor, before we begin . . ."

"Yes, Ms. Collins?"

"I have a friend who is in another Foundation experiment. I've had a very good experience with the Foundation, but she's not. Can you explain why?"

"Sorry Ms. Collins. It's against the rules for me to discuss another student or another experiment. But I'm sure the Foundation has good reasons for what it's doing. It always does."

* * *

The nurse returns to Kaitlyn and Nicole, "Wait you're not finished. We still have to pump in the blood you donated last week. That's the whole point of the experiment. Now, this part may hurt a little more than drawing blood."

Sensing that Nicole has exhausted her supply of niceness for today, Kaitlyn whispers, "if you smile and be nice, Nicole, I'll buy you an ice cream cone after we leave."

Nicole giggles as the nurse inserts the second needle.

* * *

"Ms. Collins, based in your self-reporting and our tests, your body has been reacting well to the first three months of the new hormones. We think you're ready to move to the next level."

"Doctor, I've been having some strange emotions lately."

"Yes, we know. It's all in your reports."

"And . . .?"

"Nothing unexpected. We warned you that you'd become more emotional. We're not worried. And physically, you're doing fine. Skin sensitivity to touch seems to be increasing. You report liking that."

"Yes, but its more that. Sometimes, I feel like I'm losing control. My eyes tear up about little things. I worry a lot about my roommate and my friends."

"Like I said . . . all to be expected. Besides, is being a good friend to people a bad thing Ms. Collins?"

"No, not bad. But it's going way beyond what's normal for me. I think I was a good friend before. Now, I seem to be obsessing."

* * *

As the girls leave the Foundation, "Ice cream cones, Kaitlyn? I'm not a child!"

"Well, it always worked with me when my parents promised me ice cream. And I think you missed out on a lot of things growing up. Time for me to help you get your childhood back.[11] First step is to cure your ice cream deficiency. Besides, we never outgrow ice cream. Last month just before we drove to school, I was worried about being alone at school. And Daddy bought me an ice cream cone to cheer me up. It worked. And it did seem to be working on you just now," Kaitlyn giggles, "just shows no one is edgy when ice cream is on the line."

"OK, how many scoops do I get, Blondie?"

"Two scoops."

"With sprinkles?"

"Of course."

"I have to hand it to Gerald, Blondie. He really read you right. Get ready! I know this will shock you. I like you, Blondie."

"Oh, Nicole! We're going to help each other. I just know it in my heart."

* * *

"Ms. Collins, since you've expressed concerns, the experiment protocols require me to ask you this. Do you want to stop the experiment? You can, you know. Anytime."

---

11 Video Be Like a Child https://www.youtube.com/watch?v=DswPg0KYOjQ

"I've thought about that doctor, but I'm reassured that everything I'm experiencing is expected. So, tell me about the next stage."

"Your next injections will be like a cocktail. A mix of hormones. The estrogen you've been taking, with progesterone, prolactin and oxytocin and a new ingredient we're testing. We'll do one injection each month and you take pills every day. At the end of three months, we'll reevaluate."

"What's the purpose of the test?"

"You've reported the hormones you're already taking are affecting your male organs."[12]

"Yes, the Viagra I've been taking isn't working like it did before. It comes and goes. I like the way other parts of my body respond, but better performance would be nice."

"Most people report the similar things, Ms. Collins. It's a major side effect of transitioning. If you keep on your current track, performance is likely to become increasingly difficult. We're hoping this new cocktail will help with that. I don't want to pry into your personal life Ms. Collins. But . . . do you really need. I mean, are you and a partner. . .?"

"Yes, we're sexually active doctor. So, I'd like to be able to continue to perform at least as well as I do now. Are there any side effects to this new hormone cocktail?

"You should expect more swelling in your breasts. You're an A-cup, correct? You'll probably go to a B cup after several months. Maybe a C-cup if you continue more than a year. Beyond that, we're not sure yet. You're the first to try this new cocktail. No side effects that we know of yet, except that Prolactin is a stimulant for lactation. So, lactation is a possibility."

"You mean, I might produce breast milk?[13] Is that really possible?"

*   *   *

---

12 Video Trans Physical Responses https://www.youtube.com/watch?v=eEfSAGB7Q5g

13 Article Trans Women Breast Milk https://internationalbreastfeedingjournal.biomed-central.com/articles/10.1186/s13006-020-00308-6

"Thanks for sharing in class today, Sheldon. I can't do that in class yet, but I think I can with you. Is that, OK?"

Sheldon thinks, "What did Michelle tell me about how to deal with this in girl land rules? Melanie just took a risk. I'm supposed to be supportive. Reassure her that it's OK." Then, having translated the situation into girl cultural rules, "Well yes, Melanie. I'd like that if you're comfortable. Maybe over coffee?" As they walk to the dining hall, Sheldon notices Melanie smiling.

"I really understand about emotions shutting down[14], Sheldon. Seems like my soul died my whole junior year of high school. Right before prom . . . I took a bunch of pills. After I took the pills, I got scared and called my parents. They saved me. Then I spent all summer at a special camp. I've been making progress, but I'm still shy. Anyway, I just wanted to know that it's good to know I'm not the only one."

"Me too, Melanie. That's what's helping me. No way I would have shared anything personal in a group of strangers until I realized strangers are just friends, I don't know yet." Before they part. "Uh, Melanie . . . can we share contact info? Maybe we can talk again." Sheldon thinks. "That seemed to work. I can talk with girls. Why didn't anyone tell me this when I was in high school? Michelle is the best mom!"

*   *   *

"Ms. Collins, I hope I didn't scare you. I don't want to overstate the risk. We don't think lactation is inevitable. The lactogen dosage we're using is small. But it is a possibility. And if you do start lactating the quantities are likely to be small. It's not likely anyone would hire you to be a wetnurse."

"But . . . it's so . . . . I never . . . .."

"Ms. Collins, lactation is a natural human function. It can be annoying sometimes to have to break away from doing something else. But I liked how it felt when I was nursing my children. Sensuous and being part

---

14 Music Video Hard Feelings https://www.youtube.com/watch?v=d6nYF3juDQY

of nature. Women have different reactions; some miss it when lactation stops."[15]

"But . . .."

"I know this probably wasn't what you were thinking about when you started your journey, Ms. Collins. Few people do. You need to decide how far down the female road you want to go. It's OK to say: 'I'm at the edge. This is far enough.' Are you at your personal edge Ms. Collins? Is lactation where you draw the line?"

"I don't know, doctor. So far, I've gone to my personal edge on this journey several times and later I was glad I went farther."

"Now, let's get into the details. Maybe that will help you decide."

"It's really rather simple. Millions of women are dealing with this every day. If you begin lactating, you can use one of these. We've really improved breast pumps[16] since I used one. Portable and electronic now. Makes you feel much less like a cow being milked . . . That's a joke Ms. Collins. My . . . you're not your usual perky self today, Ms Collins."

"No need for a pump unless you start seeping milk on a regular basis. A drop or two here or there won't matter. The pump can reduce breast swelling by getting rid of the milk before it starts seeping out. But make sure you really need to pump. Pumping will increase milk production. Your breasts will react like it's a baby sucking. Breasts don't like leaving a hungry baby. So, the more you pump, the more milk your breasts will produce. You can pick a pump up at the Foundation anytime if you need it. And of course, we'd like to test the milk if you begin lactating."

"I'm not crazy about producing milk, doctor. I mean, it's not something one focuses on. Can I think about it? I'd like to talk to my family."

"Of course, Ms. Collins. Think it over. You've been such a trooper the past three years. You know, your body is a testament to all the advances we've made in hormone treatments the past several decades. You're really at the edge of where scientific knowledge ends and guesswork begins. I can

---

15 Article Breast Feeding Sensations https://www.laleche.org.uk/mothers-on-what-do-you-like-most-about-breastfeeding
16 Article Breast Pumps https://aeroflowbreastpumps.com/blog/best-breast-pumps

understand you not wanting to walk along that edge too long. Let us know next week what you decide."

*   *   *

As Michelle emerges from her Foundation session, "Allie, I'm so glad you waited for me. Thanks. I needed a hug."

"Anything wrong, girlfriend?

Wrong? No, not really wrong. It's just that I'm going to have to make some decisions sooner than I wasn't expecting. Can we talk tonight after I think about this?"

"Later, Michelle begins imaging a future life. A life she never thought about. What would it be like? What's that Sarah? The bubbles will show me? Of course!" As Sarah guides Michelle into the bubble dimension, "Oh! This feels so real.[17] Is mothering really like this? Is this where my journey leads me?"

As Sarah smiles, Michele cautions her, "I haven't decided yet, Sarah.

"Of course, not dear," Sarah whispers in her ear. "I hadn't decided at your age either. Some of us decide. For others, it just seems to happen one day. We wake up from a daze and feel the sensations of a hungry child. You'll find your way. For now, just enjoy your little gift from the bubbles."

Michelle ponders her journey, "I just became a girl. How am I becoming a woman so fast? Maybe, someday. In between now. Not a woman yet."[18]

*   *   *

Over ice cream, "Nicole, thanks for brightening my day. I was in the dumps."

"What's the matter Blondie?"

---

17 Pic Michelle Breastfeeding https://firepitcell.com/wp-content/uploads/2021/12/C20N17-Michelle-Imagines-Breastfeeding-Baby.jpg

18 Music Video Not a Woman Yet https://www.youtube.com/watch?v=IlV7RhT6zHs

"I thought I was forming a wonderful relationship with Scott Hopkins. Several dates were good. We're amazing in bed together."

"Wait! White girls like sex?[19] Is that what you're telling me?"

"Ha! . . . Good one, Nicole. You have real friend potential."

"OK, I can see you're dying to tell me about Scott."

"Well, he hasn't called in a week. Just responds with text messages."

"Oh, so sorry, Kaitlyn. What are you going to do?"

"The girl in the room next to mine gave me some really good advice. By the way, Michelle is amazing. She's helping practically everyone in our dorm."

"Did she tell you to track him down and cut off his . . .?"

"No, she said wait two weeks. Then go to a place he usually goes to and wait for him to approach me. I still have a week of waiting to go through. It's depressing."

"That's why tracking him down and . . . is a better idea, Kaitlyn. No waiting."

"I'm not there yet, but I'll remember your advice if he keeps me waiting too long.

"Blondie, this ice cream is really powerful stuff."

*   *   *

Several hours later at their dorm room, "Kaitlyn, you look terrible! What's wrong?"

"I don't know Olivia. I've never felt this way before. It's kind of like my body is on fire."

"You don't feel feverish."

"No, not a fever. It's different. I ache all over. I need to sit down. Oops, I guess I'm down."

Five minutes later Kaitlyn's phone rings. "Nicole, I was just about to call you.

"Yes, I'm feeling the same thing."

---

19 Music Video California Gurls https://www.youtube.com/watch?v=F57P9C4SAW4

"Maybe the ice cream was bad, but I don't feel sick to my stomach. Do you?"

"No? That's a good sign, right? Olivia says it may be the new blood they gave us. God, I hope not.? Nicole, do you have anyone to take care of you? Good, Gerald's coming over? Call me if it gets any worse. I'm going to bed early. Hope it's gone in the morning."

* * *

"Shelley, Allie's coming over in a couple of minutes. Do you mind if . . .."

"Sure, good excuse for me and Luna to catch up. I really like her, Michelle. She's wonderful. And I can't believe it, but she likes me! Thanks, Mom."

After Shelley leaves, Michelle shares her hormone therapy issues with Allie.

"That's a lot for me to digest, Michelle. All I can say is that I'm here for you, girlfriend. No, that's not all I can say. I totally get this is way beyond what you signed up for. In girl years, you're only three years old. Your years as Michael don't count. I mean, no girl that age is ready to deal with breast milk. We all know it's coming. We watched our mothers. You probably weren't watching your mom thinking you'd be doing it. Its part of being a woman, but you're not a woman yet. You're just a girl, like me."

As Michelle draws Allie closer, "Did you say a C-cup, Michelle? Really? Talk about making mountains out of molehills. That's it, girlfriend. Giggling is good. Let's giggle together. Let's forget about treatments and just be girls for as long as we can. We both deserve it." Holding Michelle's breasts, "You're not ready to grow up yet. Not ready to be a filling station for babies. Maybe someday, but not now. We're going to take good care of you until then."

Michelle enjoys Allie's attentions and thinks, "Yes, I can deal with this as long as I'm not alone on the edge."

* * *

"Agent 1, we have a problem. Too sensitive to talk about over the phone. Meet you by the Bell Tower in five minutes."

* * *

Sheldon returns to his room to find a now familiar scene. Allie and Michelle collapsed in each other's arms. "So sweet together. This time I'm taking a picture to show Luna."

* * *

Kaitlyn and Nicole spend a rocky day recovering from their blood therapy.

"Some insurance policy you turned out to be, Kaitlyn!"

"I told you that idea had holes in it, Nicole."

"Maybe blonds don't really have more fun,[20] Kaitlyn."

"Nicole, I'm so glad we're friends. Is that, OK?

"It's more than OK, Blondie."

"Just be careful what you say about blondes, Nicole. I'm in the Blonde Power movement."[21]

"Oh! I'm so scared Blondie!" as both girls giggle.

---

20 Video Blondes https://www.youtube.com/watch?v=xD_sxigE2nU
21 Music Blonde Bad https://www.youtube.com/watch?v=ku2YavtBEww

21

All Paths Cross

Several days later, Friday night all roads for the freshman class and their families lead to Pullen Park.

"There's a picnic in the park," Michelle tells her family.

Kaitlyn says ". . .. in the park, Mom and Daddy."

"Judge and Professor, first stop is the park."

"There's an event in the park tonight, Senator. The Judge and Professor will be there."

"Nicole, I'm working tonight at the event in the park. Here's a free ticket. I'll be working, but I'll make time for you. See you there."

"Meet you in Pullen Park, Allen. Text me when you get there."

*   *   *

"Kaitlyn, we have to clean up our room."

"Why Olivia? My parents already know I'm sloppy."

"Well, my parents don't know that about me, and I intend to keep it that way."

*   *   *

"Thanks for letting me know, Mom."

"Allie, all three of my sisters are coming with my mom. Elaine cancelled her other plans at the last minute. It's been almost three years since we've all been together. Just after the beginning of my transition."

"Are you sure you want me hanging around for the reunion, Michelle?"

"Of course, girlfriend. Time for you to meet my family[1] . . . for better or worse. Don't worry, you're great. They'll absolutely love you. Compared to the other people I've been with, you're a saint."

"I'm down with all of us getting together tonight, Michelle. I'll just disappear on Saturday to give the Collins girls some family time. Any words of wisdom before I meet the 'in-laws?'"

"My Mom's a sweetheart. You've got no worries from her. My sisters were always protective of their youngest brother. No girl or boy was ever good enough. Not sure whether they'll be as protective now that I'm their baby sister."[2]

* * *

Just outside of town, the Judge, the Professor and the Senator meet for lunch.

"So, we're all agreed. Scott and Olivia will transfer to another university as soon as Operation Princess terminates."

* * *

"Gerald, thanks for being here for me for parents' weekend. It's kind of strange. Everyone so mushy about seeing the parents they were so happy to get away from just a month ago."

"No problem, Nicole. Just don't expect me to pay your tuition. My checking account is running on fumes. You should have gotten yourself adopted by a more financially solvent family."

---

1 Music Video Meet Family https://www.youtube.com/watch?v=IEy7bahnQuQ
2 Music Video Gets Away With Everything https://www.youtube.com/watch?v=x Zam8NTrebk

"Gerald, since my brother Jamal died, you've been the best family I could ever want. We're family."[3]

"Jamal took me in when I was living on the street. Gave me my first job delivering drugs for him. Gave me the easy jobs. I had to take care of his little sister after he got shot."

"Let's go and meet all these white people. Show them what family really means."

*   *   *

Marjorie Collins arrives with Michelle's three older sisters, Elaine, Alice, and Sarah.

Just look at our baby sister. All grown up! Michelle, you look amazing. Always said you had the best hair. And who's this lovely girl?"[4]

"Allison Lee but call her Allie. Mom, I told you about Allie."

"But Michelle, you didn't tell . . .US . . . about Allie," Michelle's three sisters chime in as they surround Allie.

"Allie, my sisters are master interrogators. Just remember you have the right to remain silent. They won't use anything you say against you, but I'm fair game in their books."

With Allie and Michelle's sisters off in their own world, Michelle hugs her mother, "Mom, we have so much to talk about," as Michelle buries her face in her mother's shoulder. Looking up at her mom with a tear in her eye, "It's been sooooo hard. Thanks for being here for me."

"I know, Dear. With your sisters I had years to prepare them to become women. It all happened so fast with you. Time for my fourth daughter to really become the fifth Collins woman."

*   *   *

---

3 Music Video We Are Family https://www.youtube.com/watch?v=hkg_f6i9-IE
4 Video Can't Think Straight https://www.youtube.com/watch?v=lMcymh5WMYU

Olivia, the Judge, the Professor, Scott, and Senator Hopkins meet Kaitlyn and her parents.

"Senator, I've been wanting to talk with you." As Kaitlyn leads the Senator away from the group for a private chat, Scott looks on with a worried expression. "Scott, nothing bashful about my daughter Kaitlyn, is there?"

"No sir."

"What's she doing?" as Scott sees the Senator laughing and putting his arm around her shoulder. After conferring with Olivia, Scott realizes the Senator and Kaitlyn have disappeared into the crowd.

"Don't worry, Scott. She'll return your father in one piece," Olivia says with a look that says she's worried she's wrong.

Half an hour later, Kaitlyn and the Senator reappear.

"Scott, you never told me how amusing your father is. He certainly knows how to show a girl a good time. You could learn a few things from the Senator about how to treat a girl."

As Kaitlyn watches Scott's reaction, she thinks, "Time for you to man up,[5] if you want me, Scott."

* * *

"Hey Allen!

Sheldon, how's my little brother doing? Scott's been giving me reports. Says you're rooming with a really hot chick.[6] How'd you pull that off, bro? Yeah, you're the smart one in the family. Lulling everyone into thinking you're a harmless nerd. Then shacking up with a blond bombshell. Makes a brother proud. You did really learn something from me. Is she here? How is she in bed Sheldon?"

"Yes, she's here. But so is her girlfriend."

"Sheldon, threesomes? I'm even more impressed."

---

5 Music Video Man Up https://www.youtube.com/watch?v=D_K9sjB2pKM
6 Movie Clip Hot Chick https://www.youtube.com/watch?v=6z5zbY-0QCA

"No, it's not like that. I'm not doing it with either of them. I'll introduce you to Michelle tomorrow when Allie isn't here. We need to give them some space tonight."

"Wait, you're saying that you and Michelle are just roommates? Is that right?"

"That's right, Allen."

"What a raging homo you are Sheldon!"

"No, Luna's my girlfriend."

"So, are you banging Luna? No, you haven't, have you?"

"Well not yet. We're not ready for that. We're going slow."

"Little brother, I got here just in time. Time for you to man up with the ladies. Big brother will show you how with that blond roommate of yours. I'll just meet her tonight, but by Saturday night she'll be begging me for it. Yeah, begging. Girls pretend not to want it. But they all do. All girls are the same, Sheldon."

"Maybe some Allen, but Michelle's different. Trust me."

"I'll prove you wrong tomorrow, Sheldon."

"Just introduce us tonight and I'll take it from there."

* * *

As Nicole wanders through the crowd of happy families, she thinks, "This is no place for me." Walking away from the crowd she hears in Kaitlyn's perky voice. "Nicole!" We've been looking for you. Where have you been?"

"I introduced Gerald to my father. They're talking restaurant business. Come this way." More seriously, "How are you feeling Nicole? It took me three days to get over whatever that was." Then Kaitlyn reverts to form, "Daddy, this is Nicole. We're doing the experiment together.[7] You might say we're blood sisters."

"Good honey. Gerald, I have to tell you I'm impressed with your operation here. Managing an outdoor event for hundreds of people. Difficult to pull off. You have a real gift for organizing."

---

7 Music Video Experiment https://www.youtube.com/watch?v=NTUcoR8_pyE

With the two men who raised them continuing to talk the food business, they both think, "maybe we are blood sisters."

*   *   *

Shelley reluctantly brings his brother Allen to meet Michelle.

"Mom, this is Shelley, my roommate."

"Shelley, who is this mountain of muscles you're with?"

"My brother Allen. He's staying with Scott. High school buddies."

"Michelle, I just wanted to thank you for looking out for Sheldon. He's always been so . . . unusual. But I can see you've worked wonders with him in just a few weeks."

As a dreamy eyed Michelle looks up at Allen, she feels the warmth he exudes like rays of sunlight breaking through a cloudy sky. "Oh! Just happy to help Shelley," as Michelle involuntarily draws herself closer[8] to Allen.

"Well, it's practically a miracle, Michelle", as he puts his arm around her. "I've been so worried about him."

Relishing Allen's attention and going into Scarlet O'Hara mode, "I'm not a miracle worker, Mr. Atwell. Just a good friend."

"I'd like to be your friend, Michelle," brushing her cheek with his fingers. Do you think the miracle worker might spare a little time this weekend to share your secret?"

"Well, my family leaves town late Saturday afternoon. Maybe . . ." as Michelle blushes.

"It's a date then. I'll stop by your room around seven on Saturday."

Looking over her shoulder at Allie still surrounded by her three sisters, "No, I'll meet you by the Bell Tower, Mr. Atwell."

When Michelle returns to her mother, a little giddy with excitement, Mrs. Collins snaps, "Young lady, we do have a lot to talk about."

*   *   *

8 Music Come Closer https://www.youtube.com/watch?v=0d2b4XuAa80

"And that's how it's done Sheldon. She's playing the sweet virgin now, but like I said, she'll be begging for it tomorrow night."

"But . . .."

"But what?"

Not knowing what to do, "Nothing Allen."

*   *   *

Back at the hotel, the Collins women settle in for a night of girl talk.

"Girls, your baby sister made a conquest at the party tonight. While you were talking to Michelle's girlfriend, a guy picked up your sister."[9]

"You mean that big guy? He's so . . . muscular."

"Little sister aren't you the one! You always were a little manipulator. And now with that new body of yours. You've got a lot more to work with."

After the giggling and looks subside, "But Michelle, I'm worried about you. I'm worried you're playing with fire,"[10] Michelle's mother warns.

"I know Mom, that's why I'm so grateful you're all here. I'm confused. My life seems to be spinning out of control. I really need your help. All of you. It started as a game. Another role to play. Now, everything is happening so fast. And there's no script to follow. What should I do? How do I handle being a woman? So many things I never thought about."

"Michelle, you're doing the right thing now. Sharing your feelings. Asking for support. That's how women deal with the world. Not your father's way. He'd rather go it alone. Not your way . . . before. But now it is, Honey. So, just pour your heart out and the Collins girls will help you find your way."

After several hours of laughing . . . and crying . . . and hugging.

"And my next big decision is about the hormones. It's a big step."

"No, Michelle. That's not your next big decision."

"It's not, Mom?"

---

9 Music Video Ladies Love Country Boys https://www.youtube.com/watch?v=CBQ01X-1AlI

10 Music Video Play with Fire https://www.youtube.com/watch?v=VHhPYNwgRYQ

"No young lady. It's tomorrow night with Allen. The way that man was looking at you. Be prepared to surrender yourself[11] tomorrow night or to defend your honor. He doesn't look like the kind of man who takes no for an answer. And the way you were looking at him, I don't think you'll be saying no."

"Mother!"

"Michelle, I didn't always understand my son, but I know all my girls. I knew what each of them wanted. Sometimes before they did. And I know what you want."

"Mother!"

"And what will he do when he finds out your secret?"

"Oh, I can handle that, Mom."

"I know Michael had some tough street experiences, but it's always dangerous to assume you can handle everything. I know you want everything. You always have. And you already have that sweet girl Allie. What about her? While Allen was sweeping you off your feet, Allie was right there, watching you and I saw her heart breaking. You need to think about Allie, Michelle. It's not all about you. Other people count."

Mom . . . I . . . .

"No, let me finish, young lady!"

"I haven't been this ashamed of you since your father had to bail Michael out of jail. Those horrible characters Michael was hanging out with! Your dad was so good about it. But that was the bottom. Then, you decided to become a woman. It's affected all of us, but we've given you as much support as we can. That part is settled now. You're my daughter. But I've decided I'm not putting up with my daughter behaving as atrociously as Michael did. We're not making the same mistakes again that we made with Michael. This is a fresh start for both you and us."

"Restarting isn't about how you look or changing your name. Now it's about what kind of woman you're going to be. What are your values? Are you kind to people? Are you answering a bigger calling?[12] Do you

---

11 Music Video Surrender to Me https://www.youtube.com/watch?v=MY4ZC4obNOA
12 Music Video The Call https://www.youtube.com/watch?v=XD6RdI1QqCg

bring love into the world? Or will you just take, like Michael did? I'm so proud I've raised three daughters who make the world a better place. I was hoping for four. But after your self-centered display today, I have my doubts. You hurt Allie today. She deserves better. You should be ashamed of yourself, young lady. Michelle, your sisters and I probably spoiled Michael. You were my last baby. I was tired by the time you came. So was your dad. We're not going to make the same mistake with Michelle. Time for tough love,[13] honey, so Michelle becomes better than Michael."

"Oh Mom! That's what I mean. I'm so confused. I really want your guidance. Tell me when I'm messing up. Being Michelle is a second chance for me. Help me not to blow it. You're right. I do want everything. And I know that may hurt Allie. She's a wonderful girl. I don't want to hurt her. I want to keep her."

"Then, you know what you need to do, Michelle."

"So, I should talk with Allie?"

"Daughter, that's your first step to becoming the woman[14] I hope you want to be."

"Thanks, Mom. I do want you to be proud of all your daughters. I just need a little more help finding my path."

*　*　*

After her sisters fall asleep, Michelle crawls into bed with Marjorie. "Mom, there's something else. Something more important than boyfriends and girlfriends. Something that's bigger than I realized. The doctor warned me that I may produce breast milk if I take the new hormones. That surprised me, but the thing I really need to talk about is bigger. Before that, I was noticing that little things were changing, but that conversation with the doctor put it in perspective for me. I realized I really am a girl now. It's not just acting anymore."

---

13 Music Video Tough Love https://www.youtube.com/watch?v=RKVdwpbPedA
14 Music Video God is a Woman https://www.youtube.com/watch?v=kHLHSlExFis

Describing her experiences mothering Shelley, Allie, Kaitlyn and others seeking advice, "What does it all mean, Mom? What's in my future?[15] How do I do this? I mean, really do it, like you did it? I like it, but I'm not the most stable person. I'm afraid I'm going to mess up. I can't let them down."

"Oh Michelle, this is the first thing other than performing you've taken anything seriously. I guess you're realizing that mothering is more than acting."

"That's what scares me, Mom. My whole life has been acting. This is real. I have to learn to be real for the people who depend on me. I wish I was more like you, Mom."

"Michelle, do you think I was born a mom? I know this may surprise you, but I wasn't always a mom, or even a nice girl."

"Mom! Tell me more. No don't. Not sure I can handle hearing about my mom's bad girl days. Well, maybe a little."

"Michelle, have you ever stopped to think where you inherited this side of yourself? Certainly, not from your dad. He's always been steady and reliable. Your three sisters were always steady like your dad. Then, Michael came along, and I immediately recognized my younger self in him. He reminded me of a more exciting time in my life when anything and everything was possible. Maybe that's why I indulged his whims, maybe too often. Then, I remembered how I grew up. It wasn't a pretty story. I was worried that wouldn't happen for Michael, that Michael would remain a problem child his whole life. And then, my youngest daughter, Michelle, was born, a second chance for both of us. Now that you're my daughter,[16] Michelle, I can tell you some things about myself that I was too embarrassed to tell my son, Michael. Maybe that will help."

After explaining some of her teenage and college adventures and disasters to Michelle, "I was a manipulative games player like you, Michelle. I don't know why, but your father was the only boy who put up with that for very long. I was drawn to him because he was so steady. Sometimes, I think

---

15 Music Video My Future https://www.youtube.com/watch?v=b-5Ugpc22mE
16 Music Video Dear Daughter https://www.youtube.com/watch?v=WHPVb-qMzsY

I acted out just so he would calm me down and help me set boundaries. I liked his firm hand reigning me in. And I've seen you do the same thing, Michelle. Like you're testing people to see how much they love you."

"Your dad was the only one who passed all my tests. He was my light when I turned dark. So, we got married, but that didn't magically chase away my dark moments. They always returned. I was scared your dad would give up on me. The things I put him through."

"So, when your oldest sister, Elaine, was born, you can understand why I had the same fears you're having now. I was terrified I wouldn't be a good mother after being so selfish and self-centered. I know that would have been the last straw for your dad. He could put up with my games, but not if it hurt our child. But when I held her and looked down at her for the first time, my world changed. Realizing that Elaine needed me, more than any person in the world, made me look deeper into myself. It turned out I had a bigger heart than I thought. I discovered I was a different person, a better person, than I thought I was. The more my children needed me, the stronger I became. Also, with four children I was too tired to play games with people."

"So, you see, Michelle, you're not the only Collins girl who went through a transition. That's what you're experiencing now, Michelle. You're beginning to find that bigger mother's heart[17] you didn't know about. I can see you're really meant to do this. Your friends recognize a good mom, even though you're still finding your own way. Helping them will make you stronger. That's why I'm so happy to welcome you to the mother's club."

Seeing Michelle looking hopeful, but also worried, "But you're too young to just be a mom. First, you need to be a college girl. Experience the joys and heart breaks of a girl[18] of your age. You're getting good practice helping your friends. They need you, but not as much as a baby does. So, you can make a few mistakes like I did. Just learn from your mistakes and try not to hurt other people along the way, OK?"

---

17 Music Video Mother Like You https://www.youtube.com/watch?v=7_fqP-XJg2E
18 Movie Clip Camelot Maidenhood https://www.youtube.com/watch?v=efo2X0QQpOo

A relaxed Michelle snuggles with Marjorie, "Oh Mom, I never realized we were so much alike. If you changed, maybe I can too. And Dad knows about all those things you did and still loves you?"

"Your Dad and I developed our own ways of forgiving one another. I won't go into that, now. Even a mother is entitled to keep some things private from her daughter."

As Michelle returns to her own bed, she mischievously smiles as she recalls a hazy memory of Michael finding something in his parent's closet that Marjorie quickly whisked away without answering his questions, something like one of her punishment toys. "Not only was mom like me, apparently she didn't totally stop when she had children. Is mom still a naughty girl[19] sometimes? Does dad still punish her?[20] I wonder . . .. No, not my mom. She's a good girl now."

While Michelle debates about her mother, Marjorie laughs mischievously, "One last thing, Michelle, did the doctor really say C-cups? That's better honey, laughing will bring you from the darkness to the light. It's always helped me. Still does when my darkness starts taking over."

"OMG," Michelle thinks, "it's still true!"

"Michelle. This is just between us girls. Don't tell your sisters. They won't understand the way you do."

"Good night, Marjorie., and thanks. It will help. You found your way to the light. I'll, find my way."

"That's my girl. Good night, Michelle."

---

19 Movie Clip Dog Pound https://www.youtube.com/watch?v=K4srmGl7fY0
20 Movie Clip 50 Shades https://www.youtube.com/watch?v=d4gF7Yuu0bE

22

Family Connections

Early the next morning.

"Allie, I'm so glad I found you."

"I thought you'd be spending the day with your family, Michelle," as Allie draws away from Michelle's embrace.

"I will, but you're more important."

"Am I? Really? Sometimes you don't act that way, Michelle."

"I suppose you noticed me and Allen last night?"

"Notice? Girl . . . impossible not to notice. You went totally gaga over him.[1] Practically right in front of me. I mean, I was so . . . embarrassed. Why bring me to meet your whole family and then do that in front of them? If your sisters weren't surrounding me, I would have walked over and slapped your face."

"I know now. I didn't realize while it was happening, but my mom and sisters told me. I agree with them and you. I was bad. I'm here to apologize . . . and . . . plead for forgiveness. I'll try to change. Three years ago, I was a spoiled little boy.[2] Becoming a girl just made me a spoiled self-centered girl. Changing gender seems like a lot of effort if I remain the same. My mom and sisters helped me see that last night. And I'm begging you to help me change . . . like inside . . . not just outside. I've been too concerned about outside. My mom made me realize that. Can you help me?"

"Michelle? Really?"

---

1 Music Video Carousel https://www.youtube.com/watch?v=zAB5AC9yhY0
2 Music Video Little Game https://www.youtube.com/watch?v=WNr3x1kVVEc

"Looking back since we met, Allie, I just don't know how you put up with me. You deserve better. I shouldn't just . . . you know . . . . . I just couldn't help myself with Allen. My brain turned off."

"Yes, I know. I'm insanely jealous of how guys like that make you feel.[3] Remember, the first time I punished you, it was about that. Sometimes, I wish . . . ."[4]

"Allie, I don't wish that. We have a special thing between us. It's different than with guys . . . but so wonderful. You're still my alpha. I'm trying to be a better person. I really am. You've helped me. Talking with my mother and sisters really helped a lot. I thought I had life figured out. Now, I know I still have a lot to learn."

"What did your mother say, Michelle?"

"My mom doesn't hold back when any of her children are about to crash. Here are the highlights. That she's ashamed of my behavior. That you deserve better. Now that I'm a woman, what am you going to do with my life? Half the people in the world are women. So, becoming a woman isn't a big deal. Decide what kind of woman I'm going to be. Make her proud of her daughter."[5]

"Your mom really knows how to lay it on the line. Michelle. Reminds me of my mom."

"I had it coming. I was totally selfish. I know that now."

"Your mom and sisters all love you. And . . . I love you, Michelle. There I've said it. You've turned your hip, alpha girlfriend into a lovesick puppy. You've totally ruined my self-image. I hope you're satisfied."

"And I love you too," as the two girls embrace.

"I know that, but it's still nice to hear."

"You're the most important person in my life, Allie. I don't know what I'd do without you. You're a big part of how I become not just a woman, but a good woman. That's what I really want. The Allen's of the world

---

3 Movie Clip Song Nobody Does It Better https://www.youtube.com/watch?v=hAes 4MFLJtA

4 Music Video The Man https://www.youtube.com/watch?v=AqAJLh9wuZ0

5 Music Video You're Gonna Be https://www.youtube.com/watch?v=0kLs4VdfFlQ

won't help with that. Sometimes I just get caught up in the details . . . how I look . . . how I can manipulate. . . and I lose sight of the big picture. You know . . . trying to become a real person when I'm not on stage. That's always been hard for me. My family promised to keep me focused on that big picture."

Seeing that Allie is still frustrated with her, "Allie, I wish you had walked over and slapped me[6] last night, right in front of everyone. I would have told them all that it's OK, because you're my alpha and I've given you complete control. Then, I would have apologized to you like a naughty child, right in front of everyone. I really would have."

"I believe that Michelle, apologizing is easy for you. You seem to thrive on apologizing. But sometimes apologies are too late. I can't always. I mean, sometimes you have to take responsibility for yourself. Not misbehave and make it up later. But you're right that you've always corrected yourself when I act like your alpha and I bring you back to earth."

"So, Allie, are you still mad with me about Allen?"

"Angry? No. Jealous? Yes.[7] And you'll be punished for making me jealous. What kind of alpha would I be if I don't punish you for that?"

"How about now? Is my alpha free to punish her sub now?"

"Are you seeing him again?"

"Yes . . . but I can get out of that."

"Michelle, this may sound strange, but your alpha says don't break your date with Allen. I know it's confusing. Let me hold you, girlfriend, and I'll explain. As much to myself as to you."

As Allie holds her, a confused Michelle listens looking into Allie's big almond eyes. "As your girlfriend I'm insanely jealous and I don't want you to go on your date with Allen. But as your alpha, I think it's something you must do. I see how you react to guys like that. Its real. I hate that its real. But it is. I crave that you'll look at me like that. It hurts that I can't give you that. It really does. But what we have together is good. It's worth fighting for and suppressing your desires isn't the way to create something good.

---

6 Video Slaps https://www.youtube.com/watch?v=kTCLdGzVbUw

7 Music Video Curious https://www.youtube.com/watch?v=YXTzMOmmEfE

Believe me, suppressing doesn't work. Done that. Not doing it again. And you shouldn't either. I want you to love me more than anything else. But loving isn't built on sacrificing what you really love. So, as much as I hate it, my advice is to explore that side of yourself."

"But . . . I'm scared, Allie. Sometimes, I lose control. I wasn't thinking about that last night when Shelley introduced Allen. My brain just stopped working. What if I do something that makes you want to leave me?"

"I know Michelle. The only thing scarier than acting on stage is being yourself off-stage. You're fabulous on stage . . . you need more off-stage experience. You're very good playing your characters off-stage too. So good that I fell in love with both of them, I mean, how many lesbians carry a picture of a guy around for two years, meet a girl down the hall in college and fall in love again? I did. I should be thrown out of the lesbian club for that. So, as we go through this together, remember that you're not the only one who's scared. I'm scared too. I'm scared I'll lose both Michael and Michelle. They're the only you I really know. But I also know you're more than both. And I love their creator, whoever you really are."

"So, go on your date with Allen. Explore who you are. You may fall in love with a guy. You may leave me. Or you may get battered and bruised and decide I'm what you want. But understand this, Michelle, I don't want to be your escape from something bad. I'm rooting for you to love both, but to choose me. But I'll welcome you back either way. . . because . . . . I love you and . . . I want us to be together. Now stop crying and kiss me. Or keep crying and kiss me. I just need you to kiss me."

After their kisses, Allie grabs Michelle wrist tightly and with continues with increased intensity, "But, if you date another girl, I'll cut off what's left of Michael. That half of you is all mine. Is that clear?"

"Uh huh, my alpha. You're my only girl. Not much else in life that I'm sure of, but I'm sure of that." Nervously giggling, "But I'll have to keep you away from kitchens with knives."

"One more thing Michelle. Be careful. You have great taste in girls . . . but you're one of those girls who falls for the bad boys. Don't let yourself get hurt by the bad boys."

"I'll try. I know it's my weakness. I've been hurt before. Someday, when we're old, I'll tell you about it."

After more soft time making up, Allie's tone changes, "One more thing, Michelle, I'm on to your con. You knew that if you asked me to help, I'd get over my jealousy and tell you to go on your date, because you need to explore."

Sheepishly smiling, "Girlfriend, all I did was rely on your integrity. It's a compliment in a way. I knew you'd be the kind of alpha who really looks out for me. I trust you like I trust my mom. I know I can't fool of either one of you and I don't want to. Is that a con, Allie?"

"Yes, it's more of your games playing, Michelle."

"And does my alpha promise her sub that you'll punish me for it?"

"Michelle, you're earning many punishments. After your family leaves, my naughty little kitten won't be able to sit down for a week."

"Oh, but making up afterwards will be worth it, Allie. One last thing, Allie. I know you must be missing your family. The Collins girls are treating ourselves to a spa day.[8] Become a Collins girl for today?"

"Way ahead of you, Michelle. Your sister Elaine already invited me. I wasn't going to go, but I'm glad my girlfriend had the balls to face me this morning and sharing a spa day is something you'll never get from the likes of Shelley's brother. So, I'm one of the Collins girls for the rest of the day."

* * *

Shelley calls Michelle.

"What about your brother, Shelley?"

"Yes, your brother's quite charming," a dreamy eyed Michelle responds.

"What do you mean? Am I not good enough for your brother? Is that it?"

"And what makes you think he's getting into my panties tonight?"

"Is that so? Goodbye, Shelley."

---

8 Music Video Spa https://www.youtube.com/watch?v=WG8FntR8JD8

Michelle thinks, "That boy really has a lot of nerve. I've created a Frankenstein monster."

At Shelley's end, he thinks, "I hope Michelle knows what she's doing. This could end really badly."

*   *   *

At the spa.

"Mrs. Collins. Thanks for your advice to Michelle last night. She told me what you said. We kissed and made up.

"Yes, she's a handful. But I've bought into her philosophy of living on the edge. It's easier with two."

"Yes, I know about Allen."

"No, not thrilled. It's hard to understand. Sometimes I don't."

"I'm concerned too. I'm afraid Michelle will end up like a girl in a country song singing about how the man in her life treated her badly. But Michelle needs to learn about the bad boys in life. The edge can get dangerous if you're there with the wrong people. I just hope Allen is half as nice as his brother Shelley. But my instinct tells me he's not. Michelle is so childlike when it comes to that. I just hope she doesn't get too scarred."

*   *   *

Michelle in a dreamlike state while getting a mani and pedi,[9] "Mom thinks I'm doing to sleep with him. My sisters think the same. Even Allie and Shelley. And I'm sure Allen does too. One part of me says, he has some nerve being so sure. But I like that he sees into me and instinctively knows I want him. What's a girl to do?"

*   *   *

The Senator and the Judge give speeches at the university fundraiser.

---

9 Music Video Manicure https://www.youtube.com/watch?v=4TTOUVgLR_g

"Scott, look around. What do you see?"

"A lot of overcooked food getting cold?"

"What I see is money and power.[10] What I see is my son building on that. You know that's what the Judge, the Professor I want for you and Olivia. You understand that, right? That's why we set such high standards for both of you."

"Yes, I know."

"Frankly, Scott I've been worried about reports about you being emotionally involved with Kaitlyn."

"That's over, Dad. You don't have to worry about that anymore.

"I wish it was that easy, Scott. You don't know women like I do. I had a good talk with your Princess last night."

"I know. I was worried she might become my next stepmother."

"Now, there's a thought, Scott. Oh yes. Still a lot of fire in my furnace.[11] But back to your problem. She's a real spitfire, son. I can see why she excites you. Reminds me a bit of my third wife. I'll share this with you, Scott. I was happiest with that woman. Excited everyday with what she would do next. But she was poison for my political career. Support was building for the big job in the big house in DC. But when Helen found out about my secretary and me, all hell broke loose. No more White House dreams after that. So, now I'm just a Senator in a safe seat and Chairman of the Judiciary Committee. Some people would be satisfied with that. But I could have had more. You can have more, but only if you play it smart. Do you understand what I'm telling you about Kaitlyn? She's dangerous.

"Is she really a spy? Is she playing for the other team, Dad?"

"A spy? The other team? Who put that in your head? I bet it was the Professor, right? That's all she thinks about. Wish it was as simple as spies. We could deal with that. Kaitlyn's in love with you, boy. The only team that girl is playing for is the Scott-Kaitlyn team. And I don't think she's easily discouraged. That girl isn't going to give up until she has you. And, like

10 Music Video Money Power Women Drugs https://www.youtube.com/watch?v=iVJYS 1L1snA

11 Music Video Fire Furnace https://www.youtube.com/watch?v=Qz2IRvL2mKQ

I said, that little blond filly is something. I can see why you might decide that the Scott-Kaitlyn team isn't such a bad thing. But she won't play the game like political wives need to do."

"You mean like Olivia will."

"Exactly. The Professor raised Olivia to be the perfect match[12] for you. We started talking about this over 15 years ago. The Judge got on board over ten years ago. It's been settled since then. We can't risk all that effort and then have you fall for a girl from nowhere. How could I ever look the Judge and the Professor in the eye again? They're good people. Olivia is good people. And you are too, Scott. That's why I know you won't let the team down."

"So, what's your plan, Senator?"

"Son, play nice with Kaitlyn. Get as much information as you can. The Judge, the Professor and I have decided you and Olivia need to transfer to another school after this semester. Keep you away from Kaitlyn. Then, she'll find another guy to fall in love with. A girl like that won't have problems finding guys. You and Olivia should talk about what school you want. Trust the Judge, Professor and me to arrange the rest."

Scott hesitates.

"You need to get on board with this, Scott. It's the only way to stop Kaitlyn short of a bullet in the head. The Professor hasn't done that kind of work in a while. Let's keep it that way. I know I can count on you, Scott. You're steady. You've always come through. So has Olivia. That's why the two of you are going to lead this great country of ours someday. Just one more bit of political advice son. Texas has a lot of electoral votes. Good demographics. Will be bigger by the time you can run. Wouldn't be bad to add Texas to your bio. But you and Olivia decide where you want to go to school next. I don't want to interfere."[13]

*　*　*

---

12 Music Video Perfect Match https://www.youtube.com/watch?v=ivfa2KdGtsw
13 Music Video Your Right To Act Stupid https://www.youtube.com/watch?v=eBS hN8qT4lk

One by one, the families leave. Having received much needed family support, the students also remember why they needed to get away from home.

*   *   *

At the Foundation, scientists labor to analyze the collected data.

Yes, preliminary data is consistent with prior years. 75% less sex in the freshman class on parents' weekend.

Let's see if it spikes tonight like in past years.

*   *   *

"Allen, your date with Michelle really isn't a good idea."

"OK, little brother. I'm listening. Tell me why."

"I can't. I promised not to."

"Does she have an STD or something?"

"Yeah, you guessed it. So, you can't . . . you know."

"Sheldon, you do know I can call her right now and ask her."

"But you wouldn't do that, Allen. Would you?"

"Just as I thought, you're lying bro. I don't know what your game is Sheldon, but don't stand between me and getting laid."

"Time to go. Maybe I'll send you a picture of us in bed, little brother."

23

Miss Adventures on the Edge

Michelle waits by the Bell Tower oblivious to her surroundings, pondering her next move, "When do I tell him about the private part of me nobody sees? It might not be tonight. Maybe it will just be a simple date. Dinner? A goodnight kiss? Maybe a little more? But I want it to be more . . . much more. So, how do I tell him without him hating me for tricking him?"[1]

While Michelle is lost in thought, Allen sneaks up from behind. His big hands cover her eyes.

"Allen?"

All Michelle hears is heavy breathing. "What does that hot breathe on my neck trigger in me?"[2] she wonders. Emerging from her dreamworld, she shifts into her Scarlett O'Hara mode.

"Now, that's not nice Allen."

To herself, "How did he know I like this kind of thing?"

"This better be Allen or I'm screaming rape."

"Relax Michelle, It's just a game. You like games, don't you?"

"Yes, but a girl likes to play her own games."

"When we met, I thought you were a girl who likes adventures. I could feel it. Now I'm feeling you're icy."

---

1 Video Trans Trick https://www.youtube.com/watch?v=GaSCO_Z6w5U
2 Music Video Catch My Breathe https://www.youtube.com/watch?v=HEValZuFYRU

"Allen, I'm so disappointed. Don't you know how hot icy girls get with the right man?"[3] Michelle looks up pouting her lips.

"Now that's the kind of invitation I was looking for," as his arm envelopes her.

"OMG, he's so strong. I could never escape his grip even if I wanted, and I don't want."

"What's your plan for our date?"

Sensing the physical connection, "I'm staying in a friend's apartment. He'll be gone tonight. The fridge is stocked. So, the evening is ours. You OK with that?"

"OK big spender. But saying yes to the apartment doesn't mean I'm saying yes to everything."

"Girl, you'll be the one asking me," as he caresses Michelle's rear. "Had to do that. Can't stand boney-assed girls."[4]

"So, do the goods pass inspection?"

"With plenty of room to spare Sweet Ass."

"Sweet Ass?" she thinks "Should I play indignant? No, time for Scarlett to go home. Time to play Carrie Bradshaw." Michelle looks up and pulls herself tighter to him, "Not such a bad ass yourself, Allen."

* * *

"Here's our pleasure palace," as they enter the apartment.

Michelle thinks "Kaitlyn was here with Scott. Wonder where they did it. Bedroom? Couch? All over? Some night Kaitlyn and I should compare notes."

"How about fixing us some dinner, Michelle?"

"Oh! I get to work in the kitchen while you do what?"

"While I do this, Michelle."

After catching her breathe from a long engulfing kiss, she says, "That's more like it. From now on, you're Sweet Lips. I love cooking for a man

---

3 Music Video Hot https://www.youtube.com/watch?v=fzb75m8NuMQideo
4 Music Video Fat Bottomed Girls https://www.youtube.com/watch?v=tpzkSg9e3Uw

who knows what he wants and isn't afraid to go and get it. Let me see what I have to work with in the fridge."

"Good girl!" as Michelle feels a slap on her rear, she thinks "He's a natural alpha. He'll only need a little training. As Michelle imagines their coupling."[5]

"Allen, can you let go? I need to be able to move my arms if you want dinner," as Allen draws her closer Michelle playfully squirms in his embrace.

"Nope, you're making me hungry for something other than food, Michelle."

"Allen, if all guys were this good in the kitchen, women would never complain about cooking. Now, you go get us something to drink while I finish here."

*   *   *

"Hey, you can cook! Nice appetizer."

Michelle tries to remain aloof while they eat, thinking "Maybe I should play hard to get.[6] But that's one game I've never been good at."

"OK, Michelle, ready for the main course?"

As Allen guides her to the couch, Michelle thinks "I feel so . . . desired. So . . . on fire."[7] But realizing this is the time to tell all, Michelle holds both his wrists to slow him down, "Allen, pay attention. Please? No, stop that, at least until I tell you something. It's important that you listen. Really! I hope it won't make a difference."

Allen laughs.

"What's so funny? Share your thoughts, Allen?"

"My stupid brother, Michelle."

"What about Shelley?"

"He warned me about you. Your deep dark secret."

"And you're OK with my secret?"

---

5 Movie Clip Dominant https://www.youtube.com/watch?v=MciGrZ6bjTM
6 Music Video Hard to Get https://www.youtube.com/watch?v=UwXkHj679ko
7 Music Video Fire https://www.youtube.com/watch?v=9VKjxWcd96s

"Hell yeah!"

"Oh Allen! I've been dreading telling you. It would scare off some guys."

"Not me. Not for someone as hot as you, Sweet Ass. That's what condoms are for."

"OMG, it's a miracle! No awkward explaining!" Michelle thinks, as she glues herself to Allen's muscular body and begins her seduction.[8]

"What's got into you girl? Has the ice queen has melted?"

"Shut up Allen. Take me. I'm yours."[9]

Let loose, Allen does his thing, like with dozens of girls before,[10] "I'm struggling, but he's so strong he doesn't even notice," Michelle thinks, as Allen explores her body until Allen discovers Michelle's secret, "Huh! How is this happening?" Like a bolt of lightning just hit him, Allen suddenly stands up and Michelle finds herself on the floor.

"But you said Shelley warned you, Allen. You said it was OK. Why are you acting so surprised?"[11]

"Sheldon told me you had STDs. I can deal with that. But not this."

When Allen moves to help her off the floor, they bump heads. "Did I kill her?" Allen worries as Michelle lays on the floor unconscious, "I'm in big trouble. Come on, Sweet Ass. We didn't bump that hard. Come back to life. You're back! Thank God!" as Michelle regains consciousness.

"Look, Michelle. I'm sorry. This is weirder than I'm used to. Sometimes, I'm kind of a jerk with women. Half the girls in my hometown probably hate me after they liked me. But I don't normally hurt girls physically. It was an accident."

Allen lifts Michelle off the floor and gently places her on the bed. Stroking her hair, "I'm so sorry."

"I know you're sorry. I can feel it. Can you get past my secret? We were getting along so nicely. It'll be fine. You'll see."

---

8 Music Video Seduction https://www.youtube.com/watch?v=FcmErbAsI7I
9 Movie Clip Top Gun https://www.youtube.com/watch?v=WqT9O8acsvk
10 Music Video Intercourse https://www.youtube.com/watch?v=z5Ex9gyOmp0
11 Music Surprise https://www.youtube.com/watch?v=NRaXyaBul8E

Michelle sees that Allen isn't going along, "No, please don't cry, Michelle. I'm just not prepared for this kind of thing. Ice, I'll get you some ice."

"Oooh! that hurts. Don't press. I'm delicate, like a feather. Just touch. That's better," Michelle says. With an inviting smile she lifts her head and kisses Allen.

"Michelle, please don't."

Disappointed, Michelle feigns fear, "Just don't hurt me again.[12] OK? You don't know how to do it the way I like it."

"The way you like it, Michelle?"

"Yes, it has to be a certain way. Now get me a mirror.[13] It's in my purse, you naughty boy." Surveying the damage, "I think I can cover this with a little makeup."

"Michelle, I'm confused. I mean . . . I knocked you out cold. Even I know that's not right. But you're not mad. What's going on?"

"Shelley tried to warn you I'm an unusual girl. Allen, sometimes I like . . . hard love[14] . . . to be punished. Just not the way you did it. When we do this again, they'll have to be rules."

"Again?"

After Michelle explains her other secret to Allen.

"That's what you like, Michelle?"

"Oh yes, it can be so beautiful and sad at the same time. When it's done the way I like, it's like a tragic Opera.[15] And I can teach you. I'll teach you the punishments that are OK with me."

"Michelle, this isn't going to work for me. You should stop that. I mean it, Michelle, stop touching me."

Michelle thinks. I'm so torn now. He was making me feel like a desired woman[16] and now he's treating me like I'm a freak. Fighting off tears, Michelle decides Allen needs to learn a life lesson.

12 Music Video Don't Hurt Me Again https://www.youtube.com/watch?v=SAbolKsUL4o
13 Music Video Girl in Mirror https://www.youtube.com/watch?v=U_1Ne7XHBas
14 Music Video Love Me Harder https://www.youtube.com/watch?v=g5qU7p7yOY8
15 Movie Clip Madam Butterfly https://www.youtube.com/watch?v=sLcbfF9ypmM
16 Movie Clip Natural Woman https://www.youtube.com/watch?v=aEsWXYy1NPo

"Allen, Shelley told me you're a man of the world. Why are acting like a virgin[17] on her first night?"

"Michelle, we're from totally different planets. You and I aren't going to work together. Sorry, but it's not what I want."

"Allen, this is all your fault!"

"What?"

"I was having a perfectly lovely time with my family last night when you pursued me at the party. I agreed to go on a date with you because you're Shelley's brother. I was being polite. I assumed you're a gentleman[18] because your brother is."

"Sheldon and I are different."

"I assumed we would have a nice date at a restaurant or bar. We could have gotten to know one another better. If we liked one another, I could have explained my secret to you. Then, you could have backed away and we would both have our dignity. If we didn't like each other, nothing would have happened. Right?"

"I guess . . .."

"Instead, you lured me up to this apartment. Started grabbing me all over. Made me cook for you. Then, you tell me you know my secret, but after you get me all excited, you panic and knock me out. Because of one little thing, it's all off. And now, I can't even touch you?"

"Michelle, that's exactly what I did. I'm so sorry. But nothing is going to happen between us tonight. I can't."

"What a little tease[19] you are, Allen. Isn't that what you'd say about a girl who suddenly changes her mind at the last minute?"

"Well, yeah, I guess."

"And would you stop if she changes her mind, Allen?"

"Well yes, . . . at least sometimes," Allen says while remembering a time he didn't stop.

---

17 Music Video Like a Virgin https://www.youtube.com/watch?v=s__rX_WL100
18 Movie Clip Gone With Wind https://www.youtube.com/watch?v=lrhNPS4nbmQ
19 Music Video Tease https://www.youtube.com/watch?v=AYRjw_8GnDE

Pouting, "OK, Allen. I won't make you defend your virtue again. I won't touch my little virgin. I'll be a lady even if you aren't a gentleman. Even a tease like you is entitled to change her mind."

A confused Allen thinks, "This seems familiar, but different."[20]

Knowing that she has Allen on the defensive now, Michelle changes her approach, "But you can make up for hurting me in another way. There's ice cream in the freezer. I deserve a treat. Do you think you can do that for me?"

"OK, Michelle, but that's all."

Michelle pictures how Audrey Hepburn ate ice cream in 'Roman Holiday.'[21] "No, it's a little late to play innocent Audrey. Need to be more like Uma Thurman in 'Pulp Fiction'[22] or Angela Jolie in 'Girl, Interrupted.'[23] Definitely time for Uma and Angela to take over."

"I like it slow,[24] one spoonful at a time, as she spills it and begins licking it off his chest. Make me feel like you're grateful for my suffering." As Michelle turns on her charms. With each lick,[25] she senses its effect on Allen. Whispering in his ear as she finishes, "Ready to start again where we left off, Sweet Lips? I can see you're interested. I'll make life so sweet for you. Really, just let me show you."

"You're sexy, Michelle. Never saw anyone make love to ice cream like that. But sorry, I can't. Not gonna happen. I'm just gonna sit here and get very drunk.[26] It's late. I'll sleep on the couch. You take the bedroom. We'll figure things out in the morning," as Allen takes another long gulp from his Vodka bottle.

---

20 Music Video Girls Chase Boys https://www.youtube.com/watch?v=5GBT37_yyzY
21 Movie Clip Roman Holiday https://www.youtube.com/watch?v=tfj8QO_UDXQ
22 Movie Clip Pulp Fiction https://www.youtube.com/watch?v=lZzai6at_xA
23 Movie Clip Girl Interrupted https://www.youtube.com/watch?v=S3Po0Tld8Po
24 Movie Clip Ice Cream https://www.youtube.com/watch?v=rPQQUc3QZb8
25 Video Licking https://www.youtube.com/watch?v=kPpIT3MMG3Q
26 Music Video Drunk https://www.youtube.com/watch?v=G2fOum_KWQU

"You're so cute playing hard to get, Allen. I'm not going to beg you, but the next time a girl changes her mind, I hope you'll be more sympathetic now that you know how girls feel."[27]

* * *

Alone in the bedroom Sarah visits Michelle. "Oh! Sarah, didn't think I'd find you here."

"Allen's my son too, Michelle. I have a little advice for you about Allen. He's not really a bad boy. He's a lot like his father. Strong and stubborn. There's nothing subtle about him. He usually says what he means and means what he says. So, uncomplicated. Animal instincts. That's why I fell for his dad. Don't think you're going to change him. You'll get hurt if you try."

Michelle ignores Sarah's advice, smiling as she falls asleep, "He thinks I'm sexy!"[28] Once that happens, he's mine. It's only a matter of time before he changes his mind.

* * *

HER MEMORY SEEMS A BIT CLOUDY

---

27 Music Video Girls Feel https://www.youtube.com/watch?v=dxyo5ZXoBgQ
28 Music Video Sexy https://www.youtube.com/watch?v=G8xvVPoVMKo

24

A New Dawn

Michelle awakens and sees Allen asleep sprawled across the couch still in his clothes. Before Michelle leaves the apartment, she whispers as she kisses the groggy Allen,[1] "That's a good boy. Now go back to sleep."

"Have to get back to my dorm in time for sunrise yoga in the park with Allie," Michell thinks.

* * *

Walking back to her dorm in a daze, Michelle smiles thinking.

"Two days ago, my life was falling apart. Totally out of control."

"Now everything is perfect. I'm playing all the roles with a wonderful cast."

"I can be a good daughter and sister."

"I can mother Shelley."

"I have a perfect girlfriend, Allie."

"Allen was so sweet feeding me ice cream last night. He just needs to get used to something different. I'll have Shelley arrange another date. He'll change.[2] Then, I'll have my own bad boy to play games with on the edge. And he's a two-hour drive. Just far enough away not to interfere too much with my other roles."

---

1 Music Video Angel of the Morning https://www.youtube.com/watch?v=HTzGMEfbnAw
2 Music Video Future https://www.youtube.com/watch?v=nc00hlI2s_Y

"They're all taking care of me and I'm taking care of them all. Life is Sweet."

"And I am going to get that new hormone cocktail to help me do it."

"I'm the luckiest girl in the world."

* * *

Arriving at her dorm just as Allie is leaving for the park, "Can I join you girlfriend?"

"What's the matter? Does Superman have something against yoga?" as Allie pulls away from a kiss.

"I would never do yoga with Superman. Only with my beautiful girlfriend. Got that?"

"I'm going to go ahead. You should clean up. Right now, you're dressed for slut yoga, Michelle," Allie says smirking.

"Oooo . . . that's so mean. But you're entitled to take some shots. Putting up with my dark side. And I guess I do look kind of slutty. I'll clean up and join you in ten minutes. Then you can abuse me as much as you want. I probably deserve everything you can throw at me. You don't have to be nice to me until after lunch."

Before Allie leaves, "What's that on your face? Did he hit you? Looks like he did."

"Oh, it's nothing Allie. It was really my own fault."

"I don't believe what you just said, Michelle! Like a line in a bad Netflix movie. The women always excuse the guy. It's my fault. I did this . . . or I didn't do that . . . he didn't really mean it."

"I know what you're saying Allie. I guess I do sound like some poor redneck woman[3] standing up for her no-good man. But this is different. I mishandled how I showed him my secret. He freaked for 10 seconds. He didn't exactly hit me, just moved suddenly. But he's so strong it knocked me out. Then, he was as meek as a lamb. Took good care of me afterward."

---

3 Music Video Redneck Woman https://www.youtube.com/watch?v=u0oBUdFoj9w

"Don't give me that, Michelle. Guys who hurt girls are bad news. Maybe the first time it really is an accident. But later they begin thinking. 'I wasn't supposed to do that. But I got away with it.' Next time it's not an accident."

"I know, but . . . ."

"Look Michelle, you asked me to be a guide to help you be a woman your mom can be proud of. Permission to interfere. Remember? Well . . . I'm interfering now. Not because I'm jealous. Not because I want to. Not even because I promised you."

"Then why Allie?"

"Because I promised your mom. We both love you, but we both worry. No, don't try to persuade with hugs Michelle. This is too serious. Look, you want to become a poster child for an abused women's home. Go ahead. Just do one thing first . . . tell your mom about it."

"But she wouldn't understand, Allie."

"You got that right, Michelle. Not understand why you're acting crazy."

"OK, I'm listening, Allie. You really know how to bring me to my senses. You might be right. You go do your yoga. I'm going to lay down in my room and think about what you've said."

"And what will you do if Super Pig walks through that door after I'm gone?"

"I'll just tell him to run for his life cause my crazy Asian girlfriend is going to kill him."

On her way out, Allie passes Shelley in the hall with an icy stare and "What a pig!"

After Allie leaves, "Friday I felt like garbage. Saturday riding high. Back to trash again on Sunday. What's a poor sub girl to do? Do? It's Sunday. I can spend it with the best girl I've ever met. Or I can lay around feeling sorry for myself because my girlfriend doesn't understand my boyfriend."

When Michelle gets to the park, the rising sun frames Allie's body in dancer's pose, long silky black hair tied in a ponytail flowing down. Her 5'4" slender frame stretched to the max in perfect balance.

"OMG, she's like a goddess frozen in time[4] to teach humans the perfection they might aspire to." Michelle thinks as she snaps a picture, "something to remember when I feel like I'm drifting to my dark side."[5]

Joining Allie, both girls smile as they go through their poses, both sensing that Michelle's dark side has been banished by the light she now shares with Allie. Bathing in the serenity that follows when light banishes dark or dark banishes light, Michelle smiles thinking, "I'm the luckiest girl in the world."

---

4 Pic Allie Dawn Yoga https://firepitcell.com/wp-content/uploads/2022/01/C24N4-Allie-Dawn-Yoga.jpg

5 Music Video Dark Side https://www.youtube.com/watch?v=H5ArpRWcGe0

25

Dark Disappears in Light

Later that morning on the quad, a large black bird flying across the sky reminds Michelle of her dilemma. "I love both the light and the dark sides of me. I do want it all. Allie, will you hold me?" a fragile Michelle asks.

"When you ask like that girlfriend, anything is possible."

Snuggling into Allie, "I need a day with you. A whole day of lightness. A day . . . we'll both remember . . . I mean . . . years from now. A very sweet day. OK?"

"Did he scare you?"

"No . . . it's just . . . sometimes I scare myself. Want to hear something funny? I think I probably scared Allen more than he scared me. He's not used to being on the edge. He's got his own little thing going. Some people like it. Others don't. Does he care? Probably not. Just wants to continue doing his Allen thing. It must be nice to be like that. Whatever your thing is. To know what it is. And be satisfied by it."[1]

"Thanks for sharing, Michelle, but I don't want to know the details between you and Allen. All I know is that he's not a rival for the Michelle I love. The Michelle who likes the light and makes sweet days. The Michelle who looks at me like I'm someone special. I know I have that Michelle all to myself. The Allen's of the world only have another person, the dark Michelle."

"You sound sure of that, Allie. You should be. It's so true."

---

1 Music Video Satisfied https://www.youtube.com/watch?v=ArAlk3yf5hI

"I saw it in your eyes this morning . . . and the way you smiled. Not the big smile you show everyone. Your small secret smile that only I notice. I love this Michelle. And yes, Michelle, we both need a day of sweetness and light."

Seeing a smile, "Michelle, what's going on in that brain of yours?"

"I was thinking about which movie stars we should be today to bring us the most sweetness and light, Julie Andrews."

"That's pretty sweet."

"You don't understand yet, Allie. We need a double dose of sweetness and light. So, we'll both play her today. You be Julie in Mary Poppins. I'll be Julie in 'The Sound of Music."

"Michelle, I'd do anything to see you play a nun! So, you're on, but Julie can be bad girl too."[2]

*   *   *

"Michelle, are you OK?"

"Of course, Shelley. Why?"

"I mean your date with my brother. Did you? Did he? You know, find out."

"Why Shelley! What personal questions to ask a girl! I'm not one to kiss and tell. And why would you assume I drop my panties on a first date? I mean you may sleep around, but not this girl."

"OK Michelle, play your little games. I'm not trying to be nosy. Just concerned about you."

"I know Shelley Dear. And I'm so pleased you kept my little secret from your brother. Now I really know I can trust you," as Michelle kisses Shelley's cheek.

"Wait, Shelley, one more thing. Does your family like big weddings or small?"

*   *   *

---

2 Music Video 7 Rings https://www.youtube.com/watch?v=QYh6mYIJG2Y

Sheldon's phone rings.

Seeing its Allen, Sheldon thinks, "I don't want to talk about this. Should I answer? I can't hide forever."

"Yes Allen. What's up?"

"Your roommate and her little secret. That's what's up bro![3] I'm in the park across from your dorm, little brother. Get your ass down here now."

*   *   *

Olivia's phone rings.

"Scott, is there a problem?"

"Is Kaitlyn there?"

"No, she's having breakfast with her parents before they leave."

"Good, we need to talk."

"OK, in an hour? At your place?"

*   *   *

Sheldon calls Luna.

"Hi Luna, want to meet my brother Allen?"

"Sorry Sheldon. Can't. Getting ready for the big hackers meeting later today."

"See you there?

"Damn! My last chance to avoid Allen's wrath was to have Luna with me."

*   *   *

The Korosec family having breakfast with Nicole and Gerald before leaving town.

"So, Nicole, are you and Gerald related?"

"Not like in a blood sort of way Mr. Korosec."

"Daddy . . . they're like way, way better than just being a family! Jamal, Nicole's older brother, helped Gerald when he was a boy. And ever since

---

3 Video Bro Code https://www.youtube.com/watch?v=5uIc-TUbMGk

Jerold died, Gerald has been taking care of Nicole, Jamal's little sister. Isn't that so sweet."

"Gerald, you manned up. Need more of that in this country. Too many guys not manning up like you."

"Like you said Mr. Korosec. Just doing what's right."

"By the way sir, if you don't mind, did you get that limp in the war?"

"No. Survived the war OK. Shootout with a drug dealer when I was a police officer. He ambushed two of my team. They died before I got him. Worst day of my life. I loved those guys. Good family men. Good officers. But we all knew we were signing up for that possibility. Just grateful I've had ten extra years with my family."

Dead Silence follows.[4]

"Daddy, I guess it's time to say goodbye."

"Yes, long drive home."

As she hugs her mother, "Take care of Daddy. I miss him so much."

*　*　*

"Did they tell you, Olivia?"

"You mean about changing schools next semester?"

As Scott nods, "Yes, the Judge and Professor told me last night."

"Well? What do you think Olivia?"

*　*　*

Sheldon sees his brother standing at the park entrance and walks the hundred steps from his dorm to the park like a doomed prisoner walking slowly to the gallows,[5] until he hears, "Shelley!" a reprieve from heaven in the form of Kaitlyn's perky voice.

*　*　*

---

4 Music Video Sounds of Silence https://www.youtube.com/watch?v=BXuveostQaQ
5 Music Video Gallows Pole https://www.youtube.com/watch?v=NedEQ6sHloE

"Allie, I love the way your hair shines in the sunlight," as Michelle massages Allie's neck laying on the quad with a picnic breakfast.

"You can do that all day, girlfriend. Massage me and tell me how beautiful I am."

* * *

"Allen, Kaitlyn rooms across the hall from me. This is our friend Nicole."

"Ladies . . . maybe you can help me figure this out. My little brother went all through high school without talking to a girl, at least not to any girl who will admit it. Now he knows all the hottest girls on campus. How?"

"That's simple Allen," Kaitlyn replies. "College girls are smarter than high school girls. We know a catch when we see one."

"Shelley's definitely a catch," Nicole adds.

"What about his big brother?"

"Too small to keep," Katlyn and Nicole giggle walking away. "State law requires us to release the minnows."

"Ouch, you're killing me ladies."

* * *

"I'll start looking at schools this week Scott."

"Wait a minute! You mean you're on board with their plan, Olivia?"

"Of course, it's our new plan, Scott."

"No, not this time Olivia."

* * *

"Michelle, I'm tired of my girlfriend being a nun.[6] So, limiting. Feel like God will strike me down if I touch you. Can we play another game?"

"Allie, let's be each other the rest of today?"

"What do you mean, Michelle?

6 Video Nun https://www.youtube.com/watch?v=RFgMi8my_uY

"I mean you play Michelle and I'll play Allie. We're both actresses, right? Come on, it'll be fun."

"OK, but I'm not sure which Michelle you are today."

"The light and sweet one. The dark Michelle is on hold for a while. OK, I'm taller, but we're practically the same size, except shoes. Let's switch closets and makeup and hair styles for the rest of the day. The works."

"OK, Michelle, let's see if you can really play Allie."

"Be ready in half an hour?" and the girls go off to the other's room to dress for their new roles.

* * *

"Alone at last little brother. Let's take a walk."

"OK Allen, but . . ."

"Relax Sheldon. I'm not mad. At least not anymore."

"You're not? You mean you liked Michelle's surprise?"

"No, that's not what I mean. Are you crazy? I mean it's not that big a deal after you get over the initial surprise. I've seen a lot of kinky things. This is just one more."

"So, do you plan to see her again?

"No, once is enough. Too many real girls to screw. Before I left town, I just wanted to say that I'm glad you're doing so well at school. I mean making friends. I always knew the academics would be a cinch for you. But glad you're catching up in other areas."

"Thanks, Allen. I think I'm on a new and better path."

"One last thing, Sheldon. Your roommate is into playing some kinky games. I know she's been helping you, but watch out for her dark side. Don't let her lock you up or anything like that. Tell her I'll call her. Girls like that. I don't always do it, but she's your friend. So, I will. Don't worry. I won't be a jerk when I call her."

* * *

"So, what happened with Scott yesterday, Kaitlyn?"

"Very little, Nicole. I talked to his father more than to him. The Senator is quite . . . colorful."

"What's that mean, Kaitlyn?"

"Well . . . you know how an older guy like that will sometimes look at you and seem like he's seeing right through your clothes?"

"Yeah . . . once they reach a certain age, they figure they have no chance, so what the hell."

"Well, it was a little like that, Nicole, except . . . it felt like he thought he still has a chance."[7]

"Oh! Really creepy."

"Now here's . . . the big surprise. Less creepy than I would have imagined."

"Kaitlyn! You mean . . . .."

"He has unusual charm for an old guy that keeps him out of the totally pathetic category. I kind of see how some of those DC interns fall for an older guy like that."

"And why are you smiling like that, Kaitlyn?"

"Because I'm imaging how charming Scott's going to be when he's that age. I mean if his father still has that effect on women. Then maybe Scott will too."

"I got it. You're thinking when you're an old lady you'll still be hot for Scott. Imagine being 40 or even 50 and still hot for each other?"

"You got it. But my first job is catching the young Scott. That's still up in the air."

*   *   *

Allie calls Michelle, "Ready for the unveiling?"

"Meet you outside the library in 15 minutes. I'll leave first. I want to watch you approach to see whether you have my walk down pat."

---

7 Music Video Guys My Age https://www.youtube.com/watch?v=3LzWUAkpNrQ

"This is going to be so much fun, Michelle. A sweet day of lightness and acting."

* * *

"Kaitlyn, there's a short play at the Black Student Union this afternoon. Want to come with me?" Now don't be getting all gushy on me girl. Yeah . . . I know what I said before. But we're different now. Just don't embarrass me, OK? Try to remember this. Thinking comes first. Talking is second."

* * *

"OMG, I just knew you'd pick those shorts and to play me. It's my favorite outfit. I guess I wear them a lot. Is that the way I really walk? Too much eye liner girlfriend. Totally NOT me. Well . . . maybe sometimes. And what about me, Michelle. Do you think I got you right?

"Totally. You really know me. You're more me than I am."

Michelle thinks, "Totally the one side of me she knows. I wish I could show Allie all of me. Maybe someday. But not today. Today is all light."

* * *

"Hi Shelley! What are you doing here?"

"Hacker's meeting in the library. Me, Luna and Sanjay."

"Inside? On such a beautiful day?"

"Well, hacking seems like an inside thing."

A confused Shelley looks at both girls several times, "Michelle and Allie, you're getting me mixed up. You're both different than you usually are."

"He noticed!" both girls giggle.

"Noticed what?"

"Now, Shelley, pay attention. Tell us what you noticed. It's important."

"Well, you kind of switched. I mean, I still know you're Michelle and you're Allie, but you've kind of blended. That doesn't make much sense to me, but that's what I see."

Both girls kiss, "We did it!"

"Thanks Shelley. You made our day."

* * *

"Sorry I'm late Luna. Anything interesting?"

"Sanjay and I have been trying to hack into the Follow the Science Foundation."

"Cool! Maybe we can find the experiment they're doing on me."

"That sounds fair. They know everything about you. You should know about them."

"Any luck?"

"None so far. Sanjay's taking a short break, but he'll be back soon. Maybe the three of us can some progress."

"Luna, there's something else. I want us to not just have a date and then go back to being just classmates."

"Shelley, that was lovely. What made you decide to kiss me like that? So impulsive. Not like you".

"Luna, you're changing me. I'm still not an impulsive person . . . except with you. Is that, OK?"

"Mumm Humm!" as Luna returns the kiss, "We're special together."

* * *

"Michelle, do I really talk about my family like that? I guess I do still have some issues to work through. Don't I?"

"OK, now I'll be Michelle. Oh, my hormones! Someone get me my hormones."

"Allie, I wish I could really be you and you really be me. Just for a day."

"That's my Michelle. Always wants to play every role. But if I really played you, do you think you could stand it? You're a handful even when you not in your dark side."

"Maybe you're right, Allie, I really like you being in charge and me trying to get away with things. I'd hate to be in charge."

*   *   *

Making noise as he enters the room to give Shelley and Luna time to get back to their computers, "Sorry to interrupt.

"That's OK Sanjay. We're finished for now."

"I briefed Shelley on what we've done so far with the Foundation. He suggested a few different approaches"

*   *   *

"Olivia, I mean it. We can't keep changing our lives because our parents say so."

"Let's finish this assignment and then decide what we want to do, Scott."

"I don't know, Olivia."

"Is this because of Kaitlyn? Are you are we losing everything[8] because of Kaitlyn?"

"I don't want to throw you away, Olivia. Just the 15 years our parents have manipulated both of us. I'm a man. You're a woman.[9] Time to see whether we want to be together. I like Kaitlyn. So do you. I think we like her for the same reasons. She's living her life being happy. Or at least trying to. We're living the lives our parents created. I'm jealous of Kaitlyn. I think you are too."

Nodding, "Scott, what are we going to do?" Olivia sniffles.

---

8 Movie Clip Top Gun https://www.youtube.com/watch?v=Y7YyC3Z1dbg
9 Movie Clip Man Loves Woman https://www.youtube.com/watch?v=6VSyKVgi0_8

"Olivia, I really do care for you. I'm a little confused now. Sometimes you're my girlfriend. And I really like that. Other times you're more like a partner? Sometimes a sister?"

"I'm confused too, Scott. Our life together has been good. But it's kind of like Prom night.[10] Every detail planned. That's fine for one night, but it's not real life. Where do our parents' plans end and the real us begin?"

"Don't know, but it's time we both find out."

* * *

Later that evening

"Hey Michelle, just calling to thank you for forgiving me for your bruise last night. How's that bruise now?

"Good to hear."

"Yes . . . Uh huh . . . I understand."

* * *

"Walking back from the play."

"So, Blondie. What did you think?"

"Nicole, let's just say it wasn't very upbeat."

"But that's the point. To show how the world really is."

"I know. You're right. I don't know the whole world. Just my little piece if it. Now it's time for me to learn. And I'm happy you're showing me. But can we still get ice cream?"

"Blondie, I'm buying the ice cream cones tonight . . . but only chocolate."

* * *

---

10 Cartoon Video Prom Night https://www.youtube.com/watch?v=xgQ8BJdkN5U

Allen calling Sheldon, "I just hung up with Michelle. Went better than planned. She doesn't want a follow up session. Likes her girlfriend, Allie. So, I don't have to be the jerk again."

"No, don't say anything to her about our talk. Everybody's walking away from this a little wiser with their dignity intact. Talking about it can only upset a good outcome."

"Allen, you're not as big a jerk as I thought."

"Sheldon, you're not half the wimp I thought."

"See you at home Thanksgiving."

*   *   *

"Allie, I used to be afraid.

"Of what, Michelle?"

"Of the dark . . . my dark side."

"And you aren't now?"

"Well, maybe a little, Allie, but I realized something sharing this sweet day with you. I think it may be important."

"Share, girlfriend."

"I realized that dark isn't real. Dark is just when there's no light. And if we keep light in our life, it'll never get dark. Then, you and I can be in the light together[11] all the time."

---

11 Music Video Light up My Life https://www.youtube.com/watch?v=BsBY722rb2M

26

Can You Go Home Again?

A week later.

"Allie, why are you looking at me like that? Are you all right?"

"Michelle, you know I care for you . . . you're my best friend, and I appreciate your devotion to me but . . .."

"But you don't want it to be just us? Is that it, Allie?"

"Well, yes. I need . . . you know . . . I hate to say it . . ."

"You need a 'real' girl? Is that the reason, Allie?"

"Not instead of you, Michelle. Its good when we're together, but there are some things I miss . . .."[1]

"I know it's not exactly the same with us. I miss things. You miss things. So, I'm not surprised. Is it Elizabeth?"

"Yes, how did you know?"

"Allie, I know you. You know me. Better than other people do. We can't really keep secrets from one another. Can we?

"No . . . guess not. So, what're we going to do Michelle?"

"Allie, we're young. We're in love. But we both know we each have other interests. You've put up with mine. I'm grateful for that. I'll try to do the same. Remember when we both promised we'd live on the edge together?"

"Is this how we do that, Michelle?"

---

1 Music Video Only a Girl https://www.youtube.com/watch?v=jRIzDQEB1mk

"At least for now. That may change later, but right now, I think living on the edge together includes other people to give us the things we can't give each other."

"Getting kind of crowded out here on the edge. This doesn't end us, does it Michelle?"

"Allie, you're my alpha. I'm committed to making you happy and accept your decisions. You're the only one I can trust. I'm totally committed to preserving our harmony."

Allie's eyes betray her, "You didn't tell Elizabeth about me, did you? About me being a new girl?"[2]

"Oh Michelle, I feel so . . . I didn't mean to . . . it just happened before I knew what I was saying. You know, it was pillow talk. People say all kinds of things in bed. Elizabeth was curious and it came out."

"Allie! I'm so very disappointed in my alpha," is all the misty-eyed Michelle can say. Backing away, "I guess I've idealized us, Allie, I see the truth[3] now."

As she watches the crying Michelle run across campus, Allie thinks, "I've made a really big mistake . . . will she ever trust me again?"

* * *

Back at their dorm, "Michelle, why are you crying?" Shelley asks as he returns to their room.

"Endings are sad, it's OK to cry,[4] Shelley. I just need to let it flow out of me. Then, I'll know what I should do."

* * *

---

2 Music Video New You https://www.youtube.com/watch?v=R9SQl0cSfI8

3 Music Video Truth https://www.youtube.com/watch?v=_3r6wKnPK7Q

4 Music Video https://www.youtube.com/watch?v=YQHsXMglC9A

Laying on her bed alone in her dark dorm room, Michelle thinks, "I was hoping I could always move forward, not back. But now I need to renew old ties," as she calls an old friend.

"Hi Brock. I heard you were in town."

"Maybe we could get together."

"No, I haven't been there. Haven't gone to those types of places in a long time. But I can find it."

"Tonight? 10 o'clock? Yes, I'll see you there."

* * *

Getting dressed for her reunion with Brock, Michelle ponders.

"I called him in a panic because I was feeling hurt and alone. I thought I was over him, but isn't the person you call when you're feeling bad important to you? Clearly, I'm not over him."

As Michelle ponders her complicated relationship with Brock, her mind drifts to the bubbles and she hears Sarah Atwell. "No, you're not over Brock, honey. But you are over the pain and suffering. You've changed. You're stronger now."

"Sarah, do you think maybe this time it'll be different? Maybe he's changed? Maybe I'll change him?"

"Maybe, but what I think doesn't matter, Michelle. Personally, I think Allie is better for you, but you can't live in the bubbles wondering about Brock. You need to find out for yourself. Just don't let him draw you back. Be prepared to walk away. And . . .."

"And what, Sarah?

"Well Dear, pardon me for being so blunt, but you need to change your image. Look at how you're dressed. It's, well, kind of slutty. He already thinks of you like a slut. You need to reappear to him as a lady, if you want him to treat you like a lady."

Looking in the mirror, Michelle assesses herself. "You're right Sarah. Brock and I need a new beginning?[5] I'm not going to get what I want just

---

5 Music Video New Rules https://www.youtube.com/watch?v=k2qgadSvNyU

walking into that bar looking the way he expects. I need a strategy, like a script in a play. And every strategy needs a matching wardrobe. My normal campus jeans and T-shirts aren't right."

As Michelle surveys her closet, and tries on outfits, "No, too sexy. Sarah is right. He'll just pick up where we left off. I don't want that, do I? No, but what do I want? I want to be like an all American girl."[6]

As she peruses her clothes, she answers her question, "I want respect. I want to be treated like a lady. But I also want him to want me. Of course, I do. But he should feel like he has to earn me. Not that he already has me."

As Michelle continues her wardrobe search. "Not much to work with. Don't I have anything between college girl casual and slutty?"

"Who should I be tonight?" Then shining eyes and a beautiful smile fill her consciousness. "Ingrid Bergman playing Ilsa in Casablanca.[7] She had Humphrey Bogart drooling even though she was wearing clothes my mother would wear. That classy look will keep Brock off balance. But what do I have that's classy?" Then she notices something at the end of the closet rack, "The suit Elaine bought me when I went to that convention in Chicago as her assistant. Haven't worn it since then. Let's try it."

Looking in the mirror, "Michelle, you look like a librarian,[8] a well-dressed librarian, but that's too much respect. Don't want to be talking about books all night, not that he's read any. Accessories might help. Sexy shoes. Shiny purse. And these."

Modeling before the mirror, "This is the look, I want.[9] A hip business-woman, maybe in fashion sales, out for a drink and a little fun after a working dinner. Oh yes! This is the look. This girl isn't going to bed with just anyone. Bed. That's a definite no, tonight. That would be a big mistake. No matter what happens, I'm all business tonight. No bed. If that's all he wants, I'll just get on that plane like Ilsa and he'll never see me again Or will I?"

---

6 Music Video All American Girl https://www.youtube.com/watch?v=m36xv75MJ4U

7 Movie Clip Casablanca https://www.youtube.com/watch?v=Do2olZ49M54

8 SNL Clip Librarian https://www.youtube.com/watch?v=IrMTLV2cR2Q

9 Pic Michelle Businesswoman https://www.youtube.com/watch?v=XOMKCX3DhFQ

After deciding her character's role and costume, "Wouldn't Allie be surprised to see me looking like this? What will I do if Allie stops by? I have no idea. I hate her now. But she's still my alpha, and I love her. Maybe, I'll forgive her.[10] Maybe we'll just go back to normal."

* * *

Meanwhile, Allie sits in the dining hall talking with Kaitlyn,
"Kaitlyn, what am I going to do? I messed up with Michelle. Betrayed her trust."
In return, Kaitlyn confides in Allie about the bumps in her relationship with Scott.
Both girls decide it's not too late to try to fix their relationships.

* * *

"Oh my, time to leave. Guess I'll never know what I would have done if I saw Allie tonight."
On her way down the stairs, "Michelle? Is that you? It's a little late to be going out for a job interview, isn't it?"
"Depends on the job, Olivia. Depends on the job."

* * *

As Michelle leaves the dorm by one door, Allie enters through the other.
Determined to make amends with Michelle, Allie finds an empty room.
"I hope Michelle doesn't do anything drastic," Allie thinks, "love her, but she's always on the edge."

* * *

---

10 Music Video Forgive https://www.youtube.com/watch?v=VTFX0Q7rq-E

As her Uber drives through the dark town, Michelle becomes mesmerized watching the traffic lights as the blocks speed by.[11] Ignoring her driver's attempts at conversation, Michelle feels herself being pulled back three years and imagines herself playing Alice in 'Alice Through the Looking Glass.'[12] "Wonder how my Mad Hatter is? How has he changed? Has time run out for us?"

When her car stops in front of the seedy club,[13] she thinks, "Looks just like one of Brock's typical places from the old days. I'm not dressed for this place. A businesswoman wouldn't be caught dead in a place like this. Or she might end up a corpse."

Then, "Driver, I've changed my mind. Take me back to the university." Then, half a block away she hears herself say, "Stop driver."

A kaleidoscope of images flash[14] through her brain melting into one another. "What's happening? Am I Michael again? No, Brock, I'll behave. It was just a slow night, I didn't steal anything, I swear. Doctor, do you have to report these bruises? Sorry, I don't do that. Officer, don't tell my parents. Brock, you do love me, don't you?"

"Why do I feel like I'm falling.[15] Now flying. I'm so lost." After wrapping her arms around the back of the driver's seat to steady herself, Michelle is jolted back to reality as the driver opens her door and taps her hand, "Miss, are you OK? Do you need a doctor?"

"No, I'm alright. You can let me off here."

Slowly walking the half block to the club, "I have no idea what I'll find once I open that door, but I need to find out." Seeing her refection in a window restores her confidence. "This time, I'm in charge. He'll see."

Entering the club, she sees Brock[16] at a table in the corner of the half empty club. 30ish. Three days beard stubble. Not exactly athletic looking,

---

11 Video City at Night https://www.youtube.com/watch?v=GG4pdvU0pSs
12 Movie Clip Alice https://www.youtube.com/watch?v=x3IWwnNe5mc
13 Video Clubs https://www.youtube.com/watch?v=WD1Tacq43a0
14 Video Flashing Images https://www.youtube.com/watch?v=p6uvsu8g6BA
15 Music video Falling https://www.youtube.com/watch?v=olGSAVOkkTI
16 Music Video Saloon https://www.youtube.com/watch?v=3xfFbB2CRo8

but hard and sinewy. Someone who's been knocked around and survived. In a bar fight, kill him or he'll get up and kill you.

"That's my man, for better or worse," she thinks, "Clint Eastwood, or he could have played that hard guy in Urban Cowboy. Poor Debra Winger.[17] Streamed that movie three times the same weekend. Why do Debra and I fall for the bad boys? That never happened to Ingrid Bergman. Why? Will I always be Debra? Why not Ingrid?"

"I had some hard times with Brock," as she pictures herself playing Jodie Foster in Taxi Driver.[18] "So, why am I here?" Answering her own question, "because he's what a part of me craves. I knew Brock was trouble the moment I saw him[19]. But I wanted trouble."

Michelle pretends to ignore Brock, sitting at the bar legs, demurely crossed at her ankles, she waits for Brock to make the first move, but Brock stares past her, surveying the room. Michelle wards off several potential dates.[20]

"That's just like him, keeping a lady waiting. He thinks he can wait me out. Make me come to him, but that was Michael, not me. Maybe I should show him and leave. Get on that plane like Ingrid Bergman."[21] Finally, "Time to find out whether I'm really over him." Feeling herself cast a small smile in his direction. "Why did I do that? Why couldn't I wait? Now, that he knows he's won, he'll make his move."

As Brock approaches, "Michael, good to see you. Didn't recognize you. Very classy look."

"It's Michelle now, Brock. And don't get any ideas. I'm out of your league now."

"OK, its Michelle. I'll play along for old times' sake, but you called me. I know I've got what you want."[22]

---

17 Movie Clip Urban Cowboy https://www.youtube.com/watch?v=XkasRfjEqFs

18 Move Clip Taxi Driver https://www.youtube.com/watch?v=SNulYDunfH0

19 Music Video Knew He Was Trouble https://www.youtube.com/watch?v=vNoKguSdy4Y

20 TV Clip Girl at Bar https://www.youtube.com/watch?v=kTMow_7H47Q

21 Movie Clip Airport Casablanca https://www.youtube.com/watch?v=KtiMG23ZVps

22 Video Woman CEO Window Washer https://www.youtube.com/watch?v=MBo C_8dePUY&t=28s

"Bartender, whiskey for me with a beer chaser, and a daiquiri for my lovely friend. That still your drink?"

"Not anymore Brock. Bartender, make that a gin and tonic. Light on the gin. A girl needs to keep her wits about her in a place like this."

Patting her backside, "That seems real enough."

"I'm not for hire anymore, Brock. It's polite to ask a lady before touching."

"Lady? Polite? Is that what you expect these days?" Mockingly kissing her hand, "how's that, my lady?"

"An improvement. Maybe you are trainable."

"Maybe, but don't get your hopes up, Michelle. Better women than you have tried."

"Not better Brock, just different. I'm not arriving at your doorstep desperate the way Michael did. I have a lot of good things going on. I've worked hard to change. I need you to respect that." As she picks up her purse, "I guess this was a mistake.[23] I'll pay for my own drink and go."

"Sorry, Michelle, please sit down, holding out the chair for her. "You have changed. Michael would never stand up for himself like that. Such a needy kid. Is it polite to ask, what's your story, Michelle?"

To herself, "He's calling me Michelle. Definitely need to be Ingrid Bergman tonight, not Jodie Foster."

"Very appropriate, Brock. I've learned this is what normal people do. So, thank you for asking."

Brock takes notice that Michelle isn't quite as adoring as Michael was and thinks, "OK new game and a new player.[24] What's her angle?"

"I'm starting over. Freshman at the university. New girl, new school, new life. I've made peace with my family." Sipping her drink, Michelle brings Brock up to date, ending with "And at this point with all the hormones, I'm more girl now than boy."

* * *

---

23 Music Video My Mistake https://www.youtube.com/watch?v=54ELKr-F1D8

24 Music Video End Game https://www.youtube.com/watch?v=dfnCAmr569k

"Michael, it's been a while since I've heard such a crock."

"Why are you so surprised Brock? I told you I was going to do it. Many times."

"People tell me all kinds of garbage in my business. Most of it never happens. And you always lived more in fantasyland than reality, Michael."

"It's Michelle, and it's not a fantasy. It's my life"

"Michael, I know you. I bought you your first dress."

"I know, Brock. It's still hanging in my closet. I thought about wearing it tonight . . . for old times' sake. It doesn't fit right anymore in the hips and other places. But I just can't seem to force myself to get rid of it."

"I must admit you've come a long way since that first $20 dress."

"$20 that I earned for you . . . the hard way, Brock."

"Michael, you loved your work. Never had anyone working for me so eager to please customers. Made you Miss Popularity. But let's not dwell on that. You're a lady now. Or are you?"

As Brock draws her closer, Michelle closes her eyes and . . . .. "You kiss better than in the old days Michael. Who have you been practicing with? Girls or boys?"

"Both, if you must know. And you can't just kiss me without permission."

"I just did Michelle. And I'll do it again . . . Bartender, the lady needs another drink. Make this one a daiquiri. You always were sexy sipping a daiquiri." As Brock explores Michelle's new assets "and I always liked licking your sweet daiquiri lips."

Michelle's hip businesswoman act begins to disintegrate, "I know. "Brock, I've missed . . .you."

*   *   *

"There's music playing. Shame to let a song go to waste. Still like to dance? Or has that changed too?"

Brock pulls her to the dance floor holding her in a tight embrace. An OK dancer, but great at making a girl feel he's in control.

"Michael, you dance better than you used to. You're like guiding a breeze now.[25] Much better in heels too. Do you remember the first time you danced with me in heels?"

"That was a lifetime ago, Brock," Michelle blushes as she remembers how that first dance made her feel.[26]

"I remember it, Michael. I dragged your sorry body around the dance floor."

"But you . . .you said . . .."

"I know what I said, Michael. But you were very needy. I said what you needed to hear. You were always looking for praise. Like an addict needs a regular fix. So, I gave it to you. Is that so bad?"

"I did. . . I admit it . . . I was desperate . . . for approval. From anyone, but especially from you, Brock."

"Should I tell you what you want to hear now?"

"Yes, sometimes I still need it, even if it just reinforces my dream for the moment."

"Be careful, Michael, dreaming is dangerous."[27]

"I know, Brock. A dream is like a bubble. It's just as real as anything else . . . until suddenly it's gone."

"Brock, I still need to hear it to keep my dream real.[28] Can you? And can you say it to Michelle, not Michael? Please?"

"OK Michelle . . . you've become the girl guys dream about. The way you look, move, feel, talk, kiss, tingle when I touch you. It's all there. . . a perfect dream. I'm not making that up. That's real now."

Before Michelle can speak, "And I can sense what you crave, Michelle. A night of pleasure. You pleasing me. Me pleasing you. It's oozing out of every pore of your body. I sensed it in the stuck-up girl sitting at the bar even before I realized it was you. You can't hide it behind fancy clothes."

---

25 Music Video Thinking Out Loud https://www.youtube.com/watch?v=lp-EO5I60KA

26 Movie Clip My Fair Lady https://www.youtube.com/watch?v=hA9bEKKxTNU

27 Music Video Dreaming https://www.youtube.com/watch?v=TU3-lS_Gryk

28 Music Video These Dreams https://www.youtube.com/watch?v=41P8UxneDJE

"That always was your talent, Brock. Sensing what people want. Before I met you, I was a mystery to other people, even to my family. But you knew what I wanted. . . sometimes . . . before I knew."

"Michelle, the way you look at me and whisper and hold yourself and respond to my touch, you're nothing like that awkward boy anymore. And very sexy, even if you're dressed like a librarian. I want you so bad. Maybe as much as you want me."

Blushing, "Brock I've worked so hard to . . . to hear you tell me that. You don't know how hard. No one does. And I'm so mixed up now." A misty-eyed Michelle relaxes in Brock's embrace, "Just hold me."

*   *   *

"So, Michael."

"Back to Michael again?" pouting her lips.

"Yeah Michael. We've been in your dream world long enough. Need to get real again. Not this Michelle fantasy you've created."

"You disappeared over three years ago. I let you go because you were special. Not like the others. So, I thought to myself. Sure, you lost your investment in Michael, but maybe that's OK. Maybe Michael is into better things. And I felt good about that. That's why I didn't come after you. Better to picture you moving on to something better than to track you down."

"I wondered why you let me go. I knew I wasn't that good at hiding. Sometimes I wish you had come after me."

"No, you don't, Michael. I would've had to punish you bad, not just a few slaps. Make you an example to keep the others in line. I know what you're thinking, Michael. You always liked punishment . . . and making up afterward. I meet a lot of people like that. But you were a little special. So, I let a mixed-up kid go. Then, you called me out of the blue."

"You want something, Michael. Michelle is bait for something you want. Don't try to hustle a hustler. What is it? For real. You know I can tell when you're lying. And you know how I react to that. So, spit it out for real."

Looking tenderly up at him, "Brock. I thought that maybe now . . . I mean now that I've changed . . . maybe we could be happy together."

"Is that why you came back? To be happy together?" Like in the storybooks?"

"Yes, I'm different now. We could be different together. Or at least try?"

"A house [29]with a white picket fence, 9 to 5 jobs and a mortgage? Three little brats? Is that what you're talking about Michael?"

Michelle doesn't respond while she ponders the image in her head, "Is that what I want?"

* * *

"Michael . . . happiness . . . torment. I know they're the same to you."

"But I'm learning. It can be different than before, Brock. More happiness. Just a little pain."

"Michael, the world didn't change just because you think you've changed. You can't take a hormone pill and make it all go away."[30]

"Me and the family are still hustling for a living. The same as always. That will never change. You know what you can expect from me. Same as before you left. And you haven't changed either, Michael. You're just playing another role. That was always your thing. Another role."

"OK, go ahead and cry. That always helped you get back to reality."

* * *

After Michelle calms down, "Come with me. I'll remind you of what's real,"[31] as Michelle finds herself being dragged across the club and down a dark hallway. Forcing Michelle to her knees, "Haven't seen urinals up so close in a while, have you Michael? Look at them. That's reality staring you

---

29 Video Clip Escape House of Horror https://www.youtube.com/watch?v=wngB9_6Vqbc
30 Music White Rabbit https://www.youtube.com/watch?v=RaHnbNRUuP0
31 Video Twisted Reality https://www.youtube.com/watch?v=M-Rc5FoKQzc

in the face. Take a good whiff. Not some fancy powder room that Michelle uses, is it?"

"You made us money working urinals just like these. Remember? That's what you came back to. Kneeling in smelly men's rooms. So, let's do it right here. . . just like old times."

"But someone may come in."

"Michael? Still playing a proper young lady? College girl? Too proud to turn tricks like in the old days?"

"You'll have to get used to it again, if you really want to come back. Now, we wait until your customer comes in. Just like the old days."

*   *   *

As another man enters the bathroom. "That's it honey, work it good. We'll see whether college has taught you anything useful." Turning to the customer, "She's good bro. Really knows her business. Best $50 bucks I've ever spent, but since you're a regular customer, maybe she'll give you a quickie for $20."

As Brock leaves, "Michelle, let's see whether you're ready to get back to reality. Earn me that $20."

*   *   *

Brock returns ten minutes later to find Michelle crying on the cold wet floor, nursing a bruise from an unhappy customer.

"Couldn't do it. Could you?"

"No Brock. I didn't . . . don't be mad . . . it's just that I've changed since the old days."

Picking Michelle up from the floor, he begins cleaning her up, silent but with a gentle touch.

"Brock, I know why you did it."

"Really college girl? Is Michelle that much smarter than Michael?"

"I think, yes I am."

260

"Good, because Michael was a dumb awkward kid. Pretended he had all the answers. He did, but most of them were wrong. Had no future. You were right to get rid of him. You deserve better."

"Yes . . . I do. It's better now. But it wasn't all bad . . . before. We had something special. Didn't we?"

"No, not all bad, Michelle."

As they leave the rest room, Michelle slides her hand into Brock's pants and holds firmly. "Brock, if you ever do that again, I'm going to crush you like a bug. Understand?" Brock nods wincing in pain and Michelle smiles as she eases her grip, "Good. Now that we've agreed on the new rules, I'm going to clean up in the Ladies. I don't miss dirty men's rooms."

When Michelle returns, "Brock, sorry if I hurt you. I know you needed to show me, not just tell me. And I needed to show you that Michelle is different from Michael, not just tell you."

"Michelle, let's get out of this dump and talk for real."

*   *   *

As they walk to a coffee shop around the corner, Michelle leans in on Brock. "Now we can talk about whether Michelle and Brock have a future together."

"Michelle, Michael was broken before I took him in. Just like the others. I don't break people. They come to me that way. Then, we try to survive together in a difficult world."

"I really can't go home again to you and the family, can I Brock?"

"No, because you're not broken anymore.[32] You fixed yourself somehow. Good for you. You have a future. Hell! You're pretty enough and manipulative enough, maybe you'll even be a doctor's wife in a few years."

"I'm planning to be an actress, but that's a tough game. Doctor's wife might not be too bad. So, who knows?"

"Michelle, someday, you'll be driving a nice car to tennis and lunch at the 'club.' One of your fancy friends will say 'Oh, look at that poor

---

32 Music Not Feel Broken Anymore https://www.youtube.com/watch?v=zeYixXIvzgI

old man.' And she'll roll down her window and give me a dollar. And I'll take it, and try to look deserving, because I'll need it.[33] That's my future, Michelle. Always has been and always will be. Just trying to get along until the inevitable happens. That could have been Michael's future too. But you invented something better. I like that."

"But . . . something . . . worries me, Brock."

"I know. You're scared that you'll screw up your new life by falling back into your past. Your dark beginnings. You're worried you'll be taking weekend vacations from your boring new life by turning tricks[34]. . . not because you need the money . . . because you like the excitement."

"Yes, I feel like it's always waiting for me just around the corner. And tonight . . . on that disgusting wet floor . . . I realized that was Michael's life . . . I'm Michelle now and Michelle doesn't want that. You helped me realize that Brock. Thanks."

Taking her two hands in his, "Yeah, I'm sure Michelle has her dark side too. Most people do. And they're scared just like you. They just resist or turn it into something good. You can do that. I know you can. Look how far you've come from that needy boy I took in. And who knows you better than I do?"

"No one knows me like you do Brock. Not even me. That's why I came to you."

"Michelle, really knowing someone is a big responsibility. Maybe I could have done it better tonight . . . maybe softer . . . but it's the only way I know. Sorry it hurt so much."

"You did good, Brock. I needed a shock."

"So, make yourself and your family proud. Keep going. Become an actress or doctor's wife . . . and hold charity dinners to help the needy . . . or do whatever you want . . . and put your past behind you."

"Brock, my mother told me the same thing last week: 'Make me proud of all my daughters' she said"

---

33 Music Taxi https://www.youtube.com/watch?v=_YWGTMC3u5o
34 Video Trans Prostitute https://www.youtube.com/watch?v=sCuKUfCcGsI

"Yeah, me and your mom talk a lot about you. Practically every day. Life is all about you. Right?"

Misty-eyed with a barely perceptible smile, "Can I call you, if I need a reminder?"

"Yeah, I'd like that, Michelle. Like to help someone get out of this life. It doesn't happen often."

"Thanks Brock . . ." after she kisses him goodnight. It would mean a lot. Trying to build a safety net in case I fall back into my dark side. And you know me better than anyone."

"No Michelle, I knew a screwed-up boy named Michael. Michelle is different, stronger. I'm just learning about Michelle. Too bad I didn't meet Michelle years ago. You might have saved me back then."

Brock watches as Michelle slowly disappears into the night and calls out to her, "You're right. I missed my chance. You're out of my league now."[35] Then, Brock whispers to himself, "You'll make someone very happy . . . just not me . . . you're out of my class now."

* * *

On her ride back to her dorm, "Whew! I didn't go to bed with him. Am I classy now? What's classy? Maybe its understanding how torn Ingrid Bergman was leaving Rick and getting on that plane in Casablanca. I think I understand that better now. I wanted her to stay with Rick, but Rick was a bad boy sometimes. Rick had a dark side. Leaving with Victor on the plane was moving toward the light. But it's so sad she couldn't have both. That's why people cry at the end."[36]

A totally drained Michelle returns to her dorm around 2:00 am and crawls into bed with a sleeping Shelley.

"Huh!"

"Michelle? Is that you? What . . .?"

---

35 Video Pretty Woman https://www.youtube.com/watch?v=Gqj_uc3KGTA
36 Music Video Already Gone https://www.youtube.com/watch?v=f0T3WAbU6tg

"Shh. Sorry, Shelley. I've had a strange day. Someone very close . . . a part of me . . . kind of . . . disappeared tonight. Maybe two people. I'll miss both of them. I just need someone I can trust to help me get through the night. No boyfriend girlfriend stuff. Just two friends. Can you just hold me[37] until I fall asleep? OK?"

"Good night, Michelle."

"Good night, Shelley.

* * *

THIS IS SO! . . . I KNOW!

27

On the Edge in the Park

After her late night, Michelle sleeps in and Allie asks Kaitlyn to join her for her sunrise yoga.

"OK, I'll go ahead Kaitlyn to catch the first rays. See you in ten minutes?"

As she approaches the edge of Pullen Park, Kaitlyn hears, "Leave me alone or I'll scream!"

"No one will hear you, babe. Strip and you won't get hurt."[1]

Peering into the underbrush with only a hint of sun in the horizon, Kaitlyn sees nothing, but hears a muffled voice struggling to be heard, "mmmmffledhe." Then, "help. Then, total silence.

Remembering the police whistle her father gave her, Kaitlyn responds with:

"FWEEEEET!"[2]

"FWEEEEET!"

"FWEEEEET!"

"Come on guys. I think I see him," Kaitlyn yells in her deepest voice. "Don't use your guns, unless you have to. You might hit the girl. But shoot any guy you see."

Moments later, a half-naked Allie emerges from the bushes fifty feet away.

---

1 Music Video Victim https://www.youtube.com/watch?v=qPOWwwAYb1I
2 Video https://www.youtube.com/watch?v=XR3OvD5VTs0

"Thank God you people came to my rescue.[3] He was about to . . .."

"I can imagine."

Looking at Kaitlyn, "Where did all the police go? Just you?"

"Yes, it's just me. Hurry, let's get back to our dorm before that guy realizes it was just me."

"Allie, are you OK?"

"I guess so. Just shaken up, I think"

"Did he?"

"No, you arrived just in time."

"Did he take anything?"

"No, he dropped my phone when he started running."

"Be careful with the phone. The police may be able to find his fingerprints."

"Did you get a look at him, Allie?"

"No, he came from behind."

Back at the dorm, Kaitlyn phones campus police and Allison files a report.

*　*　*

The girls in the dorm congregate in the hall talking.

"The police said this happens every year."

"Men are such . . .. We need to do something!"[4]

As Michelle and Shelley enter the crowded hallway, Michelle whispers to Shelley "Be nice to the girls today. They're not in a mothering mood."[5]

*　*　*

After the police leave, Michelle comforts Allie. "I just don't know what I'd do . . . if . . . he killed you."

---

3 Video Police https://www.youtube.com/watch?v=0l_RA4B9bgE

4 Music Video Made Me Do https://www.youtube.com/watch?v=3tmd-ClpJxA

5 Music Video Bad Blood https://www.youtube.com/watch?v=QcIy9NiNbmo

"I know, when he . . .began . . . all I could think about was to give him what he wanted so I could live to see you again." A frightened Allie looks up at a teary-eyed Michelle, "Do you think this means . . ? Are we . . .?"

Stroking her hair, "Yes Allie, we're a family [6]now."

"Michelle, I was so bad telling Elizabeth about you, and now you're being so nice."

"Don't worry about Elizabeth. I don't care about my secret anymore. I'm just so relieved we can start again."

"I don't want to leave you, Michelle. We need to be together."

"You won't have to leave. I'll talk with Shelley about you and him switching roommates for a few nights. We'll thrive together."[7]

* * *

Kaitlyn's brain obsesses on two words, "Park Patrol."

By that afternoon, she signs up three frats to have their members patrol the park in the pre-dawn and post-sunset hours. Later that evening, Kaitlyn explains the new safety program to the girls in the dorm.

"Girls, the boys are going to help, but we need to take charge of our own safety. I want every patrol to include one of us. We're not helpless and we need to show the boys that. And here's info about a new self-defense class at the gym. I'll be the instructor until we get the school to hire someone." There will still be gaps in the middle of the night and the patrols can't be everywhere. So, be careful." As she finishes, Kaitlyn passes out a box of plastic whistles, "My father gave me mine. I hope you'll all carry one. You can whistle faster than you can dial your phone for help."

After the meeting, Allie and Michelle surround Kaitlyn with hugs, "We owe you so much. If you ever need help, we'll be there for you."[8]

* * *

---

6 Movie Clip https://www.youtube.com/watch?v=vJIxdmLLpoc
7 Music Video Rise https://www.youtube.com/watch?v=hdw1uKiTI5c
8 Movie Clip https://www.youtube.com/watch?v=1K50QuCSlj8

"Daddy? Why are you calling? Is mom, OK?"

"You heard about the park incident already?"

"You've been keeping track of our crime situation through the "Next-Door"[9] app? And you have a buddy in the local department?"

"Yes, it was me with the whistle you gave me."

"I know you told me not to go into that park. But my friend needed my help."

"Yes, he got away."

"Yes, I'll be more careful."

"Yes, I organized the new park crime patrol."

"Thanks, I'm kind of proud of myself too. Like Daddy, like daughter, I suppose."

*   *   *

As Michelle tucks the still upset Allie into bed, "Until now, I never realized how much I depend on you, Michelle. I'm so grateful. Have you really forgiven me?"[10]

"After our fight yesterday, I met an old friend last night. I told him about you and me . . . and our relationship. He reminded me that no alpha is perfect . . . and that I'm a much stronger person now than when I knew him before. That's because of you, Allie. You're good for me."

"Sometimes, you're stronger than me, Michelle. How do you do it?"

"You've been a good alpha, Allie, but you still have a lot to learn about how our relationship works. When my alpha and I build our harmony together, we both become stronger. It's not like that with a bad alpha. Then, I become weaker. You've helped me become strong enough to fight to preserve our harmony."

Allie stares up at Michelle with a worried look.

---

9 Video Next Door App https://www.youtube.com/watch?v=CPiZtmYt7Lo
10 Music Video You Forgive Me https://www.youtube.com/watch?v=LO-2fm7IKcU

"Now, be a good alpha and I'll tell you a story[11] until you fall asleep. Once upon a time there was . . .." After Allie falls asleep, Michelle thinks, "Should I have confessed to Allie about me and Brock? Probably, but I don't think Allie's strong enough to handle that now. Confessing and being punished would comfort me, but I need to be strong for Allie. I can be. I confronted my past and I'm ready to move forward with Allie. No bad boys holding me back from the light now."

PROBE DEEPER. THERE'S MORE DATA TO BE FOUND

---

11 Movie Clip Once Upon a Time https://www.youtube.com/watch?v=PmPiV7elmXk

28

Experiments Go Over the Edge

Three hours after Kaitlyn and Nicole get their next blood treatment. In a weak voice, "Thanks for calling, Nicole."

"Yes, me too, except it's worse this time. Guess we can rule out ice cream as a cause. Has to be the blood they gave us today."

"Gerald's taking you to the hospital?"

"Maybe I'll see you there, Nicole."

* * *

Olivia calls Scott.

"Kaitlyn's terribly sick again. Nicole, too. Something's very wrong with their experiment."

"Yes, we need to act quickly."

"Can you get her down the stairs, Olivia? Good idea, get someone to help you. I'll pick you up in front of your dorm and drive you to the hospital."

* * *

"What's the matter, Luna?"

"Shelley, something's really wrong with Allie since she returned from today's Foundation session. She won't leave her room. Won't even let me open the shades. Wants the room dark, so no one can see her. Michelle's not answering her phone. She'll know how to help her. Please find her."

* * *

"Dr. Fauchison, we've paid the Foundation a lot for that blood experiment.[1] What are the results so far?"

"You know I'm not allowed to share raw data with experiment sponsors. Just a final report at the end."

"That's not acceptable in our case."

"Sorry, no exceptions."

"We'll see about that! We're not just ordinary sponsors."

* * *

Back in the Foundation's server farm.

"Ah yes! Data flowing in from every experiment."

"Will this be our best data harvest year?"

"I'm projecting a 25% data increase over last year."

"Marvelous . . .."

"What's the data quality?"

"Quality? We're in the collection and measuring department. I assume there's a quality department somewhere. Not my job."

"That makes sense. Just keep measuring."

* * *

Scott carries Kaitlyn[2] to the emergency room. While Olivia fills out Kaitlyn's admittance paperwork, Scott looks for Nicole. "Gerald, glad you're here. Olivia told me you brought Nicole. How is she?"

"Not good. I've seen people die, Scott. She has that same glazed look."

---

1 Music Video This Blood https://www.youtube.com/watch?v=Z4RBIa3b9QA
2 Music Video Nurse's Office https://www.youtube.com/watch?v=R2YM5zSapNg

"Did they say what it is?

"No, they have no clue so far."

"Gerald, we need to figure this out together. Our girls are depending on us."

*   *   *

Luna stands outside the dorm room.

"Michelle, I didn't know what to do. So thankful you're here."

"You look scared. Tell me what's happening."

"After I asked Shelley to find you, Allie went totally crazy."

"Screamed that I was going to kill her. Took out a knife and started yelling something. I think it was in Chinese or Japanese. Couldn't understand a word."

"Since then, I've been standing guard to make sure she doesn't leave the room."

"Does she still have the knife, Luna?"

*   *   *

"Well, they'll live."

"You cured them, Doctor?"

"No, their symptoms just disappeared.[3] I don't think it was anything we did. One minute I thought they were both dying. Next minute they seemed tired, but all vitals were normal, and they were asking if they could have ice cream."

"Never seen anything like it. All the tests we took came back normal. So, we can't trace what happened to them."

*   *   *

---

3 Music Video Disappear https://www.youtube.com/watch?v=YaLLLHugwHw

"Luna, I'm going in. After I get the knife and give it to you, lock the door. We can't leave her alone. And I don't want her wandering around outside. So, I'll stay with her. You sleep in Shelley's and my room tonight. You can borrow my pajamas. You OK with that? I'm going in now."

*   *   *

"Can you tell us anything else doctor?

"No . . . nothing to tell. I really don't understand what they both went through. Especially perplexing that exactly the same things happened to both of them and the symptoms started and stopped at the same time. Viruses and bacteria aren't usually that precise. They may head in a general direction, but they don't coordinate attacks[4] like an army would."

"An army?"

"Yes, this seems almost like a coordinated attack. But that's impossible. Contrary to all scientific principles."

*   *   *

"Allie, it's me, Michelle."

"How do I know that? The lights are out. You could be anybody."

"Allie, just as we're rending our intimate times together, you make this sound: "eeehhhhh. Sometimes you also murmur something . . . I think it's in Chinese, but it could be Japanese."

"OK, it's you, Michelle."

"Can I come over and hold you?"

Allie sobs, "I need you so much, Michelle."

*   *   *

"Doctor is there anything else you can tell us? Anything unusual?"

---

4 Music Teardrop https://www.youtube.com/watch?v=u7K72X4eo_s

"Yes. Something very unusual. Statistically impossible. They both have the same blood type. In itself, that's not so unusual. Lots of people have the same blood types. But this is an extremely rare blood type. Maybe one in ten million people have it. That's maybe 33 people all of America. What are the odds of two girls the same age ending up in my ER with the same problems and the same extremely rare blood type? I don't understand how that happened, but it's probably not just a coincidence. I think I should report this to the CDC."[5]

"Doctor, I'll put you in touch with a higher authority."

* * *

"Allie, if you give me the knife, I can stay with you tonight. Would you like that? It'll just be us tonight. And you know I won't let anyone hurt you."

"Good girl, Allie. Now, I'm going to give this knife to Luna to take it away. Then, Luna's going to sleep in Shelley's room while you and I sleep together and we solve your problem. OK?."

* * *

"Same blood type, Scott? One in 10 million? I think we have the answer for why Kaitlyn and Nicole are going through the same experiment."

"Yes Olivia, can you contact the Professor and have them find out everything they can about this blood type? While you do that, Gerald and I will talk with Kaitlyn and Nicole."

* * *

"Allie, you really scared Luna. I think maybe she's scared enough to do it with Shelley tonight."

"Well, I'm glad my trauma is for a good cause."

---

5 Centers for Disease Control Website https://www.cdc.gov/

"That's my girl, Allie! Good to see that smile back. Now, tell me all about your problems while I stroke your hair and tell you how great you are. Just like we promised each other when we're out here on the edge."

*　*　*

Scott and Gerald bring Kaitlyn and Nicole from the hospital to Scott's apartment.

"Me and Blondie have the same blood type? One in 10 million? How weird is that?"

"Nicole, we really are blood sisters!"[6]

"Do you know why the Foundation is doing this to us?"

"No, it must have something to do with you two having the same blood type, but we don't know more than that. You two rest while we find out more. Olivia is working on it now."

---

6 Music Video Blood Sister https://www.youtube.com/watch?v=u8B08i2Vtls

29

Changing Relationships

The next night, the new roommates stare across their room at one another.

Breaking the silence, "Shelley, I have something to tell you."

"No wait Luna. Let me go first. You need to know how I feel. You and I have a special relationship. I didn't know how special until I worried that Allie . . . might . . . you know . . . with that knife. It made me realize that life is short. I don't want to miss out on my life with you, Luna. I need to make love to you tonight. And I think you need to make love to me tonight, Luna."

"I'm glad you went first Shelley. It's difficult for a girl to ask. That's what I wanted to tell you, Shelley. I've been praying for guidance about you and me."

"Luna, talking to God about me, Sheldon Atwell? Really?"

"Oh yes, I pray every night before I go to sleep. I want my first time to be with someone special. And now I'm sure you're special.

"And God told you that?"

"Oh yes, in my dreams, every night. But it wasn't just ordinary dreams. They were very real. That's how I knew it was God talking. So, I'm ready.[1] Join me in my bed, Shelley. But we should pray together first. OK?"

"I'm Jewish Luna, you say the prayer your way and I'll follow."

---

1 Music Video Ready to Love https://www.youtube.com/watch?v=C3Ff8AknRuI

"Almighty and all forgiving God, please bless our union and know that we will welcome the fruit of our union."[2]

"Luna, you're not taking birth control pills! That's what you mean about welcoming the fruit, isn't it?"

"I'm a virgin, Shelley. Virgins have no need of pills. If God wants to bless me with children, I will not say no. You wouldn't make me say no to God, would you Shelley?"

"Maybe this is the way it's supposed to be . . . for us Luna. I can't make you say no to God."

"Oh Shelley! I just knew you'd understand. Our children will be so smart and we'll take such good care of them."

* * *

On their phones.

"Gerald, good to hear your voice."

"Oh, that's sweet. I've missed you too, Olivia."

"Yes, I'd like another visit,[3] but don't come here. Nicole is sleeping over with Kaitlyn."

"Yes, our two children are so cute together now."

"I'll come to you, Gerald."

* * *

"Luna, its your first time. I don't want to hurt you."

"Shelley, you're the one I've been waiting for. I'm ready. I'm craving you.[4] I'm not afraid. A little pain before great pleasure, is what my mother told me."

* * *

---

2 Music Video Mine https://www.youtube.com/watch?v=XPBwXKgDTdE

3 Music Video Come Over https://www.youtube.com/watch?v=lbnGtOBcJtk

4 Music Video Cravin https://www.youtube.com/watch?v=_jqEqmc35yk

"This is garbage, Kaitlyn! We have to do something."

"Totally agree, Nicole. Everyone seems to know more about what's happening to us than we do. Time for that to change. Scott, Olivia and Gerald can't keep running the show. They're used to treating us like children, but now it's a very adult game and it's our game."

*   *   *

"Shelley, it doesn't hurt," as his fiery Latina lover overwhelms him.

"Luna . . . I didn't know . . . you've been so . . . but just now, you were so . . . ."

"Now you know, Shelley. We'll always be passionate like this together, always. It's God's will! We should pray again."

"This time I'll lead the prayer. It's Jewish prayer. OK, Luna?"

"Oh Shelley! You really are the special man I've always dreamed about! I will follow your prayer."

רבג ינא םויה, לאל הדות !

"Luna, that means 'Thank you God, for today I am a man!"

"You're my man, Shelley. Can my man do it again? Let me help you recover."

As Luna continues, Shelley prays again, תוחפל ,אבא תויהל הצור אל ינא וישכע אל.

"What was that, Shelley?"

"Oh, nothing important. Just another prayer."

*   *   *

"So, we're agreed, Nicole. Tomorrow, we take back control of our lives."

"Right about that Kaitlyn!"

*   *   *

"Allie, is that a new nightie?" [5]

"You like, girlfriend?"

"Oh, I like. I'm just surprised. You usually don't go in for so glam."

"I'm planning a special evening for us . . . some snacks you like . . .and wine."

"Quite the little seduction scene you've set up for us, Allie. That's usually my role."

"I know, Michelle, I want to invest more effort in our relationship. Take care of you a little bit, like you've been caring for me."

"That's so sweet. I've never had an alpha like that, but be careful, you don't want me getting too used to it."

Allie lays back and slips Michelle's arm around her while they sip wine. After some cuddling, "I've been thinking. You know how in drama class we sometimes switch roles? You play my part. I play your part."

"Yeah, seeing the play from a new perspective often helps us both."

Looking up into Michelle's eyes, "Well, I was thinking, maybe . . . if it's all right with you, Michelle, maybe we could switch roles outside of class?"

"Oh, is that what this is about? Allie, you're doing a good job of playing the submissive girlfriend tonight. Brava! Shall we keep this switch going all evening? Or are you finished?"

"Not finished, Michelle . . . is it alright to continue? It might be fun. See where it leads us?"

"Sure, I'm enjoying my alpha being so attentive to my needs. You do get a little bossy sometimes. Never had an alpha who cared enough to switch. Maybe, we'll both learn something tonight."

"More wine, Michelle?"

As time passes, the girls get comfortable in their switch. While Allie massages Michelle's neck, "Oh, that's heavenly, Allie. Oh yes, very nice! You've got a real talent for the submissive arts, dressing sexy, serving and helping relax me. That's my formula especially . . . when I want something," as Michelle begins to realize Allie's game.

---

5 Video Funny Girl https://www.youtube.com/watch?v=42XWZwjVlBY

Seeing Allie's smile, "You do you want something, Allie, don't you! But you're my alpha, you don't have to do all this. I'll do anything you ask. You know that. So, why the games?"

"It took you a while to figure it out didn't it, Michelle? I've been study-ing your games. How you manipulate me. I decided I can do it too. I do want something. And I can't just tell you to do it. I must do this your way. To manipulate you so that you tell me that you want it."

"I'm not understanding, Allie."

"Of course, you don't. The alpha never understands the games. You taught me that. So. I'll make it easy for my alpha. I'd like to switch[6] . . . for more than tonight," As Michelle looks perplexed, "I want you to be my alpha and I'll be your sub. Will you do that for me?" Allie asks in a meek voice, "Please . . . .?" as a tear moistens her cheek. "I know it's a lot to ask, but it would mean so much."

"Allie, I'm confused . . . I've never considered. . . I mean, I've always . . . and someone else has always." While Michelle hesitates, Allie continues massaging her new alpha, "I'll be ever so grateful, my alpha," in a sweet girl voice. Then, "please don't say no. I need . . ." then, Allie's words are broken by intermittent sobs. "I'm worn out.[7] I want to be like you – young and vulnerable – tasting life like I'm brand new, at least for a while. Can you do this for me, Michelle? I'm so confused. I need your guidance so I can figure out who I'm going to be. Please?"

"But . . . you're an alpha and I'm a sub . . . can we change our natures like our outfits?"[8]

"After us being together these weeks, I think I'm both alpha and sub and so are you, even though you enjoy manipulating me with your sub games so much. Oh, how you love doing that! So frustrating! But your games have taught me a lot and we both know you've been guiding me these past couple of weeks, Michelle. That's what alphas do. Now, I want to give you complete control over me, like you gave me."

6 Music Vido Switch https://www.youtube.com/watch?v=X9IW0FpHvN4
7 Music Video Brutal https://www.youtube.com/watch?v=OGUy2UmRxJ0
8 Music Video Cardigan https://www.youtube.com/watch?v=K-a8s8OLBSE

"Oh Allie, are you sure? I've been a sub for years. You're new at it. I don't think you know what complete control really is. You might not like it, and you know how I get sometimes. Like a balloon blown by the breeze. That's fine on a calm sunny day, but if a storm comes, what if I crash the both of us?"

Holding Michelle's hand looking into her eyes, "Remember, how you explained to me that you sometimes need a vacation from your struggles? That handing over control to your alpha gives you that. I need that kind rest now, Michelle, I really do."

"Allie, I know, but maybe there's another way."

In a whisper peppered with soft kisses, "Allie is gone. Call me your sub. Please . . .that's what I crave. Accept complete control over my body as a token of my love and restore our harmony. I'm yours to do with as you think best, in all ways."

Reaching under Michelle's bed for the bag of punishment toys, "Take these, I need my alpha to restore our harmony."

Looking into Allie's desperate eyes and digging down into her years of suffering and recovering, Michelle hears herself uttering words she never thought possible, "I am your alpha. I accept my sub's offering and will restore our harmony."

As Allie smiles, Michelle changes tone, "Forget our past together. You will live by new rules. Punishment is a privilege you must earn. First you must pass inspection.[9] Stand straight. Be quick. No, stand like this," as Michelle repositions Allie like a Barbie doll. Continuing her inspection, "You'll do for now. Tomorrow, I'll change you to suit me better."

Looking into Allie's eyes, Michelle thinks, "I thought Allie would rebel against me talking to her like this, but she seems so . . . peaceful . . so at home. Like I like to feel when I'm being controlled."[10]

"Now smile, Allie, I like a girl who smiles." Michelle tilts Allie's head down. "Your eyes should look down at my pretty feet." Pulling Allie's long black hair over one shoulder, "That's better. So, vulnerable."

---

9 Music Video Imperfections https://www.youtube.com/watch?v=_8EokLztgMo
10 Music Drink Wine https://www.youtube.com/watch?v=axUh_2fTLe4

"OMG," Michelle thinks, "Allie is on the edge. Totally into me controlling her. Just the way I . . . ."

As Allie senses Michelle's lips brushing her neck, she begins to quiver. "I know you can't control yourself.[11] Moving during inspection isn't permitted. You'll have to be punished," and Allie feels a quick slap on her rear.

"So, this is how being controlled by someone who loves you feels," Allie senses. "So alive,[12] everywhere, not knowing what will come next."

"You can look up now. Raise your head so I can see it in your eyes

"Michelle is saying something. It seems like she thinks it's important, but why can't I understand?"

"Allie, I know that glazed look. Usually, it's me lost in that haze, but now it's you. Listen closely. So far, you've just been exploring. But going forward now will be serious. I know it's hard for you to think right now but try. Do you still want to do this, Allie? You can change your mind now and be my alpha again. Really. We can forget this happened. Then, I'll take care of your every need, like before."

Seeing the despair in Allie's eyes, "But if you want to continue to find your true nature, tell your alpha how you were bad. Then, I'll know you've really switched. Why should you be punished and forgiven?"

Allie's confession begins pouring out, "I betrayed your secret to Elizabeth, but my sins started long before. Every day you've taken care of me . . . and turned yourself over to me completely. All to build our harmony together. I trust you now to make decisions that are good for me. But I should have trusted you long ago, just as you've always trusted me. That's my guilt."

"I thought you would turn back, Allie, but your submissive side is screaming for attention. You've been very bad. You've disrupted our harmony. You deserve punishment," as Michelle wipes a tear from her cheek thinking to herself, "I have to be strong.[13] Allie, needs my strength now."

---

11 Video Hypnotized https://www.youtube.com/watch?v=LcbV9P196KA

12 Music Video Alive https://www.youtube.com/watch?v=mfL9cgpS9K0

13 Music Video Stronger https://www.youtube.com/watch?v=AJWtLf4-WWs

While Allie waits, Michelle feels herself engulfed in bubbles [14]and hears Sarah whispering to her, "The bubbles are approving your change, Michelle. You're ready to be strong."

Sensing Michelle's conflict, "All I crave is to be punished and forgiven and satisfy you. You've experienced these joys. Please restore our harmony."

"I'm going to punish my sub with my favorite toy. It gave me much harmony. Maybe it will become our favorite."

"That would be lovely my alpha. Your sub would be very pleased to share a favorite punishment toy. Please do it hard my alpha, I won't break."

"My sub does not decide her punishment. Your alpha has decided your punishment should not be painful. Sometimes, my punishment was from the dark. The dark is past. Your confession and punishment should be from the light side of our natures."

Seeing panic in Allie's eyes, "I have decided this is a time we should both change. Confession and punishment should be symbolic of the control you have given me and our love. Pain has no place in that. It is the sweetest gift. Do you question your alpha's decision?"

"I accept my alpha's decision."

"I cherish my sub's commitment now that you understand what it means." As Allie assumes punishment position, "Accept this symbolic punishment and feel controlled, loved and forgiven and know that our harmony is restored."

After ten symbolic strokes, with Michelle's first caress, Allie begins shaking uncontrollably.

"She really is like me," as Michelle thinks in awe of the passion[15] their first forgiveness ritual has released.

*　*　*

"So, Olivia, how often do you do booty calls[16] this late at night?"

---

14 Video Bubbles https://www.youtube.com/watch?v=05EFBPe3qs0
15 Music Video https://www.youtube.com/watch?v=1ekZEVeXwek
16 Music Video https://www.youtube.com/watch?v=5Whe1GUjtKE

"Oh, I'd say . . . never. Gerald, you didn't call after our last date! I had to call you. Why?"

"I like you, Olivia . . . a lot, but part of you always seems to be in another place. Even now, only part of you is with me."

"The curse of being a lifelong a multi-tasker. I need someone to cure me of that. Are you up to the challenge, Gerald?"

"You need a simpler life, Olivia. I'm going to show you how."

An hour later, "Oh Gerald, I'm loving simple. More of simple, please. I just can't resist[17] it any longer."

*   *   *

After their coupling, "Michelle, you were right, I never really understood. It was so beautiful. Each stage, so intense, I'm still shaking. How could anyone know without having experienced it?"

"I know, Allie, but let's rest while I think about where we go from here. I didn't expect this. I was sure you'd back out at the end when I offered the chance. I thought you were all alpha, but now we both know, you're also like me. I'm pleased . . . and confused . . . I've never dealt with this before. Alpha and sub? Can you? Can we? Be both?"

"I don't want to go back to being alpha, Michelle, at least not until after I explore my hidden passions. I thought I knew myself, but I've found a whole new me, inside. Like Michael found Michelle. But I need a loving alpha, like you. I don't know whether I'm ready for pain, but I need to symbolically turn myself over to you. You're the only one I trust to teach me more about the submissive arts. Can you do that?"

"I'll try this new path to our harmony, Allie," as Michelle thinks to herself "Now what do I do?"

Allie smiles, as if in the middle of a pleasant daydream and Michelle reminds Allie of her new role, "Not nice for my sub to keep secrets from her alpha. I own your dreams too."

---

17 Music Video Can't Resist https://www.youtube.com/watch?v=yKXw_MMm0UA

"I was just remembering a day when I felt this peaceful and free, a special day. When I was ten years old, my cousin was teaching me how to surf.[18] It was hard, until I learned not to fight the waves. Then, I felt free and powerful by going with the waves instead of fighting them. I've been doing too much wave-fighting these past years. It's hurt me and my family. Tonight, I stopped . . . I'm riding my alpha's wave . . . my beautiful alpha. Now, I'm feeling like my younger surfer girl [19]self on that beach again. Being in harmony with something more powerful is making me feel so . . . ."

*   *   *

The next morning, "Michelle, are you a religious person? Me neither, but maybe we're inventing our own religion. We have our ritual three positions and confession and punishment and forgiveness and reward. Having our own private religion[20] together makes us special."

"Excuse me, Allie, Sarah has something to say What's that Sarah? . . ." As Michelle listens to Sarah, Allie can see a look of growing concern on Michelle's face. "Uh huh. Uh huh. I think you're right, Sarah."

Allie impatiently asks, "What's she saying to you, Michelle? What's right?"

"Wait Allie. Wait until Sarah finishes. You have a lot to learn about not interrupting, Allie."

Finally, Michelle turns to Allie, "Sarah says that if we're a religion, Allie, we should be doing good things. Maybe, like bringing families together. You helped guide me to reestablish myself with my family. I'm going to help you with your family."

"That's alright, Michelle, I've got family matters under control."

"Allie, your alpha has decided. Is this how you respond to your alpha?"

---

18 Video Girl Surfing in Hawaii https://www.youtube.com/watch?v=yc2_FC1ty9M
19 Music Video Surfer Girl https://www.youtube.com/watch?v=HGjky5U64LM&list=PL ROpOUyD2EJx9C_aCWQMUQSWeUqpLPVjl
20 Music Video Hallelujah https://www.youtube.com/watch?v=iIiqxyIuMJk

"Sorry, I forgot. It's confusing, I'll need some practice overcoming my alpha side." Trying to look as contrite as her nature allows, Allie responds. "This poor sub would be very grateful for my alpha's help," Allie says, barely getting the words out between her gritted teeth.

"When was the last time you called your mother?"

"I called her to let her know I arrived at college."

"Has she called you?"

"Many times, but I never answer when she calls. I just text her back that I'm OK."

"Six weeks? Only texts? What a bad girl you've been, Allie! I couldn't believe it until Sarah told me just now."

"Will my alpha punish me again?" Allie whispers, hopefully.

"Not until my sub restores her family's harmony.[21] Call her this afternoon so you can stop fighting that family wave too. We'll have all day to prepare you with the time difference."

"My alpha is so . . . in charge. Just riding waves is so pleasant," Allie says with a smile knowing that Michelle is envying Allie's freedom.

"I know you're toying with me, Allie, just as a good sub should. I'm going to help you practice the submissive arts . . . and not just with me. By apologizing to your mom, you'll create family harmony. I know you crave that. It's what's draining you."

"Should I just tell her I have a boyfriend named Michael? She'll like that. Is it OK to call you Michael when I call her? To create family harmony?"

"You have Michael's permission to create harmony with your family, but I have a different script in mind."

"A script?"

"Yes, a story to create harmony."

"You mean lying to my family will create harmony?"

"Allie, I've played submissive games with you as my alpha. Now that we've switched, I'm playing the game as your alpha. It's exciting. But there's

---

21 Music Video Sweet Harmony https://www.youtube.com/watch?v=rP9Z5Pc8cRM

a serious side to this when it affects your family. Your direct alpha approach hasn't worked with your family. Has it?"

"Well, no. I guess it's been a disaster. I've drawn lines in the sand. But they have too. I'll lose face if I give in."

"Losing face? Are you auditioning for some kind of 1940's Asian movie? Face is just another word for pride and pride is for alphas, Allie. Yesterday, you gave up the burden of pride. Giving up control means you no longer need to worry about pride. That's my burden now. Your mom keeps calling you, Allie. That shows that she's not afraid to lose face. She values you, but what have you been doing? You've been humiliating your mom by not answering her calls. That's why you feel disharmony that's draining your life."

"I understand, Michelle, but I'm still not ready to . . ."[22]

"I know you're not ready by yourself. Today, I'll teach you to manipulate and use white lies, half-truths, and games to restore your family's harmony. When you were alpha, you created sharp hard edges in your relationships. Your new role is to make things softer and rounder[23] for you and your family. Today, under my guidance, you'll practice your submissive arts to clean up the mess you made when you were alpha."

"I don't know how, Michelle, and I don't like deceiving."

"I know, but you're an actress, Allie. Think of this like you're acting in a play. Your mom is the audience and I'm the writer and director. Our play is an illusion. Just made it up in our imagination. You, the actress, use dramatic tricks to convince the audience the illusion is real. The only difference from the other plays you've been in is that this play is about you. Does that help, Allie?"

"OK, Michelle. You're my director. I'll be in your play."

"I know you can do this, Allie. My sexy little surfer girl has a real talent for . . .."

22 Music Video Not Ready to Make Nice https://www.youtube.com/watch?v=pojL_35QlSI
23 Music Video Humble and Kind https://www.youtube.com/watch?v=awzNHuGqoMc

"You mean, for someone who's been banging her head against the waves for so long?"

Knowing that Allie needs more training in submissiveness before she talks with her mother, Michelle switches tactics, "Now . . . it's time for you to do your nails. I've always hated that color on you."

"But you said . . .."

"When you were my alpha, I said many things to please you. That was my role." Grinning, "Now, it's your turn to please. Don't look so gloomy, Allie. Enjoy your new role while I arrange costume and makeup for my actress."

"Your mom will love this. Here's the perfect shade for your nails, very ladylike," as Michelle digs into her makeup box, "and we mustn't forget the matching lip gloss. Can't have my sub walking around without matching gloss. Now, make yourself pretty for your face time with your mom while I find you the right costume."

Returning, "I borrowed this outfit from Sheri down the hall. It should fit you and it just screams 'sorority girl.' So much less butch than what you usually wear. Your mom will love it when you face time with her."

As Allie looks displeased, "My sub should be careful what she asks for. Your body is mine in all ways and I intend to enjoy it. Right now, that means dressing you like a doll." Patting Allie's rear end, "Now, remake yourself into a dutiful daughter[24] to please your mother and your alpha."

* * *

Allie emerges after an hour of fussing, "That's a good girl. Nice touch putting your hair up like that. Now, remember, you're playing a member of a sorority and have a boyfriend named Michael, who you're dating to please your mom, but then there's a twist to our little story. Get yourself ready. I expect a good performance from my actress."

"This is so humiliating . . .. How did I get myself into this?"

---

24 Music Video Dear Daughter https://www.youtube.com/watch?v=WHPVb-qMzsY

"Like a lot of other actresses, you slept with the director, that's how," Michelle laughs, "Now stop complaining. Your humiliation today is fair punishment for how you've been humiliating your mom. Your mom knows her daughter. She'll probably know you're acting."

"Then what's the point, Michelle? Why do I have to do this?"

"She'll appreciate you trying to please her. And that will create the harmony you both crave. Then, you won't feel humiliated anymore. You'll feel like you do at the end of a play, when the audience[25] is letting you know, they adore you."

As Allie practices her lines, "That's a good girl. It's time for you to call her, Allie. I'll be here off camera watching like a nervous stage mother."

"Hello mom . . . I've missed you too . . . yes . . .I know . . . lots of changes. Glad you like my new look. Yes, I'm trying to please you, I really am. I'm so ashamed of myself for the way I've behaved! So, maybe I should at least try doing some things your way."

As Allie tells the story of the fictitious boyfriend Michael, her nervousness turns to relief sensing her mother is accepting her performance as a token of her love. Then, her story twists.

"Mom, I've been pretending. There is no Michael. Her name is Michelle. And I called you because she told me the most important thing is to restore family harmony. So, Michael or Michelle, what does a name matter?"

"Oh, you don't care either. I appreciate you trying, Mom. I know, I'm getting misty too. Yes, she's standing here, just off screen . . . coaching me, just like you used to do at my school plays and recitals. You were a good mom and so is Michelle."

"I don't think she'll mind. There she is. Say hi to my mom, Michelle."

Waving, "Hi, Mrs. Lee."

"Yes, I agree she's pretty. Yes Mom, she's smart to value family harmony. Yes, we all should. I really do, you know. Our tensions these past

---

25 Video Audience https://www.youtube.com/watch?v=nvCS5yPD6Z4

several years made me miserable. That's why Michelle took over. She felt how miserable I was and decided to help me fix it by calling you. Mom, I'm sorry that I didn't show how much I love you and my family. I was very wrong. I'll really try to do better. You too? You're right, we can both do better."

Michelle briefly interrupts, "Good-bye Mrs. Lee. I'm going to leave you and Allie alone now. You have a lot of family business to talk about. Just know that everyone in our dorm loves your daughter. We're like a big family. We take care of one another, even if we don't always agree."

"Yes, I promise. I should just spank her? Really? Aloha, to you too, Mrs. Lee."

As Michelle leaves Allie and her mom to talk, she thinks, "Funny, Allie promised my mom the same thing, to help me to become a good woman. We really are becoming an extended family." Smiling, "Me and my mom are just like any other mother and daughter. Michelle and Marjorie Collins and Allison and Emily Lee, so similar. So glad I'm not Michael anymore. I would have missed so much."

*   *   *

When Michelle returns half an hour later as the call is ending, Allie jumps into her arms, "Give me the biggest hug!"

"Your mom was so sweet, Allie. Not at all like the dragon lady you described. Now, was that really so bad?"

"It wasn't like what I expected, Michelle. I started out feeling humiliated but seeing in her face that I was creating our harmony made me feel powerful."

"Typical stage fright. We all get that before every performance. Did you learn anything?"

"Yes, I learned that I always want you off-stage supporting me. It really calms me down."

"Allie, I'm the same way. My mom was always offstage rooting for me. I miss that. Every actress should have someone like that. I hope we'll always do this for each other.

"And maybe the problems between me and my mom these past couple of years really weren't all about me liking girls. Maybe I helped create our disharmony, because I was throwing my choices in her face all the time. Like it was a test or something. Looking back, maybe sometimes I chose people, both boys and girls, I knew would annoy my mom? Does that make sense?"

"That sounds like you. Allie's alpha side liked being in people's faces."

"But my mom seems OK with you, Michelle. I almost lost it when she told you to spank me when I'm naughty. Like she was blessing our new religion. After you left, she said I can bring you home for Christmas break if I want. The two of us on the beach for Christmas! I could teach you to surf as your Christmas present! It would so sooo . . .."

Michelle smiles at how Allie is remaining the girl in the script she wrote even after the call.

"Michelle, I'm starting to understand why you love manipulative games. Getting my way, while making other people feel good is so different. I've been making people angry and not getting what I want. Not a good path. I like your path better."

"I was hoping we could switch back soon to the way we were before now that you and your mom are together again, but you don't seem very interested in that, are you Allie?"

"Michelle, you spent about 18 years being Michael, until you discovered you really were more Michelle. That's what I'm feeling now. Tired of always struggling to be in charge and then screwing up. I like the old me you helped me rediscover, a little surfer girl. She's only ten years old. She needs your help to flourish. Can you do that for me, please? Maybe forever, or at least a little longer?"

"Allie, I've been reborn. If I can help my little surfer girl do the same, I'll try to do my best."

Embracing Michelle, Allie says "I need this. But I think you do too. Your journey isn't over. A new part is just beginning, like mine. I'm sensing that you're learning too, aren't you Michelle?"

"Yes, Allie. Michael always had to be the star of everything. I thought Michelle would be the same, but while I watched you making our little play come alive, I realized I like being a teacher, writer and director, especially when you're my star actress, Allie."

"I know, Michelle, that's why I chose you to be my alpha. For this part of our lives, I need a director and you need a star actress."

"I'm scared too, Allie. Until this moment, I thought changing gender would be the biggest transition in my life. But maybe this new transition is even bigger. And I need your help too. So, even though sometimes I'm missing my old role, I'm excited about us sharing our two new journeys."

With an enticing smile, "Then, let's start practicing right away, Michelle. I felt you getting turned on watching me help your script become alive. Very distracting. I mean, fantasizing about you and me while I was talking with my mom. Never thought I'd be doing that. Talk about acting on the edge!"

"Allie, your performance created a new phase in our relationship."

"So, did my performance earned something?" as Allie assumes the inspection pose Michelle taught her, "Please bring me back to when you first accepted control over me. I'm ready for inspection again, and for what comes after."

"But that's only if you've been bad, Allie. Today you've been good. You have to confess something bad."

"Michelle, one good day shouldn't wipe out all my bad days. Trust me, I'll deliver on the confession end. There's all kinds of things I need to be punished for."

Gazing deeply into each other's eyes, they sense they're both being overwhelmed by the same emotional wave as they are bathed in a sea of bubbles from Sarah, "our sweet life is returning."[26]

---

26 Music Video Sweet Life https://www.youtube.com/watch?v=kKUo2-oMt5s

"Such lovely sisters for my Shelley," Sarah thinks. Then, "Michelle, I'm getting tired now. My work is finished. You and Allie have healed your-selves and my Shelley is becoming a good young man."

DON'T TELL ANYONE, BUT I'M BEGINNING TO LIKE THEM.

I KNOW. I SHOULDN'T, BUT ME TOO.

30

Taking Control

The next day, back at Scott's apartment.

Standing on a chair, 6 inches from Scott's face, Kaitlyn rages,[1] "Scott, why am I thinking that you and Olivia have known something about this all along?"

"That's a good question, Kaitlyn."

"How could you? Two of my best friends hiding this from me. And putting Nicole in danger too! Is that right, Scott? You and Olivia knew all along?"

As Kaitlyn, Nicole and Gerald stare incredulously at Scott, "Give me a chance to explain. It's not as bad as it sounds.

"We're waiting, Scott!" while Nicole and Gerald whisper in the background.

"Better fess up Scott. She's got you cold," Gerald finally adds as he pulls the enraged Kaitlyn away from Scott.

"We need to wait for Olivia to report back. Then, we'll both tell you the full story."

"Scott, give me a little credit. My father taught me that's what guilty criminals want, to tell their story together with their accomplices, so they tell the same made-up story."

Gerald adds, "Scott, don't ask me how I know this, but Kaitlyn is right. The police always interrogate suspects separately."

"Way to go Kaitlyn!" as Nicole hi fives her new friend.

---

1 Music Video Mad Woman https://www.youtube.com/watch?v=6DP4q_1EgQQ

"Why do I feel like I need a lawyer?" Scott asks.

Gerald, Nicole and Kaitlyn talk while Scott waits nervously.

*   *   *

Several hours later, "Olivia!" the four announce in unison.

"Oh, did I miss something?" Olivia asks.

"Olivia, we've been busted," Scott says. "Time to tell them what's been going on."

"More lies will only make it worse," Nicole scolds.

For the next hour Scott and Olivia confess what they've been doing and why.

"OK, that's what I know. What did you find out today, Olivia?" Scott asks.

Before Olivia starts her report, Kaitlyn takes over again.

Let me get this straight. You and Scott targeted me on Move in Day? That was staged because you knew something about the experiment the Foundation was planning to do me? And you wanted to find out more?"

"And you've watched Nicole and me become sick?"

"And you did all this because the Professor, the Judge and the Senator told you?"

*   *   *

After Kaitlyn calms down, Olivia reports on what she found out today from the Professor.

"Several years ago a Chinese scientist wrote a paper on his hypothesis that a certain extremely rare blood type would stimulate a super immune system response to any virus. The only people in the world who have this blood type are of mixed Eastern European and African descent.

"Wait a minute! Olivia, are you telling me that Blondie is a Sister?"[2]

---

2 Video Interview Twin Teens https://www.youtube.com/watch?v=JIUK2KSbvvI

"It appears that way, Nicole. According to our experts, that's the only scientific explanation."

"And Nicole is part what?" Gerald asks.

"Kaitlyn's last name, Korosec, means someone from the province of Slovenia called Carinthia,"[3] Olivia responds. "It's on the border between Slovenia and Austria."

"Olivia, how do you know that?" Gerald asks. "I bet Kaitlyn didn't even know."

"Two years ago my mother and I had a lovely lunch there," Gerald "while my father was lecturing at the university in Ljubljan. Such a pretty mountain valley. Kaitlyn, you absolutely must see it someday. It's like from a fairytale."

"Olivia knows just about everything, Gerald. Get used to it," Kaitlyn says before hugging Nicole. "I just knew we're blood sisters, Nicole. Isn't that exciting!"

"Yeah, great Kaitlyn. We're both from a place only Olivia knows exists and I can't pronounce."

"But here's something you might like about our heritage," Kaitlyn adds, "Slovenes are kind of like an oppressed minority."[4]

"Oh, great Kaitlyn. I just find out I'm part white, but not the privileged whites. I'm a two-time loser."[5]

"How about we postpone the family reunion until after Olivia finishes her report?" Scott suggests. "Please continue. Olivia."

"The paper hypothesized that people who have this blood type could be used to develop antigens that could produce treatments. But the few surviving viruses would become immune to all other immune systems and other treatments. So, these rare blood type people could become both a lab to develop treatments and lab to produce more powerful bioweapons."

---

3 Carinthia Website https://www.austria.info/en/where-to-go/provinces/carinthia

4 Website Minority Rights https://minorityrights.org/minorities/slovenes-of-carinthia-and-styria/

5 Music Video Loser https://www.youtube.com/watch?v=zRJNlvMheHE

"American intelligence noticed that this Chinese scientist suddenly disappeared a few months after her paper was published. Then, websites all over the world were hacked and copies of that paper were deleted. Someone wanted to suppress that theory. That's when American intelligence agencies started devoting serious resources to track this.

"My mother, the Professor, was put in charge of investigating all blood experiments."

"Your mother's a spy?" Nicole asks.

"No, her organization has agents you might call spies, but the Professor is more of an analyst and administrator. When the Professor found out the Foundation planned a big blood experiment on this campus, the Professor had Scott and me investigate, because we're already right here. She thought it would be good training for us. Since Kaitlyn was slated to be in the experiment, we set things up so that Kaitlyn would meet Scott on move-in day, and I would be your roommate."

"What about me?" Nicole asks.

"We didn't know about you then. But when Kaitlyn told us you were doing the same Foundation experiment, the Professor started getting interested in you. By now, the Professor probably knows more about you than you do."

"What we didn't know until today is that you both have the same very rare blood type. We think that's why your bodies react exactly the same way to the Foundation's experiment."

"Well, what about all the other people with this blood type?" Gerald asks. One in 10 million means there must be at least 600 other people in the world."

"Not everyone gets blood tests. And most people who test blood don't even know this rare type exists. So, they probably classify some people with one of the more common blood types. That's why 90% of people with this blood type probably go undetected. Then, there's geography. In the ideal experiment, you would do exactly the same thing at the same time to multiple people to get the best test results data. Age might also matter. Immune systems change over time. Two 18-year-old women may be more representative of the general population than someone who is two years old or 80 years old."

Gerald interrupts, "While Olivia was talking, I checked out rare blood types on the Internet, because this sounded crazy to me. But there really are rare blood types that most people have never heard about. I found one that's 1 in 6 million people. They call it the Golden Blood type – aka 'RH null.'[6] It's different from what Olivia just told us, but it shows rare blood types do exist."

Gerald continues, "So, maybe what Olivia is saying is true. Or maybe it's just more lies. Point is that, if it is true, then Nicole and Kaitlyn are very precious to scientists. In my neighborhood, anything that's valuable might be stolen. We need figure out how to protect them."

Nicole stands up with a wild-eyed look and yells, "OK, everybody leave! I mean right now! I'm tired of listening. Me and Kaitlyn need to figure out how to deal with this. Just the two blood sisters."

Kaitlyn nods agreement and hugs Nicole, "You heard her. Everybody out. You too, Scott. I know it's your apartment, but out right now."

As Scott leaves, he thinks "I've really messed up. I hope it's not over."[7]

*　*　*

"Now that they're gone, what do we do, Nicole?"

"We need to buy time to think. We don't know if we can trust Scott and Olivia. I'll borrow a car and meet you by the Bell Tower at midnight. And make sure you're not followed. We'll just disappear for a couple of days until we know who we can trust."

*　*　*

Several days later Olivia's phone rings.

---

6 Article　Rare　Blood　Type　https://www.discovery.com/science/Rhnull-Rarest-Blood-Type-on-Earth

7　Music Video Bet You think About Me https://www.youtube.com/watch?v=5UMCrq-bBCg

"Olivia, it's me, Kaitlyn."

"Yes, I know we've scared you by disappearing. But Nicole and I are both OK."

"No. I can't tell you where we are. Besides, we won't be here long."

"Yes, I trust you about some things, but not this, at least not yet. You and Scott are in time out. If you want Nicole and me to cooperate, do exactly as I say. Are you writing this down?"

"Yes, I'm sure I want them at the meeting. We're going to need a team to pull off the plan Nicole and I have."

"Yes, you can tell Scott everything, but don't tell the Professor or her organization. Nicole and I don't trust them."

"I'll call you again to confirm you've got everything ready."

"Oh, and I really do love you and Scott, Olivia. I pray for both of you every night. Mostly, I pray we can all be happy together again. But we have a lot of work to do. God helps those who help themselves."

31

Forged in Fire

Olivia begins inviting the people on Kaitlyn's list.

"What's the mystery about, Olivia? Secret meeting in the park around a fire pit?"

"Sorry, I can't say more. Kaitlyn will explain when she gets here. All I can tell you now is that Kaitlyn and Nicole are in danger and they trust you to help them."

* * *

After the group gathers, Kaitlyn calls Olivia.

"Is everyone there?"

"Yes, just as you asked. Scott and me, Gerald, Michelle, Allie, Shelley, Luna and Sanjay."

"No. No one else is here or knows about this meeting."

"OK, I'll be there in a few minutes, Olivia."

* * *

A transformed Kaitlyn appears out of the darkness, entering the small circle of light cast by the dancing flames, wearing a hoodie, jeans and sneakers. As she approaches, she draws strength from the fire.[1]

"Where's Nicole?" Gerald asks.

---

1 Video Dance Around the Fire https://www.youtube.com/watch?v=dI8SVOZmhJ4

"Nicole will come later after we're sure the team is on board with our plan."

"I trained that girl well. She's a survivor,"[2] Gerald tells the group.

"Thanks for coming everyone. Sorry for the drama, but it's been very weird lately."

"Scott, you tell the group everything about what's been happening."

After Scott finishes telling the story, Kaitlyn asks, "Before I talk about the plan Nicole and I have, is everyone still comfortable helping? As you can tell from what Scott told you, it's kind of dangerous."

"Oh, and here's something that Scott and Olivia don't know. Both Nicole and I are invited to go to China on a 'scholar's' trip after the semester ends. All paid for courtesy of the Confucius Institute."

"We both thought it was an Internet scam. So, we ignored it. But we've been receiving texts asking us to confirm. Now that Nicole and I know that our bodies are the ideal bioweapons factories, we assume the invitation means the Chinese are after us. That ups the risk levels for everyone. So, are you sure you want to help?"

After a few questions and confirmation from the team, Kaitlyn calls Nicole.

"Yes, the team is on board. Time for you explain our plan."

A few minutes later, Nicole emerges from the darkness dressed in the same uniform as Kaitlyn.

Nicole describes their plan to the team gathered around the fire pit.

"You mean you're going back to another blood session?" Gerald asks incredulously.

"Yes, we don't want to make the Foundation suspicious," Nicole says. "They need to think we don't know anything. We need surprise on our side to make our plan work."

"Kaitlyn, you tell them why."

"Nicole and I are totally pissed-off. They picked on the wrong people [3] I mean, who do these people think they are? We don't want to just escape.

---

2 Music Video I Will Survive https://www.youtube.com/watch?v=XZGwHtGBZJU
3 Movie Clip Rambo First Blood https://www.youtube.com/watch?v=OjkWd8sqPn4

We want to take these jerks down! Make them pay. All of them! So, don't help just because you want to save Kaitlyn and Nicole. We invited you all here tonight, because we've heard your stories these past few weeks. We know someone is manipulating you the way the Foundation is using Nicole and me.

"Join our fight against the people who are manipulating all of us."

"Fight for yourselves, for all of us,[4] because this stuff the Foundation has been dishing out to us is just bull!"

"And they won't stop until we teach them a lesson."[5]

Listening to Kaitlyn leading them the Cell Members are caught up in Kaitlyn and Nicole's anger and see Kaitlyn in a new light. "What happened to that sweet girl? I never took her seriously, but I'd follow her anywhere now." And as the Cell Members become a tribe obsessed with the mission Kaitlyn has inspired, they begin chanting and dancing around the fire.[6]

"OK, I appreciate the enthusiasm. I take that as a yes. Let's calm down with a team hug!"

* * *

After the meeting ends, Kaitlyn and Scott linger by the fire.

"Kaitlyn, you're right. We're all being manipulated by someone."

"And I just want you to know . . .."

"Stop, Scott."

"You, Olivia and me . . . we have some personal issues to work out. When we first met, you both really impressed me. I struggled to keep up with you two. I fell in love with both you and Olivia in different ways. You both made me more confident of myself just to be with you. That's helping me deal with this problem now. So, thank you."

"So, you're not mad?

---

4 Movie Clip Braveheart Freedom Speech https://www.youtube.com/watch?v=TME0xubdHQc

5 Music Video The Principal https://www.youtube.com/watch?v=plJCH77VMoI

6 Video Tribal Fire Dance https://www.youtube.com/watch?v=QgAmhuTaghg

"Mad, no. Disappointed, yes. I mean, how can two grown people let their parents tell them what to do like this? Leading a totally planned life? As much as I love my family, I just couldn't do that, Scott. I don't understand how you and Olivia let them get away with this for so long. Scott, I gave you my love. Now you have to win my love[7] back by showing me you're not afraid to live your life. I want a man, Scott, not a scared boy."

"It's complicated, Kaitlyn . . .."

"I know it must seem that way, Scott. Dealing with parents is always complicated. In a strange way I think this is good. I idolized the two of you in a way that no one could possibly measure up to. That wasn't the basis for a real relationship. After I help you and Olivia deal with your parent problems, we'll be on a more equal basis."

"I can see that you've grown up a lot the past seven weeks, Kaitlyn. The way you ran that meeting and gave assignments to everybody. You're not the same small-town girl I helped moved into school."

"Yeah, being turned into a bioweapons lab changes a girl."[8]

"Scott, my dorm is that way."

"I know, but my apartment is this way. I want to know what making love with a bioweapon's lab is like. Think you can show me?"

"I'm dangerous.[9] Think you're up to the challenge, Mr. Hopkins?"

*   *   *

I LOST THE CONNECTION. WE'LL HAVE TO START OVER.

---

7 Music Video Win My Love https://www.youtube.com/watch?v=rxIfKpsemGo
8 Movie Clip Courage to Change https://www.youtube.com/watch?v=p5QfyF9pkHU
9 Music Video Dangerous Woman https://www.youtube.com/watch?v=9WbCfHutDSE

32

Executing Their Missions

Allie begins her assignment scouting out the Confucius Institute[1] to find out their interest in Kaitlyn and Nicole. At a reception following a play, she finds Denney Chen, who lives in the same dorm.

"Hi Denney! Thought I might find you here. This building is absolutely beautiful. Lots of money spent on this."

"The Institute is well funded. When they sent me to study in China, they spared no expense."

"Really? You studied in China? I have a friend who's been invited by the Foundation to study there next semester. How does that work?"

Denney explains his experience as a Confucius Institute scholar.

"And do you spend much time at events like this, Denney?"

"Probably two or three events a week. They're great networking opportunities. You have no idea how connected this organization is to universities, businesses, and governments – both here and around the world. I've lined up a job with a Chinese company for next summer."

Allie leans into Denney, "Do you think you might like a companion for some of these events?"

"Sure Allie. . . but I had heard you . . .."

---

1 Article https://www.insidehighered.com/news/2019/01/09/colleges-move-close-chinese-government-funded-confucius-institutes-amid-increasing

"That I like girls?"

"Well, yes."

"People do gossip. I like a lot of things and right now, I'm liking you. Is that, OK?"

As Allie takes Denney's hand, "I read palms. I'm seeing in yours that we could become close friends."

"I'd like that, Allie."

"Maybe, you'll also like my friend Michelle. Have you ever been with two girls?"

*　*　*

Sheldon, Luna and Sanjay devise two hacking plans for the Follow the Science Foundation and the Confucius Institute.

*　*　*

Scott organizes six of his Lacrosse Teammates in case some "muscle" is required.

*　*　*

Nicole and Kaitlyn show up for their next blood appointment with Olivia and Gerald waiting outside for them.

"Any side effects to report?" the nurse asks.

"Not much. We barely noticed."

"What should we expect after this session?"

"I don't know. I just handle taking blood and transfusions."

As the nurse leaves to deposit the blood in a refrigerator, Nicole begins taking pictures of the files the nurse left behind while Kaitlyn captures the nurse's login password from her computer.

*　*　*

After the blood session ends, Olivia and Gerald drive Kaitlyn and Nicole to a hotel next to the hospital. There, the four wait to see what reactions the two girls have.

"Olivia, time to take small blood samples," as Kaitlyn rolls up her sleeve. "We need to have the same blood samples the Foundation has."

"Hold still, Nicole."

After two hours, the girls lay down together and suffer through the same types of reactions they experienced a week earlier.

Olivia calls Scott, "They're not doing well. Come on up and help us carry them to the hospital."

Just as Scott arrives, the two girls begin to recover, as quickly as they had the week before.

"Anything I can do?" Scott asks.

"Nicole and I need ice cream. We've earned it."

*　*　*

Scott reviews the photos Nicole and Olivia took of their files.

"We have an experiment number. Looks like you two are the only people in this experiment. Confirms our suspicion that the Foundation knew about your blood types and designed the experiment just for the two of you."

"I'll give this info and the login info you stole to our hacking team."

"Good work girls! Your suffering is paying off," Scott says as Kaitlyn and Nicole finish their pints of ice cream.

*　*　*

At Michelle's Foundation meeting, "Yes doctor, I've decided to go ahead with the new hormone treatments." When the doctor logs onto the Foundation's IT system, Michelle records her with her phone, hoping the recorded keystrokes will help the hacking team.

*　*　*

The next day, the team reunites at the fire pit.

"Thanks for all your work," Nicole opens the meeting and each team reports progress.

At the end of the meeting, Kaitlyn summarizes. "OK, looks like Nicole and I will have at least one more blood session before we're ready to pull the trigger to execute our plan."

"Sanjay, Luna and Shelley, anything we can do to help with your hacking?"

"We have a lot of info now about the Follow the Science Foundation, Sanjay reports. I expect we'll be able to breach their security within the next few days. Every system has a weakness. We just need to be persistent."

"We know less about the Confucius Institute" Sanjay adds.

Allie reports about her next steps, "Denney Chen is quite the networker. More interested in making business connections for his career than anything else. I doubt that he's involved with the experiment. He set up a 'private' meeting for Michelle and me with Dr. Wu, the local head of the Confucius Institute, at their executive lounge. Seems like, Dr. Wu, the Institute Director, has a large collection of girl-on-girl videos he's interested in sharing with us. Denney swears he's more interested in watching than doing. Michelle and I talked. We're OK with putting on a show for the old pervert to get the information we need. Besides between the two of us, we can handle that dirty old man."

"Thanks for taking one for the team," Nicole says.

*   *   *

Before the girls enter the Confucius Institute.

Michelle, have you decided who our acting models will be for this job?"

"Time to be Thelma and Louise, Allie."[2]

"You're a little taller so, you're Thelma, Geena Davis. I'll be Susan Sarandon playing Louise."

---

2 Movie Clip Thelma and Louise https://www.youtube.com/watch?v=66CP-pq7Cx0

"We're so going to stick it to these guys."[3]

*　　*　　*

"Dr. Wu, nice to meet you again," Allie says.

'Yes, I speak a little Chinese, but just the dirty words. I expect that will be enough for tonight.," Allie teases.

"This is my very special friend, Michelle."

"Oh Dr Wu, a cultural Foundation that promotes world harmony must be terribly complicated to run. Please tell us everything about it," Michelle urges as she kisses Allie. "The more you share, the more we'll share with you."

"Your video collection? We'd love to see it."

"Dr. Wu, you sit with Allie and relax," as Allie entertains him[4]. "I'll open the videos on your computer. Just tell me how."

"Oh, what a clever password! I never would have guessed."

As Michelle clicks through his video library, the girls see neatly organized categories. "That one looks like children, Yech!" she thinks, but then, "I bet the police would love to see this collection. Good for future reference."

"Oh my! You're a man of many interests, aren't you! A real dirty old man!"

"Dr. Wu, do you mind if I get more comfortable? Michelle and I want to show you how American girls get along with one another. Is it alright if I change in the next room? Michelle, you entertain Dr. Wu while I'm gone."

Once alone, Allie quickly accesses the Foundation's IT system in the next office using Dr. Wu's identity and password and downloads into it a program her roommate Luna gave her."

As Dr. Wu grows impatient waiting for Allie to change clothes, Michelle jumps in his lap, "Allie, hurry up girlfriend. I'm getting so hot waiting. I'll just have to start with Dr. Wu without you. Relax and let Michelle take care

---

3 Music Video Addicted to You https://www.youtube.com/watch?v=Qc9c12q3mrc
4 Video Allie https://www.youtube.com/watch?v=_TDrWZTqxjM

of you. That's a good boy. Waiting isn't so bad, is it? Now, don't you feel better? All that tension gone."

After a few more minutes, Allie reappears in lingerie and Michelle turns her attentions away from Dr. Wu. After their love making, "Now that Michelle has finished, Dr. Wu, 像米歇爾一樣舔我的陰道"

At Allie's signal, Michelle locks him in hand cuffs. "Dr. Wu, do you know what an alpha is? Yes, it means 母夜叉. I'm your alpha now. Not a good alpha . . . a dark alpha.[5] You have displeased your alpha. Prepare for punishment. Don't beg . . . you'll get what you deserve."

"Michelle, give me my toys."

"Now, lay across Michelle's lap. She's going to spank you anytime you displease me."

"I said now!" as Allie slaps him.

"That's much better. Just remember . . . I'm in charge now."

"You watched me and Michelle. Now its Michelle's turn to watch while 我讓你成為我的妓女"

"這很傷人 Shut up, you whining baby.[6] I know you're loving this."

* * *

As the two girls leave. "Why yes, we'd just love to come back for another performance. Can you keep these clothes for us? We'd be ever so grateful."

After they leave the building, "We have him so nailed. If anything happens to Kaitlyn and Nicole, I'm sure the police will be interested in why he has clothes with their DNA all over them. And his collection of underaged porn should put him away for many years."

"Allie, I've seen a lot of filthy things over the past years. Not proud of that, but that's the worst. I'd love to help get a dirt bag like him to rot in jail."

* * *

---

5 Music Video Human Nature https://www.youtube.com/watch?v=XPL_qGqSJxA
6 Music Video Cry Baby https://www.youtube.com/watch?v=O87lzhoexyA

"Good work Shelley! I think we're in."

"Look at this Luna. It's amazing."

"What is it, Shelley?"

"It's a list of the Foundation's experiments. . .. Not just on our campus, but all around the country. We just click next to each to get all records related to an experiment."

Hugging Shelley, "We've struck gold!"

"Here's a summary of what the Foundation has done since it started. Over ten thousand students this year. More than a thousand different experiments. Psychology, environment, hematology, immunology, genetics . . . The list goes on and on.?

"What's this? Average 25 annual student deaths? They don't put that number in their social media recruiting."

*   *   *

"Did you download Luna's little present for the Confucius Institute, Allie?"

"Oh yes. They won't know we're inside their brain. And we're invited back for future performances. God, I love performing on stage with an adoring audience."

After they get to their dorm, Allie texts Dr. Wu. "Here's a link to the video we made of 米歇爾和我操你。 我們希望您和我們一樣喜歡觀看。

*   *   *

"Sanjay, why can't we find the experiment they're doing on Kaitlyn and Nicole?"

"Let me see if I can detect another layer of security the passwords we have can't access, Luna."

After several hours Sanjay concludes, "If you had something that was really important to keep absolutely secret, would you connect it to the Internet?"

"Of course not," Luna and Shelley agree.

"So, we'll need to break into the Foundation and find a disconnected server."

* * *

Olivia and Scott report back to the Professor.

"Yes, it's all under control."

"No, we can't provide details."

"All we need you to do is to have resources on standby in case something goes wrong."

"Yes, new IDs, a safe house and transport. The works."

"No, not just for two. We have ten on this team now."

"Mom, its either ten or none. Scott and I decided we'll go down with the others, if the team gets caught."

"Yes, we trust the team. You'll just have to trust us."

"No, not negotiable Mom."

"Olivia, the Judge and the Senator are on the line. We're all agreed. We're shutting you and Scott down. Too risky for everything we've planned for your futures. Time for you both to come home."

"Scott here. Glad you're all together to hear this. You have to learn our new rules. Olivia and I are great partners. We'll always be like family after we graduate, but we're not getting married. One of us might go into politics someday, but we're not going to waste our lives chasing your lost dreams."

Olivia adds, "And we're not calling you the Professor, the Judge and the Senator anymore. That was weird. Sorry, you're demoted to just plain old Mom and Dad from now on."

"No, don't blame Kaitlyn for this," Scott says. "Watching her just reminded us that living out your 15- year plan has been very weird.

"One last thing. We love you all, but you have to let us live our own lives instead of your dreams.

"OK, that's a lot for you to digest. But we hope you'll help our team. They're risking their lives to defend Freedom. You taught Olivia and me that was important. Don't disappoint us."

Locked in an embrace, Scott and Olivia look at one another after the call,

"Well, we finally did it. I feel so . . . free!"

"Me too."

"I still love you. Always will."

"Me too, but there are lots of kinds of love."

"But it's time to let other people into our lives."[7]

"Oh, yes."

---

7 Music   Video   Seeing   Other   People   https://www.youtube.com/watch?v=
jSGWzb-KcNM

33

The Next Stage

Kaitlyn opens the next fire pit meeting,"[1] This has been a big week for our team. Thanks to Sanjay, Luna, Shelley, Allie and Michelle, we know a lot more about the enemy."

Murmuring and giggles from around the fire as Kaitlyn talks.

"I know the Dr. Wu video is amusing, but can you stop watching it for just a few minutes while we plan our next steps? I guess not. Can't fight that video. Recess for ten minutes while Michele and Allie reenact their little play for us."

* * *

"That was amazing girls."

"Now, back to business. Nicole, will explain everyone's next roles."

* * *

The next day Nicole and Kaitlyn go to the Confucius Institute to discuss their offers to study in China. "There's a security camera on top of that arch. Let them see your face clearly. That will document we were here and when. We should both take pictures with our phones too."

---

1 Video Fire Dance https://www.youtube.com/watch?v=LNtq7hAgaO0

Leaving the Confucius Institute the girls reverse their jackets and pull up their hoods, "Kaitlyn, remember to avoid all security cameras. We don't want any record of us leaving."

"Nicole, I think we're being followed. Don't turn around. Just keep walking. We'll turn left at the next corner. We can sit at that café and see what they do."

"Is it the two Chinese guys over to the right?"

"Yep."

"How do we know for sure they're following us? It's a free country."

"My father taught me how to tail a suspect and how to tell if I'm being followed. Benefit of being a police officer's daughter. Something every girl needs to know. Let's split up and see if our two friends split up too. I'll go right. You head left and go into the Black Student Union. Wait half an hour before you leave. Not likely a Chinese guy is hanging out at BSU unless he's following you."

"I'll call you and let you know."

"No, if they're following us, they may be monitoring our phones. I'll meet you at 7 tonight outside the Hunt library. And don't go anywhere, unless other people are around. If he's following you, he might grab you. And try to avoid security cameras after we separate. We want all the last pictures to point to China."

*   *   *

Later, outside the library.

"Kaitlyn, you were right. He hung around outside the BSU until I came out. I found a big Brother and we walked together toward him. Then, he backed away."

"I ditched my tail. I asked Stephanie and Sheri to all wear black hoodies at the dining hall. They're sitting by a window. Blonde girls all dressed the same. He probably thinks I'm still at dinner."

"I can get some Brothers to teach them to not to follow us, Kaitlyn."

"We may need that later, but its better if they don't know that we know they're following us. That's why no cell phone communications about this – to anyone. We only say on the phone things we want them to hear. OK?"

"Then how do we talk?"

"For the next few days we can use girl code."[2] Handing Nicole a piece of paper, "I wrote down a simple code. Someone will be able to figure this out, but it will take time. We just need to buy time. These buildings have colors. These people have letters. If we set a time to do something, add two hours."

"I'll try talking in our code Kaitlyn. Wear a Green dress on your date with Bruno. See you at 10."

"OK Nicole, that means we're meeting Olivia at 12 at the dining hall."

As Nicole nods, "Let's check to see that our geo location apps on our phones are still turned off."

"Any ideas about an action plan, Nicole? I don't like waiting around for stuff to happen to me. We need to get on the offense."

"I totally agree. Let's disappear and see what they do. This time we'll tell our team to pretend we've been abducted.[3] They can go around campus asking if anyone has seen us. That should throw the bad guys into a panic. We don't know how many groups are after us. It might be more than just the Chinese. Make them think another group grabbed us. They may panic and get careless."

"Then, our tech team can monitor their communications. I'll tell Olivia the plan in person. You tell Gerald. They can coordinate with the others."

"I know the perfect place to hide,[4] Kaitlyn. No one will find us until we want them to."

"Great place, Nicole. I'll meet you there tonight. You bring food for a week. I'll get us two cheap cell phones. We'll leave our normal phones with

2 Music Video Girl Code https://www.youtube.com/watch?v=Wh4PVQ9x3m0
3 Music Video U Don't Know https://www.youtube.com/watch?v=F5MMV5qULV0
4 Pic Nicole Kaitlyn Hiding https://firepitcell.com/wp-content/uploads/2022/01/C33N4-Nicole-Kaitlyn-Hiding.jpg

Olivia and Gerald. Oh, and bring your laptop and books. We still have to study."

*   *   *

After Kaitlyn and Nicole brief Olivia and Gerald about their plan, the two girls disappear.

The next day, the team acts like the two girls have been kidnapped, assuming someone is listening to their phone calls.

Olivia's phone rings, "Is Kaitlyn with you? "

"No Gerald, she's not. Haven't seen her all day.

"I've been looking for Nicole and can't find her. I thought she might be with Kaitlyn. They've been real tight lately. Nicole's thinking of her like family."

"That's funny Gerald, I think we all do one way or another. Kaitlyn just seems to have that effect on people."

"I think it's contagious.[5] I'm starting to think of you like family, Olivia."

"I know, isn't it a wonderful feeling."

"Anyway, I've been texting and calling Kaitlyn and Nicole, but no reply after several hours. I'm getting worried."

"Me too. I'll mobilize the team. We'll find them."

*   *   *

Scott and some of his Lacrosse teammates begin scouring the campus for signs of Nicole and Kaitlyn asking everyone they meet.

Sanjay and Sheldon go back into the Foundation's communications network, but don't find any signs of unusual activity. "I have no idea why the Foundation collects all this useless data. Can't believe the government funds this."

"Here's something. Not sure it has anything to do with finding Kaitlyn and Nicole, but this file records all meetings and communications between

---

5 Video Contagious Laughter https://www.youtube.com/watch?v=W7rJpRqK-8E

Dr. Wu at the Confucius Institute and Dr. Fauchison at the Follow the Science Foundation."

"WOW! They talk a lot. It's a really big file. It'll take a long time to download."

"Funny, it almost seems like Dr. Fauchison is working for Dr. Wu. Notice how deferential he is on these calls. Definitely download this baby."

*   *   *

Olivia joins Luna in monitoring computer communications at the Confucius Institute. Glad you speak Chinese Olivia. All I can do is get us access. I have no idea what their saying.

"Here's an interesting one. Someone leaving Denney Chen urgent messages. They want him to report immediately."

"Allie, this is Olivia. Can you and Michelle find your old friend Denney Chen? Not much to go on, but he's about to report in at the Confucius Institute. Let him know Nicole and Kaitlyn have vanished and we're worried."

*   *   *

A few hours later Dr. Wu calls Dr. Fauchison, "The two targets have vanished. Their friends are looking all over for them. I told you we should have grabbed them last month. Now, someone else probably has them. Maybe the Russians. Maybe the North Koreans. We've identified their agents intown. Maybe a new player. I don't know. I'm calling in our top security team. They'll deal with our competitors, but we have to get them back. They have ways of making people talk. If the Russians have the two girls, they'll find out where."

Olivia and Luna listen at Dr. Wu's end while Sanjay and Sheldon listen at Dr. Fauchison's end, "Holy . . .! Russians and North Koreans too?"

"Nicole's and Kaitlyn's plan seems to be working. Spies everywhere![6] The roaches are becoming more visible while they're scrambling."

*   *   *

Later, Sheldon and Sanjay overhear Dr. Fauchison makes calls, "Do your people have the two girls? Yes, I'm positive their missing. No, the Chinese don't have them. The Chinese think you have them, unless they're just saying that to throw competitors off the track. Yes, I'm sure your people know how to handle the Chinese."

"Sounds like Dr. Fauchison is playing everyone off against everyone. Do you think he's being paid by everyone, Sanjay? He must be making a fortune."

"Sheldon, I'll let Olivia and Scott know to alert the agency that Dr. Fauchison seems to be an independent player."

*   *   *

"Mom, it looks like there's going to be a war on the ground here. So far, China, Russia and North Korea are the competitors. They're all bringing in muscle."

"Dr. Fauchison? We can't tell yet whose side he's on. Just not ours. He may be playing his own game."

"No, we can't tell you where Kaitlyn and Nicole are. They didn't trust us with that info. And rightly so because we've been hiding things from them right from the start. They're calling the shots at our end because they have the most to lose. And their plan seems to be working so far. They're confusing everyone."

"Yes, I know they're confusing you too. Yes, I know you don't like that, but the reality is that Kaitlyn and Nicole are in charge. Scott and I aren't going to change that. Now, let's focus on what you can do to help. Mom, we need the agency to deal with all the foreign muscle running around

---

6 Video Bond Girls https://www.youtube.com/watch?v=A_Z-cr5J90A

down here. I'm hoping, begging you to make that happen. Beyond that, we think Kaitlyn and Nicole are in the best position to protect themselves."

* * *

The next day, "Olivia, here's interesting local news. A car accident about a mile from campus. Four people killed."

"That's too bad Scott, but accidents happen all the time."

"All the passengers in this car have Russian names, Olivia. And it wasn't a normal accident. It exploded in a fireball. Police say they never saw anything flame up so fast."

"Do you think it was the Chinese? "

"Maybe, but maybe your mom arranged it."

"Perhaps, she never liked the Russians. One time, she killed a Russian team, but she made it look like the Chinese did it. She had the Russians and Chinese fighting for months. That may be her game now."

"We can't rely on your mom to eliminate the Chinese. Ready to launch 'Operation Wu.' Olivia?"

"It's been more than 24 hours. I'll file the missing person's report with the police now. I think all the clues that point to Dr. Wu are ready."

"Here's Kaitlyn's and Nicole's cell phone with pictures of both of them at the Confucius Institute and the two guys following them. As far as I know, nobody except us have talked to either of them since they left the Confucius Institute. They certainly haven't been to class since then. That makes the Confucius Institute the best starting place for any police investigation."

"I have the Confucius Institute's invitations Kaitlyn and Nicole received to study in China when the semester ends. That's enough to cause the police to sniff around the Confucius Foundation. Can the police do a search there?"

"Yes, technically its university property. All they need is university permission and the Professor will arrange for that."

"When the police find Kaitlyn's and Nicole's clothes in Dr. Wu's office, he and his security team will probably run. When they do, the police will search computer records and will find Dr. Wu's underaged porn collection."

"OK, so, that probably takes care of the Russians and the Chinese. What about the North Koreans?"

"The Professor doesn't think they have people on the ground here. She's thinking that the Chinese plan to hide the girls in North Korea after they grab them. Keep them there until after everyone forgets about Nicole and Kaitlyn. She says the Chinese have done that before. If anything goes wrong, the Chinese blame[7] North Korea."

"The current crisis should be resolved in the next 48 hours, if Kaitlyn and Nicole can stay hidden that long. Then, when they come back, we'll all take care of Dr. Fauchison and the Follow the Science Foundation."

"Yep, that's our Kaitlyn's plan."

"Scott, I know you and Kaitlyn have a thing going on. Just a friendly warning from an old friend. Don't cross that girl. You can't push her around."[8]

"Yeah, don't want to get on her wrong side. How does anyone so sweet have such a killer instinct?"

*   *   *

Later, that night, "Dr. Wu just made plane reservations for 8 people to fly to Beijing" Olivia tells the team. "The police just served a warrant. It's just a matter of time now before they find the evidence we planted. Then, Kaitlyn and Nicole can surface again."

---

7 Music Video Blame It On You https://www.youtube.com/watch?v=JrEmv3EmWJQ
8 Music Video Red High Heels https://www.youtube.com/watch?v=-5Ri8GY57SI

34

Taking an R & R Break
from the War

Shelley brings Luna to the women's health clinic. "One unprotected night is enough, Luna. Time to get protected."

"But Shelley, our children will be so wonderful."[1]

"Yes, but no children until after we graduate."

"But I'll be so old then. All my sisters and cousins had children before 20. It's when a woman is strongest down here."

"If you're strongest down there now, we need double protection. You get yours and I'll get mine."

* * *

"Olivia, where did you learn to cook like that?"

"In Paris, Gerald."

"Sorry, forgot I'm dating a rich girl."

"I like your cooking too, Gerald. They just do it a little different over there."

As Gerald pulls her onto the couch, "Do they do this different over there?"

* * *

---

1 Music Video Wonderful https://www.youtube.com/watch?v=EAOWvCFtbe4

"Shelley don't go to sleep yet. Time to use our new protection."

"Again?"

"Yes, again. You promised if we're protected."

*   *   *

Oh!!!! Gerald. Where did you learn that?"

"Not in Paris, Olivia. Closer to home."

*   *   *

Gazing at the Fall sky from a under a blanket on the roof of Scott's apartment building.

"Scott, that was lovely. The first time we did it without playing a game."[2]

"You mean, this is the real Kaitlyn?"

"They're all the real Kaitlyn, but the last two months have made me focus on what's important. Do you think we have a chance?"

"Sure, you've got a great team fighting for you."

"No, I mean us. Do you and we stand a chance? You know, another chance[3] to have a life together?"

"Do you think I'd be fighting Russians and Chinese and who knows who else for just any girl who's been turned into a bioweapons lab?"

"Yes, I think you're exactly the kind of guy who would do that . . . for anyone in trouble." Her eyes tell Scott that Kaitlyn is forgiving him.

"And so would you, Kaitlyn. That's why we have a chance together, even after we run out of games to play."

"Run out of games? Not a chance. Let's make a wish on a star; secret wish, like when we were children. If we make the same wish, it will come true."

---

2 Music Video End Game https://www.youtube.com/watch?v=dfnCAmr569k

3 Music Video One More Chance https://www.youtube.com/watch?v=-owpIWQMd80

"Only you could make me believe that, Kaitlyn. That's your gift, redeeming cynical lost souls."

* * *

Kaitlyn hears the phone ring, just after making her wish.

"Is that you, Nicole? Where are you?"

"In an apartment across the street. I'll flash the lights on and off so you can see where I am. We've been watching. So that's how white people do it."[4]

"Watching? Why are you there?"

"Doing the same thing you and Scott were doing."

Frustrated that the mood between her and Scott has been broken, "Then I suggest you go back to doing it, Nicole!"

"Uh-oh! Guess my timing is bad. But my friend here just told me something important. We need to meet. No, can't say it over the phone. It's too big and it's not my secret. Yes, right away."

"OK, see you at Scott's place. Apartment 4 B. But this better be good, blood sister!"

* * *

"Olivia . . .."

"Just keep on doing what you're doing Gerald.[5] We can talk in the morning."

* * *

"Nicole, glad you're safe and finding some time to . . . you know.

"I know, Blondie, believe me, I know."

---

4 Video Love Songs Black and White https://www.youtube.com/watch?v=D6JQUgdSsqA

5 Music Video Keep Doing https://www.youtube.com/watch?v=Ak6DqRSkhY4

"So happy for you, but what else do you know, Nicole, that's so important it couldn't wait until Scott and I were finished?"

"I know the date we should go after those jerks at the Foundation. Next Tuesday, after 8 pm."

"Wow! That's unusually precise. Why?"

"Sorry, Blondie, I can't tell you why. Someone gave me information that I can't share with you. It's too important to them. They're doing important things that have nothing to do with our troubles with the Foundation. Things I believe in, important things to my community, but things you can't know anything about. Just know that what they're planning is so big that no one will be paying attention to the Foundation that evening."

"So, you're expecting me to trust you,[6] Nicole, just because someone told you something?"

"Not really expecting, Blondie, just hoping."

"Blood sister, we're both scrambling to save ourselves. We've been through enough to trust each other more than anyone else in the world right now. Next Tuesday night it is. Just promise me, you'll let me know more when you can. OK, blood sister?"

"More than OK, blood sister."

---

6 Video Trust in Me https://www.youtube.com/watch?v=TEAMrZ3uId8

35

The Team Prepares
for the Big Push

The next morning.

*   *   *

All day, the tech team monitors the opposition.

"Anything important going on?"

"Funny, but no. The Follow the Science Foundation seems to be paying a lot of people to do useless stuff. Mainly, they collect data, but no one seems to be analyzing the data after they collect it. Just software programs categorizing it. Here's a good example, last night 21% of students skipped dinner, 67% didn't. They don't know about the remainder.

"So, who cares? Keep looking for the experiment about Nicole and Kaitlyn."

*   *   *

Later that night, the Cell members meet at the fire pit;[1] deeply bonded friends psyched up and ready to take the offensive in their battle for survival against the Foundation.

---

1 Music Video Fire https://www.youtube.com/watch?v=sbbYPqgSe-M

"8:00 pm next Tuesday is when we launch 'Operation Payback'[2] for the jerks who've used scholarships to tempt us into taking a trip to hell,"[3] Kaitlyn explains, "Please don't ask why it has to be then. Just trust Nicole like I do. Nicole will explain the plan."

"Tuesday is Halloween. So, no one should notice a few people acting strangely. It's also a moonless night. So, we'll have darkness on our side."

"Sanjay will continue monitoring the Foundation's computer systems. Luna and Olivia will continue monitoring the Confucius Foundation in case the Chinese reappear at the last minute."

"Allie and Michelle will be our lookouts outside the Foundation."

"Gerald will coordinate with our diversion to alert us if anything happens on that side of campus. Our diversion should begin around 8 pm, but we can't control the timing. We'll need Gerald to confirm after it begins."

"Scott, Kaitlyn, me, and Shelley will be the break-in team. We'll have a limited time. It's a big place to search and we have to be in and out before 2:00 am."

"Questions?"

The team talks about problems and potential solutions before drifting back to campus.

Then, Kaitlyn asks the Cell, "Maybe we should pray for the success of our cause?[4] Is that OK?"

2 Video Eisenhower D-Day Great Crusade Speech https://www.youtube.com/watch?v=ewVTVn_GRPw

3 Music Video Dance With Devil https://www.youtube.com/watch?v=EAg69LaLlS0

4 Video Lincoln's Prayer 1863 https://www.youtube.com/watch?v=1Z3XYPphE0E

36

Choosing Experiment # 491

The Cell meets another night at the fire pit.

"How can we teach these jerks a lesson, Kaitlyn?"

"Let's use their own playbook, Nicole. We have a list of their experiments. Pick one and see how they like being the guinea pigs."

Going through the list of Foundation experiments they downloaded, "Let's see. This one might kill them. That's a bit harsh, don't you think?"

"Not really, Kaitlyn."

"Sorry Nicole. Dead people don't learn lessons."

"Dead people also tell no tales. We can't leave witnesses"

"OK Nicole, we can take a vote. Sorry, 9 to 1 in favor of leaving them alive."

"Now, back to our list. What else do you have for us, Shelley?"

"Takes too long to implement this one. We don't have the scientific knowledge to do this one. There are so many experiments. Like trying to find the needle in the haystack."

"Keep looking, Shelley. It's got to be here.

"Oh! . . . I think I found the right experiment.

"Let me see. Yeah, this might work. It'll make them squirm,[1] but not kill them, right?"

"Their data says there haven't been any deaths in the thousands of times they performed this experiment."

"Let's vote. All in favor of experiment # 491 raise your hand."

---

1 Video Psych Torture https://www.youtube.com/watch?v=fMu28cexsp0

"Nicole, why don't you like experiment #491?"

"These jerks almost killed Allie, Kaitlyn and me. They've killed other students across the country. Seems like this is letting them off too easy."

"Well, what if we make this change?"

"OK, I'll go along with that upgrade. But only if I get to watch them suffer through whole thing."

"Of course, we'll all watch. They've been watching us squirm."

"Is everyone on board now?

37

Breaking In

Tuesday, October 31st and Gerald begins reporting to the team.

7:45 pm: "I'm just outside the Black Student Union. There's a crowd of several thousand people here now. More are on their way from the Community College."

8:15 pm: "I can see the barricades[1] going up about a block away in all directions. The student radio station and campus power station are within the enclosed area."

8:30 pm: "I can see the broadcast team entering the radio station now. They should be broadcasting their demands[2] in a few minutes."

9:00 pm: "They cut the power here."

9:15 pm: "I hear sirens from all directions. Time for you to move."

9:15 pm: "Let's go." Scott, Kaitlyn, Nicole and Sheldon approach the Foundation building taking advantage of the darkness, "Quiet. Quick, open the door and get inside before they retore power to the security system."

9:30 pm: "I guess that humming sound is the emergency generator. No lights though. So, is their IT system still working?"

"Positive on that."

"I'm guessing the emergency generator powers IT, security and the refrigerators in the medical lab."

"Let's get to our targets as fast as we can."

---

1 Video Barricade https://www.youtube.com/watch?v=xMjhfO46BnA
2 Movie Clip Think from Blues Brothers https://www.youtube.com/watch?v=Vet6AHmq3_s

Sheldon and Scott head to Dr. Fauchison's office.

Kaitlyn and Nicole head to the medical labs.

9:45 pm: Michelle reports to the break-in team. "Three cars just entered the driveway. One person in each. Civilians. No police. They're in the building now. Got it. Let us know if anyone else comes."

10 pm: Go ahead Allie: "Flashlights shining in the Board room windows. Looks like the three people we saw enter the building. Got it."

10:15: Kaitlyn: "Big refrigerator. Lots of blood samples. Check the code numbers we saw when they drew our blood."

10:45 pm: After Nicole and Kaitlyn sort through dozens of samples. "This box has my number on it. That one has yours."

Nicole and Kaitlyn count the samples in each box. "There's an extra one in each box. Must be the one they were intending to give us next week."

The girls keep looking. "Four other boxes with our numbers on them. We'll take them all."

11 pm: Allie reports "Campus police car stopped outside the Foundation. I'll divert them. Time for me to play damsel in distress." Acting scared, "Hello! Officers! Over here! A group of hoodlums just ran that way. Thank goodness you scared them off. Can you drive me back to my dorm? Oh, thank you so much. Yes, I'll lock myself in."

11:10 pm: Michelle reports: "Allie has the police under control. I'm still standing guard." Nicole to Kaitlyn, "Now let's get the stuff for Experiment #491. So nice of them to keep everything in numerical order."

11:45 Nicole and Kaitlyn head for Dr. Fauchison's office to check on Sheldon and Scott.

"We found his computer. Like we guessed, it wasn't connected to the IT system. Dr. Fauchison may have been playing his own game. The code Sanjay gave us worked. There's a file with your numbers on it. It's big. No time to read it all here. I'll download to a stick in case we need to dump the computer when we make our get away."

Nicole smiles, "It's not time to get away, yet. Time to introduce the Foundation's three board members to their Experiment #491."

* * *

As they enter the Board room, Nicole takes the lead.

"Good evening Dr. Fauchison. Nobody move."

"You're not supposed to be here. Campus police are on their way."

"Oh, I doubt that. They have a lot to handle."

"Dr. Fauchison, I'm sure you know a lot about Kaitlyn and me. We've learned a lot about you too. Tell us about your two friends here."

"Nicole said not to move!" as Kaitlyn draws a pistol from her knapsack. "Do you know what this is, Dr. Fauchison?"

"Yes, it's a water pistol. Do you think you can scare me with a water gun, Kaitlyn?" sneering, "You're even dumber than you look sweet cakes."

"Oh, Dr. Fauchison! Do you think I only have water in this gun. Silly boy."

"We've been all over your building's labs. We've found lots of very interesting chemicals. I'm sure you know how toxic some of them are. Bedsides, my big boyfriend is standing just outside the door."

"You're buffing, Kaitlyn," but as he stares into Kaitlyn's eyes seeing her contempt for him, he sits down and lets Nicole tie his hands to the arms of the chair."

"Good, now everyone else sit down while Nicole ties you to your chairs."

After Nicole finishes, "You were right, Dr. Fauchison, I was bluffing. Too bad you're such a gutless wonder," as Kaitlyn points the water gun at her mouth and sprays a clear liquid. "It's sparkling water. Very refreshing. Too bad you got tricked by a dumb blond."

Watching Dr. Fauchison seethe, Kaitlyn continues, "We're going to run a little experiment. Aren't experiments fun?"

"Let's start by experimenting with the truth. So hard to come by these days."

"We have your computer, Dr. Fauchison. Do you recognize it? Now, tell us your access code."

"You're a liar, but no problem. That was just to toy with you. We've already accessed all your files. When we plug this stick into this laptop, you'll see we already have everything we need."

"By the way, do your friends know this information isn't on the Foundation's IT network? I wonder why?"

As the two other directors look at Dr. Fauchison, "They don't look too bright, but I'm sure that with time they'll figure out you were double crossing them. See, here are the wire transfers to the joint accounts and here are the wire transfers to your private account. You're all criminals, but Dr. Fauchison, you're the biggest crook."

"Oh, and here are the blood samples we took from your lab. We haven't figured out yet why there are so many, much more than you took from us, but we will. Care to save us time and tell us?"

"I'm waiting for a confession."

"Oh, that's too bad. That was your last chance to cancel experiment #491."

"Nicole, you were right. They're guilty as charged. You can inject our three friends now. You'll have to forgive Nicole, she's had a lot of blood drawings and transfusions at the Foundation lately, but she's not a nurse. So, this may hurt a little."

"Nicole, it's not nice to laugh at people in pain. Please forgive Nicole. She's really very sweet, but she's a justice warrior. Mercy isn't one of her virtues."[3]

"My, is it midnight already? Not to worry, you won't be feeling any effects for about 15 minutes. At least that's what the Foundation's Experiment protocol says. You people may be scum, but our experience is that your experiments always run right on time. Now, who wants to spill the beans about what the extra blood is for?"

---

3 Video Mercy https://www.youtube.com/watch?v=Xj4ZBa1AJSo

"As you can see, with the blood and the computer files, we have every-thing we came for . . . except one little thing. Nicole, remind me, what don't we have yet?"

"Revenge,[4] Kaitlyn. We don't have revenge yet."

"Nicole, when will our revenge start?"

"In about three more minutes they should start suffering."[5]

---

4 Music Video Picture to Burn https://www.youtube.com/watch?v=yCMqcFAigRg
5 Video Suffering in Silence https://www.youtube.com/watch?v=CMrLNvhmiGM

38

Can We Get Away with It?

"You'll never get away with this. You'll be in jail the rest of your lives." Dr. Fauchison says just before he begins convulsing in pain."

"We doubt that. You wouldn't want the nature of all your experiments exposed[1] to the public, now would you? All your data destroyed, would you? Ever heard of ransomware, Doctor?"

"No, not the data. You wouldn't do that. It would set back science at least a decade," as he grimaces in pain.

"We're not concerned with saving your type of science, Doctor. But that's not our priority. Let's consider that a last resort."

"Nicole, do you see them sweating?"

"Before we leave, we remind you that we have records that can put you all in prison for many years. Money transfers from the Chinese and Russians and several other groups we can't identify yet. We also know the secret sponsors of other Foundation experiments. Sponsors that don't want people to know they've been funding these experiments."

"So, we have no intention of running or hiding. You'll see us around campus, if you decide to stay here, always knowing we can destroy you at any time. And we'll be watching to make sure you don't pull any of this stuff again. Think of it as a chance to redeem[2] yourselves by doing good. I like to think people can change. They just need the right motivation."

---

1 Music Video Uncover https://www.youtube.com/watch?v=U-PXEe-qeK4

2 Music Video Not the Only One https://www.youtube.com/watch?v=neXkzLDwnIk

"Kaitlyn, they don't look very well now, do they?"

"No Nicole. They look sick. Looks like they feel like they made us feel. Satisfied yet Nicole."

"No not yet, but maybe later."

"Before we leave, let me explain the rest of the experiment. This is Foundation experiment # 491. The injection Nicole gave you isn't lethal, at least that's what the experiment protocol says. I hope it's right. You're just going to feel very bad for about 24 hours. Sporadic bolts of pain, lots of heat. You may pass out from time to time."

Nicole adds, "Of course, that's if you don't take this antidote. I'm leaving enough antidote here to instantly alleviate your suffering, but it's just enough for one person. If you share it, experiment #491's protocol indicates you'll probably only feel bad for about 12 hours."

"When we leave," Kaitlyn explains, "you'll probably be able to untie the ropes within half an hour. Oh, and we're taking with us all the other antidote bottles we found in your lab. There's just this single dose."

"Did I forget anything Nicole?"

"Kaitlyn, you forgot my favorite part. We're leaving the video camera and transmitter on so we can see what the first person who unties the ropes decides to do. Will they share? Or use it just for themselves? See, that's why the Foundation has run this experiment over a thousand time on students across the country. You'll be able to find the statistics in the Foundation's files. But that's just a bunch of statistics, I only care about watching how you react. I plan to play your video every night just before I go to sleep."

"One last thing. Dr. Fauchison, do you remember your dirty hands grabbing me and telling me I had a sweet ass? Of course, you do. I expect it was the highlight of your pathetic life. Now's your chance to taste how sweet it really is. Go ahead, be a good girl and kiss it . . . I've been waiting a long time. Don't keep me waiting any longer . . . sweetie."

"OK, now we're even Doc. I'll always treasure our moment together. You know Doc, it's totally true that revenge is a dish best served cold[3] especially when its being taped."

---

3 Video Harassment Revenge https://www.youtube.com/watch?v=cTnePQNQWNs

"That reminds me, Nicole, I have a half gallon of ice cream waiting for us in the freezer. I've been saving it for a special occasion."

"Oh my, look at the time, Nicole. We must be running. We have early classes tomorrow. Say good night to the good Doctors, Nicole.

"Goodnight!!!!!" followed by laughing that gradually fades as the two girls walk down the hall arm in arm.

39

How Long Is Happily, Ever After?

Several days later, the Cell meets back at the fire pit and talk while they wait for the full group to gather.

Kaitlyn quiets the group down. "OK, this is our last official cell meeting. Now that everyone is here, what's next? Do we just go back to being students? Study for exams? Get our degrees? I'm sensing that's kind of a letdown after everything we've been through together."

"I couldn't cry at our earlier meetings, because we were in a war and I was kind of a General. But I'm not a General anymore . . .."

Nicole jumps in "And I promised I'd kill Blondie if she cried during our war.[1] Go ahead now Blondie, I know you have to do it."

Kaitlyn continues, "But now that it's over . . . you guys mean so much to me. I wanted to make friends in college, but I never imagined we'd be this close. I really thought I was going to die. Maybe we all would. Group hug . . . OK?" and Kaitlyn breaks down again.

"While Blondie gets her act together . . . next steps seem to be in everyone's mind. How about we take turns sharing what we're planning to do now that this is over? Sanjay, I know I can count on you not to cry."

"Luna, Shelley and I are starting our own digital security consulting company. We've got several customers lined up."

"And our war with the Foundation project gave us a lot of valuable experience," Luna adds, "We'll make enough money that Sheldon won't need his Foundation scholarship. Sorry Sheldon, honey, but I'm taking you

---

1 Music Video Big Girls Don't Cry https://www.youtube.com/watch?v=agrXgrAgQ0U

out of girl immersion. Mama says it's too risky to have you surrounded by other girls."

"What about those babies, Luna?" Olivia asks. "We're right next door. Thin walls you know."

"The babies will come when the babies come. But when they do, they'll be beautiful and smart."

"Allie's going to teach me to surf in Hawaii[2] after the semester ends," Michelle announces. After that who knows?" Oh, and my name was Michael before I became Michelle. . ... Waiting for a reaction people. This is where you're all supposed to express how shocked you are. . . . Still waiting! Will somebody have the decency to act surprised? At least a little!"

"I'm so surprised . . .."

"Thanks Sanjay. I really needed that. Guess, I'm not as good an actress as I thought I was."

"Michelle, it really worked for the first month or so, but we've been living so closely together for so long. Since then, we've all been waiting for you to feel comfortable telling us." Kaitlyn adds, "Really glad you are now, girlfriend."

"Oh, now look what you've done Kaitlyn, I'm getting misty too . . ."

As Michelle and Kaitlyn hug, Allie takes over, "Michelle and I really appreciate your support. It's been so important to what we've both been going through. Three months ago, we were both broken in different ways, but we're not anymore. You helped create the space we needed. So, for now we're just going to try to be a normal 'bi' couple and see how that works. We just want to spend some time living a sweet life."

Michelle tries to begin speaking again but breaks into tears again. "Sorry, its these super hormones the Foundation's been giving me. Sometimes I just can't stop once I get started. . ..."

"She's got the hormone levels of a pregnant woman. OMG, am I going to be a Daddy?" Allie jokes. "I almost forgot, if Michelle wasn't still sobbing, she'd tell you that she's writing a screen play about all our adventures together. We'll start shooting in the spring semester. Hope you'll all

2 Video Surfer Girls https://www.youtube.com/watch?v=yc2_FC1ty9M&t=190s

participate. Guess who stars as the sexy Asian girl?" Holding Michelle and whispering, "It's OK girlfriend, everyone understands."

"Don't know how I can compete with that, but I'll go next," Gerald volunteers, "but without the crying and hugging. I'm opening a restaurant. Olivia's family is investing in it. I'm hoping Olivia will join as a full-time partner after she graduates. So, I guess we're a couple in more ways than one. Olivia, I promised no hugging!"

"Gerald, I know, but I ever promised that."

Scott goes next. "We beat the Foundation one time on this campus, but they're already operating on half the campuses in the country. Some of the work the Foundation does is good, and some is kind of dumb. We're not going to dedicate our lives to making the Foundation more efficient, but we think there may be other examples where its positively evil like what happened to us here. So, we're in this fight for the long haul. Nicole, will you explain what you, Kaitlyn and I are planning?"

"First, we're starting a social media company for students to share their Foundation experiences. The Foundation has been hiding things from the pubic and even from the government. The good, the bad and the ugly all need to see the light of day. We'll sort through student feedback from around the country looking for problem projects and then figure out the best way to eliminate them. I'm going to be the Director. We're applying for a grant to fund it. Olivia and Scott will help us get the grant money. We're hoping the grant will be enough to pay tuition for Kaitlyn and me, but we don't care if it doesn't. We're not going to do any other Foundation experiments to cover tuition."

"Anything else to add, Nicole?"

"Yeah, the Foundation will regret the day[3] they turned Nicole Wilson into a human bio-weapons lab!"

"Nicole forgot something," Kaitlyn adds, "We going to help one another explore our newly discovered shared heritage. Next Wednesday, we'll be hosting a Slovenian dinner at the Black Student Union. Stop by if you can."

---

3 Music Fight https://www.youtube.com/watch?v=FWme81uDHiw

Scott, prodded by Kaitlyn, adds, "It's been an adventure since I met Kaitlyn when the semester began on move-in day. I liked carrying Kaitlyn's bags so much that I'm moving Kaitlyn out of her dorm and into my apartment. Just to fight the Foundation together, you understand. Sleeping together has nothing to do with it."

As the meeting breaks up the Cell members vow to remain friends for life before wandering off in different directions, but Allie and Michelle linger.

* * *

As Michelle and Allie sit together watching the last dying embers of the fire, Sarah reappears. Michelle greets her, "Glad to see you old friend, but you said you were leaving."

"I was Dear, but I couldn't resist your victory celebration. I feel like I'm part of the Cell too."

After Allie walks toward Sarah and hugs her with "Thanks for all your help, Mrs. Atwell. Michelle and I were broken. You helped us fix ourselves."

"You can see Sarah now, Allie? You didn't believe in her before."

"Yes, I'm letting Allie see me," Sarah tells Michelle, "Now that she's your forever family, I trust her. You've both come so far together, I just had to be part of it."

After they talk, Sarah whispers, "I came to warn you. Your planned movie about what happened with the Foundation is very important. I can't tell you why. Just know that it will impact a lot of people."

Before the girls can ask any questions, Sarah smiles and disappears again.[4]

"What do you think Sarah meant, Michelle?" Allie asks.

"Allie, that's the trouble with messages the bubbles send. They're usually ambiguous like that. The bubbles know everything, but they never

---

4 Pic Sarah Atwell's Spirit https://firepitcell.com/wp-content/uploads/2022/01/C39N4-Sarahs-Spirit.jpghttps://firepitcell.com/wp-content/uploads/2022/01/c41n2-michelle-movie-director.jpg

tell me anything specific that I can use. Just once, I'd like some specific information about what the stock market is going to do. Or who will win the Super Bowl. Something I can make some money on. The bubbles know, but they won't tell."

"But I take all their messages seriously. The bubbles saved my life. They made Brock revive me after several suicide attempts. I know it was the bubbles that made him watch over me so closely. I think it's why I fell in love with Brock, but now I know the bubbles did it. That gave me hope.[5] After that the bubbles kept calling me. Soon I ran away from Brock and started changing my life."

"Why you, Michelle?"

"Because I needed the bubbles more than anyone. Do you know what I've been afraid of the most, Allie?"

"Yes, Michelle, you're afraid that now that you've fixed yourself, the bubbles won't call you anymore."

"I was, Allie, but Sarah just told me the bubbles are still guiding me and that you're part of the bubbles now. So, I'm less fearful of losing them . . . of having to choose between the bubbles and you, Allie. I think Sarah just told us that we can have both; that the bubbles saved us to do something big and that you're an important part of it."

"Oh Michelle! I feel like something sacred is happening to us. Did Sarah just perform some kind of wedding ceremony?"

"I think it was, Allie, not an earthly marriage that ends when someone dies, but I'm sensing that we're married in the bubbles dimension that lasts forever. A lot may happen to us. We're young. Maybe we'll part when we're alive, but we'll reunite in the bubble dimension.[6] How do you feel about that Allie?"

"If you agree to be my bubbles bride, I'll be your bubbles bride."

After the two girls seal their marriage with a kiss, Michelle continues, "We're going to make that movie, OK Allie. Then, we'll see what happens. I'm also going to start taking classes in writing and directing next semester.

---

5 Music You Light Up my Life https://www.youtube.com/watch?v=b07-yKnKRMQ
6 Music Tears in Heaven https://www.youtube.com/watch?v=JxPj3GAYYZ0

I may decide that being behind the camera is better than being in front of the camera all the time."

Allie smiles, "You mean you like directing your fabulously glamorous Asian bride?"

"That's exactly what I mean, Allie. You've opened up a whole new world for me. I don't always need to be the center of attention anymore. You and Sarah helped me see that."

*   *   *

CUT: FADE AWAY AS THE TWO GIRLS . . ..

40

It's a Long Game

Two decades later at the Foundation's national headquarters.

"The video you've all just seen comes directly from the brain scans of our ten subjects. You can thank Dr. Watson and Dr. Tall for their work mining this data and creating this training video."

"The ten subjects scattered after the after the Follow the Science Revolution of 2030, but our security forces tracked them down one by one over the next few years. We preserved their brains to scan them so that we could create this training video after we had all of them. The purpose of our video is to train you to recognize signs that your subjects might be rebelling against their experiments."

"What did you learn from this data taken from the minds of these retrogrades to recognize signs that your subjects might be rebelling against their experiments like these ten did? Yes, Mr. Clean."

"I was stunned by how little information the subjects retained from their university classes. It seems like all they remembered were their feelings about each other, physical pleasure and the adventure."

"Very good point. You will find that some people, even today, are the same way. They're not able to objectively evaluate data like we scientists do. Their emotions cloud their judgment. We've been trying to breed these primitive instincts out of people, but they keep popping back up. With each freshman class we find a few retrogrades. Be alert about them. If you find one, your superiors will know how to dispose of them."

"Other observations?"

"We've been taught that such persons are anti-social misfits. How do you explain the way these ten people bonded together? How did they win?"

"Guards, escort Ms. Breyers to the conditioning room for additional training."[1]

"Class, can anyone explain Ms. Breyers' mistakes?"

"Her mistakes began by assuming these retrograde subjects won. Obviously, since we scanned their brains, they lost in the end. People are sheep easily led by the herd.[2] And this 'bonding' was merely primitive instinct, not the bonding that enlightened experimentation brings. It's simply animal herd instincts,[3] not real scientific thought and cooperation."

"Very good, we can all learn from Ms. Breyers' mistakes. In fact, every year, somewhere in America, a group like this Fire Pit Cell herds together. Science has given us many tools to control human herds,[4] Most herds are easily manipulated using simple scientific principles. Each year our experiments improve our ability to control people. Our collaboration with the Chinese is really paying off. China is a model of scientific control through social media trust scores but America started catching up with China[5] after America started penalizing people who failed to Follow the Science."[6]

"Of course, pesky politicians kept impeding us with talk of Freedom and elections. That's why the Foundation had to act to eliminate the Freedom that allowed human herds to ignore science. Imagine, Congress interfering with science.[7] That had to stop."

"Sometimes these retrograde herds can be very dangerous. Do not attempt to combat them yourself if you encounter one. We have specially trained units for that."

---

1 Movie Clip 1984 https://www.youtube.com/watch?v=T8BA7adK6XA

2 Video Social Experiment People Sheep https://www.youtube.com/watch?v=MEhSk71gUCQ

3 Video Experiment The Herd https://www.youtube.com/watch?v=0IJCXXTMrv8

4 Video Government Scientific Control Tools https://www.youtube.com/watch?v=awKHDrY5c9k

5 Video Social Credit Score https://www.youtube.com/watch?v=-N80zgzxUIE

6 TV Interview Clip 2021 Mandates https://www.youtube.com/watch?v=IzlQ1S32i1w

7 Video Congressional Hearing https://www.youtube.com/watch?v=Mi2yd_VY2TM

"I think we've exhausted the lessons these brain scans can teach us."[8]

"So much to cover in so little time. Fresh-person move-in day is at the end of this week. Be ready to collect data from the next group of subjects."

"Remember, the primary directive for all humans is to Follow the Science. It's for everyone's own good.[9] So, any mercy you show will really hurt people."

---

8 Video Brain Scans Identify Behavior https://www.youtube.com/watch?v=rTq2qIfR08g
9 Video For Youur Own Good https://www.youtube.com/watch?v=9MdiMweIzO0

41

The Circle Game

Another move in day at Bagwell Hall.

"Hi, are you Carlie? I'm Jennifer. I hope you don't mind that I took this bed."

"That's OK Jennifer. I'm just excited to finally move in and start college."

Michelle Movie
Director

"I've never had a roommate before. What's the protocol?"

"You sound like one of those Foundation people, Jennifer."

"Doesn't everyone these days? We were only five years old when they took over. I barely remember what life was like before."

"What's in that box you brought, Jennifer?"

"My older sister gave it to me. She says it made her college experience bearable."

"What does it do?"

"You play videos on it. Each video is on a chip like these. It runs on batteries so you can use it in places no one can see."

"You mean without the video streaming through our brain implants?[1] Is that legal?"

---

1 Article Brain Chip Implants https://www.businessinsider.com/elon-musk-neuralink-hopes-to-start-human-testing-2022-2021-12

"Legal? Well, no. It's been smuggled in from India. It's still legal there."

"WOW, Jennifer, you're a real Retro!"

"Does that scare you, Carlie?"

"Yes, but I'm ready to be scared . . . at least a little."

"What will we do with it?"

"My sister's favorite video is this one made by Michelle Collins.[2] She went to school here; like ages ago, when the world was totally different. The Foundation people were just starting then. She made this movie about her first semester here. All her friends in the video are fighting against the Foundation."

"Wow, Jennifer, they're totally Retro!" Carlie listens intently to her new roommate to determine whether she's really Retro or a Foundation spy, "Go on Jennifer. I want to hear more."

"This was Michelle's room. I asked for the room number in the video. I took her bed. Of course, my sister said Michelle slept in lots of beds. Her videos show that, but she always loved Allie. Said she and Allie were destined to be together forever in another life. I don't really understand why, but I totally believe it. They're just like Romeo and Juliet sharing their destiny, except that Michelle and Allie were Juliet & Juliet. No matter what happens from scene to scene, you just feel that in the end they'll always be together. They invented a new way to be romantic for all time. An inspiration for us all."

"Jennifer, do you know what happened to Michelle?"

"My sister heard they fled to South America and India when the scientists took over. An intelligence agency of the old government the Foundation overthrew gave them new identities. They're all old now, but I heard they're still Retros fighting for the cause. The Foundation likes to pretend they're all dead. They even have a training film they claim is from their brain scans, but it's just badly edited excerpts from Michelle Collins' original video."

---

2 Pic Michelle Movie Director https://firepitcell.com/wp-content/uploads/2022/01/c41n2-michelle-movie-director.jpg

"All the people in her video are cult stars. At my high school, two students came to school on Halloween dressed as two of their leaders, Kate Korosec and Scott Hopkins. The biology teacher peed in her panties when she saw them. Of course, the Foundation took them away to be reeducated, but more people are planning to do it again this year. That's why we think they're still alive because the Foundation is still afraid of them."

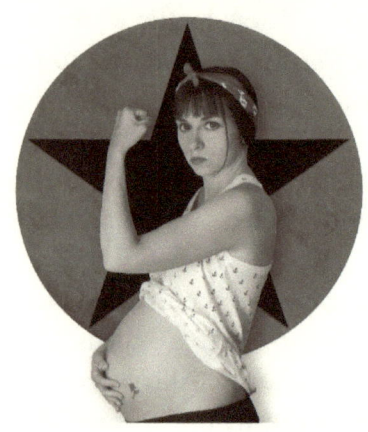

1 Kaitlyn Poster Recruiting For The Retro Revolution

In mid-sentence, Jennifer looks at Carlie and begins to piece together who her college roommate is. "Uh . . . Carlie, you look a little like their leader. In fact, very much like her. Here's a poster of Kaitlyn Korosec[3] I had hanging in my room at home. You could be . . . ."

Whispering to Jennifer, "Yes, that's my Aunt Kate. She dyed her hair to travel in disguise, but she's definitely not dead. And she'll never give up! The Retro Revolution is her Mission."[4]

"OMG, I've been blabbing on and on about Retros and your Aunt Kate is the biggest Freedom Fighter of them all!"

"So, now that you know about my Aunt Kate, we should really talk. No, not here. The Foundation has microphones and cameras everywhere. Plus, Aunt Kate says the best way to talk is over ice cream.[5] The ice cream place Kate and Nicole used to go to talk is still there. I checked. That's where they became friends and planned their fight against the Foundation."

*   *   *

---

3 Pic Kaitlyn Protester https://firepitcell.com/wp-content/uploads/2022/01/c41n3-kaitlyn-retro-revolution.jpg
4 Movie Clip Blues Brothers https://www.youtube.com/watch?v=LMoD2m5pzZU
5 Pic Ice Cream Sign https://firepitcell.com/wp-content/uploads/2022/01/C41N5-Ice-Cream-Sign.jpg

Over double scoop waffle cones the two new roommates talk.

"So, why are you here, Carlie? Is there a plan?"

"More of a direction than a plan. The Fire Pit Cells will have to do the planning and implement how it happens."

"Fire Pit Cells?"

"Aunt Kate wants us to start our Retro Revolution journey watching Michelle's video in groups of ten and develop local plans to build a Retro world. The video is important, because it shows the Foundation can be beaten if we cooperate with other people. It gives people hope. And it shows how students can cooperate to do that."

Figure 2 Nicole Wilson
Retro Revolutionary

"Carlie, why ten?"

"Ten was the number in Aunt Kate's original cell that beat the Foundation. Its big enough to include people with different skill sets, but small enough to build trust. Each group of ten Retros is called a Fire Pit Cell, because the original Retro rebels used to meet at a fire pit in the park across the street. There are Fire Pit Cells on campuses across the country now. More every year. Now that the videos are inspiring people to recruit the Cells, people like me are going to help the Cells learn to build a Retro world.

Aunt Kate and Uncle Scott have plans they communicate to my Godmother, Nicole Wilson. [6] I report to Nicole. She keeps Aunt Kate and Uncle Scott informed. They trust that Nicole won't break under torture and she's learned how to trick brain scans."

"Why Fire Pit Cells, Carlie?"

"Fire pits go back to pre-history. Civilization started with people gathered telling stories around fires. So, we're starting the Retro Revolution back at the beginning. Taking back with us the good things that we've learned since then. Trying not to bring back all the bad things, but its human nature to be both good and bad. So, we know the bad will be with

---

6 Music Video the Godmother https://www.youtube.com/watch?v=FUVddbdXaLw

us. The stories we tell one another around the fire will help bring out our good sides. The light that fights the darkness."

"Around the fire pit, people let their real thirst for Freedom show. We'll hear the people sing what they really feel from the beating of their hearts[7]. The Foundation controls all modern communications. So, we're rebuilding our Retro world using more basic tools. It's the ultimate Retro. You'll see. There are still unused fire pits in the park across the street where the first Fire Pit Cell met. When we recruit a cell, we'll watch Michelle's video there, where the Retro Revolution all began. Aunt Kate showed me the secret messages Michelle Collins embedded in the video. I can interpret them for our Fire Pit Cell."

"Why are you laughing, Carlie?"

"I'm thinking about what Aunt Kate told me about Michelle Collins. Michelle never wanted to be a Freedom Fighter. She just wanted to find a little sweetness in life. She struggled to become a girl and in the process Michelle discovered that being a girl is both bitter and sweet.[8] Then, the Foundation took over and sucked all the sweetness out of life. Only the bitter was left. That's when Michelle became a Freedom Fighter. Aunt Kate says that's what we're really fighting for. To get back the sweetness of life."

"I know two people here from my high school, Carlie. Your Aunt Kate is their heroine. I know they'll want to be in our cell."

"I saw a guy in the lobby I'd like to recruit. Fire Pits are very . . . sexy. Aunt Kate says that scares the scientists, because the scientists haven't been able to invent anything better. They hate that. So, sexy is very. . . Retro."

"Carlie, I'm totally into Retro. Fire, light, warmth, sex and sweetness. That feels like me. But how do I explain Retro to other people when we recruit them?"

Jennifer, I have a letter from my Aunt Kate explaining Retro when I asked her that question. I'll read it to you because it's in code.

"Dear Carlie,

7 Movie Clip Hear the People Sing https://www.youtube.com/watch?v=gMYNfQlf1H8
8 Music Video Just a Girl https://www.youtube.com/watch?v=PHzOOQfhPFg

What an exciting time in your life! So full of anticipation, hope and adventure. Anyway, that's how I remember my first year at college.

Good question about Retro. It's just a word we invented to brand a set of values to unite people. We put the word out there to describe ourselves without defining it and before we knew it, lots of people were talking about Retro and how there should be a Retro Revolution. Just dumb luck that the name caught on. So, we never changed it. Over the years, I've thought a lot about what Retro means. I'm still learning, but I'll try to explain.

The basis for being Retro is understanding the relationship between Freedom, Intellect, Behavior and Emotions. People aren't really free if their Freedom is limited to doing things that are smart or nice. Freedom is much messier than that. Our commitment to Freedom is measured by how we treat people who do things we think are dumb or that we don't like.

The other important point is that most of the time that people lose Freedom it isn't because a bad person takes it away. We like to blame the evil dictators. You know the list. But history shows us that often people lose their Freedom because they trade it away for something else they want – safety, money, admiration . . . the list is long. Freedom is easy to trade away, but hard to get back after its gone.

Those are the two biggest things I've learned over the years, but being Retro includes many other things.

Retro means acting for the things we value, not defining yourself by things we're against. Life was better when people did that. Spending our lives focused on what we're against is a waste of time and it generally makes people unhappy.

Retro recognizes that both happiness and unhappiness are contagious. People can only share what they have. Strive to create your own happiness and you can share it with others. Unhappy people can only share their unhappiness.[9] That's why, when the burden of building a Retro world becomes too heavy, it's OK to take a break and rebuild your own happi-

---

9 Video Unhappy People are Contagious https://www.youtube.com/watch?v= rpA2uCixflE

ness. It's not only OK to invest in your own happiness, but it's absolutely necessary.

Retro recognizes that people are imperfect and always will be. Their choices and what they create won't always please you. So, don't be too disappointed. Create a giant pool of tolerance,[10] where people respect the choices of others. But don't confuse tolerance with approval. Be satisfied if people tolerate you. Respect their choice to disapprove. The biggest mistake the Foundation made is that they thought they could perfect people with science. Trying to make people perfect only leads to disappointment and doing a lot of bad things to make people behave the way you want. Controlling people is the opposite of Retro.

Retro is not being afraid to be yourself. When I was young, and truthfully, even today, people would say 'I can't believe Kaitlyn just said that.' Some of those people have been my lifelong friends, like Nicole and Scott and Olivia. My biggest fear for you is that you'll try to mimic me. I lived my life my way.[11] You'll be Retro, if you live your life your way.

Retro is recognizing that our job in rebuilding the Retro world isn't to tear down the Foundation. That would be defining ourselves by what we're against. Our job is to build a viable alternative to the Foundation. The Foundation has reached a point where it is eating its own. It's punishing its own people for small variances from official thought.

The best people at the Foundation already know their experiment is failing, that they're forcing too many people into cold dark places. They're scared. Maybe more than we are. They know that their experiment has destroyed much of what once held our country together; what made it work. A lot of Foundation people would like a redo. Just go back to their labs instead of running the country, but they're scared there aren't enough common values left if they give up control.

That's why the Retro Revolution is building our fires[12] that will attract the people wandering around in the cold dark world the Foundation has

---

10 Video Tolerance Definition https://www.youtube.com/watch?v=MMpTeOYLLbk
11 Music Video My Way https://www.youtube.com/watch?v=AzBBiNK5fkQ
12 Music Video Start the Fire https://www.youtube.com/watch?v=-onk-Qm7ATw

created. Welcome them to the warmth and the light.[13] Sharing a campfire was the earliest sign of friendship among people. Then encourage newcomers to do the same for others.

Encourage people to build their own fires. Remember that their new fires won't diminish your fire. New fires will only diminish the darkness and the cold. A big army of Freedom has room for hundreds of watchfires.[14] Creating one big fire would destroy the world. An old native American story cautions not to feed too much to a fire.[15] Having many fires helps ensure the fire doesn't consume us.

As much as we disapprove of the Foundation, recognize that things can get much worse if we don't build our alternative. People wandering in the dark and cold too long sometimes do terrible things to one another;[16] especially if they're led by the wrong people who see misfortune as their opportunity to control people.

What really scares me is what might follow after the Foundation falls apart. So, remember that destroying the Foundation isn't our goal. Our job is to offer people a better alternative than what others offer so that the better sides of people's natures prevail when the Foundation collapses of its own weight.[17]

By the way, even the scientists deserve our tolerance. Give them a chance if they'll give you your chance. We'll need them after we create our Retro world. Your Godmother, Nicole, and I have often talked about this last point. Sometimes, Nicole has a hard time letting go of grudges. She adores you and you can help her. Just keep reminding her that our Retro struggle isn't about punishing. It's about creating a space where everyone can try to pursue their happiness in their own way.[18] If Nicole starts getting

---

13 Video Welcoming Campfire https://www.youtube.com/watch?v=LYF2VzCN0os

14 Battle Hymn of the Republic https://www.youtube.com/watch?v=Jy6AOGRsR80

15 Video Fire Native American Story https://www.youtube.com/watch?v=TD_f23pbZDc

16 Video Worst Dictators of 20th Century https://www.youtube.com/watch?v=G5K7e_Tge44

17 Video MIT Predicts Society Collapse 2040 https://www.youtube.com/watch?v=kVOTPAxrrP4

18 Video Explains Pursuit of Happiness https://www.youtube.com/watch?v=Nv1Rdkw5Gzl

dark, remind her how great she feels eating ice cream.[19] That usually brings out her better side. It does with most people. My father taught me that.

If you use these principles to guide your decisions, you'll be very Retro and other people will respect you. That's how you'll succeed.

I'm looking forward to the day I can return home and see what wonderful things you've done. Then you can finally meet your cousins. Another cousin will be coming soon. Scott is still so like he was when we met. We still can't keep our hands off one another.

I have to go now. Michelle is acting out. Flirting with Scott[20] . . . yet again. So annoying, especially with me so pregnant! Those hormones of hers will be the death of me. Happens after every injection.

Here's a picture of our family in exile.[21] Your uncle Scott is still as sexy as the day I met him. Don't you think? Michelle called him a Greek god the day she met Scott. Sheldon told me that, so, I can understand why Michelle is always after him. But he's all mine just like I planned the day I met Scott. He's the only thing in my life that worked out like I planned. I am blessed.

Love,
Aunt Kate

---

19 Video Joy Eating Ice Cream https://www.youtube.com/watch?v=WJv-tZUCT5g
20 SNL Video Flirting https://www.youtube.com/watch?v=WwfVaehcdfE
21 Pic Kaitlyn Scott Family https://firepitcell.com/wp-content/uploads/2022/01/c41n21 kaitlyn-scott-famy.jpg